WHERE THE HEART IS

Also by Annie Groves

Ellie Pride
Connie's Courage
Hettie of Hope Street
Goodnight Sweetheart
Some Sunny Day
The Grafton Girls
As Time Goes By
Across the Mersey
Daughters of Liverpool
The Heart of the Family

ANNIE GROVES

Where the Heart Is

HarperCollins*Publishers*

HarperCollins*Publishers*
77–85 Fulham Palace Road,
Hammersmith, London W6 8JB

www.harpercollins.co.uk

Published by HarperCollins*Publishers* 2009
1

A catalogue record for this book
is available from the British Library

ISBN: 978-0-00-726593-0

This novel is entirely a work of fiction.
The names, characters and incidents portrayed in it are
the work of the author's imagination. Any resemblance to
actual persons, living or dead, events or localities is
entirely coincidental.

Set in Sabon by Palimpsest Book Production Limited,
Grangemouth, Stirlingshire

FSC is a non-profit international organisation established
to promote the responsible management of the world's forests.
Products carrying the FSC label are independently certified
to assure consumers that they come from forests that are managed
to meet the social, economic and ecological needs
of present and future generations.

Find out more about HarperCollins and the environment at
www.harpercollins.co.uk/green

For my readers who have so kindly and generously supported me. I hope you are all enjoying reading about the Campion family as much as I am enjoying telling their story.

Acknowledgements

I would like to thank the following for their invaluable help:

Teresa Chris, my agent.

Susan Opie, my editor at HarperCollins.

Yvonne Holland, whose expertise enables me 'not to have nightmares' about getting things wrong.

Everyone at HarperCollins who contributed to the publication of this book.

My friends in the RNA, who always have been so generous with their time and help on matters 'writerly'.

Tony, who as always has done wonders researching the facts I needed.

PROLOGUE

Christmas Day 1941

Katie Needham couldn't wait any longer. It was Christmas Morning, after all, even if it wasn't even six o'clock yet, and she had been soooo very patient, promising herself that she wouldn't open Luke's letter until it was Christmas, hoping that saving it to read then would help to make up for his being so far away in Egypt, whilst she was here in Hampstead.

Her small attic bedroom in the house where her parents were currently living with friends, now London was being heavily bombed, was freezing cold, and Katie thought longingly of the cosiness of her room in her fiancé, Luke's, family home in Liverpool. She was missing the warmth and bustle of the Campion household already and she had only arrived here yesterday, she acknowledged guiltily. She felt under her pillow for Luke's letter, her guilt dissipated by the heady warmth of her love and excitement as she retrieved her precious letter, and then reached out to switch on the bedside lamp.

A tender smile curled her mouth as she traced her own name on the envelope. One day, when this awful war was over, she would be Mrs Luke Campion.

Mrs Luke Campion.

Quickly she opened her letter – from the side as she had been taught to do working for the Postal Censorship Office – her heart skipping a beat when she saw Luke's signature at the bottom.

Oh, Luke. Tenderly she pressed her lips to it, closing her eyes as she did so, as though somehow she could conjure up Luke himself, to put his strong arms around her, his dark head bent over her own, his warm lips on hers, kissing her.

Oh, Luke . . .

She mustn't cry. After all, there were thousands of young women who, like her, were facing Christmas without the men they loved – some of them knowing that their men would never be coming back to hold them and kiss them.

Katie's hand shook slightly as she smoothed out the airmail letter and began to read.

'Katie . . .' Just Katie? Not even 'Dear Katie', never mind 'Dearest'. But then Luke was on active service in the desert.

Katie,
    I am writing to tell you that I wish to bring our engagement to an end.

What? No! There must be some mistake.

Frantically Katie read the cold matter-of-fact sentence again, and then a third time, her distress

2

growing with each read, tears of shock and disbelief blurring her vision as she tried to read on.

> Through the good offices of 'a concerned
> friend' I have been warned that you have
> been seeing someone else – no doubt believing
> yourself safe from discovery with me out here
> in the desert.

A concerned *friend*. Who? A horrible certainty,
mixed with a dreadful sinking feeling, invaded her
tummy. Carole. It had to be. But surely not; she
knew how much Katie loved Luke. She and Carole
had been such good pals, working together and
Carole dating one of the men under Luke in his
role as the unit's corporal. But then Carole had
got involved with an Irish boy they had met at the
Grafton dance hall and her head had been turned
by his attentions.

Katie hadn't deliberately got Carole into
trouble when she had told their supervisor about
these Irishmen asking so many questions, but
the reality was that Carole had broken the
Censorship Office rules of secrecy and she had
been dismissed.

She had blamed Katie for that, and had threatened retaliation. But to write lies to Luke about
her . . .

> There's no point in you writing to me saying
> that it isn't true, as I won't be opening your
> letter. I should have known something like
> this would happen. After all, I saw what you

were like that time you flirted with that
cyclist.

The cold words almost leaped off the page like
physical blows.

'That's not true,' Katie protested aloud. 'You
know it wasn't like that.'

Luke's jealousy had been the one flaw in their
relationship and her happiness. Sometimes she had
felt as though he almost wanted to find her out in
some kind of betrayal. It had hurt her dreadfully
that he didn't trust her love for him.

If we're honest we did rather rush into things,
and I dare say that without the war we'd have
realised pretty quickly that we weren't suited.
    The last thing a serving soldier needs is the
worry of wondering if his girl is being
unfaithful to him behind his back, and it
seems to me that I shall be a good deal
happier without that worry.

Tears welled in Katie's eyes and splashed down
onto the letter, making the ink run. Surely if Luke
had loved her as much as he had said he did he
would never have been so unkind and hurtful.
Instead he would have understood how much she
loved him and that she would never ever so much
as look at another man because of that.

Before they had fallen out, Carole had told
her that Andy, her boyfriend, had written to her
that Cairo was filled with pretty girls. Perhaps
Luke was glad of an excuse to break off their

engagement. Perhaps in fact he had already met someone else . . .

A savage pain gripped her, tightening her chest and trapping her breath.

> I am writing to my parents to tell them that our engagement is over, although for their sake, especially my mother's, I don't intend to tell them what you have done. I shall simply say that we have grown apart and the engagement is over.
>
> Luke

As Katie tried to gulp back her tears the light from the lamp shone on the engagement ring Luke had given her just before he had been posted overseas.

That had been such a special day, filled with sunshine and happiness. She had felt so happy, so proud, so delighted, not just that she was going to be his wife but that she was going to be a member of the family she had come to love so much.

Jean, Luke's mother; Sam, his father; his sister, Grace, now married to Seb who was ostensibly with the RAF but working for the intelligence agency known as the Y Section, and then the twins, Lou and Sasha, had all welcomed her so warmly into their family and she had felt so at home there, so safe and protected and loved.

She hadn't just lost Luke, Katie recognised, she had lost them as well.

The diamonds in her engagement ring seemed to quiver beneath her tears. Her fingers trembled as she slipped it off and put it in the envelope that had contained Luke's letter.

From now on, for her, no matter how long she lived, Christmas Day would always be the day she remembered that Luke had destroyed their love and broken her heart.

ONE

Mid-February 1942

Lou Campion eased her regulation WAAF duffel bag off the luggage rack. She had packed everything so carefully, warned by the more experienced girls of what she could expect if she didn't, but still somehow or other she had ended up with the sharp edge of one shoe catching in the net as she tried to roll the bag clear.

The February afternoon was already fading into dusk, the seemingly endless frost-rimed flat fields the train had carried them through on the long journey from Crewe now wreathed in fog. Lou was tired and hungry and feeling very sorry for herself, already missing the familiarity of Wilmslow where she had done her initial 'square bashing' training along with dozens of other new recruits.

They were a jolly crowd, even if she had been teased at first for her naïvety when they had found out that she had joined up with dreams of learning to fly.

'Have you heard this?' one of the girls, a chirpy

cockney who seemed to know everything, had asked the others. 'Lou here reckons she's going to learn to fly. No, love, what the RAF wants you for is to mend the planes, not fly them.'

Lou remembered how she had gone bright red with discomfort when the other girl burst out laughing.

'You've got a lot to learn and no mistake,' the girl had continued. 'The only flying you'll be doing is off the end of the sergeant's boot on your back-side if she gets to hear what you've just said. Hates women pilots, the sarge does. Says they shouldn't be allowed. See, the thing is, it's only them rich posh types in ATA that get to do that; them as already can fly before they get taken on – savvy? No, love, wot you'll be doing is filling in forms and fixing broken engines – and that's if you're lucky.'

'Leave off her,' one of the other girls had called out. 'The poor kid wasn't to know. It's not as bad as she's making out,' she had told Lou comfort-ingly, 'especially if you get put in a decent set of girls.'

The last thing Lou had expected when she had originally signed on for the WAAF was that she would end up being sent for training as a flight mechanic. However, flight mechanics were a Grade Two trade and, as such, Lou would be paid two shillings a day more than less skilled personnel.

She had felt quite pleased and proud of herself then, but this morning, standing on Crewe station with the other new WAAFs, waiting for the train to take them to Wendover – the nearest train station to RAF Halton, the RAF's largest training station and the Regimental HQ – she had wondered what exactly she had let herself in for. If Wilmslow in Cheshire had seemed green and rural compared with Liverpool, travelling through the pretty Buckinghamshire countryside had had Lou studying the landscape with wary curiosity. Such clean-looking picturebook little towns, so many fields and trees.

The train had slowed down. Betty Gibson, a bubbly redhead who kept them all entertained during the long cold journey with her stories of how accident-prone she was, had jumped to her feet announcing chirpily, 'We're here, everyone.'

There were five girls altogether, all from the north of England, although Lou was the only one from Liverpool. They'd soon introduced themselves and exchanged stories. Lou had discovered that she was the youngest, and a chubby placid girl named Ellen Walters, from Rochdale, the eldest. Of the others, Ruby Symonds, Patricia Black and Betty Gibson, Lou suspected that Betty was the one she had most in common with, and she'd been pleased when she'd learned that, like she, Betty was down to do an eighteen-week flight mechanic course. Lou had enjoyed their company on the long journey but that hadn't stopped her missing her twin, Sasha.

'Fancy you being a twin,' Ruby had commented when they had all introduced themselves, 'and her not joining with you.'

'I bet the WAAF wouldn't have allowed them to train together even if she had,' Betty had said.

'Just think, though, the larks we could have had if she had joined and you'd both been here.'

A frown crinkled Lou's forehead now as she remembered Betty's comment, and the miserable feeling she hated so much began to fill her, bringing a prickling sensation to her eyes. She did miss Sasha. Being without her twin felt a bit like losing a tooth and having a hole where it should have been, which you just couldn't help prodding with your tongue no matter how much it hurt – only worse, much much worse.

Not that Sasha would be missing her, of course. Oh, no, Sasha had got her precious boyfriend to keep her company, the boyfriend whose company she had preferred to Lou's.

The train had stopped now, and all the other girls were grabbing their kitbags.

'These things weigh a ton,' Betty complained, 'and I hate the way no matter how carefully you pack a kitbag you still seem to end up with something sticking into your shoulder.'

'It's not surprising they're so heavy when you think of our uniforms and everything we have to pack into them,' Lou pointed out.

'Item, one air-force blue battledress and beret, one dress jacket and skirt with cap for best wear, three blouses, one pair black lace-up shoes, two pairs grey lisle stockings and three pairs of grey knickers, two pairs of blue and white striped Bovril pyjamas,' they all began to chant together, before dissolving in a shared fit of giggles.

'At least it's not as bad as the ATS uniform,' Patricia said.

'Come on,' Ellen warned them. 'If we don't get off we'll end up at the next station, then we'll miss our transport and then we shall really be in trouble.'

Still laughing the girls picked up their kitbags and hurried off the train, Betty going first and Lou bringing up the rear, scrambling down onto the platform just as a military lorry pulled up on the other side of the fence separating Wendover station from the road.

'Are you from Halton?' Betty called out cheerfully to the uniformed driver, who had climbed out of the lorry.

'That's right. Climb on board, girls,' the driver invited.

'I've heard that Halton is quite some place.' Ellen remarked once they'd all clambered into the back of their transport. 'It's even got its own cinema. And a big posh house that used to belong to the Rothschild family that the officers get to use as their mess.'

'A cinema? Who needs films when there's a camp full of handsome RAF men to keep us entertained?' Betty laughed.

'I thought there were rules about not fraternising with the men,' Ruby said.

'Well, yes,' Betty agreed, 'but just think of the fun we can have breaking them. I don't know about the rest of you, but fun is definitely what I want to have. What do you say, Lou?'

'I agree,' Lou replied, more out of bravado than anything else, because the very last thing she wanted to do was to get involved with any man – in or out of uniform. She had learned her lesson where the opposite sex was concerned with Kieran Mallory and, although she hated admitting it, deep down inside that lesson still hurt.

It was because of him that she and Sasha had lost the closeness they had once shared and which Lou had taken for granted would always be there. He had driven the initial wedge between them by pretending he was sweet on Lou when he was with her and sweet on Sasha when he was with Sasha.

Lou had thought the rift had been mended when they had both sworn off boys, but then Sasha had got involved with the Bomb Disposal sapper who had helped to rescue her when she had been trapped in an unexploded bomb shaft.

She mustn't think about Sasha and all the things that had made her feel so miserable, Lou warned herself. She was a Waaf now, and her own person, even if sometimes being her own person felt so very lonely.

As the lorry lumbered towards their destination Lou smothered a yawn. It had been a long day, so long in fact that she was actually looking forward to going to bed, even though that meant sleeping in a hard military bed with its three-part-biscuit mattress and itchy blankets, in a hut filled with thirty girls. It was amazing what you could get used to.

'I hope they give us something to eat before we bed down,' Betty said.

'We'll be lucky if they do,'

Ellen replied. 'It's gone nine o'clock now. I reckon

it will be a quick admission, and then we'll be marching into our billets. And to think I could have trained as a postal clerk.'

'Looks like we're here, girls,' Lou told them as she saw the start of the camp's perimeter fence from the open back of the transport, the wire shining in the moonlight.

The lorry slowed down by the guardhouse and the barrier was raised to allow them through. Another five minutes and they were clambering out in front of a brick building, easing cramped cold limbs and shouldering their kitbags.

'Watch out,' Betty warned as the door opened, and a sergeant and another NCO stepped out, the latter holding a clipboard.

One by one she called out their names and numbers, then told them, 'You're in Hut Number Thirty. Sergeant James here will escort you to the mess for your supper, but you'll have to look sharp. It's lights out at ten p.m. I don't know what you've been taught or told wherever it is you've come from, but here at Halton we pride ourselves on doing things by the book.

'You'll be woken up at six by the PA system. No one gets to go for breakfast until the corporal in charge of their hut has done a proper inspection of beds and uniforms. After breakfast, everyone musters for a proper parade. There's no slouching around and turning up at classes individually here. We've got a reputation to maintain and it's the job of us NCOs to make sure that it *is* maintained. You have been warned.

'Now tomorrow morning, since it's your first

day, after parade you'll all present yourselves to the MO for medicals and vaccinations.

'One day a week here we all have to wear our gas masks. Anyone found not doing so will be put on a charge. All right, Sergeant, you can take over now.'

Obeying the sergeant's command to fall in, Lou decided tiredly that she was relieved that Sasha wasn't here to tell her that she'd have been much better off staying at the telephone exchange, because the way she was feeling right now she might just be inclined to agree with her.

Tucked up cosily in bed with her new husband in the pretty bedroom with its dormer window and cream-painted walls, on which she had carefully stencilled pink roses to match their pink eiderdown, Grace gave a deep sigh.

The wonderful intimacy of being married still made her colour up a little self-consciously, and she felt excited inside now Seb came into their bedroom from the bathroom, in his blue and white striped pyjamas, freshly shaved, smelling of soap.

'What, not fed up of being married to me already, are you?' Seb demanded in mock outrage.

'No, of course not. I love being married to you,' Grace assured him fervently.

'Do you now? Well, I'm very glad to hear that because I certainly love being married to you,' said Seb, before drawing her into his arms so that he could kiss her.

Naturally it was several minutes before Grace could speak again, but when she could she told him,

'I was just thinking about Mum, Seb. She's ever so upset about Luke and Katie. She thought they were perfect for one another – we all did – and now Luke's gone and broken off their engagement.

'Perhaps it's for the best.'

'How can you say that?' Seb had released her now and Grace shivered a little, despite the warmth of the flannelette nightdress she was wearing, the neck tied with pretty pink ribbon. 'Mum is heartbroken, and Katie will be too. She loves Luke so much. Anyway, I thought you liked Katie.'

'I do,' Seb assured her, reaching up to pull the cord to switch off the two wall lights either side of the bed.

'Then—'

'I know that Luke is your brother and of course you love him. He's a fine soldier, and a good brother, but it seemed to me that whilst he loved Katie, he hurt her quite a lot with his lack of trust. You can't build a good marriage without trust, or at least not in my book. Perhaps without this war Luke and Katie could have married and not had any problems, but war changes things, it sharpens and intensifies so much.'

Grace sighed again, as she snuggled into Seb's waiting arms and put her head on his shoulder. They were so lucky. They had one another, and they had this cosy cottage where she was so happy making a home for them both. She knew that Seb was right, but she still couldn't help feeling sad. They had all liked Katie so very much.

'I'm so lucky to have found you,' she told her husband, 'but I do feel guilty about not being in

Liverpool to help Mum. She's got so much to worry about now, and so has Auntie Francine. Mum told me that uncle Brandon is very poorly and going to die soon. They've been married such a short time.'

'We'll go and see your mum the minute we both get leave, if that will help put your mind at rest.'

'Yes, it will.'

'Good. Now it seems to me that it's an awfully long time since I last kissed my wife.'

'Oh, Seb.' Grace gave a small giggle and then said nothing at all as her husband's arms wrapped lovingly around her.

TWO

'It can't be morning already,' Lou heard Betty complain as the public address system announced that it was six o'clock and time for them to get up.

Inside the cold darkness of the hut, all the young women were waking up, and going through the automatic actions of pulling on clothes and making beds, ignoring slowly numbing fingers as they hurried against the clock.

In common with accommodation huts at bases all over the country, theirs housed thirty girls with a small separate 'room' for their corporal. Two stoves supposedly kept the place warm although only those with beds close to them actually felt their benefit.

At six thirty on the dot their corporal appeared. The girls stood stiffly at the end of their beds whilst she walked up and down the line, inspecting them.

Lou quailed a little inwardly when the corporal looked at the buttons on her jacket. Lou had learned whilst square bashing that it was a matter of pride to look as though one belonged and wasn't 'new', and so she had paid a small amount to swap her buttons for those on the uniform of another girl who was leaving the WAAF on medical grounds. She felt immensely proud of her well-polished buttons but now she wondered if swapping them was going to get her into trouble.

To her relief, Ruby, who was standing next to her, suddenly gasped and put her hand on her tummy as it rumbled loudly, distracting their corporal's attention, although Lou didn't relax properly until the corporal commanded them to 'Fall out' and they were all free to go for their breakfast.

Without anything being said, the five new arrivals kept together, waiting until some of the other girls were ready to leave the hut and then tagging along behind them, Ruby complaining that she was 'starving'.

'Yes, we all heard,' Ellen pointed out.

'Ablutions block is over there, just in case no one told you that when you arrived,' one of the girls ahead turned round to tell them. Sturdily built, with a mop of chestnut hair and bright blue eyes, she nodded in the direction of another brick building. 'I'm Hawkins – Jessie Hawkins – by the way, and these two here are Lawson and Marsh.'

Taking her lead, Lou and the others quickly introduced themselves, all using their surnames.

'You'll find that Halton takes a bit of getting used to if you did your square bashing somewhere small,' Jessie Hawkins informed them. 'We're pretty close to Chequers here, of course, so we get an awful lot of top brass coming in. You'll find that the officers and NCOs are pretty hot on discipline. Do you remember that girl who got court-martialled for jumping into a Lancaster?' she appealed to the other two.

They nodded silently.

'For a Waaf to fly is, of course, a court-martialling offence,' she continued, 'and whilst we all know there are some places where you can get away with it, you can't here. One wrong move and you're out.'

Lou felt a shiver of apprehension run down her spine at the thought of that happening to her and her having to return home in disgrace to face her parents. When she had broken her news to them after Grace's wedding her father had been not just angry with her for enlisting without their permission but also scathing in his opinion that she wouldn't be able to 'stick it out' since she had spent her life finding ways to get round the parental rules he and her mother had put in place to protect all their children.

'In fact,' Jessie continued warningly, 'there's a bit of competition between the huts to get good reports, and the best pass-out rate from the courses. Our hut came second last year and this year we're hoping to be first. I'm just telling you so that you know what's what and to make sure that there's no letting the side down.'

Behind Jessie's back Betty pulled a face at Lou as they were forced to quick march behind the others to keep up, and whispered, 'I thought it was the corporals who were supposed to tell us what to do, not one of our own. I reckon she's going to be on our backs all the time, bossing us and spoiling

19

our fun. Part of the reason I joined up was so that I could have a bit of fun.'

Although it wasn't daylight yet, the length of their march toward the mess indicated how big their new base was, the more practical-looking buildings dominated by the big house to the rear of them.

'So what's that posh-looking place then?' Ruby asked cheekily, gesturing towards it.

'Top brass and high-ranking RAF officers' mess,' Jessie told her promptly. 'And strictly off limits to you lot.'

Under cover of Jessie's answer Betty dug Lou in the ribs and giggled, 'If some handsome officer tried it on with Jessie, I reckon the first thing she'd say to him would be, "No, it's strictly off limits."'

Betty was fun, Lou acknowledged, as she struggled to keep her own face straight.

'I suppose the officers still get a plimsoll line painted round their baths?' was Ellen's comment, referring to the new practice of painting a line to mark the five-inch depth of water one could have in one's bath.

'You can forget about baths here,' Jessie told her. 'It's showers for us and if you aren't quick enough it will be a cold shower.'

Although Lou hadn't seen much of the base yet, what she had seen of it seemed to be immaculately spruce and smart, a regular showplace compared with her brother's old army barracks at Seacombe and the small base in Wilmslow where she had trained. Halton was smarter and prouder of itself, somehow. The Buckinghamshire countryside around them looked far less war weary than Liverpool.

There was no doubting the pride of the girls here. Backs were ramrod straight, shoes were highly polished, and the girls themselves all seemed so neat and confident. Would she fit in here, with her renowned untidiness? Lou hoped so.

The mess was huge, or so it seemed to Lou, and filled with girls either already eating or queuing up for their breakfast, whilst the smell of frying bacon and toast filled the air.

Soon the five newcomers were tucking in to a very welcome meal.

'At least the grub's good,' Ruby announced with relish when she had polished off her own breakfast. She looked at Lou's plate. 'Are you going to eat that toast?' Then, without waiting for Lou's response, she removed it from Lou's plate to her own, with a cheeky grin.

It was left to Betty to say what Lou suspected they were all thinking. 'I think we've all done very well getting posted here. Halton's got everything anyone could want to have a good time, and that's what we're going to do, isn't it, girls?' she demanded, lifting her cup in a toast.

Half an hour later, marching on the parade ground flanked by the RAF regiment, led by its sergeant major with its mascot – a goat with a dangerous-looking set of horns – Lou knew that she dare not look at Betty to see if she was sharing her own desire to break into nervous giggles. There had certainly not been anything like this at Wilmslow. Halton quite obviously took its square bashing very seriously indeed.

Those Waafs already on courses were marched to their classrooms until only thirty or so girls were left, to be marched over to the medical facility ready for their medicals.

'I don't know why we have to have another medical and more inoculations,' Betty grumbled.

'They're probably testing our pain threshold,' Lou grinned, quickly standing to attention when a medical orderly appeared and shouted out her name.

'Bye, Mum. I'm off to work now.'

'Well, you take care, Sasha, love,' Jean Campion told her daughter as they hugged briefly, 'and no dawdling home tonight, mind, because your dad's got an ARP meeting and he'll be wanting his tea on time.'

Jean shook her head ruefully as the door closed behind Sasha. Automatically wiping the already pristine sink, she tried desperately not to think about the unexpected and unwelcome changes the last few weeks had brought to the family, and the grief and upset they had caused. There was still a war on, after all, and, as Sam had said, life had to go on, no matter how they all felt. It was their duty to put a brave face on things. But to suffer two such blows, and over Christmas as well. Her hand stilled and then trembled.

It had been bad enough – a shock, even – to learn that Lou had volunteered for the WAAF and not said a word about it to anyone, including her own twin sister, without getting that letter from Luke, saying that he and Katie were no longer engaged.

Jean looked over to the dresser, where the polite little letter Katie had sent them was sitting, her engagement ring still wrapped up inside it, to be returned to Luke. Jean's caring eyes had seen how the ink was ever so slightly blurred here and there, as though poor Katie had been crying when she wrote it.

Jean had done as Katie had asked in her letter, and had parcelled up her things and sent them on to her, obeying Sam's command that she must not try to interfere in what had happened, but it hadn't been easy.

'It's their business and it's up to them what they do,' Sam had told her when she had said that there must be something they could do to put things right between the young couple.

'But Katie's like another daughter to me, Sam,' Jean had protested. 'I took to her the minute she came here as our billetee.'

Sam, though, had remained adamant: Jean was not to interfere. 'No good will come of forcing them to be together because you want Katie as a daughter-in-law, if that isn't what they want,' he had told her, and Jean had had to acknowledge that he was right.

She did miss Katie, though. The house seemed so empty without her, for all that she had been so gentle and quiet.

Jean had her address; she could write to her. But Sam wouldn't approve of her doing that, Jean knew.

She couldn't help wishing that Grace, her eldest daughter, was still living in Liverpool, and popping

23

home for a quick cup of tea as she had done when she'd been working at Mill Street Hospital. She could have talked things over with Grace in a way that she couldn't with Sam. But Grace was married, and she and Seb were living in Whitchurch in Shropshire, where Seb had been posted by the RAF.

The house felt so empty with only the three of them in it now, she and Sam and Sasha.

Jean wiped her hands on her apron and looked at the clock. It was just gone eight o'clock and she had a WVS meeting to attend at ten, otherwise, she could have gone over to Wallasey on the ferry to see her own twin sister, Vi.

Although they were twins, Jean and Vi weren't exactly close. Vi liked to let Jean know how much better she thought she had done than Jean by moving out to Wallasey when her husband, Edwin's, business had expanded.

Now, though, things had changed. Just before Christmas Vi's daughter, Bella, had told Jean that her father had left her mother, and that she was worried about her mother's health because Vi had started drinking.

It was hard for Jean to imagine her very proper twin behaving in such a way – a real shock – but beneath her concern at what Bella had had to tell her, Jean felt a very real sympathy and anxiety for her sister, despite the fact that they had grown apart.

She had tried to imagine how she would have felt if her Sam had come home one day and announced that he was leaving her to go off with some girl half her age – not that Sam would ever do something so terrible, but if he did then Jean knew how hard to bear it would be. She knew that the shame alone would crucify her twin, with her determination not just to keep up appearances but always to go one better than her neighbours.

For all her Edwin's money, there was no way that Jean would have wanted to swap places with Vi. Edwin could never measure up to her own reliable, hard-working Sam, who had always been such a good husband and father. And for all that she was so disappointed about Luke and Katie splitting up, at least her son hadn't gone and got some poor girl pregnant and then abandoned her to marry someone else, like Vi's Charlie had.

Then there was Bella. She was doing well now, running that nursery she was in charge of, and Jean freely admitted that she was proud to have her as her niece, but there had been a time when Bella had been a very spoiled and selfish girl indeed.

Sam had made it plain over the years that the less the Campions had to do with Vi and her family the better, but things were different now, and Jean felt that it was her duty to to try to help her sister.

Tomorrow morning she'd walk down to the ferry terminal and go over to see her twin, Jean decided.

She looked at the dresser again. They'd had a letter from Lou this morning telling them that now that her WAAF induction period was over, she'd been selected to go on a training course to be flight mechanic.

Sam had merely grunted when Jean had read the letter to him, but then Sam was a bit old-fashioned about what was and was not women's work, and he would much rather that Lou had stayed at home working at the telephone exchange with Sasha. Jean would have preferred to have had both twins at home as well, but what was done was done, and she didn't want any of her children ever to feel that they weren't loved or wanted every bit as much as their siblings. Sasha had always been the calmer, more biddable twin, and Lou the impatient rebel. It was hard sometimes to think of the twins as being the age they were. It didn't seem two minutes since they'd been little girls. Jean sighed to herself, remembering the time Sam had been giving the pretty yellow kitchen walls their biannual fresh coat of distemper, and somehow or other Lou had hold of the paintbrush when Sam had put it down, wanting to 'help' with the work. The result had been yellow distemper on everything, including the twins. The memory made Jean smile, but her smile was tinged with sadness. Keeping her children safe had been hard enough when they had been small and under her wing; she had never dreamed how much harder it would be when they were grown. But then, like all who were old enough to remember the First World War, she had not believed that such dreadful times would ever come again.

How wrong they had all been.

THREE

It was strange now to recall how nervous she had been the first morning she had turned up for work at the Postal Censorship Office in Liverpool, Katie thought tiredly as she got off the train at Holborn tube station, hurried along with the flow of passengers along the tunnel and then up into the daylight and cold of the February morning, carrying her suitcase, so that she could go straight from work to the billet that her new employers had found for her. Her parents' friends had been willing to allow her to stay in their attic room but she had been told that there was a billet going in a house in Cadogan Place, off Sloane Street, which had been requisitioned by the War Office, and that it would make much more sense for her to move in there. Of course she had agreed.

Like Liverpool, London had been badly blitzed by German bombers, the evidence of the damage the city had suffered inescapable, that same air of weary greyness evident in people's faces here, just as it had been in Liverpool.

Of course the new rationing of soap wouldn't

27

help, Katie acknowledged. A lot of Londoners were up in arms, declaring that their allowance should be increased because of London's hard water and the soap's reluctance to lather. Katie had felt rather guilty about the small hoard of Pears she had acquired over Christmas and had immediately offered both her parents and their friends a bar each.

The Postal Censorship Office was situated in High Holborn, and Katie huddled deeper into her coat, glad of her scarf and gloves, knitted for her by Jean and lovingly given to her before she had left Liverpool for London just before Christmas.

She must not cry, she would not cry, Katie told herself fiercely, but she was still forced to blink away the moisture blurring her vision.

A newspaper vendor standing on the street, stamping his feet, caught her eye. The papers were full of the dreadful news of the fall of Singapore. What had she got to cry about compared with what those poor people had to endure, Katie rebuked herself.

The war was wearing everyone down. There seemed no end to the bad news and the losses amongst the British fighting men. The spirit that had got them through the blitz was beginning to wear thin under the burden of worry loss and deprivation. You could see it in people's faces – and no doubt in her own, Katie realised.

When she finally reached the building she was looking for Katie hesitated for a moment before going in. It was impossible not to contrast how she was feeling now with what she had felt that first morning at the Postal Censorship Office in Liverpool; hard too not to think of Carole, who had been so kind to her then, and who she had thought of as her friend. She must just tell herself that in causing Luke to end their engagement Carole had done her a favour, Katie warned herself determinedly. How could she ever have been truly happy with Luke, no matter how much she loved him, when he refused to trust her?

Once she was inside the building the well-built uniformed guard on duty directed Katie towards the reception desk, where she produced the letter confirming her position. She didn't have to wait long before someone came to collect her, a calm-looking older girl, as different from Carole as it was possible to be, Katie thought gratefully as the other girl introduced herself as Marcy Dunne.

'You'll be on my section,' Marcy explained. 'I'm the most senior of us, although not a supervisor. We deal with the mail coming in from and going out to our POWs, and I must warn you that it can sometimes be difficult – we get to read an awful lot of Dear John letters. It looks like you're moving to a new billet?' she commented, eyeing Katie's suitcase.

'Yes,' Katie confirmed. 'I've been staying with some friends of my parents, but I've been offered a billet within easier reach of here.'

When Marcy said, 'Good show,' Katie wasn't sure whether her approval was because of the billet or because Katie had been careful not to give any details of where or what her billet was.

'You'll need to go to Admin first to get yourself

sorted out with a pass, and a number to write on the correspondence you deal with.'

Katie nodded. It was the rule that everyone who checked a letter had to write their Postal Censorship number on it.

An hour later, when Katie had been given her pass and her number, Marcy reappeared to take her to where she would be working.

The room they eventually entered was set up very much the same as that in Liverpool, although here the desks were individual, like school desks, rather than long tables. Marcy showed Katie to what would be hers, and then introduced her to the half-dozen or so girls who were already at work – naturally, with it being her first day, Katie had been keen to arrive early – including one named Gina Vincent, who gave Katie a warm friendly smile that made her feel that she was genuinely welcome.

'You'll soon settle in, I'm sure,' Marcy assured Katie. 'There's a Joe Lyons not far away, and a decent British Restaurant, although you'll find that it gets pretty busy, what with so many government departments around.

'As you've done this kind of work before you'll know the ropes. If anything strikes you as suspect, inform your supervisor. We've got fairly senior representatives from all the services here, as well. Any questions?'

'No, I don't think so.'

'I've put you next to Caroline for today so that you can work together until you get the hang of the way we do things here,' Marcy added.

'No doubt Mrs Harper, the supervisor for our group, will have a word with you when she arrives.'

At least she had been able to get a transfer from Liverpool to High Holborn, Katie comforted herself as she diplomatically allowed Caroline to show her how to open the envelopes from the side, so that the letter inside wasn't in any way damaged, although of course she already knew the procedure. She couldn't have borne to have had to go back to her old desk, with all its memories, and she certainly couldn't have gone back to her billet with Luke's parents. The head of her department at Liverpool's Postal Censorship Office had told her that her request for a transfer to London would make the London Office very happy indeed as they were short of staff, whilst the return to Ireland, of the young Irishmen who had caused Katie so much heart-searching had also meant that there was no longer an ongoing covert operation to keep a check on any mail they might have sent or received whilst living in Liverpool. She must forget about Liverpool and all the memories it held, she told herself, and try to focus on the present instead. She had a job to do, after all, and worthwhile one.

Because of her experience working in Liverpool and the excellent report she had been given, she had now been upgraded to work on more sensitive mail and cablegrams here in London and, modest as always, Katie hoped that they weren't thinking she was better at her job than she actually was.

'I'm sure you'll like it working here,' Caroline assured her, having given Katie's dexterous opening

31

of the small pile of envelopes she had handed to her an approving smile. 'Our first office was in a converted prison, but this is much better. And conveniently central too. Not that we didn't have a bit of a time with it during the blitz, mind you.'

Katie nodded, but Caroline's reference to the blitz reminded her of Luke and his kindness to her when Liverpool had been bombed, and she had to blink away her tears. She was trying desperately hard not to think about Luke or Liverpool, or anything connected with her poor broken heart, but it wasn't easy. The last thing she wanted to do, though, was to break down completely and make a fool of herself.

Perhaps another kind of girl would have written right back to Luke and firmly put him right by explaining just what had really happened, but Katie just hadn't had the heart to do that. Not when Luke had made it so obvious that he didn't trust her. She wasn't the sort to cling on to a man when she felt in her heart that he had fallen out of love with her and that he was glad of an excuse to break things off.

FOUR

Emily decided that it was a good job that Tommy, the boy she had found half starved and freezing, living off scraps at the back of the theatre in Liverpool where her good-for-nothing husband was the manager, wasn't here to see her peering anxiously out of the kitchen window like this. He'd be bound to ask questions. He was a bright boy, was Tommy, and no mistake, and all the brighter too since they had left Liverpool and come to live here in Whitchurch. Happy as larks, she and Tommy were, with their tacit agreement that neither would reveal to anyone else his or her past or the fact that they were not even related, never mind aunt and adopted nephew, as everyone now believed them to be.

Or at least Emily had been happy. Until last week when she had gone and spoiled everything, like the silly fool she was, by going and giving Wilhelm, the German POW who kept her vegetable garden so productive for her, a pair of thick woollen socks she had knitted for him.

Of course he wouldn't want to come here any

more now that she had gone and made a fool of herself – yes, and probably made him feel like a fool as well, embarrassing him with her gift; her, a plain woman who had never been what you might call pretty even in her youth, and who no man, especially a handsome, well-set-up man like Wilhelm, would want to think admired him. A daft lonely married woman, who had no right to be knitting socks for any man other than her husband. Not that he would have welcomed hand-knitted socks. A bit of a dandy Con had always considered himself.

Poor Wilhelm had probably had his fellow POWs laughing their heads off at him on account of her gift. Why hadn't she just left things as they were instead of behaving so daft and losing Wilhelm's company into the bargain?

It was over a week now since she had given him the socks and she hadn't seen him since. Normally he appeared most days, not spending as much time here as he had done in the summer, of course, since it was winter and there was plenty to keep him busy at Whiteside Farm where he and some of the other POWs worked, but he'd been here most days, tidying the vegetable garden and even insisting on doing other little jobs for her, like fixing that loose handle on the back door and sorting out the gutter blocked with autumn leaves.

She'd enjoyed the few minutes they'd usually shared together when she took him his cup of tea and a bit of something to eat – looked forward to them, in fact – and now it was all spoiled thanks to her own stupidity. What on earth had possessed her? Hadn't she learned anything from the misery of her marriage to Con? Her husband had been unfaithful to her from the day they had married, and the truth was that she'd been glad to leave him behind in Liverpool.

The trouble was that she hadn't really thought through just how her knitting Wilhelm those socks might look. All she'd thought of was his poor cold feet in those thin Wellington boots he always wore. It hadn't been until she mentioned after church on Sunday about knitting the socks, and Biddy Evans, who was related to old Mrs Evans and her daughter, Brenda, who ran the local post office, had given a little tinkling laugh and said so loudly that everyone around them must have heard her, 'Knitting socks for a POW! Well, I never. You'll have him thinking you're sweet on him next,' that Emily had realised just what kind of interpretation others, including Wilhelm himself, might put on her gift.

Thankfully her kind neighbour Ivy Wilson had immediately said that Biddy was talking nonsense and that Emily was to be applauded for her charitable act, but of course the damage had been done by then and Emily had hardly dared look at anyone since when she went shopping, she felt so uncomfortable and self-conscious about what Biddy had said.

She was glad that it was still winter and the days short. That way Tommy wasn't going to start asking when he came in from school why Wilhelm hadn't been round. Proper fond of Wilhelm, Tommy was.

It did a boy good to have a decent hard-working man around, not like that feckless husband of hers. Not that he had approved of her taking Tommy in, not for one minute. But then it was her money they'd been living on and her house they'd been living in, and for the first time in her marriage Emily had stuck to her guns and told her husband that if it came to a choice between him and Tommy then she was choosing Tommy.

Now that she had done exactly that she was happier than she had ever been in the whole of her life, or at least she had been until she had gone and made a fool of herself with those socks and frightened Wilhelm away.

'What are you still doing here, Lena? Your shift finished half an hour ago. Gavin will have something to say to me, I'm sure, if he thinks I'm making his wife work longer than she should,' Bella teased her billetee, before bending down to look into the pram where Lena's nearly three-month-old baby daughter, Janette, named after Gavin's mother, Janet, was smiling up at them both, her big brown eyes wide open, her soft dark curls escaping from under her white knitted bonnet, one fat little hand lying on top of the smart white coverlet embroidered with yellow daisies that had been made from an old dress of Bella's.

'And how is my precious, precious niece, the prettiest angel that ever was?' Bella cooed at the baby, who immediately dimpled her a delighted smile.

'Spoiled rotten by you and Gavin, and Gavin's

mum, and just about everyone else that she winds round her little finger, that's how she is,' Lena laughed, but it was plain that she adored her baby.

Behind them the walls of the nursery, painted a bright sunny yellow by Lena's husband, Gavin, gave the day room an air of warmth no matter what the weather was outside, the small tables and chairs spotlessly clean, just like the cots and small beds in the 'sleeping room' beyond the day room, where the children had their afternoon naps, in comfortable and safe surroundings, watched over by Bella's carefully selected and trained nursery staff.

'I was going,' Lena continued, 'but Mrs Lewis was late picking up her Cheryl, and so I hung on because I wanted to tell her about Cheryl being a bit off colour and not wanting her dinner.'

Bella was very proud of the nursery in Wallasey, of which she was the manageress. All her girls were handpicked by Bella herself, but there was no doubt in Bella's mind that Lena was the best of them all. Even so, she didn't want Gavin thinking that she was taking advantage of Lena and expecting her to work longer than she should. Gavin and Lena were newly married, after all, and the last thing Bella wanted to do was to cause trouble between them.

Lena loved Gavin, Bella knew that, but Lena also felt a strong sense of gratitude towards her. Such a strong sense of gratitude, in fact, that Bella felt she had to be especially careful never to do or say anything that would in any way hurt Lena.

It had been totally out of character for her to

take Lena under her wing, Bella would have been the first to admit. Before knowing Lena, she had been selfish and uncaring. But the war and the problems it had brought her, along with the responsibility she felt towards Lena, had changed her, and now Bella knew that she was a very different person from the Bella she had been in 1939 on the eve of her own marriage.

That Bella seemed so alien to her now.

It had taken betrayal by her husband, widowhood, falling in love with the wrong man, having to cope with her father's desertion of her mother, and her brother's abandonment of Lena, the girl he had so carelessly impregnated before marrying someone else, to change her into the Bella she was now: a Bella who truly knew the value of friendship and kindness and doing one's bit for others and a Bella who had suffered the pain of forbidden love and the sacrifice that had entailed for the sake of others. A Bella who no longer felt the need constantly to scheme to make sure that she was considered the prettiest and most sought-after girl in the area, and a Bella who longed only to be the very best person she could be. The Bella who was truly worthy of the love of the man who could never be hers, but who she knew she would love for ever – Jan Polanski, the Polish Air Force pilot, whose mother and sister had been billeted with Bella at one time, and whose marriage to the daughter of a close family friend meant that no matter how much he and Bella loved one another, they could never be together.

'Well, you must go now,' Bella warned Lena,

'otherwise there will be no dinner on the table for Gavin when he comes home from working on the river.'

Gavin was a junior river boat pilot – one of the men who brought safely into dock the convoys of ships that crossed the Atlantic in such dangerous conditions to bring much-needed supplies into the country.

'However, before you do go, there's something I want to say to you. It's about the house.'

Immediately Lena gave Bella an anxious look. Lena and Gavin were now living with Bella in the house Bella's father had given Bella and her husband when they had first married, and which now belonged to Bella. Guessing what Lena was thinking, Bella gave a quick shake of her head.

'No, it isn't anything for you to worry about. It's my mother, Lena. I don't have to tell you the situation.'

Lena knew that Bella's mother, Vi, who had been living on her own since, shockingly, her husband, Edwin, had left her to live with his secretary, had been very badly affected by her husband's departure.

'It's ever such a shame that she's taken your dad going off the way he did like she has, and I know how much it upsets you, her drinking like she does, and showing herself up in front of her neighbours. Oh . . .' Lena paced her hand over her mouth and looked guilty. 'I'm ever so sorry, Bella. I shouldn't have said that. I didn't mean to speak out of turn.'

As though Janette had sensed her mother's

concern she gave a small cry. Bella smiled down at her whilst Lena rocked the pram soothingly.

One of the things Bella insisted on was that no baby in her nursery was ever left to cry.

'You could never do that, Lena. I don't have any secrets from you,' Bella assured her younger friend. 'It's true that Mummy is causing both herself and me embarrassment with her drinking, and it's not good for her health either. Her doctor has told me that. When I called round the other day the cooker was left on. Lord knows what might have happened if I hadn't decided to go and see her. That was the last straw really, Lena.' Bella closed her eyes for a moment, remembering what a terrible fright it had given her to walk into her mother's kitchen and see the ring on the cooker burning. 'I can hardly sleep these days for worrying about her, so I've decided that little though it is, it's what I want to do—'

'You're going to move her in with you?' Lena guessed, adding immediately, 'You'll want me and Gavin to find somewhere else, I expect.' Lena tried not to sound as low as Bella's news made her feel. She knew how lucky she and Gavin were, and how generous it had been of Bella to let them live with her.

'Would you mind, though, Bella, if just for now perhaps me and Gavin could move into Janette's room with her? I don't want to put you out, not when you've been so good and generous to us, but Gavin was only saying the other night that Mrs Stone, his old landlady, has let his room, and—'

'No, Lena, please stop,' Bella pleaded, holding

up her hand to stem Lena's outpouring of words, horrified that Lean would think that she would ask them to leave. 'Of course I don't want you and Gavin to find somewhere else. Lena, I thought you knew me better than that.' Bella gave Lena's arm a loving shake. 'Haven't we both already agreed that we are the sisters to one another that neither of us ever had? And isn't little Janette here my niece, my own flesh and blood, and Gavin so clever and kind about doing things around the house and here at the nursery that he saves me a small fortune?'

All of which was true, Bella thought, mentally running through all the small jobs that Gavin did so willingly, often noticing that they needed doing before Bella did herself, and not just at the house but here too at the nursery, fixing rattling windows, cleaning out gutters and downspouts.

But more important than any of that was the love Lena gave her, the kind of generous freely given love that Bella had never known before, and that Bella truly believed had changed her and her life for the better.

'Do you really think I would want to lose any of that, and most especially you? No,' Bella answered her own question, 'what I have decided to do is to make you and Gavin my official tenants for my house. That way you'll have a spare room for when Gavin's mum wants to come and stay, and I will move in with my own mother.'

For a few seconds, as she struggled to take in the generosity of Bella's offer, Lena couldn't speak. When she could she protested, 'Oh, Bella, no.

You've always said as how you value your own independence and how you could never go back to living under your mum's roof.'

'That was before,' Bella replied calmly. 'Mummy can't possibly be left on her own any more and I'd never forgive myself if . . . well, if anything happened.'

As Bella's voice fell away she couldn't bring herself to look at Lena, knowing what she would see in the younger girl's eyes. But she had no choice, Bella reminded herself firmly.

Lena's tenderly sympathetic, 'Oh, Bella . . .' prompted her to admit, 'I haven't said anything before, but to be honest, Lena, Mummy isn't looking after herself or the house properly. When I went round the other day there wasn't a clean cup anywhere, and Mummy was looking dreadfully untidy. When I think of how smart she was, and how house-proud.' Bella bit her bottom lip. 'I feel guilty, Lena, because I've been pretending not to know how bad things are, not to see how much Mummy needs me to be there with her. I've been trying to blame my father—'

'And why not? It was his fault, after all,' Lena defended her best friend fiercely.

'Yes, but, well, I've made up my mind, Lena, and tonight when I come in I shall start packing up my things so that I can move in with Mummy. It is all for the best, for you and Gavin and Baby, as well as for Mummy. You are a newly married couple, after all, and you should have a home all to yourselves,' she told Lena generously.

'Oh, that is so typical of you, Bella – that you

put everyone else before yourself,' Lena told her emotionally. 'I shall miss you dreadfully, you know.'

'And I you,' Bella admitted. 'But we shall see one another every day here, and I dare say that you and Gavin will invite me round for tea some Sundays,' she added teasingly.

Lena's 'Oh, Bella,' was muffled as she reached out and hugged Bella tightly.

After Lena had gone Bella turned to go to her office and then stopped, unable to resist giving the nursery a swift look of pride. The air was filled with the hum of quiet industry and sounds of contented babies and children. Bella had even managed to expand the facilities modestly in order to provide simple little lessons for those children who were ready for them – just learning their letters and that kind of thing, Bella had explained earnestly to Mr Benson, the senior civil servant in charge of the Government administration of nursery care for the area, an initiative allowing young women to work to help the war effort.

He had been very generous in his praise for her expansion, and had even managed to find her nursery some little slates and an easel from somewhere.

It was Bella's ambition to have 'her' little ones ready for school, with their letters and figures all learned by the time they were ready to leave the nursery.

Their small kitchen provided simple nourishing meals for the children, satisfying the Government's stringent rules and directions on nutrition. There was no cost-cutting in Bella's nursery so that those who worked there could benefit at the children's expense, and in fact Bella had a growing number of little ones under her wing who by rights should not have been there, but who, Bella had learned, were in need in one way or another, and who she had felt compelled to help: little ones who might not otherwise have had a good hot meal, or a bath, or a clean bed, to sleep in.

She had been astonished, and more than a little wary at first, when her auntie Francine had turned up at the nursery with her young American husband during their visit to Liverpool to attend Bella's cousin Grace's wedding, and had shown such an interest in the children and their welfare. The Bella she now was had been acutely aware of the sadness in her aunt's face when she had played with the children, knowing how terrible it must have been for her to lose her own little boy – not once but twice – the first time when she had given him up to her sister, Bella's mother, to bring up, and the second time when he had been killed when the farmhouse to which he had been evacuated had been bombed.

Bella looked at her watch. Her mother's neighbour, Muriel James, had agreed to keep an eye on her mother until Bella could move in herself later this evening. Privately Bella was dreading going back to her childhood home to live. It had taken Lena to show her how devoid of true family love and happiness that home had been, and now Bella's heart was chilled by the very thought of that emptiness. How she would miss the happy, chatty atmosphere of her own kitchen with her and Lena cooking together; the evenings when they read their books and listened to the radio, or sometimes played cards.

It was selfish to feel so low, Bella warned herself. It would do Lena and Gavin good to have some time to themselves. Gavin was a really decent sort who loved Lena and little Janette, and who deserved to have his wife to himself. It wasn't as though she was never going to see Lena and her baby again, was it?

'Four kings.'

The young American was sweating with triumph as he placed his cards down on the rickety baize-covered table in the upstairs room of the Pig and Whistle pub. He and Con were the only ones left in the game now. The other four Americans, and two stagehands from the Royal Court Theatre to whom Con gave a few quid to join the game so that he wasn't the only one at the table not in uniform, had dropped out. Con knew he must be careful. The last thing he wanted was to arouse anyone's suspicions. Con might like winning at cards and might not mind cheating to do so, but he certainly didn't like the kind of trouble that involved fists and accusations flying everywhere.

'Sorry, mate.' Shaking his head, Con spread his own four aces on the table, and then swept up the pot whilst the Americans were still grappling with their disappointment.

Not a bad evening's work. The Yanks put down five-pound notes like they were ten-bob notes, and

Con reckoned he'd got himself a good hundred pounds or so in tonight's haul. Not that it was all profit, of course. He'd have to give that lazy good-for-nothing pair Stu and Paul a tenner apiece to keep them sweet, and then there'd have to be another tenner to Joe the landlord for the use of his upstairs room and no questions asked, seeing as gambling was illegal.

'Look, lads,' he told the Americans, putting his arm round the shoulder of the one his aces had just trumped in a false gesture of bonhomie, 'seeing as you've been such good sports, I'll treat you each to a drink. Show's almost over at the Royal Court and there'll be plenty of pretty girls wanting to be taken out for a bit of supper, so why don't you all come back with us?'

It worked like a charm every time, Con congratulated himself as the young men immediately forgot about the money they had lost and accepted his offer with enthusiasm. Or at least all but one seemed to have accepted it. The soldier whose kings Con had just so cleverly trumped – with the aid of some trickery that had allowed him to remove the aces from the deck right at the beginning of the game and keep them concealed within his own hand of cards – was glowering at him.

'You know what Ah reckon, boys?' he announced in an accusatory voice. 'Ah reckon that this guy here's been cheating on us.'

'Come on, Chip. Don't be a sore looser,' the first soldier to drop out of the game cautioned him. 'It's only a few bucks, after all. Let's go and see these girls.'

46

'That's right, it's only a few bucks,' Con immediately agreed, smiling genially, urging them all towards the door. Once he'd had a couple of drinks and been introduced to the chorus line, the young soldier, who was still glaring at him, would soon forget about his 'few bucks'. The last thing Con wanted to do was antagonise this new source of income he had discovered. What Con wanted was for these young soldiers to feel they'd had such a good time that they encouraged their friends to ask for an introduction to him for 'a friendly game of cards' and the chance to meet pretty girls.

Funny how things turned out. Who would have thought that those card tricks of old Marvo the Magician, who did the panto every Christmas, would come in so handy?

Oh, yes, Con was well pleased with himself. After he'd given Joe his tenner, Con gave the barmaid a wink and patted her on the bottom on his way past.

''Ere, get your hands off of that,' she warned him, but the smile she was giving him told Con that she'd be more than willing if he wanted her to be.

He'd always had a way with women – had his way with them, and all, Con thought to himself, grinning at his own mental joke as he paused briefly as he left the pub to check his reflection in the glass partition that separated the entrance from the taproom, smoothing down his still thick and dark hair. When it came to women you either had it or you didn't, Con acknowledged, and he had 'it' in spades.

47

Life had really been on the up and up for him since the Americans had started to arrive in Liverpool. It was only natural that they'd find their way to the Royal Court Theatre; Con prided himself on having the best-looking girls in the city in the Royal Court's chorus. Then when he'd found out about their free-spending ways, of course he'd wanted to channel some of that money in his own direction.

It had been one of the girls who'd told him that an American had been asking her if she knew anywhere where they could join a poker game, and Con had immediately seen a golden opportunity to make some extra money.

Con whistled happily to himself as he shepherded his little group of newly fleeced lambs through the blackout's darkness of the narrow back alleys towards the Royal Court Theatre.

FIVE

Katie had been surprised by how quickly her first day had passed. She'd accepted an invitation to go for lunch with several of the girls she was working with, queuing alongside young women both in and out of uniform, and men as well, in a nearby British Restaurant for a bowl of unexpectedly tasty soup and a cup of tea.

Now, having taken the Piccadilly Line from Holborn to Knightsbridge, she was walking a little uncertainly down Sloane Street towards her new billet.

She knew the area, of course, having lived in London most of her life before she had gone to work in Liverpool. Her mother had always loved going to Harrods and looking at the expensive clothes, but Katie, whose tastes were far more simple, had never imagined actually living in one of the elegant squares with their private gardens, which had looked very smart before Hitler's bombs had caused so much damage to them and the city. It had shocked and hurt her to see just how much damage had been done.

The gardens belonging to Cadogan Place were split in two, bordered on one side by Sloane Street itself and on the three others by what she remembered as elegant four-storey properties, although it was impossible actually to see much of them in the dark and the blackout.

Her destination lay on the far side of the square and it was with some trepidation that, having found the house, she climbed the steps and knocked on the door.

She was still waiting for it to be opened when someone bumped into her from behind, almost knocking her over.

'Oh crumbs, I'm most awfully sorry.'

'It's all right,' Katie assured her. 'No harm done.'

The other girl was wearing an ATS uniform, her cap rammed onto a mop of thick dark red curls.

'Are you visiting someone?' the small whirlwind of a figure, or so it seemed to Katie, asked as she produced a key to unlock the door.

'Actually I'm supposed to be billeted here,' Katie told her.

'Oh, you've got poor Lottie's room then. So dreadful for her when Singapore fell, with her parents both being out there. She was quite overcome by it, poor girl, and the medics have sent her on sick leave. I don't think she'll be coming back. Well, you wouldn't, would you, not if you were her, and your parents had been killed – murdered, really – in such a shocking way? Her mother was at that hospital, you see, the one where the Japanese bayoneted those poor people.'

They were inside the house now, the front door closed, and a single gloomy light bulb illuminating what in happier times must have been a rather grand entrance, Katie suspected. Now, though, denuded of furniture, its walls bare of paintings and the stairs bare of carpet, the house looked very bleak indeed. But not as bleak, surely, as the outlook for the girl whose room she was taking, Katie thought soberly.

'Oh, you haven't got anyone out in Singapore, have you?' the other girl asked, looking conscious-stricken.

'No.' Not Singapore, but Luke was fighting in the desert, even if he wasn't hers any more, and the news from there was hardly much better than it was from Singapore.

'You're in luck with your room; it's one of the best. Sarah Dawkins, one of the other ATS girls here, wanted to move into it but our billeting officer put her foot down. Jolly good show that she did as well, if you ask me, because Sarah gets a bit too big for her boots at times. Oh, no, now you're going to think badly of us. We all get on terrifically well together, really.'

The front door suddenly opened and another girl in an ATS uniformed rushed in, exclaiming, 'Oh, Gerry, there you are. I couldn't remember where we said we'd meet those RAF boys tonight, Oh—' she broke off and looked questioningly at Katie.

'Katie Needham,' Katie introduced herself. 'I'm the new girl.'

'Hilda Parker.'

The other girl shook Katie's hand whilst 'Gerry' grinned and announced, 'And I'm Geraldine – Gerry, for short – Smithers.'

'There are six of us here in all, including you: me, Gerry here, Sarah, Peggy, and Alison. Peggy's newly engaged to a corporal she met at Aldershot. She's a darling but she tends to spend her time reading and knitting and writing to her chap—'

'Whereas we spend ours looking for handsome men in uniform to take us out. If you are fancy-free then you'd be very welcome to come out with us. As far as chaps are concerned it's the more the merrier where girls are concerned,' Gerry added with a giggle.

'Don't pay too much attention to Gerry here,' Hilda warned Katie. 'The truth is that in a way we feel that it's our duty not just to keep our own chins up but to try to bring a bit of cheer into other people's lives as well, if we can. I think it comes from working at the War Office. One sees and hears so much about the importance of good morale, as well, I may add, Gerry,' she punned, 'as good morals.'

It seemed the most natural thing in the world for Katie to join in the laughter as Gerry herself laughed good-humouredly at the small joke against her.

Katie couldn't help but feel her spirits lift a little. The ATS girls might initially have portrayed themselves as a fun-loving, slightly giddy bunch but Katie felt that Hilda's comment was far more true of what they really felt, and that beneath their pretty hair, and the smart chat that matched their smart uniforms, they were all young women who took their responsibilities towards their country and the men fighting to protect it very seriously indeed.

Perhaps it would do her good to adopt a little of their outward attitude to life herself, Katie reflected. After all, the last thing she wanted to do was to cast a pall of self-pity over the house just because of her own heartache. There was a lot to be said for keeping up other people's spirits in these dreadful times, the darkest times of the war in many ways, people were saying.

'It's a pretty decent billet really,' Hilda continued, 'although you have to watch out for the rules—'

'No shaking of mats or cloths out of any of the windows, no hanging of laundry out of the windows, no spooning on the front step, definitely no bringing men into the house, and no gawping at Lord Cadogan when he's on home leave and you see him walking past,' Gerry broke in again, this time leaving Hilda to explain.

'Lord Cadogan – Earl Cadogan, actually – owns the property. He owns most of the houses here, in fact, although the War Office has requisitioned some of them.'

'I'll take you up to your room, shall I?' Gerry offered, leaving Katie to follow her as she started to climb the first flight of stairs.

Katie's room was two flights up and was a very good size indeed, with a window overlooking the street and the garden beyond.

The room was furnished with a narrow single bed, a utilitarian dressing table and a wardrobe. It had a fireplace and, to Katie's delight and astonishment, there was a door that led into her own personal bath-room. Luxury indeed, and yet after Gerry had left her to unpack, and despite her good intentions, Katie acknowledged that she was missing the cosiness of her room at Luke's parents' house quite dreadfully, and the loving kindness of Jean, and the company of Luke's teenage sisters even more.

She must not think like that, she chided herself. She must put Liverpool and Luke behind her and get on with her life as it was now, doing all she could to play her own part in the war effort. perhaps right now this four-storey town house, with its cold air smelling of damp khaki and cigar-ettes, instead of being filled, as the Campion house had been, with the warmth of Jean's cooking and her love for her family, might seem alien and lonely, but she must get used to it, and fit into it and with those living in it, and make a new life for herself. She was, after all, alive and in good health, and not suffering as so many people were in this war, and in so many different ways. All she had to live with was a broken heart. The newspapers were full of the most horrific stories of what was happening to others: the people taken prisoner by the Japanese, the Jewish people forcibly transported to Hitler's death camps. She must put her whole effort into doing her bit instead of feeling sorry for herself.

Francine looked at her husband with some concern.

'Are you sure you want to go to this reception at the American Embassy tonight, Brandon?' she asked gently.

'Sure I'm sure.'

They both knew that what she really meant was, was he well enough to attend the reception being given by the American Ambassador at the Embassy in Grosvenor Square, to mark the arrival of the first American troops on British soil?

Their marriage was an unconventional one in many people's eyes: Francine was older than her husband by nearly a decade, and he was wealthier than her by several million dollars. What they did not see or know, however, was that Brandon was a young man living under a death sentence because of a rare incurable illness, and that their marriage was one between friends rather than lovers. Brandon had chosen Fran as the person he wanted to accompany him to the end of his personal road, and she had willingly taken on the responsibility of that role. She had lost so much in her life already: her son, Jack; Marcus, the man she loved, the major with whom she had fallen in love in Egypt and who she had lost thanks to the spitefulness of another member of the ENSA group they were both in. She knew and understood what loss was. What she felt for Brandon was a combination of womanly pity and a desire to offer him what comfort she could in memory of the child – the young son – who had died without the comfort of her presence and the warmth of her arms around him. She could not go back and change things where Jack, her son, was concerned. For him she could only grieve and bear the burden of her guilt. But in doing what she was for Brandon, she was, she felt, making some kind of atonement in her own small way.

'Besides,' Brandon continued, 'you don't think I'm going to miss out on celebrating the fact that America has finally officially joined this war of yours, do you?'

Francine knew better than to try to dissuade him.

Neither of his divorced parents knew of his condition. His father, according to Brandon, would simply refuse to accept that his son could suffer ill health, and his mother would threaten to have a nervous breakdown.

'Poor little rich boy,' Francine had sometimes teased him when they'd first met, but now that she knew how apt the description was she no longer used it.

They had met the previous autumn when Fran, as the lead singer in a London theatre revue, had been invited to attend a diplomatic event to help entertain some visiting American top brass.

She knew that her sister Jean had been worried by the speed with which they had married – until Francine had taken Brandon home to Liverpool with her to attend Jean's daughter Grace's Christmas wedding and had had a chance to explain the situation honestly to her older sister. Her family might know that Brandon was poorly, but only Jean knew the reality of Francine's marriage.

Francine had stopped working for ENSA. Brandon's needs came before anything else now. And for that same reason she had felt that it was wiser for them to live in a service flat at the Dorchester rather than rent a flat of their own. As an entertainer she was used to living in hotels, and

Brandon's service flat was positively palatial compared with some of the accommodation she had had. Not only did it have two double bedrooms, each with its own bathroom and sitting room, there was also a dining room, a small kitchen and a maid's room. Not that they had or needed a maid, but they both knew that the time would come when the services of a full-time nurse would be required.

Francine was determined that Brandon would be nursed 'at home' and amongst the benefits of being at the Dorchester was that, along with room service meals, there was a doctor on twenty-four-hour call.

Brandon was insistent that no one outside Fran's family was to know about his condition unless they absolutely had to.

Tonight was a very special occasion for Brandon, as an American, and Francine could almost feel his pride a couple of hours later when they were waiting in line inside the American Embassy to shake hands with the line up of American military top brass standing with the Ambassador.

The double doors to the room in which the reception was being held were guarded by American servicemen looking far smarter than their war-weary British counterparts. Just the sight of British Army uniforms, though, was enough to remind Francine of Marcus. So silly of her when it was all over between them . . .

The guests being, in the main, American airmen – commanding officers waiting impatiently for the agricultural land of Norfolk and the South East to be turned into the hard surface airfields on which their huge bombers could land and take off, – there were far more men in uniform than there were female guests, although the Ambassador had obviously done his best to even up the numbers by inviting several women whom Francine recognised as senior members of the American Red Cross, as well as a sprinkling of women in uniform, along with other women such as Mollie Panter-Downes, the London correspondent for the *New Yorker*.

Eventually it was Francine and Brandon's turn to shake hands, the Ambassador discreetly stressing Brandon's name, or so Francine, with her trained ear, felt, as though wanting to underline for the benefit of the Military top brass just who he was.

As an American billionaire, Brandon's father was a hugely influential political figure, but Francine knew that despite his obvious pride in his country's decision to join the war, later, when they were on their own, Brandon would be cast down by the sense of personal worthlessness he often felt, that came from being 'the son of' his father rather than being valued for his own achievements, however modest.

The American Embassy had originally been owned by the Woolworth heiress, who had given it to the American Government, and was an elegant backdrop for tonight's well-dressed gathering. Not wanting to let Brandon down, Fran had decided to wear one of the outfits she had had made in Egypt: a beautiful full-length gown in palest blue slipper satin, which followed the curves of her body without clinging vulgarly. High in the neck at the front, at the back the dress dipped down to below her waist, where it was embellished with embroidery in the shape of a butterfly sewn with tiny seed pearls, blue and green beads, and diamanté. A wrap of sheer silk organza dyed the same colour as the dress and sprinkled with seed pearls and diamanté covered her bare arms and back, and Francine carried with her an evening bag made from the same fabric as her dress.

She knew that her appearance – and no doubt her lovely dress, she thought with rueful amusement – was attracting a good deal of attention as they circulated amongst the other guests, but Francine was more concerned about Brandon. She was trying to keep a subtly careful eye on him, whilst at the same time concealing her concern for him beneath the 'public' cloak of charm and her well-honed ability to put other people at their ease, which she had acquired during the years of her singing career. Francine was not someone who would ever compromise her own principles or cultivate anyone's friendship to aid her own prospects. She had far too much staunchly Liverpudlian independence and spirit to do that, along with a Liverpudlian sense of humour, but she did feel that easing the wheels of social discourse was an asset that it made good sense to acquire. Old-fashioned good manners, her own mother and her sister Jean would have called it, she reflected, as she listened politely whilst a general, smelling richly of bourbon, boasted to her about how the Americans were going to 'show you Brits how to bomb the hell out of Hitler'.

'Stands to reason you ain't gonna hit much with them little toy planes of yours,' he told her with a self-satisfied grin, 'especially at night. Why, we've got bombers ten times their size, with a hundred times their accuracy, that we can send out in daylight raids to hit an exact spot.'

Francine had worked in Hollywood for a while and was familiar with a certain type of bombastically overconfident American attitude, so she held her peace.

Not so, though, Brandon, who immediately swallowed back his own drink and then announced grimly, 'Sir, we might be able to outdo the Brits with the technical abilities of our bombers, but when it comes to sheer guts and bravery, we've yet to prove we're one hundredth as good as the RAF.'

There was a small uncomfortable silence before someone, Francine couldn't see who, started to clap their hands in agreement and then within a very few seconds the whole room was clapping, causing the general to propose a toast to 'The brave men of the RAF'.

'That was so good of you,' she whispered to Brandon, her own eyes filming with silly tears. 'As a British woman, I thank you; and as your wife, I am so very proud of you.'

'Nowhere near as proud as I am of you,' Brandon whispered back.

A pianist hired for the occasion had started to play some popular American numbers, and what with all the American accents, the music, and the bottles of Coca Cola that a Marine behind the bar was swiftly opening and handing out, the Embassy felt very much like a small part of America, right in the heart of London.

Francine made a point of joining in the banter and bonhomie.

'This is exactly the kind of homey American atmosphere we want to create for our boys here in England. After all, it's the least we can do for them,' one of the American Red Cross women told her enthusiastically, only to break off with an anxious exclamation that had Francine turning round to see what was happening.

Brandon had semi-collapsed and was being supported by the anxious-looking lieutenant he had obviously lurched into.

Excusing herself, Francine went immediately to his aid, her concern on his behalf not helped by the careless, 'Damn fool boy obviously can't take his drink,' she overheard from a cigar-chomping Texan.

White-faced, with beads of sweat standing out on his pallid forehead, Brandon was making a tremendous effort to brush off the incident, and tears of pity and pride stung Francine's eyes as she saw the looks of disapproval he was attracting as he tried to straighten up and then swayed as he made to reach her.

Her whispered, 'Don't worry, darling, I've got you,' was for his ears only, her seemingly light touch on his arm, in reality a protective supportive grip that was straining her muscles.

As he leaned into her she could see that he was trying to say something, but his voice was so changed by his weakness that it took her several seconds to recognise that he was saying, 'I'm sorry.'

As he spoke he tried to straighten up but somehow instead he lost his balance and crashed to the floor, his flailing arms sending glasses flying from a nearby table as he did so.

In the silence that followed it was possible to hear the sound of liquid from the broken glasses dripping onto the floor, accompanied by the occasional nervous clearing of a throat. These small sparse sounds gradually gathered volume and pace as they were joined by hushed whispers and speedy footsteps; then the Ambassador's voice reaching down to Francine as she kneeled on the floor at Brandon's side, asking curtly, 'Is he all right?'

Knowing exactly how Brandon felt about his condition, and his determination that no one else was to know about it, Francine could only say shakily, 'He hasn't been very well,'

Above her she could hear other voices: 'He must be drunk . . .' 'How dreadful . . .' 'Shameful . . .' 'But what do you expect? I mean, he's married that showgirl . . .'

Ignore them, Francine told herself. They know nothing, mean nothing. Brandon was what mattered.

He wasn't unconscious, thank heavens, but she could see how shocked and humiliated he felt from his expression. She reached for his hand and held it tightly in her own. His doctor had warned them about this happening: a sudden weakness that would rob him of the ability to move, and perhaps even speak, that would come out of nowhere and then pass – at first – a sign that his illness was advancing.

'I'll get you some help,' the Ambassador was saying and within seconds two burly Marines had appeared and were helping Brandon to his feet, their expressions wooden but their manner fault-lessly correct and polite as they went either side of Brandon to support him.

'It's the bourbon, I guess. It's a mite too strong after London's watered-down whisky,' one wit was suggesting as Francine made their apologies to the Ambassador and explained that they would have to leave.

'But I still don't understand what you're doing here, Bella. After all, you do have a house of your own.'

Bella tried not to feel too low as she sat with her mother in the kitchen of Vi's house. It wasn't just her mother's attitude that made her feel so unwilling to be here, Bella acknowledged, it was the house itself. Her mother might have insisted on Bella's father fitting out the whole house with everything that was new and up to date when they had first moved into it a couple of years before Bella had married, but now that she knew what really made a house a home, Bella could see how cold and barren of loving warmth her mother's house was. Somehow the house was cold and unwelcoming – just like her mother?

'I have to say that I think it very selfish of you not to have made such a dreadful fuss about it that your poor brother and dearest Daphne felt unable to move into it. It's your fault that they aren't living up here, you know. Daphne would have been such a comfort to me, and of course if Charlie had been here working with your father,

63

as he should have been, then that wretched woman would never have got her claws into him. It's all your fault, Bella. You do realise that, don't you?'

Her mother's voice had risen with every imagined injustice she was relaying, causing Bella's heart to sink even further. There was no point trying to reason with her mother when she was in this frame of mind, Bella knew. Although her mother's neighbour, Muriel, had assured Bella in a conspiratorial whisper as she had left that 'Your dear mother hasn't had any you-know-what whilst I've been here, dear,' Bella suspected that her mother's current overemotional mood had its roots in alcohol.

'Did you hear me, Bella?' Vi demanded. 'It is your fault that I'm in this wretched state, and that your father has left.'

Bella wanted to be patient but her mother's selfishness and the injustice of her accusations, never mind their inaccuracies, tried her temper to its limits.

'I don't want to hear another word about Charlie or Daphne, if you don't mind, Mummy,' she began firmly, but once again her mother overruled her.

'Well, that's just typical of your selfishness, isn't it, Bella, not wanting a poor mother to talk about her beloved son? Isn't it enough for you that you practically drove poor Charlie away with your selfishness is not giving him that house? That poor boy, forced to stay in the army – and live apart from dearest Daphne when they could have been living up here, and all because of you.'

Bella put down with some force the kettle she had been just about to fill and turned to her mother.

'Mummy, that is ridiculous. You know perfectly well that why Charlie is still in the army and not up here working for Father is because he tried and failed to get himself dismissed from the army on the grounds of ill health and they very sensibly, in my opinion, saw through him and have insisted that he must do his duty, like all the other young men who have had to enlist. As for Daphne, it seems to me that she was only too pleased to have an excuse to go home to her own parents.'

'You are a very unkind sister and daughter, Bella. And it's all because of that dreadful . . . that person.'

Even now her mother could not bring herself to mention Lena by name, and blamed her and not Charlie for the fact that Lena had had Charlie's baby.

Bella felt angry on Lena's behalf, but she also felt that now that Lena was so happily married to Gavin it could do more harm than good to keep reminding her mother that Charlie was the baby's father and not Gavin, who was, after all, being a far better father to the little girl than Charlie, married to someone else, and who had refused point-blank to accept his responsibility towards Lena, could ever have been.

'I think you should go home now, Bella. I've got an awful headache, I really must go and lie down.'

Her mother's voice was thin and fretful, and Bella could see that she was plucking at the edge of the stained tablecloth, a habit Bella had noticed she had developed. A wave of pity and defeat washed out Bella's earlier anger. She lit the gas under the kettle, then went over to her mother and said lightly, 'I am home, Mummy. Remember, we talked about it this morning and I said that I would come and live here with you for a little while so that you wouldn't feel as lonely.'

'Did we? I don't remember.' For a moment her mother looked so lost and confused that Bella's heart ached for her.

'Why don't I make us both a nice cup of cocoa, Mummy, and then we can listen to the news together?'

'The news? Is it that time already?'

Bella had a particular reason to want to listen to the news today.

Half an hour later, on the pretext of going upstairs to unpack her suitcase, Bella made a quick inspection of her mother's bedroom. Its general untidiness, along with the unmade bed, was upsetting, all the more so because her mother had always been so fastidious.

At least she wasn't drinking any more like she had been when Bella's father had first left. It had been such a terrible shock for Bella to discover her mother drunk, buying gin from a criminal selling it on the black market.

Bella was so grateful to her mother's doctor for the help he had given, sending Vi to a nursing home where she could be probably looked after. But she was not the person she had been, Bella knew, although whether that was because of her drinking or because her husband had left her, or a combination of both, Bella did not know. It was impossible to imagine Bella's auntie Jean or her auntie Francine behaving as her mother had done. They were both so much stronger in their different ways, women to be admired, not pitied. Bella now felt so much closer to her auntie Jean, who had been such a rock and so very kind to her since Bella had taken her courage in both hands and gone to tell her what had happened. She didn't feel she deserved the love and kindness Auntie Jean had shown her, but she was very grateful for it.

Her aunt had been coming over from Liverpool to visit her mother at least once a week all through the winter and the bad weather, but Bella had no intention of allowing Auntie Jean to be put upon. It wouldn't be right.

Automatically she picked up the clothes her mother had left scattered around the room, putting those that needed washing aside, pulling back the bedclothes and remaking the bed. The furniture – bought new when her parents had first moved to the house, and of which her mother had been so very proud – like the rest of the house had an air of neglect about it.

The Bella who had lived in this house, spoiled and selfish, wouldn't have had the first idea about how to keep house or cook, or do anything that the Bella she was now did with such accomplishment and pride, and all the more so because they were lessons hard-learned and self-taught.

She and Lena had had such fun learning to cook together. Her own kitchen had been filled with the sound of laughter as well as the smell of food, both seasoned with love.

Her poor mother. Bella couldn't think of anything worse than being married to a man like her own father, a cold-hearted bully who thought of no one but himself, but her mother continually made it plain that she would rather be married to him than deserted by him.

Back downstairs Bella filled two hot-water bottles, one for mother's bed and one for her own.

It was eleven o'clock before she finally went to bed herself, having seen her mother safely up, and then having gone back downstairs to make a start on cleaning the kitchen. Now physically tired, she should have been ready to sleep but instead, as though it sensed her weakness and that her guard was down, the news of Bomber Command's continuing raids on enemy targets allowed her thoughts to slide towards Jan, who was a fighter pilot and not a bomber pilot, but whose life was still in danger with every mission he flew, and who she had no right to be thinking of at all. They might have admitted their love for one another and shared a little precious time together, but Bella had told him then that there must be no future meetings, no letters, and even no thinking of one another in their most private thoughts because Jan was married. She had meant what she said.

Bella knew she had made the right, indeed the only possible, decision but there were times when the temptation to let Jan into her thoughts betrayed her. As she knew all too well, letting him into her thoughts was only a heartbeat away from letting him into her imagination – and her memory – and that once there, in no time at all she would be remembering how it felt to be held in his arms, and to hold him back. How it felt to be kissed by him and to kiss him back. How it felt to be loved by him and to love him back, and then the pain would begin all over again. A double-edged pain – for herself and for the woman Bella believed she was betraying with her thoughts. She loved Jan beyond any shadow of doubt, and loving him surely meant wanting the best for him, and the very best future happiness for Jan would be for him to be happy with his wife. That was what she must pray for and hope for him, no matter what the cost to herself, because any other kind of lesser, more selfish love was not the love Bella believed her wonderful Jan deserved.

SIX

'I can't believe we've been here over a month already,' Lou announced as they all lined up outside their hut, ready for morning inspection, blinking in the late March bright morning light.

'A month? It feels more like a year,' Betty groaned, shivering in the cold wind that seemed to whistle round the base. 'It's all right for you, Lou,' she complained. 'You're so good at what we're supposed to be doing, but I just can't seem to get the hang of it.'

'Watch out, Corp's on her way,' Ellen, always the cautious one, warned them. They all stiffened into a dutiful silence as their corporal started to walk down the line of uniformed young women in her charge, checking the cap angles, hair length, shoe and button shines.

She was finding that she had a natural aptitude for what they were being taught, Lou admitted as she stood to attention. Perhaps it came from the fact that her father was, as they said, 'good with his hands' and worked for Liverpool's Salvage Corp, although her father had never in Lou's memory suggested that his daughters understand what a plane or a vice or a file was, never mind try to use one. The very thought was enough to make Lou grin.

'Something funny, is there, Campion?'

Oh Lord. She'd been so lost in her thoughts that hadn't realised that the corp had reached her.

Somehow managing not to make any retort but instead to stand to attention and look straight ahead, Lou cursed herself inwardly. Their corp – Corporal Carter, to give her her full name – was a real tartar, and had seemed to take a dislike to her after she had made the mistake, during her first week, of mentioning that her brother was also a corporal in the army. She'd only been making conversation but obviously the corporal had thought she was trying to be clever or, even worse, to curry favour, and since then she'd been coming down hard on her, finding fault as often as she could, or so it seemed to Lou.

If it wasn't the shine on her shoes that wasn't bright enough, then it was the curl in her hair, or – on one occasion – the length of her eyelashes, which the corporal had accused her of darkening with either mascara or shoe blacking, both of which were banned whilst the women were on duty.

The last thing Lou wanted now, with Easter only ten days away, was to provoke the corporal into putting her on a charge, as she had threatened to do the last time she had given her a telling-off. The pettiness of the rules and the discipline irked her at times, Lou admitted, but on the other hand she was enjoying what she was learning, even if she still felt disappointed about the fact that she was never going to get to learn to fly.

All the recruits were looking forward to their promised long weekend off over Easter, and Lou had already written to her family telling them that she would be coming home. She'd even got Sasha to promise that the two of them would go out together to the Grafton Dance Hall on Easter Saturday – just the two of them.

Lou had missed Sasha, but she still felt a bit on edge at the thought of being reunited with her twin.

She'd have so much to tell her family and, of course, so much that she couldn't tell them. Halton was a busy base with, if the grapevine was to be relied on, any number of top brass being flown in and then out of it almost daily.

'They've got some American military top bass coming down today, so I've heard,' Betty whispered excitedly to Lou a bit later whilst they were queuing for their breakfast. 'Bomber Harris is going to be here as well.'

A fully fledged leading aircraftwoman in the queue ahead of them had obviously overheard and turned round to give them each a reproving look. 'It's Air Marshal Harris to you, and we don't make a fuss about Yanks here. This is an RAF base, remember?'

Lou and Betty exchanged rueful grimaces, whilst Ruby, cheeky as always, pulled a face behind the other Waaf's back.

'I'm surprised she didn't start reminding us that walls have ears,' Betty grumbled, when they were sitting down with their breakfasts. 'Anyway, everyone knows that the American military are here and that

72

they're going to be flying those enormous bombers of theirs out of all those airfields that are being built for them. I've got a cousin who's based in London. She's been out with one of them already – one of the Yanks, I mean. She says they really know how to treat a girl.'

'A lot of people think it's fearfully bad form to step out with one of them when our own boys are overseas fighting,' was all Lou felt able to say, remembering how anti the Americans her own brother, Luke, had been when they had first arrived in Liverpool the previous year.

'I'm really looking forward to Easter. It seems ages since I saw my family – or wore civvies,' Betty complained. She heaved a heavy sigh. 'I can't wait to go to a dance wearing a dress and decent shoes. My ankles were black and blue the other Sunday, from being kicked accidentally by chaps in uniform, after we'd all been to that dance in the mess.'

'Well, at least the RAF boys get to wear a pretty decent uniform,' Ellen reminded them, coming to sit down with them just in time to catch what had been said. 'Not like the poor army boys.'

The table was full now and whilst the other girls embarked on an intense discussion about the merits and demerits of various service uniforms, Lou let her thoughts slip to their Easter weekend break.

Easter was quite late this year, which meant that her dad would already have been busy in his allotment, and although there wouldn't be any chocolate eggs because of rationing, Lou suspected that there would be wonderfully fresh eggs from the hens the allotment keepers had clubbed together to keep. Her mother was a wonderful cook. Naafi food had been an eye-opener for Lou, but she had made herself get used to it; she didn't want the others thinking she was a softie, after all.

It would be heaven to sleep in her own bed again in the room she shared with Sasha. Her sister Grace had written to tell her that although she would be on duty at the hospital in Whitchurch, where she was now working, for most of the Easter holiday, she had got Easter Monday off, when she and Seb would be coming over to Liverpool to see everyone.

There would be no Luke there, of course. He was fighting in the desert with the British Army, and there would be no Katie either, because she and Luke weren't engaged any more.

They were all upset about that, but especially her mother, Lou knew. She was never going to let herself get daft about a lad. It only led to problems and misery. She had made enough of a fool of herself over Kieran Mallory to know not to do the same thing ever again. Just look at the way it had changed Sasha. Lou just hoped that her twin would keep to her promise about just the two of them going out together on Easter Saturday, she really did.

'Auntie Jean!' Bella exclaimed with genuine delight when she stepped into the kitchen to find her aunt sitting there with her mother.

Although Vi and Jean were identical twins, the way they had lived their lives now showed in their faces so that, in their mid-forties, Jean Campion's expression was one of warmth and happiness, whilst Vi Firth's was one of dissatisfaction and irritation. Vi's hair might be iron neat in the scalloped rigid permanent wave she favoured, her twinset cashmere and her skirt expensive Scottish tweed – like her twinset, dating from before the war – but it was her auntie Jean, with her slightly untidy soft brown curls, and the kindness that shone from her hazel eyes who looked the prettier and happier of the two, Bella thought. Not that her auntie didn't look every bit as smart as her twin sister, and a good bit slimmer. Unlike Vi, Jean had kept her neat waist, and if her jumper and skirt weren't the exclusive models worn by Bella's mother they were still of good quality. The pretty lilac of the jumper her auntie was wearing with her navy serge suit enhanced her colouring. But it was the quality of her auntie's lovely smile that really showed the difference between them. Her own mother rarely smiled properly, which was why her mouth turned down, giving her a permanently dissatisfied and cross look, whilst her twin's mouth turned upwards, drawing attention to her smile and the kindness in her eyes.

Her mother might once have enjoyed showing off to her twin and boasting about the way she had moved up in the world but it was Auntie Jean who was truly the happier of the two of them and, bless her, she hadn't said so much as a single unkind word about how her twin might have brought some of her unhappiness on herself, Bella acknowledged as she hugged her aunt affectionately.

'I'm really glad now that I delayed having my

lunch so that I could pop home this afternoon to remind Mummy that it's our WVS night tonight,' Bella told her aunt, 'otherwise I'd have missed you. It's so good of you to come all this way, Auntie Jean.'

'Nonsense. It's only a matter of coming over on the ferry and then catching the bus,' Bella's mother objected immediately.

'I'll put on the kettle, shall I, Bella love?' Jean asked, giving her niece a motherly look. It meant ever such a lot to her to have this new relationship with her niece and to feel that Bella was now within the fold, so to speak, and a real part of her own family. Her own mother would have been that pleased. She'd always felt strongly about family sticking together.

Watching her aunt busy herself, Bella admitted to a small sad stab of loneliness. Living here with her mother wasn't easy, and she desperately missed her own house and Lena's company, even though she knew that in coming home she had done the right thing – for Lena as well as for her mother.

'I had a letter from Grace the other day saying that she and Seb are hoping to come up to Liverpool over Easter,' Bella told her aunt.

'That's one of the reasons why I'm here,' Jean said. 'I was wondering if you and Vi would like to come to us for your tea on Easter Monday. It won't be anything much, what with the war and every-thing, but Grace and Seb will be there, and Lou's got leave as well.'

'Well, I don't know about that, Jean,' Vi began

before Bella could say anything. 'I don't know what Charlie and Daphne's plans are yet.'

'We'd love to come, Auntie Jean,' Bella overrode her mother.

'But what if Charles and Daphne are here?' Vi asked.

'Well, they'd be very welcome too,' Jean hurried to assure her sister.

'I thought you said that when you wrote and asked Charlie what they were doing for Easter, he wrote back that Daphne's parents were having some friends to stay, and that he didn't even know if he would get leave,' Bella reminded her mother.

Personally the last thing Bella wanted was for Charlie to come home. There was the matter of Lena and the baby, for one thing, and there was no way she wanted her young friend upset or embarrassed in any way by Charlie's presence.

After they had drunk their tea, and Bella and Jean had finalised the arrangements for Easter Monday, Bella offered to travel back to the ferry terminal with her aunt.

'Oh, Bella, that's kind of you but there's really no need,' Jean protested.

'No need at all,' Vi agreed. 'I can't for the life of me think why Jean would need you to go with her, Bella, especially when she knows that I'm here on my own day in and day out with no one to speak to until you come home from that nursery. I don't know why you work there, I really don't. Not when you could have been working for your father, and if you had . . .'

Her mother was working herself up to one of

her angry outbursts, during which she'd blame her for Pauline's presence in her father's life, Bella recognised, stepping in quickly to deflect it by saying calmly, 'It was Charlie Daddy wanted to have working for him, Mummy, not me. Now, why don't you go and start getting ready for the WVS tonight?'

'Oh, the WVS. I don't think I want to go, Bella. Mrs Forbes Brown cut me at church last Sunday.'

'Don't be silly, Mummy. She just didn't see you, that's all.'

'Bella, you are such a good daughter to your mother,' Jean praised her niece later as they walked to the bus stop together, Jean now wearing a neat little navy hat she had trimmed up last year with a scrap of cream petersham ribbon.

Jean thought approvingly that Bella's businesslike dark green suit and a matching beret had a bit of a look of a uniform about it and certainly suited her niece's trim figure. A pair of court shoes showed off her dainty ankles, and Jean thought how well that style would suit Grace, who had to wear such ugly shoes for her work.

'There's really no need for you to come all the way down to the terminal with me, Bella,' Jean insisted. 'I know how busy you must be.'

'We are,' Bella agreed with a smile, 'but not so busy that I'm prepared to give up the opportunity to spend time with you, Auntie Jean.'

As Jean said to Sam later, once she had returned home and the two of them were sharing a cup of tea in the warmth of the kitchen before Sam went out to take advantage of the last of the daylight to work on his allotment, 'You'd never know our Bella for the same girl. She's changed so much, and for the better. I feel sorry for her too having to put up with Vi, the way she is, always finding fault. I know that Vi's my own sister, my twin, and heaven knows I feel sorry for her after what she's been through with Edwin treating her like he has, but she doesn't make things easy for herself, Sam, or for those around her.'

'Well, you know what I think,' Sam responded. 'Your Vi and her Edwin were a perfect match for one another, both of them as selfish as bedamned, but I know you, with that soft heart of yours, never able to resist helping others even when they don't deserve it.'

Jean gave her husband a tender smile. They'd had a good marriage, her and Sam, a happy marriage, but she knew how uncomfortable 'soppy' talk made him feel so instead of telling him how much she loved him and how glad she was that she had married him, she asked him anxiously, 'Do you think those Jersey potatoes of yours will be ready for Easter, Sam? Only there's nothing quite like your Jerseys with Easter Sunday lamb, and any that's left over will do nicely cold on Easter Monday.'

As she had known he would, Sam puffed himself up slightly with male pride and assured her, 'I reckon they will be ready, but I'm not promising,' he warned her, 'and I'm not having my Jerseys pulled up before they're ready, no matter what.'

Which Jean knew from experience meant that

she could relax and they could all look forward to the delicious treat of home-grown new potatoes with their Easter Sunday lamb.

'It will be a funny Easter this year, Sam, what with Grace married and Lou in uniform. We won't be having our Luke dropping by either.'

As she reached for her handkerchief Sam leaned across the table and took hold of her hand in his.

'Aye, love, I know.'

'It's not as bad as if he'd been in Singapore, but . . .'

Sam's hand tightened over hers.

'What do you think will happen, Sam? I thought that we were winning in Egypt, but now . . .' Anxiety thickened Jean's voice. The news from the desert – or rather, what they were allowed to know was going on – was increasingly worrying. In January Rommel's tanks had started to push back the British Eighth Army with which Luke was fighting, and which had been doing so well the previous year.

'They don't call Rommel the Desert Fox for nothing,' Sam acknowledged. 'If you ask me, Churchill should have recalled Ritchie.' Lieutenant-General Ritchie was in charge of the war in the Western Desert, and there was growing criticism of him, blaming him for the Eighth Army's current plight.

Jean knew from the sombre tone of Sam's voice that she had good cause to worry for Luke, but being the woman she was, instead of giving way to her tears, she withdrew her hand from Sam's and blew her nose very firmly.

Changing the subject she said, 'Sasha's told me that Lou has written to her suggesting that they go out dancing together, just the two of them, when she comes home at Easter. As luck would have it young Bobby has got leave over Easter himself, but seemingly he's told Sasha that he's going to go home to Newcastle to see his family. He's ever such a nice lad,' Jean concluded approvingly.

The other person who was in her thoughts was her younger sister, Francine. Fran wrote regularly, funny, witty letters – she had always had that gift – but although she mentioned Brandon she didn't say anything that gave Jean any clue as to how the young American's health was.

At Christmas Fran had promised that she would let Jean 'know when there is anything you need to know', and since she had not done so Jean could only hope that Brandon was holding his own.

'Dr Forbes is admitting a new patient today, Nurse, a German POW suffering from blood poisoning.'

Grace nodded briskly as she listened to what Sister O'Reilly was telling her. She was enjoying working at her new hospital. They dealt with a variety of cases, some military and some civilian. Matron had made her feel very welcome and had told her how pleased she was to have her, and Grace was glad she was able to put her training to good use.

'In the circumstances I think perhaps he should go in the private room at the end of the ward. To us a patient is a patient, and that is exactly how it should be, but some of our other patients may have other views.'

Grace knew exactly what sister meant. The new admission was one of their enemy, and some of the other men on the ward might either be upset by his presence or antagonistic toward him.

As a nurse, however, Grace couldn't help but feel sympathy for the German when he was eventually brought in. His lower right leg was swollen to double the size of his left leg, the flesh red and hot to the touch and drawn tight over the swollen limb. A bandage had been wrapped around what Grace guessed must be the site of the wound, but above it she could see quite plainly the telltale red line of infection.

Her heart gave a flurry of beats, the sight taking her back to the time when she had been training and Seb had been admitted to her hospital with a shoulder wound that had threatened to give him blood poisoning. She had been so afraid for him, so determined to do everything she could to help him, cleaning the wound and packing it with hot kaolin paste, making sure that he took his M & B tablets regularly.

The guard who had come in with the POW, an army squaddie, stationed himself outside the small room, telling Grace, 'You won't have much trouble with Wilhelm here. He speaks English.'

Summoning a junior nurse, Grace began to remove the dressing from the German's leg. He was a pleasant-looking man with unexpectedly nice eyes, and if she hadn't known he was a German she'd probably have thought of him as a decent sort.

The wound, once she'd removed the bandage, might not look much – a single small puncture wound that had healed over – but Grace knew how serious it was. It would have to be opened and drained of the poison inside it, the rotting flesh removed, and that telltale red line brought down because if it wasn't, well then at best the POW could lose his leg and at worse, his life. His 'Thank you' as she made him as comfortable as she could to wait for the doctor surprised her and caught her off guard. A little guardedly she smiled at him. He may be 'the enemy' but as a nurse it was her duty to take care of him.

Why doesn't Wilhelm come any more?' Tommy asked Emily when they were sitting having their tea.

'I dare say he's got better things to do. Now how about you and me starting to read *A Tale of Two Cities* tonight?' she suggested, wanting to change the subject.

Not for the world did she want anyone, including Tommy, guessing how upset she was over Wilhelm.

'We could ask the farmer, and tell him that we want Wilhelm to come back,' Tommy continued, ignoring her suggestion about the book.

'We'll do no such thing.'

'But I liked him,' Tommy protested.

'That's as maybe, but Mr Churchill's got better things to do with POWs than send them to places because little boys want him to,' was all that Emily could come up with to bring an end to the conversation. After all, Mr Churchill's decisions carried a lot of weight with Tommy, as they did with the whole country, and were not to be questioned.

SEVEN

'Come on, Lou, don't let her get away with it,' Ruby called out mischievously and challengingly, as a sponge filled with water hit Lou on the side of her face.

'Yes, come on, Lou,' Betty, who had thrown the sponge, teased her.

'I'm going to get you for that,' Lou warned mock threateningly as water ran down her face.

They were in the showers, in their bathing suits, having just been put through their paces in the gym by the PT instructor, and were in high spirits knowing that their Easter weekend break was only a handful of days away, especially Lou, who only the previous day had been praised by their instructor for her riveting skill, an essential component of their training to become aircraft repair mechanics.

Still laughing, Betty threw another water-laden sponge at her, mocking, 'You'll have to catch me first,' as she did a triumphant dance on the tiled floor outside her shower cubicle.

Spluttering and laughing herself, Lou set to work soaking both sponges, along with her own and a fourth she quickly grabbed from Ellen, who was standing just outside the shower adjoining her own, Lou's back to the room as she worked to gain her revenge, knowing that Betty would be working equally hard to beat her.

The silence that now filled the room as the others obviously waited for her return attack only added to her determination to score a hit so, when she turned round, a dripping sponge in each hand, she was already raising her arm to let fly, only realising when it was far too late that the reason for the silence was the presence of a sergeant between her and her intended victim, watching her, a sergeant whose face and uniform was now soaked in the water from the two sponges. Betty was now standing white-faced behind the dripping sergeant with a mixture of guilt and shock. It might seem a small offence and nothing more than a silly prank, the kind of thing that Lou herself would have shrugged off dismissively in her old pre-WAAF life, but, as she had quickly learned, Forces life was very different from civvy life. Once you were in uniform very strict and rigid rules controlled every aspect of your life, right down to the smallest detail. That breaking the rules was a serious crime had been dinned into them all from the moment they joined, and now Lou felt sick with the same shocked horror she could see so strongly in the faces of her pals. No one was laughing now. What Lou had done, no matter how innocently inspired, and despite the fact that her sponges had been intended for someone else, was tantamount to an assault on an NCO. And for that she could be drummed out of the service in absolute disgrace.

Where the old Lou would have had to fight back laughter at the sight of her unintended victim, her hair and the shoulders of her uniform wet, the new Lou was instead filled with stomach-curdling dread, and a very deep sense of regret.

The sergeant – not one Lou knew – looked so implacably stony-faced that Lou didn't even dare try to stammer an apology in case it was interpreted as an attempt on her part to cheek her unintended victim. The atmosphere in the showers, so light-hearted and filled with laughter only a few minutes ago, was now thick with apprehension, and no one, Lou knew, felt that more strongly than she.

Easter was only a matter of a few days away. Katie had volunteered to work over the holiday, feeling that she would far rather one of her colleagues enjoyed a well-deserved break than that she herself was off with time on her hands and nothing to do but think about last year when Luke had loved her.

She was on her way for her morning tea break when Gina Vincent, who had been so friendly since Katie's first day, called out to her to wait.

'Look, I know we're both down to work over Easter, and that we're getting a long weekend leave to make up for it later in the month. I was thinking of going away then for a bit of a break. I've always wanted to visit Bath – I'm a Jane Austen fan – and I wondered if you'd like to come along. No offence taken if you don't, mind, but it's always more jolly if you've got a pal to share things with.'

'I'd love to,' was Katie's immediate and genuinely delighted response.

It was the way of things now with the war: friendships were often quickly made, people seizing the moment because time was precious; people, especially young women working together, finding that they were making friends with a speed they might never normally have done and with girls from a wide variety of backgrounds. Katie was by nature solitary, enjoying her own company and hesitant about 'putting herself forward', but the warmth she had found within the Campion household had shown her how much happiness there was in being close to like-minded others.

She might only have known Gina for a few short weeks but what she did know of her she liked.

Tall, with mid-brown wavy hair and a calm manner, Gina was friendly to everyone, but not the kind of girl anyone would ever describe as 'bubbly' – not like Carole, whom Katie had once thought was her best friend.

'Good show,' Gina smiled, putting her arm through Katie's. 'We'll have tea at Joe Lyons one evening, shall we, and make plans? I have a pal in the navy – we grew up in the same village. He recommended an hotel in Bath to me that he says is pretty good.'

Katie nodded.

Living and working in London as a single young woman, as the ATS girls were keen on proving, meant that one need never be short of a date.

The city was constantly full of men in uniform on leave, determined to enjoy themselves.

Katie had quite got used now to being stopped in the street and asked for a date by some young man eager for female company on his precious time off. One learned to accept that eagerness and not be offended by it, whilst determinedly checking it – or not, if you happened to be the kind of girl who was as keen to enjoy all the fun that came your way, just in case there was no tomorrow. 'Good-time girls', some people referred to them disparagingly, but not Katie. She felt she understood what lay behind their sometimes desperate gaiety, and she sympathised with them.

Not that the number of testosterone-fuelled young men visiting the city was without its problems. Already there had been 'words' and a distinctly frosty atmosphere in the billet because Gerry had been dating an American serviceman.

The six of them – Sarah, Alison, Hilda, Gerry and Peggy as well as Katie herself – had been in the small dark basement back kitchen at the time, and Peggy Groves, who had been making tea for them all, had been unusually outspoken on the matter, making it plain that she disapproved, and asking pointedly, 'What about that Royal Navy chap you've been writing to, Gerry?'

'What about him?' Gerry had responded with a defiant toss of her head.

'Peggy's right,' Hilda had stepped in. 'He isn't going to be very happy when he finds out that you're dating someone else, especially an American.'

'Who says he's going to find out?' Gerry had

challenged. 'A girl has to have some fun, and Minton is fun.'

There the matter rested, for now, but privately Katie agreed with Peggy and Hilda.

As a result of the sponge incident Lou had been put on a charge and had been marched out to the guardroom, which was a small room in the admin building, in which she had been locked for twenty-four hours before being taken in front of the WAAF commander to have her case heard and punishment handed down.

She had been left in no doubt how serious her assault on an officer was, even if it had merely been a prank and its intended victim not the NCO but her pal. Now she wouldn't be going home for Easter. Lou felt sick with misery and close to tears, but of course she wasn't going to show that. Not when she was standing in front of a grim-looking commanding officer and about to be marched back to the guardhouse.

Not only was she on a charge but her hut had also had twenty points removed from it because of her behaviour, and she herself was going to have to do 'jankers' as punishment for seven days.

Lou had learned enough about being in uniform to know that there would have been no point in her protesting that she had simply been retaliating to another's deliberate provocation, no matter how strongly she had been tempted to speak the hot words in her own defence. The Forces didn't care about the whys and wherefores that might prompt an offence, only the offence itself. Not, of course, that Lou would have given Betty away anyway; that was simply not done. No, it was her own fault for not realising what the silence meant and checking before she had thrown those sponges. Her fault. How many times when she and Sasha had been growing up had she been told off for being 'too impetuous' and 'not thinking' through the consequences of her actions? Then she had shrugged off those criticisms because there had always been Sasha to share the blame with her, the two of them together against everyone else. Now, though, Lou was beginning to see that she had always been the one to institute things, dragging Sasha along with her whether or not her twin shared her desire to be rebellious. Then she had hated and resented rules of any kind, and having to do what other people did because someone else said so, but now that she was in uniform she was beginning to understand that discipline was necessary in order to achieve goals. Even something simple, such as parade ground marching, had a purpose to it. How would it be if they all marched in their own way and to their own tune? What a muddle it would cause. More important, though, than enforced discipline was, Lou recognised, learning the virtue of self-discipline, and of thinking for oneself – knowing one had to think beyond one's own immediate wishes and look to what was right for everyone in a group. Lou had a great deal of respect for the manner in which the services' way of doing things made a person feel different about themselves. For the first time in her life she was actually enjoying working for praise, and aware of how horrid it felt to be criticised and told off. Poor Sasha, was that how she had sometimes felt when she, Lou, had got them both into trouble? She'd make it up to her, tell her how much she had learned and how sorry she was for the way she knew her own past rebelliousness had sometimes upset her twin.

Sasha. Only now could Lou admit how desperately she had been longing to see her twin. But now she wasn't going to. She'd been thinking about her parents too. Her mother had been upset over Christmas when she'd told them out of the blue that she'd joined up, and her father had been angry. Then she'd shrugged aside their reaction, but even though she'd written to them telling them how happy she was, and had received loving letters back from them, Lou felt that she owed them an apology for not discussing her plans with them first and for not being grown up enough to explain how stifling and depressing she had found the telephone exchange, instead of going off like that and joining up behind their backs.

'Halt.'

Obediently Lou stopped walking. They were outside the WAAF guardhouse again. Her stomach was churning with misery in a way that reminded her of being a little girl and wanting to cling to her mother and Sash on the first day at school, but there was no Sasha here now to share that feeling with her, and no mother either to hold them both tight for a few precious extra seconds of comfort.

Her mother would be disappointed and upset

when she learned that Lou wasn't going to be home at Easter. For a few desperate seconds Lou tried to think of some suitable excuse she could make that would enable her to conceal the truth from everyone, but there was no story she could tell that her mother would accept. She had felt so proud about being able to go home and tell them how well she was doing, but now that wasn't going to happen.

At least Sasha's boyfriend would be pleased, Lou reflected bitterly, as she heard the guardhouse door being locked with her inside it.

Doing jankers would no doubt mean that she'd be set to work in the mess, peeling potatoes, washing up and scrubbing dirty floors, and of course everyone who saw her there would know that she was being punished.

Now that she was finally on her own, a solitary tear was allowed to escape.

'Oh, Mum, it's so good to see you,' Grace greeted Jean as they exchanged hugs in the Campion kitchen.

'Here, let me have a look at you,' Jean demanded, holding her eldest daughter at arm's length. 'Your face looks thinner.'

'Well, if it is it isn't for any lack of food,' Grace assured her, as Jean turned to hug Seb. 'You'd never guess what a difference it makes living in the country, Mum. I had a farmer's wife come round the other day and bring me some of her own butter as a thank you for me bandaging up her little boy's leg after he had fallen almost outside our front door. I suppose I should have refused, but, well, with me coming home I thought that you could use it.'

'I dare say you should have said "no",' Jean agreed, her eyes widening as she saw the good half-pound of butter Grace was handing over to her. Two ounces was the ration, that was all. 'But I have to admit that I'm glad you didn't. Best not say anything to your dad, though, love. He's just gone down to the allotment to water his lettuces but he should be back any minute. He's been asking me since first thing what time you were due.

'I hope she's feeding you properly, Seb,' she smiled warmly at her son-in-law.

'Impossible for Gracie not to be a good cook with a mum like you,' Seb assured her.

'Where are the twins?' Grace asked, as she took off her coat and the pretty, rather gay little hat that had been perched on top of her curls – both 1939 buys, but Grace had a good eye and was now learning to be clever with her needle, thanks to treasured copies of *Good Housekeeping* that one enterprising member of the WVS had organised to be handed on to those who put their name down on the requisite list and paid a penny for the privilege of reading it.

Jean's expression changed immediately to one of disquiet. 'We got a letter from Lou on Thursday telling us that she's been put on a charge, 'she began as she went to light the gas under the kettle she had filled earlier. She was using her special tea set, the one that Grace had given her for Christmas the year she and Seb had got engaged.

Grace and Seb exchanged glances.

'You can imagine how your dad reacted to that, Grace. I'm just glad in a way that Lou wasn't here, because he'd have torn a strip off her and no mistake.'

'What did she do? To get put on a charge, I mean?' Grace asked as she went to get the milk from the cold slab in the larder to fill the milk jug, mother and daughter working harmoniously together. Grace was a housewife herself now, after all.

'Well, as to that, from what she wrote – and of course the letter had been censored – it seems she was involved in some sort of prank that went wrong. It's like your dad said, that's Lou all over, acting first, without thinking, being too high-spirited. I don't know, Grace. I just wished she'd talked to us first before going and joining the WAAF. She's never taken kindly to rules and regulations and I've been dreading something like this happening. I just wish . . .' Jean looked out of the kitchen window, her hand still on the handle of the teapot she had just filled.

Grace knew what her mother wished: that Lou had stayed at the telephone exchange with Sasha.

'It's not the end of the world,' Seb tried to re-assure Jean, stepping in in a calm reassuring way that made Grace smile gratefully at him. 'The services are tough on sticking to the rules, but they aren't the place for people with no back bone, and Lou has plenty of that.'

'Yes, Mum,' Grace agreed quickly, picking up

on Seb's attempt to cheer her mother up. 'And from what Lou wrote to me in the letter I got the other week, she's taken to this course she's on like a duck to water.'

Jean had begun to lift the teapot but now she put it down again, smoothing her hand absently over the scarlet poppy embroidered on the starched white linen tray cloth. The tray cloth and its matching napkins had been a Christmas present from the twins before the war.

'Oh, well, yes, but that's another thing. Your dad isn't happy at all about this business of her training to mend aircraft. He doesn't think it's women's work at all.'

Grace pulled a face, setting about buttering the bread her mother had already cut and covered with a cloth.

'Well, you know Dad, Mum, but the fact is that women are having to do men's work because the men are fighting for this country, and I dare say that the pilots and crews are glad enough to have their aircraft working properly not to turn up their noses at a woman doing that work.'

'You're right, of course, love, but it might not be a good idea to say too much to your dad.'

Grace had been married less than four months but already she seemed to have grown up so much, no longer a girl, but a woman with her own opinions and ready to state them, Jean thought, torn between a sense of loss and pride.

'Your dad's temper's a bit on the end at the moment, with all this bad news from the desert,' she warned Grace.

'Have you heard from Luke recently?' Grace asked immediately.

'We had a letter in March saying not to worry and that he's well, but of course we do worry.' A look at both Seb and Grace's sombre faces confirmed to Jean that they shared her feelings.

'Rommel's a first-rate commander,' Seb said at length, 'but our lads are good fighters, good men.'

Jean nodded. Of course they were good men – her Luke was one of them – but being 'good men' wasn't going to keep them safe from Rommel's tanks, was it?

'I've got to admit that I'm still ever so sad about Luke and Katie splitting up,' Jean told them in a valiant attempt to take their attention away from the desert and the fact that the British Army was being beaten back by Rommel and his tanks. 'I'd have liked to keep in touch with her but, bless her, being the thoughtful girl she is she said that it wouldn't be right or fair to Luke . . .

'Oh, we've got Vi and Bella coming round for tea. Vi's running poor Bella ragged, and her with that nursery to run. Not that I don't feel for Vi, I do, but she doesn't make it easy for herself or for anyone else. Anyway, Grace, love, tell me your news. Are you liking it at the hospital in Whitchurch?'

'Yes, I love it,' Grace answered her truthfully. 'I wasn't so sure at first, because it's so much smaller than here, but you do get to see a bit more variety. Mind you, I had ever such a moment a few weeks back, Mum. We had a POW in, a German – a nice chap,' she emphasised when Jean frowned. 'Speaks good English and seemingly was one of those forced to enlist. Anyway, he was sent in by a local doctor because he'd got a puncture wound to his leg that had gone bad. The POWs are sent out to work for the local farmers and this chap had had a pitchfork in his leg – an accident. I really thought he was going to lose his leg and it brought it all back to me how Seb had been so poorly with his own wound.'

'So what happened to the POW?' Jean asked, concerned on the man's behalf in spite of herself.

'Oh, he's made a full recovery. The doctor is a friend of a friend of someone who wanted to try out this new stuff. Penicillin, it's called. It's like a miracle, Mum, but it's all a bit hush-hush at the moment.'

'Well, I dare say it's all right giving him something like that, since he's got better, but I wouldn't have wanted them trying it out on one of my own. Say it hadn't worked?'

Grace exchanged looks with Seb. She loved her mother dearly, but Jean could be a bit old-fashioned about some things.

Emily could hardly believe what had happened. It was like something out of a book, or a film – well, almost – and she was still all aflutter over it. She'd hardly slept last night and now here she was, all fingers and thumbs over her knitting, as she set about making socks for Wilhelm, who had come round yesterday afternoon to say especially to her how much he appreciated the pair she had already knitted for him, and asking her if she would let him come back to work on the garden. If she minded!

A pink glow warmed her face, a slightly dazed but very happy smile curving her mouth.

Who would have thought yesterday morning, when she and Tommy had set out for church together, what the day would bring?

Of course, there'd been a good turnout for the eleven o'clock service, it being Easter Sunday, and not just from the congregations. All the scouts and guides and the like had been there, along with the Boys' Brigade and a band. Those members of the WVS who had wanted to do so marched into church in their uniforms. Emily had chosen instead to wear her own clothes and stay with Tommy, but she had still felt a thrill of pride seeing her fellow WVS members looking so smart and businesslike.

There'd been a handful of young men and women in uniform, those lucky enough to have leave, and of course there'd not been a dry eye in the church when, after the service, their vicar had read out the names of the newly fallen from the parish.

It hadn't been until after the service, when people were chatting outside the church, that Emily had allowed herself to look discreetly in the direction of the POWs with their uniformed escort. Wilhelm hadn't been to church since she'd given him the socks, and she had known why. It was because he hadn't wanted to see her.

But then yesterday he'd been there, and she'd been so taken by surprise to see him that she'd flushed up like a fool and looked the other way, wanting to get Tommy away before he noticed and said something or, worse, wanted to go over and talk to Wilhelm.

Shamefully she hadn't even noticed that Wilhelm was using a crutch until Ivy from next door had commented on it, saying, 'Well, I never. There's that POW that used to come and do your garden, Emily, and he's been in some kind of accident, by the looks of it.'

Of course, that had her forgetting her own feelings and turning round immediately to look anxiously at Wilhelm. And sure enough, there he'd been, standing with the other men.

She'd seen often enough at the pictures what she had thought of as daft scenes in which a couple would look at one another in silence whilst some soppy music played and you'd just know that this was IT, but she'd thought it was all so much nonsense, especially after her experience with her own husband. A right one for giving those kind of looks, he was, and to any pretty girl who took his eye. But then Wilhelm had looked right at her, and she'd looked back, and then he was saying something to the soldier guarding them, who had looked across at her and nodded, and then Wilhelm had come towards her, and Ivy had given her a bit of a nudge in the back and said, 'Go on, he wants to say something to you and you surely aren't going to make him walk all the way with that bad leg?' And somehow they had met in the middle of the lane, still thronged with churchgoers, and he had explained to her about having had a nasty accident and being too poorly to come to work, and she had been so concerned that she had asked him a lot of anxious questions and then she had been jolted by someone by accident and

Wilhelm had reached out to steady her – he had ever such a lovely touch – the feel of his hand on her arm warm and steady and kind.

Of course, when he had asked if he could come back to continue doing her garden she couldn't have said 'no' even if she had wanted to, could she, as she had said to Ivy, not with him having that bad leg, and her worrying about Tommy missing out on his fresh veggies.

And it had been then that he had said them, the most wonderful words, just as though somehow he had known, which of course he couldn't have done, and right in front of Bridget, who being the busybody she was had made sure that she got close to them to find out what was going on.

'The doctor told me that I was very lucky that the pitchfork missed my vein, and I have your kind gift to me to thank for that. The socks you knitted for me spared my life with their good strong wool and your excellent knitting.'

Oh, what a moment that had been. Emily's chest swelled with pride and joy just to remember it.

But that hadn't been all.

'I have the socks still,' Wilhelm had told her quietly, the words for her ears alone. 'They are my good luck and I shall treasure them always.'

'I'll knit you another pair,' Emily had promised, half dizzy with happiness and the triumph of it all.

Tommy, who had been playing with some of his school friends, had arrived then, delighted to see Wilhelm and demanding to hear the whole story.

Emily had been itching to ask Wilhelm back to have lunch with them, but she had known better than to do so. He was a POW, after all, and rules were rules. He'd be having his dinner at the POW camp with all the other men there.

But today, even though it was Easter Monday, he was coming round. Just to check the state of the garden, of course. What a bit of luck it was that she'd had just enough butter and sugar put by to make that bit of a cake. She'd sent Tommy up to the farm to beg some cream, and she'd got the jam she'd made in the autumn.

It had been a lovely afternoon at Auntie Jean's, even if her mother had refused to enter into the spirit of things and had insisted on reminding them all of how badly done to she was, Bella reflected, as they walked the short distance from the bus stop to her mother's house. Auntie Jean's home was always so cosy and welcoming, and Bella had had a lovely chat with Grace and had accepted an invitation to go to Whitchurch to visit her there as soon as the weather warmed up a bit. There was nothing like being part of a loving family to give you a warm happy glow, Bella acknowledged. Her inner reflections made her glance ruefully at her own mother, looking more like her old smart self these days now that Bella was there to encourage her to take a pride in her appearance again. What a shame it was that her mother wasn't closer to Auntie Jean. Her aunt had done every-thing she could this afternoon to make them welcome, and Bella felt that her mother could have made more of an effort at least to look as if she was enjoying herself.

They had reached the house now, and as they walked up the short drive Bella saw that Lena was sitting inside the open porch on one of the small stone benches that ran either side of the inside walls.

Immediately Bella ran forward, exclaiming worriedly, 'Lena, what are you doing here?'

Lena, her face pale but set and determined, answered, 'There's something I've got to tell you, Bella.'

'Something's wrong?'

Lena's expression confirmed that she was right.

'What is it?' Bella demanded. 'Is it Janette?'

Lena's expression immediately softened into a maternal smile. 'No, Janette's fine. I've left her with Gavin.' Lena reached for Bella's hand and held it tightly. 'I need to talk to you on your own,' she told Bella quietly, her expression so grave that Bella's heart lurched.

'What's going on? What's she doing here?' Vi demanded.

'You go inside, Mummy,' Bella instructed her mother, quickly unlocking the door and urging her mother in before closing it again.

'Lena, what is it?' she asked anxiously. 'Your hands are cold. You shouldn't have waited outside like this. How long have you been here?'

'Not long. Oh, Bella!' Lena lifted her free hand to her mouth, her eyes filling with tears. 'There's been such a terrible thing happened. I don't know how to tell you, I really don't.'

Bella's heart was now pounding. Had something happened at the nursery? They were closed over the Easter holiday but there could have been a fire or—

'I . . . I didn't want to telephone. Me and Gavin talked it over and he agreed that I should come,' Lena interrupted Bella's anxious train of thought.

'Is it the nursery?' Bella asked. 'Has there been some kind of accident? Lena, please tell me what it is.'

'Oh, Bella, I wish I didn't have to tell you this. It's the most dreadful thing.' Lena shuddered. 'Your Jan's mam and sister came round just after dinner, I mean lunch, Lena corrected herself, whilst Bella refrained from picking her up on 'your Jan' for fear of delaying hearing what had happened even longer.

'Jan? Something has happened to Jan?' she demanded frantically.

'Not Jan,' Lena gulped. 'They was wanting to see you but when I told them that you had moved back in with your mum and that you'd gone over to your auntie Jean's for the day they told me and asked me if I would tell you so as you'd know.'

Not Jan. Bella barely registered Lena's explanation, she was so relieved. For a minute she had truly thought the worst and that something terrible had happened to him. But if it hadn't . . .

'Well, if it isn't Jan, then—' Bella began.

'It's Jan's wife, Bella. She's dead. Got knocked down and killed by a car.'

Jan's wife! Jan's wife was dead. Her relief that it wasn't Jan was quickly swamped by guilt for that relief, as Bella sank down onto the other stone bench, her hand to her lips, repeating almost pleadingly,

'Oh, no, Lena . . .' When Lena didn't respond Bella said shakily, 'I dare say you'll think that I'm just pretending to be sorry and that really—'

'As if I would think any such thing, me as knows how good and kind you are,' Lena assured Bella stoutly. 'And your Jan's ma and sister don't think that either, before you go saying that maybe they do.'

'Lena, you mustn't call him "my Jan",' Bella begged her weakly. 'He isn't and he never was.'

'He loves you and you love him, and don't you go telling me any different because I saw how he looked when he talked about you.'

She didn't feel glad that Jan's wife was dead, and that he was now free, Bella knew. Instead she felt numb – numb and anxious and desperately shocked.

'Was . . . was Jan with her? Did they say . . . ?'

'All they said was that there'd been this accident, although . . .'

When Lena hesitated, Bella looked at her, her anxiety suddenly intensifying. There was something that Lena hadn't told her yet, something that Lena was reluctant to tell her.

'Although what?'

'Well, it was Jan's sister, Bettina, who told me. Took me on one side on purpose, I reckon, whilst her mother was making a fuss of Baby. She said that the driver of the car that hit her said as how she'd walked out in front of him deliberately.'

'No! No, Lena, tell me that isn't so?'

'I'm ever so sorry, Bella, but Bettina said that it was best that you knew. She said to say as well

104

that the poor lady had been having medical treatment because of how she was mentally, and that the doctor had got a nurse staying at the house with her because he didn't think it was fair to her dad that he had the worry of it all whilst Jan wasn't there, but that the nurse said she'd slipped out without her noticing. Of course, for the family's sake it's best that it's left as an accident, but Bettina said she thought you ought to know.'

'Yes . . . yes, of course . . .'

Jan's wife had committed suicide. Bella couldn't bring herself to look at Lena. She felt sick with shock and disbelief. She had known that Jan's wife suffered mental problems caused by the German invasion of her home town, but she had never imagined that they would lead to her taking her own life. How dreadful. Bella shuddered to think of the mental suffering Jan's poor wife must have endured. She couldn't imagine what it must be like to have one's country invaded, its men killed and taken away and its women . . . Bella bit down hard on her bottom lip. Jan had told her how his wife had witnessed soldiers raping another girl and how it had damaged her mentally.

'Bella, how long are you going to be out there, only my bed needs a hot-water bottle?'

'Coming now, Mother. Lena, you'd better go. Gavin will be worrying about you. I'll telephone and tell him that you're on your way back.'

'I'm ever so sorry that I've had to give you such bad news, Bella.'

Bella nodded. As grateful as she was to Lena, all she really wanted was to be on her own.

'You're not to go dwelling on it now, mind, and upsetting yourself, Bella. Promise you won't,' Lena appealed to her.

'Of course I won't,' Bella assured her, but they both knew that she was lying.

Jan's wife was dead – had deliberately killed herself. It was gone midnight and Bella was still wide awake, lying in bed, her eyes burningly dry because she couldn't cry, and her heart filled with bleakness and guilt.

It was impossible for her not to ask herself if her love for Jan and his for her might have played a part in the appalling tragedy. If somehow his wife had sensed that Jan had given his love to someone else and that had tipped her over the final dreadful edge into self-destruction.

She had told Jan, and he had agreed, that he was married and that because of that there could be nothing between them; that they must not even think of one another, never mind communicate or see one another. They must, she had told him, remember, respect and uphold the vows he had made to his wife, in their thoughts as well as their actions. She had sworn to use her love for him to help him to be a good husband to his wife. She had told him that the only way she wanted him to prove his love for her was by being that good husband and loving his wife. She had said that in loving his wife he would be loving her, Bella.

'I could never live with myself if I thought that I had contributed in any way to your wife's unhappiness,' she had said and she had meant those words, even though the pain of knowing that they could not love one another had been tearing her apart – and still tore her apart whenever she slipped and gave in to the temptation to think of him and what might have been.

Bella didn't blame Jan for marrying someone else. He had had his reasons. Good reasons, reasons that proved what a wonderful man he was. His wife was – had been – the daughter of close friends of Jan's own parents. She and her father had escaped to England from Poland but it had only been after their marriage that Jan had realised the damage the atrocities she had witnessed had done to her emotions and her mind.

Jan could have had his marriage annulled. Their marriage had not been a proper one nor ever would be, Jan had believed, but Bella had sensed that despite her behaviour towards Jan, his poor damaged wife needed him, and so he must stay, and she must step back.

Giving Jan up had never ceased to cause her pain, a deep inner private pain that had become a constant companion, a new part of herself that she had to embrace and accept as the price of loving him. The news Lena had brought her would not end that pain. How could it? If Bettina was right and his poor deranged wife had taken her own life, then there could be no future happiness for her and Jan as a couple. Her ghost and their own guilt would forever stand between them, and they *were* guilty, Bella was sure of it. Guilty of loving one another; guilty because that love might have contributed to Jan's wife's death.

107

And yet a part of her longed to go to Jan, to be with him to comfort him and to share this burden with him, to offer him the full measure of her love for him in whatever way he chose to take it, from her words, from her presence, from her touch and even from her body. There was nothing of herself she wanted to hold back, and everything of herself she wanted to give to him. But of course she could not do so; must not do so.

She must instead remember that hers had been the roof under which Jan's mother and sister had been billeted, and that Jan had been the son who had visited them there, and that was all. She must in every way behave as that role dictated, and no other way – not now, not ever. She would not besmirch the status of the young wife who had died, or the love she herself had for Jan by doing anything that would tarnish them.

In the morning she must write to Jan's mother, expressing her sympathy, and ask her to pass that sympathy on to Jan and his father-in-law. She must ask about the funeral arrangements, and organise sending flowers, and she must . . . she must not cry. But it was too late, she was already doing so, acid tears that burned her heart.

EIGHT

'So you didn't see Lou, then? And there was me feeling jealous because I thought the two of you would be out dancing together and that she'd be doing her best to persuade you to drop me and join the WAAF.'

'That's the last thing I'd want to do,' Sasha assured Bobby, as they strolled hand in hand down to the ferry. Bobby had got a rare whole Saturday afternoon off, and so had she, and so they were going to take the ferry over to Wallasey and enjoy themselves. His wholesome good-natured face shone with happiness, his dark brown hair ruffling slightly in the breeze despite the application of brylcream, and his bright blue eyes sparkling. Everything about Bobby made her feel safe and comfortable, Sasha acknowledged. His jokes made her laugh, and she really liked listening to his soft north-east accent, but it was that lovely safe feeling that being with him gave her that she liked best.

'I'm quite happy working at the telephone exchange.'

'Oh, and there I was thinking it was me you didn't want to leave.'

Bobby was laughing but Sasha could see the question in his eyes.

'You know that Mum and Dad made me promise that we wouldn't start going steady properly,' she reminded him. 'They think I'm too young.'

'A baby,' Bobby agreed, adding unsteadily and with fierce emphasis, 'my baby Sash, and one day, I hope, not just my girl but mine for ever.'

'Oh, Bobby.'

There was a corner up ahead of them, and noone in sight, so Bobby took the opportunity to pull Sasha close and hold her tightly in his arms, whilst he kissed her fiercely.

Sasha felt her heart leap against her ribs. She'd be for it if her parents knew what she was doing, but she loved Bobby so very much.

'It's so unfair,' she told him when he had released her, both of them checking they hadn't been seen, before continuing to walk towards the ferry. 'Mum wasn't much older than me when she married Dad. I know how I feel, and with this war . . .' She shivered and Bobby knew that it wasn't because of the cool April breeze.

Bobby was a sapper with a bomb disposal unit, wearing the uniform that belonged to those men who had the shortest life span of any within the armed services. Since Sasha had known him, which was not even a year yet, two of the men in his unit had been killed when a bomb they had been disarming had gone off, and three more had been so badly injured that, according to Bobby, if he'd been them he would rather have been dead.

The wind coming in off the sea tousled Sasha's short curls, and Bobby brushed them off her face. She was so pretty, his Sasha, and he loved her so much that sometimes he felt when he was with her that his heart was going to burst with all that he felt for her.

'Nothing's going to happen to me,' he reassured her. 'I've got nine lives, like a cat, according to me mam.'

'Does she know about me?' Sasha asked him.

'What do you think?' Bobby teased her tenderly. 'Of course she does.'

'What did you say to her about me? What did she say?'

'I said, Mam, I've met the girl who's going to be your daughter-in-law, only she's got this twin sister who doesn't want her to have anything to do with me, and this mam and dad who say she's too young to be going steady, but her and me, Mam, well, we know different. We know how we feel about one another, and given me own way, her and me would be wed just as soon as we could get the banns read.'

'You never said that to her,' Sasha protested, half scandalised and half thrilled.

'Well, I would have done if she'd had the time to listen to me for more than half a second. She'd got our Pauline round and her kids, and me other sister, Jane, had come home on account of her having a set-to with her hubby, and me nan and granddad were there as well, putting in their two pennyworth about everything, so I just sort of let them know by mentioning your name and saying as how you were the prettiest girl in the whole of Liverpool.'

Sasha pulled a face. 'You know that's not true. Grace is the pretty one in our family and—'

'It's true for me,' Bobby told her, 'and I meant what I said about wanting us to get married, Sash. Promise me that you will when your mum and dad say you can?'

'I promise,' Sasha told him gladly.

They were across the road from the ticket office for the ferry now, and if they hadn't been in full view of the people jostling amiably to form a queue Sasha knew that Bobby would have kissed her again and that she would have let him.

'I haven't told you properly about Lou yet,' she reminded him when they joined the queue. 'Mum was ever so upset, I could tell, even though she didn't say much.'

'What happened?'

Bobby was always pleasant enough about Lou but Sasha knew that he resented Lou's attitude towards him, which was one of open hostility. He knew, though, that Lou was Sasha's twin and that she loved her, and so because of that he didn't say too much about her.

'She couldn't come home because she'd been put on a charge.'

Bobby made a sound of disapproval mixed with resignation.

The ferry was in now, its passengers disembarked, and it was ready for them to start boarding.

'I thought when it came out that she'd joined up that there'd be trouble. If she couldn't take the discipline at the telephone exchange she certainly won't be able to take it in the Forces,' Sasha told Bobby as the queue moved forward, allowing them to get on board and find seats. 'I think she was really enjoying being in the WAAFS before this happened. I just wish that . . .'

'That what?' Bobby asked once he had made sure that they had found somewhere out of the wind for Sasha. He was kind and thoughtful, Sasha thought appreciatively, slipping her hand into his beneath the cover of his jacket and her cardigan.

'Well, that she wasn't quite so much like she is, Bobby. Why couldn't she have stayed here in Liverpool at the telephone exchange? It was what Mum and Dad wanted her to do. She could have partnered up with one of those friends of yours you tried to introduce her to, and we could have gone out as a foursome. It would all have been so perfect, but Lou had to go and be difficult.'

There was genuine misery in Sasha's voice, which caught at Bobby's heart.

'You don't want to go getting yourself all upset over her, Sasha. I know she's your twin but she's not like you.'

'No, she isn't,' Sasha agreed sadly. 'I could never have done what she's done, Bobby – you know, joined the WAAF. Lou's always been the brave one. I do miss her, but just lately whenever we're together we seem to end up falling out about . . . about something.'

'About me, you mean,' Bobby corrected her.

He was a fair-minded young man, and he loved his Sasha more than enough to want her happiness above everything else. 'I dare say me coming along put Lou's nose out of joint a bit,' he continued when Sasha didn't say anything, 'and I dare say too that I'd have felt the same in her shoes.'

'But you and me being like we are didn't have to mean that me and Lou had to fall out. I don't want it to be with me and her like it is with Mum and Auntie Vi, Bobby. Lou's put out with me because after . . . well, you know, after that dancing business that I told you about she wanted us both to promise that we wouldn't let any boy come between us, but that was before I knew how it was going to be with you and me.'

'She'll come round,' Bobby tried to comfort her. 'You'll see.'

Sasha realised that Bobby wanted to reassure her, but she knew Lou better than he did, and she knew how stubborn her twin could be when something or someone got her back up. They weren't children any more, though, and unlike in their schooldays she wasn't going to give in and do as Lou wanted for the sake of peace and quiet.

'Ah, Connor, you are a very good man. You make my visit here to your theatre where I sing for the people of Liverpool a most wonderful experience.'

Con flashed his trademark wide smile in the direction of the large-bosomed woman who was currently the Royal Court's leading female singer.

'Only the best is good enough for the Royal Court's artistes, Eva,' he responded.

They were only halfway through the evening's show, and Eva had caught him just as he had been about to sneak out to the pub to warn the landlord that he was going to need his upstairs room tomorrow night for a card game.

'You are so kind,' Eva breathed, placing her hand on his arm, the rings on her fingers catching the light. 'Kind, but something here within me –' Eva touched her magnificent chest in a theatrical gesture before looking deeply into Con's eyes with burning intensity – 'here in my heart, that power I have inherited from my forebears, tells me that you are a very lonely man, Connor. A man who yearns for the comfort and the pleasure that only a very special woman can give him.'

Or, in fact, several very special women, Con thought, especially when one of them was the luscious young dancer who had just joined the chorus line, blonde, with legs up to her armpits, baby-blue come-to-bed eyes, and a certain something about her that told Con that his planned conquest of her was going to be successful.

'You are a little alarmed, I think, that I should have this power to see into your heart,' Eva was telling him, 'but you must not be. I am a woman of great passion, a woman who knows how to please a man who is worthy of her.'

Eva was moving closer to him as she spoke, pressing her body up against his on the narrow staircase.

Alarm bells began to ring inside Con's head. Eva was making up to him, there was no doubt about that, and he couldn't afford to offend her,

115

there was no doubt about that either, but as for what he suspected she was suggesting . . . She was closer to thirty-five than eighteen, and not his type at all.

'I am right, aren't I?' Eva was demanding.

'What? Oh, listen, there's the interval bell ringing,' Con warned her, determinedly stepping back from her so that she was forced to release him. 'You don't want to be late for your second half solo.'

'I shall sing just for you,' Eva assured him, 'and then after the show we shall have dinner together, and open our hearts to one another.'

Over his dead body, Con thought as he smiled at her again, whilst inwardly cursing the fact that Harriet Smith, his now retired secretary, who had been with the Royal Court Theatre for years and who had known exactly how to protect him from women like Eva, had taken it into her head to leave Liverpool and go and live in Bournemouth with her brother.

Stu and Paul were waiting for him outside the stage door to the theatre, falling in behind him as Con headed for the pub tucked down a back alley behind St John's Market, ignoring the shells of buildings, casting dark shadows in the moonlight, that had been bombed in the dreadful air raids that had nearly destroyed the city in the early part of May 1941.

Striding ahead of his henchmen, Con ignored them. He prided himself on being a snappy dresser, even in these times of rationing and utility clothing. Like the wide boys and spivs who sold their illegal goods on the black market, Con favoured pinstripe suits, although he liked to top his with a smart camel-hair top coat, with a nice bit of velvet on the collar, just like the big impressarios of the West End, whose photographs he'd seen in *Variety*, liked to wear.

Con liked to arrive at the pub before the Americans but tonight, thanks to Eva, he was running late and reached the pub to find they were waiting for him.

One of them was Chip, the young American who had had to be warned not to be a sore loser. Con shrugged inwardly. If Chip wanted to lose even more money then why should he care?

'Good to see you, boys,' he smiled as he directed them towards the side of the building where the door that the landlord had left unlocked for him led straight to the stairs to the private room.

'We've brought Ricky with us tonight,' another of the Americans told Con once they were all upstairs.

'Once I'd heard they'd found a good poker game there was no way they were going to stop me joining in,' Ricky told Con as Con reached out to shake his hand.

Con prided himself on the firmness of his own handshake but the American, for all that he wasn't particularly tall or even thickset, had a grip that left white pressure marks on Con's flesh.

'Chip says you play a mean game of cards,' Ricky told Con as they all sat down at the table, Ricky deftly beating Stu to the chair next to Con's.

Con shrugged, assuming the affability of a man with a clear conscience. 'I've just been lucky.'

'Well, I'll just to have to hope that some of your good luck rubs off on me,' Ricky responded, smiling at Con as he reached into his pocket and removed a pack of cigarettes, offering Con one, which Con refused, going instead into his own pocket to get one of his favourite brand of cigars, along with two packs of playing cards. The cigar was black market, of course, but Con could afford them, thanks to the Americans.

Con knew another chancer when he met one, and the American had that confidence.

With the cigar clamped between his teeth, Con shuffled the cards several times, and was just about to start dealing them when Ricky leaned towards him, producing two brand-new packs of cards from his own pocket.

'Would you mind if we use these,' he asked Con. 'I've got this thing, you see, about using only new packs. It's kinda a bit of a superstition with me. Seems like I never win unless I'm using a new pack.'

As he spoke, Con caught the grin that Chip was giving him. So the sore loser had been suspicious about his loss, had he? Well, too bad, and as for the new packs of cards . . . Con shrugged his magnificently broad shoulders.

'Of course I don't mind, if you don't mind if I shuffle them?'

Check them he meant, of course, and Ricky knew it. As Con well knew, a pack could be marked and put back in its box and the box made to look

118

as though it was sealed and untouched. Old Marvo had known all the tricks there were to making the cards fall in his favour.

'Sure, you go ahead,' the American agreed.

It wasn't just big strong shoulders that Con had, he had big strong hands as well, surprisingly swift and deft big strong hands, certainly skilled enough to palm the aces as he shuffled the pack and then handed it back to Ricky, telling him, 'You deal.'

Ricky began to deal.

All he had to do now, was to exchange the cards he had been dealt for the aces, and then replace the extra cards in the pack during the course of the game every time he picked up a new card. Easy. He drew on his cigar and sat back, ready to enjoy the evening.

'Gimme those cards.'

Con had just produced his four aces and had been about to scoop the pot – over two hundred pounds tonight, thanks to Chip's increasingly wild betting, until he, like the other three soldiers, Stu and Paul, had been knocked out of the game, leaving only Con and Ricky to battle it out between them. But Chip had suddenly got to his feet, lurching towards the table, grabbing the discarded cards as he did so.

'Hey, kid, calm down,' Ricky advised him as he too stood and reached across the table to place his hand on the angry young soldier's arm.

'He's cheatin' us, man. There ain't no way anyone has that kind of luck. It's like I told you.'

So he had been right, Con acknowledged. Ricky

had come with them to see if he could catch him out. Well, it would take far more than an undersized American soldier to catch him on the hop, Con thought triumphantly, as he shuffled the pile of fivepound notes and then folded them into his pocket.

'Now look here,' Con began, drawing himself up to his full impressive height. Con stood six foot in his socks, taller than anyone else in the room. 'If you're trying to accuse me of cheating—'

'It's OK, Con, the kid's just a bit upset at losing so much money. Come on, Chip, Con won fair and square. I watched him deal the cards, and they were both new packs, you know that,' Ricky assured the younger man, going round to him and putting his hand on his arm.

'Ain't no way a man can come up with four aces two games in a row and be playin' fair and square,' Chip protested, shaking off Ricky's hand, and scowling.

'Well I'm not a man to hold a grudge,' Con assured them. 'You're all welcome to come back to the theatre with me to catch the finale of the show.'

'What, and get fleeced a second time by those hookers he's got working there?' Chip said bitterly – a comment that Con affected not to hear, as he reached for his coat from the back of his chair.

Bella had a splitting headache. It hadn't been a good morning. They'd had a young mother in a desperate state, her three-year-old in the nursery, and the news just arrived that her husband had been killed in action. She'd been beside herself, saying there was no point in her going on living, and Bella had had to calm her down and remind her that she had a little boy who needed her and that her dead husband would have expected her to be brave and look after his son.

She'd started to unwrap her sandwiches from their greaseproof paper, but somehow she didn't have the appetite for them. Her mother had been very difficult over the weekend, insisting that Bella didn't understand how she felt about her husband leaving her, and practically blaming Bella for what had happened.

Bella had tried to occupy her thoughts with other things over the weekend. Since Gavin had been working she had gone round and spent both Saturday and Sunday afternoons with Lena. Janette was almost four months old now, sitting up and showing off the two new teeth she had cut. The minute she had seen Bella she had held out her arms to her to be picked up. The feel of her soft weight and the smell of her baby skin had almost been too much for her, Bella admitted now, bringing back as it had done memories of the baby she had lost and underlining the fact that she would never now hold a child of her own – Jan's child. The pang of grief that ripped through her was so intense that it made her cry out, a low groan of mortal pain as though her body was crying out in protest.

She mustn't be like this. It wasn't right.

She looked towards the window of her small office, removing her handkerchief from the sleeve of her cardigan as she did so. She must not cry here at work, sitting behind her desk with the door open. What would everyone think? What—

'Bella.'

The sound of Jan's voice gave her such a shock that she almost knocked over her cup of tea as she turned to look at him.

'I had to come.'

'No.' She shook her head fiercely in denial. 'No.'

'Yes,' Jan told her, reaching out to stop her as she pushed back her chair.

Please don't let this be happening when she felt so weak, so pitifully weak and so much in need of him. She could feel her gaze being drawn to him, famished, desperate, greedily drawing in the familiar sight of him. He had lost weight. His face was thinner, his cheekbones sharper, emphasising his masculinity, giving his features a chiselled maleness that had her heart turning over.

She had retreated as deep into her chair as she could to avoid the hell of self-betrayal that would come with his touch.

'Yes.' His voice was as stark with pain as the look in his eyes as he kicked the door shut, isolating them in the dangerous privacy of her office. No one would come to her rescue, to save her from herself. The rule was that no one knocked or came in when the door was closed.

'You shouldn't be here.'

'I had to see you. I can't stay long. I've driven my mother and Bettina back from . . . back, but I'm due at my base tonight. We're flying almost nightly missions over the Channel, providing air cover for Bomber Command.'

'You shouldn't be telling me that.' The words were automatic. After all, anything was better, safer, than talking about . . . that other . . . his wife . . . her death . . . her own pain.

'Magda's father was very touched by your letter. My mother showed it to him.'

'Stop it.' Her voice was frantic with panic and fear.

'The doctor was very good. He stated that it was an accident, although she'd threatened to do it – to kill herself – because of me . . . because . . .'

'Because she'd guessed? Because she thought you didn't love her?'

'No! My love was the last thing she wanted. She told me that. She told me that she hated men, even her own father, because he hadn't saved the others. She said that there were voices in her head telling her that she should kill us both, that she should kill all men. I should never have married her. Without marriage she might have had a chance of avoiding sinking into the dreadful confusion that was responsible—'

'But you did marry her. She was your wife.'

'I did marry her, but she was never my wife.'

'You can't repudiate her now like that. I won't let you.'

'I'm not repudiating her. How can I repudiate what I didn't have?'

'You should be grieving for her as your wife.'

'I can't. I can only grieve for what she could have been. I want you, Bella. I need you. I need your sweetness and your warmth. I need your being alive and your love. I need *you*.' He was reaching for her. 'Come with me, back to your house. Let me love you and be loved by you in return.'

His voice had thickened and she could see, almost feel and smell the desire coming off him.

It would be so easy to do what he wanted, to let him take her, commit to her, knowing that once they had stepped over that barrier and crossed that boundary, there would be no stepping back. Once she had given herself to him Jan would want the banns read and his ring on her finger, she knew. It was so tempting, so much what she wanted – all that she wanted – to be his, to be loved by him, to take him within her body, to have his child, to hold that child to her as she had held baby Janette at the weekend. She wanted all of that so much, but even here in this office, her domain, she could feel that agonised shadow of his dead wife, reminding her of what was owed to her as his wife.

'No,' Bella told him. 'We can't do that. I won't do it.'

'I love you. I need you more than you can know. Time, life, are so precious, and who knows how little of them we may have? Please don't deny me, Bella; don't deny us. Let me have the sweetness of your love, let me have that memory.'

He was coming round the desk to her. In another moment he would be touching her, and once he did she would be lost. She wanted to be lost but it was wrong; they could not build their future on his wife's death. Panic flared and burned inside her. If she couldn't find the strength to send him away then she must make him go away, but how?

She looked at her desk. Her desk, her office, her nursery, her life, all were dependent on her respectability, her acceptability by her community, and she knew what to say. She took a deep breath and stood up.

'I can't and won't do what you ask, Jan, because, you see, if I did, if I behaved as you want me to behave, it could cost me my job and that is a price I am not prepared to pay.'

'You said you loved me.'

'I did, but now I've discovered that I love my job more. You surely didn't really think that I'd be prepared to sit around and think of nothing else but you, did you? You were a married man. I decided that couldn't allow myself to love you.'

'So you gave your love to this place instead.' His voice was harsh with bitterness and disbelief.

'Yes,' Bella lied. 'I really wish that you hadn't come here like this. We'd agreed that we wouldn't see one another again. I had hoped that my letter of condolence made my feelings, and the fact that I now see you merely as an acquaintance, plain.'

'Bella, please don't do this. Please tell me that you don't mean any of this. Please tell me that you love me.'

'I can't do that. I think you had better leave, Jan. My staff will be wondering what's going on, and I have an appointment to interview a new nurse in half an hour.'

She took advantage of his stiff disbelieving silence to skirt past him to the door and pull it open.

'Goodbye.'

'Bella, I know you love me.'

His face looked gaunt, deep hollows of pain beneath his cheekbones, his eyes sick with pain. Just looking at him made her feel as though someone was tearing out her heart. *Jan, Jan, my love, my heart, my life.* But if she let him stay, if she let him do what he wanted to do, how might he feel when the urgency of his immediate need had faded, and when he looked back and saw their loving as a betrayal, and her as someone who had aided him in that betrayal? What would that do to their love? For his own sake she could not give in. She knew Jan. She knew his integrity and his honesty; she knew what it would do to *him*, when this madness of despair and longing and need had lifted. He would hate himself. She said nothing.

'Very well. If that's what you want.'

Bella nodded, only when she could see him striding away from her, tall and handsome and strong, giving in to her own need to say a mental prayer for him – that he might be safe, that his heart might be healed, that one day he would understand the sacrifice she had made for him in not allowing their love to be tainted by the betrayal that would have been done if she had given him her hand and let him lead her to the place she really most wanted to be.

Sacrifice. Such an old-fashioned word, a word she herself would once have openly mocked and scorned, but which now went hand in glove with their wartime lives.

NINE

'Well, the rooms seem to be OK,' Gina announced with evident relief, as she stood in the open doorway to Katie's hotel bedroom. They had arrived just over half an hour ago and had been shown up the elegant flight of stairs of the tall four-storey house in the Royal Crescent, the most famous of Bath's elegant terraces, to their rooms on the second floor, by an ancient porter, who had accepted their tip with an uncommunicative grunt.

'Too used to desperate men in uniform, oblivious to what they're tipping, I suppose,' Gina had whispered to Katie once he had gone, a reference to the fact, as they had been told by their driver, and observed for themselves during their taxi ride from the station, Bath was filled with Admiralty and navel men, evacuated to the city at the beginning of the war.

'I've checked the bathroom. It's lovely and clean, and there are proper beds with springs – heaven. Doubles, as well – double heaven.'

Katie laughed. It would indeed be 'heaven' to sleep in a proper comfortable bed again instead of her utilitarian single, which felt so hard and resembled a bunk rather than a proper bed.

The hotel had an air of faded shabby splendour about it, the furniture and the fabrics obviously good quality and equally obviously well worn.

'We can't expect too much from the food, I don't suppose.' Gina pulled a rueful face, and then looked at her watch. 'It's not quite two o'clock yet; what do you say we go out and have a look around and see if we can find a tearoom?'

'That sounds a good idea,' Katie agreed. She had already unpacked her small case and put her change of clothes tidily away in the wardrobe and the dressing table drawers. Not that she had brought much with her: a smart but plain dress for the evening 'just in case'; the mackintosh that she had travelled from London in but now didn't need as there was a clear sky and sunshine; a change of underwear; a clean blouse; and a cotton dress in case the weather should turn warm, plus her night things and sponge bag.

They had had a dreadfully cold winter, but it was April now so she felt reasonably safe to go out for their exploratory stroll wearing one of the mandatorily only-to-the-knee-length skirts that was all the Government allowed in order to conserve fabric and the time spent making it up. In a soft off-white linen, Katie's had been made from curtain her mother had found in one of her trunks, and Katie was wearing it with a favourite white silk blouse patterned with black Scottie dogs wearing red bow collars, from before the war, underneath her old blazer, which fortunately steamed up well and still looked respectably smart.

A pretty scarlet scarf with white polka dots knotted at her throat brought a brave touch of colour to her outfit, although Katie would have liked something a bit more delicate than her thick lisle stockings to wear with her white T-strap shoes.

Living in the Campion household had given her an interest in her clothes and a confidence about what suited her that she had never imagined having before she had gone to Liverpool. It had been a shock to find that Jean Campion had parcelled up with her other things, and sent to her parents' address, the gorgeous silk dress Katie had worn the first time she had danced with Luke – a dress that rightfully belonged to Jean's sister Francine, but Jean had put in the loveliest little note saying that Katie was to have the dress 'in memory of happy times'.

Katie knew, though, that she would never ever wear it again. She couldn't because if she did she would think of Luke and then she wouldn't be able to bear being without him, and she must not weaken and let that happen. Instead she tried to tell herself that the Luke she had loved did not really exist because that Luke would never for a minute have doubted her or her love for him.

Gina was wearing a similar outfit, although Katie felt that Gina, being taller, had a more – and rather enviable – sporty look about her.

By mutual agreement they set off to explore the famous Georgian area of the city first.

'Oh, isn't this heaven after poor old London, with its bomb sites?' Gina enthused as they both stopped to admire the elegance of the Georgian buildings.

'Yes,' Katie agreed. 'I'd almost forgotten what it's like to be somewhere that hasn't been bombed.' She gave a small shiver. 'Liverpool might have had the heart bombed out of it, but Hitler couldn't bomb the heart out of its people.' It was lovely, though, she admitted to herself, to be somewhere that the war hadn't touched and where there was no destruction, somewhere that was a reminder of how life used to be.

'This is such a beautiful place,' she told Gina. 'I'm so glad we came.'

Gina was an excellent guide, and made no attempt to hide her delight in recognising so many places she knew from Jane Austen's books. Visiting the Assembly Rooms, which had only been reopened in 1938, after many years of neglect, so they had been told, had been a particular delight, as had Gina's face when she had said to Katie in an awed whisper, 'Just imagine, Jane Austen was actually here, in these rooms.'

They'd had afternoon tea at the Assembly Rooms, feeling deliciously self-indulgent although, as Katie had said ruefully, their clothes were rather utilitarian compared with the beautiful gowns of Jane Austen's era, and tactfully managing to decline without offence the two-pronged approach made on them by a pair of smartly uniformed naval lieutenants.

'Obviously looking for you-know-what,' Gina had observed wryly once the lieutenants' suggestion that they joined up with Katie and Gina 'to leave a table free for other people' had been declined.

'"Life's short, we should all have what fun we can whilst we can" types you mean? Yes, I thought so too,' Katie replied as she and Gina left the Rooms.

They were out longer than they had anticipated, agreeing that there was so much to enjoy in Bath that it would need far longer than a mere weekend to see it all.

When they came across a shop tucked down a pretty Georgian street, with a sign in its window advertising 'Good-quality second-hand Ladies' Garments', Gina urged, 'Do let's go in.'

The aroma of good scent and mothballs inside the shop reminded Katie of the smell from the trunks in which her mother kept all her stage costumes.

'Just look at this.' Gina lifted the long skirt of a pale grey silk gown embroidered with darker grey bugle beads.

'You've got a good eye,' the woman behind the counter told Gina. 'It's real silk, that is.'

'Why don't you try it on?' Katie suggested.

'Only if you try something as well,' Gina agreed, going back to the rail and picking out a pretty floral-patterned silk tea dress with a soft peach background. 'This will suit you perfectly.'

Half an hour later, flushed and happy, the two girls left the shop carrying their new purchases. In addition to the grey silk, Gina had bought a beautiful cream satin blouse and Katie was the owner of the peach tea dress and a darling little navy-blue knitted cardigan with white banding and white bows on the pockets.

'You'd never get anything like this in London any more,' Gina justified their extravagance.

They agreed that it was time for them to head back to the hotel. However, somehow they took a wrong turning and by some small miracle, as they happily agreed, they found themselves in a cobbled street that led to an open area with a pretty green on which was being held a small fair. Eager shoppers were clustered around the stalls. After sharing a mutual look of enthusiasm, the two girls headed for the nearest stall, Gina's eyes widening with delight as she pointed out to Katie the basket filled with what looked like long ribbons of coarse lace.

'Do look at this. It's so pretty.'

With trimmings of any kind so very hard to come by, Katie was as enthusiastic as Gina.

'It's called "tatting", my love,' the elderly woman managing the stall told them in a broad country accent. 'I make it myself.'

'How much is it?' Katie asked.

'Fourpence a yard. Or fivepence if you want the wider one.'

'It would be silly not to buy some,' Gina told Katie, 'even if we don't need it now. It's so pretty and would trim up an old blouse beautifully.'

Having both bought four yards of the tatting, the girls moved on to stall selling second-hand books and prints.

'Gina, do come and look at this.' Katie showed Gina several prints of Regency ladies in elegant gowns.

'Oh, what a marvellous find!' Gina enthused, happily parting with five shillings for four of the prints after some brisk bargaining with the stall holder.

Arm in arm the two girls went from stall to stall, learning as they did so that it was an annual event and that a lot of the stall holders had come into Bath from the country to sell their home-made wares.

'We could walk down to Pulteney Bridge after church tomorrow and explore round there,' Gina suggested as they strolled back to their hotel still arm in arm, pausing every now and again to admire the tranquil beauty of the city and its wonderful buildings.

'I'd love to,' Katie told her.

Gina smiled. 'You know, I can say now that I was a bit worried after I'd suggested we do this. It was a bit of a spur-of-the-moment suggestion, and afterwards I wondered how we'd actually get on. I don't know about you but I can honestly say I can't think of a woman friend I could better have enjoyed today with.'

'Me neither,' Katie agreed. She certainly couldn't imagine Carole enjoying Bath. She'd have been complaining that she couldn't see any dance halls.

Luke would have liked Bath. How easily and dangerously the treacherous thought slid serpent-like into her head and her heart.

It was still daylight but getting chilly now, and both girls started to walk more briskly.

'I'm glad we saw that notice for Sadler's Wells outside the Theatre Royal, and booked seats for tomorrow night as well as what we're seeing tonight,' Gina continued. 'I don't about you, but I'm not really one for sitting in a cocktail bar.'

'The theatre will be an ideal way to finish off

the day,' Katie agreed, glad she had brought along a dress suitable for going out in the evening.

Katie could tell that Gina had a well-to-do background, not just from her accent but also from her clothes. Katie's mother adored clothes and had taught Katie how to recognise good-quality fabrics. Thus Katie suspected that the simply navy jacket Gina was wearing was cashmere, and her pearls real. Not that Katie was the kind who wanted to compete with other girls, but naturally one didn't want to let the side down.

'How do you rate our chances of getting a decently hot bath?' Gina asked as they re-entered their hotel.

'Small, unless we're quick,' Katie answered wryly, eyeing the largish group of junior naval officers clustered in the hotel lobby, and, since one of them was collecting keys, concluding they were also hotel guests.

'You're right,' Gina agreed, whilst Katie determinedly pretended not to notice that one of the naval officers, fair-haired, tanned and blue-eyed, was eyeing her appreciatively.

Somehow they managed to skirt round the men without indicating that they were aware of the flow of compliments they were sending their way, such as, 'And to think I thought it was only Wrens that had good legs', 'I do like a girl with brown curls', 'And pretty eyes', 'And red lips', to reach the stairs to their rooms.

Dinner, as both Katie and Gina agreed, was rather better than they had feared. Unused to a choice of three courses, they decided to skip the soup and have a pudding instead. Their main course of lamb with new potatoes, carrots and cabbage was actually lamb, and not the mutton that everyone had learned to dread, and if the Bakewell tart that followed it was more stodge than jam, at least it was filling.

Katie was glad that she'd worn her dress when she'd seen that Gina was also wearing something appropriately dressed up, in brown jersey with a cowl neck, which made Katie wish she were tall enough to carry off a style so smart.

Rationing being what it was, Katie had borrowed an evening cape from her mother, bought originally in the twenties, the black silk heavily embroidered with bugle beads. It was an elegant item and one Katie had decided to bring with her only at the last minute, but when she saw the approving glance Gina gave it she was glad that she had.

They left the hotel in plenty of time for the theatre, taking their time and chatting happily as they strolled. The city was busy with people also obviously dressed for an evening out.

At the theatre they had to queue for a little while before they got inside and were shown to their seats in the circle.

Sadler's Wells would no doubt put on a good show tomorrow night, Katie acknowledged, as she heard other people around them talking about the ballet company as they settled into their seats, but she couldn't help reflecting that the Campion twins, Sasha and Lou, had they been with her, would no doubt have been complaining that ballet was dull compared with their own favourite jitterbugging.

The musicians would be first class, of course, and Katie wondered if any of her father's fellow musicians and friends would be part of the orchestra.

The show they had come to see was enjoyable and entertaining.

'That was lovely,' Gina sighed happily when the company had taken their final bow, and the orchestra had played 'God Save the King'.

Katie agreed as they turned to file out. It was a bright clear evening, the air cool, but the mood of those clustering around the theatre lobby and the area outside it warm, as people praised the performance.

'What a beautiful night,' Katie couldn't help saying softly as she looked up at the stars, a sudden attack of melancholy gripping her. Such a night was surely meant to be enjoyed by those in love, like some of the couples she could see, standing as close together as they could, holding hands, in some cases a woman's head leaning on a strong male shoulder, intensifying Katie's own feelings of loss and sadness. When Luke looked up at the stars, did he ever think of her, and if he did, was it with sadness and regret, and perhaps a wish that they were still engaged? No, of course not.

Snap out of it, Katie warned herself, her breath escaping in a soft whoosh of shock as someone behind her stepped back and bumped into her so hard that she almost lost her balance.

'I say, I'm most awfully sorry. Are you all right?' The man who had swung round to apologise was

136

holding her arm to steady her, recognition lightening his expression. 'You're the girls from the hotel, aren't you? The Lansdowne? I saw you there earlier.'

It was the young naval officer with the fair hair and the nice smile.

'We are staying there, yes,' Gina confirmed, stepping in with a cool nod.

The young officer was still holding on to her arm so Katie gave it a little shake and told him firmly, 'Thank you, I'm fine.'

The blue eyes twinkled. 'Ah, yes, your arm. I'm still holding on to it. My apologies, but it is a very pretty arm. Are you heading back for the hotel now? If so, may I escort you both?'

'I think we can manage to find our way back quite safely unescorted,' Gina told him drily,

He took his dismissal with good grace, releasing Katie's arm and smiling at them both as they turned to leave.

'I hope I didn't do the wrong thing,' Gina asked Katie a few minutes later as they walked down the otherwise empty street. 'You might have wanted his company. He was very personable, I have to admit.'

'No,' Katie assured her, stiffening as they both heard the sound of anti-aircraft batteries rattling out gunfire.

The air-raid siren that followed the gunfire had Katie's stomach churning, bringing back as it did memories of the Liverpool blitz.

'Don't worry,' Gina began, 'they'll be heading for Bristol. You can—' But her voice was drowned out as a chandelier of incendiary bombs showered down so close at hand that the explosions that followed shook the ground.

Both girls looked round, automatically seeking the nearest shelter.

'Not that way,' Katie warned Gina as she looked back towards the theatre. 'Any shelters there will be packed.'

'Where then?'

'I think there was one in the next street.' Katie reached for her hand. 'This way.'

Down towards the river they could hear the sound of further bombs exploding, the sticks of incendiaries followed by the telltale whine of the much bigger and more destructive high-explosive bombs. It was said that such a bomb landing in an enclosed space could blow a person into a thousand pieces, and yet at the same time there were those found dead after a bombing raid with no mark on them at all, the impact of the bomb having fatally damaged their internal organs.

Red tracer bullets lit up the sky.

'Get down,' Katie screamed at Gina, pulling her with her as she dropped down flat as close to the gutter as she could get, whilst machine-gun fire from the bomber she had just seen over the top of the houses hit the road as it flew over them, reminding her of the dreadful incident she had witnessed in Liverpool when a German pilot had raked an entire busload of people with bullets.

'We've got to find a shelter,' said Gina as they scrambled to their feet.

'They seem to be concentrating on bombing down by the river,' Katie pointed out, ducking automatically as yet another bomb exploded close at hand, sending plumes of dust and debris up into the air.

They had, of course, passed street shelters on their way to the theatre, but she couldn't remember just how far apart they had been. It made sense, though, to head back to their hotel because that was away from the area which the Germans were bombing, and had a reinforced cellar as its air-raid shelter.

Katie could hear someone running up the street behind them and when she turned round she saw the young naval officer coming towards them.

'Thank heavens you're both all right. I was worried about you,' he told them. 'Come on, the nearest shelter's a couple of streets away. No, get down,' he commanded, grabbing them both and pushing them down, just in time to duck out of the way of another Dornier spattering the road with bullets.

'It looks like Kingsmead's taking a hell of a pounding, which means they're probably after the gas works,' he informed them, once they had scrambled back onto their feet, raising his voice as a fire engine came racing past them.

At an ARP post on the corner, a warden broke off instructing a young messenger to shout out to them, 'There's a shelter next street but one, and look lively.'

They broke into a run. Above them the night sky was alive with the noise of the German Dorniers and the threat of death. That clear bright moonlight Katie had been admiring such a short time ago was now not something beautiful, but to be feared, allowing the German bombers to find their targets.

They had just reached the far end of the street and were about to cross over when a Dornier appeared over the chimney pots, flying so low that Katie thought he must clip them, so low that she could see the pilot inside the glass cockpit. Gina gave a small gasp of shock, but the plane sped over their heads, leaving them unharmed. Katie turned to watch it. A stick of incendiaries burst into fire, the men from the ARP post running out to smother them with sand. Katie heard the telltale whine and tried to warn them but it was too late. The high-explosive bomb that had followed the incendiaries made a direct hit on the post. From the ARP post to halfway down the road the glass was blown out of the house windows and covered the street, bright and shiny in the moonlight. Just like the glass over which Luke had carried her that night they had first met when the Germans had bombed the Grafton Dance Hall.

Automatically Katie started to move towards the ARP post, only to be dragged back by the lieutenant.

'It's no use,' he yelled, his voice rough and raw against her ear. 'We can't do anything to help them. Come on . . .'

Katie knew he was right. In the clearing dust she could see that where the post had been there was nothing, and that the house next to it had been ripped open from its attic to the ground, like a dolls' house with the front taken off, only no

140

little girl would ever have allowed her dolls' house to look like this house did, with its furniture falling out, soot blackening walls and huge gaping holes in the remaining walls.

In the moonlight Gina's face was devoid of colour, her expression fixed rigid with shock. Her own face must look the same, Katie knew.

It was like some dreadful nightmare in which you were fleeing from a terrifying horror, Katie thought, as behind them the bombs continued to fall, making her think that if she looked back, like Lot's wife, terrible fate would overcome her.

'I'm sorry, girls, but you're going to have to go on without me.' The lieutenant was holding his arm, his fingers covered in blood from the spreading stain darkening his jacket.

'You're hurt.'

Katie and Gina looked at one another, both shaking their heads as they said together, 'We aren't leaving you here.'

'I'm afraid you're going to have to. Ruddy glass seems to have cut an artery.' As he smiled at them, he pitched forward. Both of them grabbed hold of him and lowered him to the floor.

'I've done some first-aiding,' Gina told Katie. 'I can probably put a tourniquet on his arm, if we can find something to use as a bandage and—'

'Here.' Katie immediately removed her waist slip and then delved into her handbag for the pencil she always carried with her.

'Clever you,' Gina approved. 'From now on I shall make sure I always have one with me. Can you help me get his jacket off? We'll have to be

141

quick, he seems to be losing an awful lot of blood.'

They were, and he was, and he had also lost consciousness, but Gina was steadfast and determined, and somehow as she concentrated on doing what she could to help her, Katie was able to forget about the bombers overhead and their own danger.

'It's a bit make-do-and-mend, and we'll have to keep loosening it to make sure he doesn't end up with gangrene. It will be best if we stay here and don't try to move him, I think, in case the tourniquet doesn't hold. He's lost such a lot of blood already. But if you want to find a shelter—'

'And leave you here on your own? Don't be silly. We're probably as safe out here as we are anywhere else,' said Katie, with more conviction than she actually felt.

'There's bound to be someone along soon, a policeman or an ARP warden,' Gina agreed.

The sound of the bombers had receded, but the sights and smells of the destruction they had caused were all around them, fires burning brightly into the night sky.

'It smelled just like this in Liverpool when it was bombed,' Katie said quietly. 'I hate this war, and what it's doing, destroying families and lives. I'm sorry . . . it's just that earlier tonight, when we came out of the theatre, I couldn't help thinking about Luke. We were engaged, but then he broke it off. I keep telling myself that I must stop loving him, but somehow I can't. Some people seem to think that you can just transfer your feelings from one man to another, but I can't. Luke will always be the man I love.'

Katie hadn't intended to speak so openly, but somehow their situation had brought the words to her lips, as though if they were killed sitting here in the gutter, with a possibly dying man between them, it was Luke's name on her lips and Luke himself in her heart that she wanted to be her very last breath and her very last thought.

'I know what you mean. We weren't engaged, but, well, John and I both knew that it was just a matter of time, but the trouble was we didn't have any time. He was in the navy, and his ship was torpedoed, no survivors.'

They looked at one another in mutual sympathy and understanding.

'We're both obviously one-men women, you and I, Katie. More fool us, I dare say some people would say.'

'Well, what I say is that I wish every man fighting for his country, who worries about his girl, could have heard what I've just heard. Girls like you two are true angels, and what every chap wants.'

The sound of the lieutenant's weak voice had them looking at him, their shared confidences forgotten.

'We need to get you some proper medical attention,' Gina told him. 'Do you think—' She broke off as the all clear suddenly sounded, she and Katie exchanging relieved looks, which turned to even more relieved smiles when two policemen came round the corner.

In no time at all they were helping the lieutenant

to his feet and telling the girls that they would see the lieutenant safely to the nearest first aid post, which was only a matter of a few yards away, leaving Katie and Gina free to make their way back to their hotel.

As they parted outside their respective bedroom doors, Katie knew that she and Gina had forged a friendship that would be with them for the rest of their lives.

Once inside her bedroom, Katie sighed over the state of her clothes, dusty but thankfully not otherwise damaged, washing herself down as best she could in the hand basin in her room, before putting on her nightclothes.

She was so dreadfully tired, but somehow, despite the comfort of her bed, she just couldn't sleep. Instead her head was full of thoughts and memories of Luke. She *would* always love him, she knew, but she must still try to get on with her own life and not be one of those women who were always feeling sorry for themselves. She had *some* pride, after all.

Katie closed her eyes. Images ran through her head, of broken glass, and broken hearts, of Luke's strong arms round her . . .

What was that noise? The air-raid siren, of course. Katie was up and out of her bed before she was fully awake, pulling her raincoat on over her pyjamas, grabbing her handbag, opening her bedroom door, to find Gina opening hers.

Together they joined the other guests quickly making their way down to the cellar, the hotel owner waiting by the cellar door with a list of their names, which he ticked off as he counted them.

If this building should take a direct hit and collapse, then they would be buried down here, Katie couldn't help thinking as she went down the steep stone steps.

'We'll be safe down here,' the hotel owner assured them once they were all inside.

The cellar was large, with fresh air circulating in it, and proper electric light. It had obviously been especially equipped for just such an event because there were camp beds and cooking facilities, and even a door marked 'WC'.

In the end it was gone four o'clock in the morning before the second all clear sounded. As they exchanged weary 'Good night's outside their bedroom doors, Katie and Gina agreed that once they had some sleep they would have to discuss cutting their visit short.

'I doubt that we'd be able to do much to help, and we'll be extra mouths to feed and bodies to find beds for, especially if the Germans come back,' was Gina's opinion, and Katie was inclined to agree.

It wasn't running away. Had either of them had the kind of skills that could have been put to good use then Katie knew they would have volunteered them, but as it was, as visitors, they would only be in the way, and really could do nothing much to help.

Morning and a late breakfast confirmed their decision.

They were told by their waitress that the gas works had been hit and was still burning, that houses in the Kingsmead area of the city, which they had walked close to the previous night, had been seriously damaged and whole streets flattened. There had been terrible loss of life when the bomb shelter close to the Scala Cinema had been hit, and a doctor had been killed in The Paragon, which was relatively close at hand. In addition to that there had been many deaths, with stories of people thought to be still trapped under the rubble. The city's officials were evacuating as many people as they could, especially those who were now homeless, sending some of them to a nearby army camp, whilst others were already saying that they planned to trek out of the city for the forthcoming night rather than risk staying in their homes.

As they listened, Katie looked at Gina. After the waitress had gone, leaving them with little appetite for their kippers, Gina told Katie practically, 'Well, that's it, then. We can't stay now. We'll have to leave.

They were just finishing their second cups of tea when the hotel manager came in, heading straight for their table, bringing a naval officer.

'Captain Towers has asked me to introduce him to you,' he explained. He wants to thank you for helping his lieutenant last night.'

The captain, medium height, older than the lieutenant – in his mid-thirties, Katie guessed – his expression rather austere, had removed his cap to reveal neatly close-cut dark hair. Although he was wearing clean clothes and looked as though he

146

had only recently shaved, Katie could see that he looked tired.

'Why don't you sit down, Captain Towers, and have a cup of tea?' she suggested.

Immediately the austerity vanished from his expression, to be replaced with a grateful smile.

'As Mr Gale has just said, I wanted to thank you in person for what you did last night. Very quick-thinking and brave. The navy is indebted to you, and so am I. You see, Eddie, Lieutenant Spencer, is actually my cousin. I would have thanked you before now but I've been at St Martin's Hospital most of the night, checking up on some of our chaps who were billeted in the area. Dr Kohn and the nurses are doing a fine job but . . . there have been some terrible tragedies – whole families gone, and one poor chap who'd lost his wife and four children.' The captain shook his head.

'Terrible . . .'

Whilst he had been speaking Katie had poured him a cup of tea, which she now pushed towards him. There was, of course, no sugar to offer him, but he drank it gratefully none the less

'How is the lieutenant?' Katie asked.

The captain smiled, small creases fanning out around his eyes as he did so. Even when he smiled there was somehow a shadow of sadness in his eyes, Katie thought, wondering what had put it there.

'He's fine, thanks to your quick actions, and he asked me to pass on to you his thanks.'

'It was Gina who knew what to do.' Katie felt bound to praise her friend.

147

'But knowing what to do wouldn't have been any use without your . . . help,' Gina pointed out, giving Katie a teasing smile.

'Ah, yes, thank you for reminding me. Eddie did say something about a pencil and, er, a . . .'

The captain looked so embarrassed that Katie told him immediately, 'There's no need to worry about that,' whilst she and Gina exchanged amused looks.

'I must go,' the captain said then. 'I've got two men still unaccounted for, and one poor chap who brought his family here sitting by his wife's bedside. They don't think she's going to make it, and his two children are dead. One has to notify people and write reports and so on.'

'We won't keep you, then,' Katie assured him.

After he had gone, she said to Gina, 'I'm so glad that the lieutenant is all right, but how awful for that other man, losing his wife and children like that.'

'Yes, it can't be easy. The captain seemed a decent sort, though, and concerned for his men. Rather shy, though. He was awfully embarrassed about your slip, wasn't he?'

'Very,' Katie agreed, as they both laughed. 'Mind you, I'd rather a man be a bit embarrassed about mentioning women's underwear than too knowing about it, if you know what I mean.'

'I totally agree. One hears of chaps overseas bringing home for their girls the most unsuitable kind of things. I had a friend whose chap brought her back a belly dancing outfit from Egypt – and tried to tell her how to dance for him wearing it.'

'Oh, surely not!' Katie protested, trying to look serious but not quite managing to do so, with the result that the two of them went off into smothered peals of laughter.

'She ditched him, of course. Such a dreadful lack of good taste,' Gina commented, setting them both off laughing again.

'Should we go out for a stroll and stretch our legs, before we pack?' Gina suggested when they had calmed down.

Shared laughter was definitely a good way of getting over one's nerves after the kind of night they had endured, Katie acknowledged to herself as she agreed.

They were not laughing, though, when they stared in shocked dismay at the pall of smoke hanging over the city. They didn't go very far; there wasn't much sign of any bomb damage in their immediately vicinity, but the air was full of dust and smoke and the smell of burning, and by the time they had reached The Paragon and seen the gaping hole in the street where the doctor's house had been, they both agreed that they were ready to go back. Katie wanted to weep for the cruelty of the destruction of something so very special as this city. It seemed impossible that this was the same place they had admired less than twenty-four hours ago.

'Why Bath?' Katie asked, choking back her tears.

'I don't know,' Gina answered. 'Maybe they were aiming for Bristol and the aircraft factory there.'

'What a terrible tragedy for such a beautiful city.' Gina agreed, equally upset.

'It's a pity that we're going to have to cut our stay here short and miss the ballet, but it hardly seems reasonable to think about that when so many people in the city are facing what they have to face,' Gina told the hotel owner when they informed him that they were going to leave.

'Poor Bath,' was Gina's mournful comment when the two girls climbed on board the train that would take them back to London. 'Jane Austen would be shocked.'

TEN

Lou kicked morosely at the damp grass. It was not really light yet, but she hadn't been able to sleep so she had dressed quickly and quietly, slipping out of the hut, and had come down here to the end of the runway where it gave way to the surrounding countryside, so that she could be alone with her thoughts and her misery.

Her punishment was over now, but she was acutely conscious of the points she had cost the Hut, and whilst her chums had welcomed her back, she was all too aware of the cool frostiness of the others. It wasn't that they were ignoring her or had sent her to Coventry or anything like that, but it was because of her that they were not only not the top hut any more, but not even in the top four. She felt bad about that, really bad, though not at all like she had felt when she and Sasha had been in trouble. It was different now. When she and Sasha had broken rules it had been fun, something they had shared, something she had enjoyed doing because she had enjoyed challenging the restrictions the rules had put on them. She had liked being 'the naughty one' and she admitted she had sometimes gone out of her way to be naughty because she had enjoyed being a bit of a rebel.

But now she could understand why Sasha had sometimes been reluctant to go along with her, why she had argued for them to be 'good' and not 'bad'. Now Lou was not enjoying the reputation she had earned for herself. It didn't make her feel good and that bit braver and more daring than the other girls. In fact it made her feel isolated and alone and miserable.

As a child, when she had seen other girls being praised for 'being good', she had mocked them to Sasha, making fun of their goodness, and their curls, and their immaculate white socks, and hair that the ribbons did not fall out of. They had belonged to a group she had had no wish to be part of. Here, though, in the WAAF, the good young women were the ones whose skills earned them the praise of their superiors, young women who were dedicated to being the best they could be, and who were proud of what they were learning. Lou wanted very much to be one of those. For the first time in her life, *she* wanted to be an insider and not an outsider. She wanted to be part of that group of girls who clustered together after lessons to talk enthusiastically about what they had learned, and who were already looking forward to the postings they would be given where they would be doing a real job, which would be important – work that was needed and valued.

The truth was, Lou admitted, she really liked being in the WAAF. She didn't even mind the parading or the rules – not really – because for the first time in her life she had found something that mattered to her. Dancing had mattered, of course, but part of that had been the thrill it had given her when her dad had complained about the music, and the excitement of planning to go on stage when she knew her parents disapproved. Now that she had discovered how much more satisfying it was to do something she loved and work hard at it to be praised for her skill, the thrill of breaking the rules was something that felt not just silly but shameful, pinning on her a label she no longer wanted.

She had liked feeling proud of herself when her tutors had praised her, and now she felt not just that she had let others down, but that she had let herself down as well.

Betty had apologised to her and said that it was partly her fault for starting it but Lou had surprised herself by responding that she had chosen to retaliate and so the blame was her own.

It was like the corp had said to Lou when she had taken her on one side when she had returned to the hut: in the services everyone worked as a team, for the greater good of that team. They put the team first, not themselves. By not doing that Lou had cost the team of her hut something everyone else had worked hard for. Lou sniffed back the tears she could feel blurring her eyes. What she had done this time couldn't be made right by giggling about it with Sasha. She didn't even want to, for one thing, and for another, Sasha probably wouldn't even understand why she felt the way she did.

She had changed, Lou realised; she wasn't the Lou who had left Liverpool . . .

The sound of an approaching plane broke into her thoughts.

Lou whirled round and stared up into the sky. The sound was coming not towards her, approaching the end of the runway, but from behind her, sounding as though the plane intended to fly in over the base itself. Halton was mainly a RAF training base; planes, when they did fly, in came in during daylight hours, not with their engine whining like this one.

Lou strained her eyes, searching the sky. From the sound of it, it was a heavy aircraft of the type used by Bomber Command on its nighttime raids on German towns and defensive positions, perhaps. Bomber Command HQ was at High Wycombe, but their airfields were further to the east. For a bomber to try to put down here must mean that it was in desperate trouble.

Then she saw them: airmen tumbling from the grey bomber into the dawn mist, their parachutes opening over the farmland on the other side of the base, whilst the plane flew on, losing height fast. Automatically Lou noted that she was right and that it was a Wellington, one of the older bombers still in use. Her heart was in her mouth as the plane only just cleared the base's buildings. Then she saw that one of its two engines was on fire and that the undercarriage had been shot away.

Somehow despite her anxiety for the crew who had ejected from it, and the pilot who was still in it, there was still space in her thoughts for a rush of emotional pride in their skill and bravery, their mauled and savaged aircraft witness to the bloody fight they and it had had to survive.

Trailing smoke and flames, the bomber was now lurching to one side as it came towards her. The pilot wasn't going to make the runway, Lou realised; the plane was diving too steeply and too fast. It thudded down and then lifted so close to her that she could feel the heat from its burning engine along with the draught of its flight.

On the far side of the base, lights were coming on and she could see movement. Soon the rescue squads would be here with a fire engine and medical staff.

Lou heard a terrific thud, the ground beneath her feet shaking, forcing her attention back to the bomber, which had now come to rest with its nose almost buried in the ground, flames licking at the wing and reaching greedily forward. Why wasn't the pilot getting out?

Lou started to run, her heart hammering into her ribs. Ignoring the smoke and the flames, oblivious to the risk to her own safety, she reached up to the pilot's door – unluckily the fire was on the pilot's side but luckily the plane had slewed to that side, so that it was relatively easy for her to wrench open the door. Coughing and choking on the thick smoke, she could feel the heat of the flames, but she ignored them. Inside that plane was a man who needed her help, a man prepared to risk his life in the service of his country. How could she refuse to risk hers to save him? She couldn't, Lou knew, as she refused to give in to the heat

155

threatening to burn her skin and the smoke filling her lungs.

The pilot was slumped over his controls, a trickle of blood coming from his nose, but he was alive, she knew because he was groaning. Alive now, but not for much longer unless she could get him out of the plane.

Their tutor was thorough, and how glad Lou was now that he had insisted their learning every detail of the interior of the RAF's planes. Miraculously, somehow her fingers were reaching automatically for buckles and fastenings, as she released his para-chute harness, the better to get him out of the cockpit.

'You've got to help me,' she yelled in the pilot's ear. 'Come on unless you want us both to be burned alive.'

She could smell aviation fuel. If that caught fire then they would have no hope of surviving. The plane would explode into a fireball. Her stomach cramped with a panic she refused to let take hold of her.

Somehow her words must have reached the pilot because she felt him move with her as she struggled to tug him out. She could smell burning hair and fabric, and her hands were stinging and hot. Every second was so precious and they had so few of them left. The smell of fuel was growing stronger. Out of the corner of her eye she could see the lights of the vehicles racing down the runway towards them.

Gritting her teeth, Lou pulled harder, muttering to herself, now more than to the pilot, 'Come on. Come on . . .' unaware that she had succeeded in pulling him free of his seat until the weight of him falling against her drove the breath out of her lungs, sending them both tumbling to the ground, and then rolling away from the plane.

The lights and noise of proper rescuers were closer now but Lou knew that she couldn't wait for them. Desperately she held on to the pilot and rolled them both with the last of her strength as far from the plane as she could, grimacing against the pain in her hands as she did so.

Flame had engulfed the plane, the heat intense, the smell of aviation fuel heavy on the air. When the fuel tank ignited with a fierce crumping sound, Lou pushed the pilot to the ground and flung herself protectively over him. Something – a spark or a piece of burning wreckage – hit the back of her leg, the pain stinging, sharp and so intense that momentarily she thought she might pass out.

Then help was there, people scrambling over the fence as she had done earlier to get to them, a crisp male voice reaching through her sickening dizziness to announce, 'Atta girl. Just keep still for us for a minute and we'll soon have you on a stretcher. Careful with her,' the voice continued. 'Her hands are burned and there's what looks like a piece of ruddy fuselage in her leg.'

A stretcher. Burns . . . fuselage in her leg? Lou was indignant. She was perfectly all right, and she was determined to say so.

'I don't need a stretcher. I can walk. It's the pilot who needs help,' she began, but then out of nowhere pain overwhelmed her, and she blacked out.

* * *

'I'm really glad that Wilhelm has come back. I missed him, and I don't care what Davey Burrows says.'

Emily looked at Tommy's downbent head with maternal concern. 'Well, of course not.'

Obviously encouraged by this support Tommy continued, 'Davey Burrows says that it's treason to like a German, and that if I don't watch out Wilhelm will put me in an oven and burn me to death like Hitler is doing all the Jews.'

Emily put down the carrot she was dicing for their evening meal. 'It would only be treason if you were telling Wilhelm things about this country that might put us all at risk,' she told Tommy firmly. 'And then of course Wilhelm would have to pass what you told him on to someone in Germany who could use that information against us. You and I know, because Wilhelm had told us, that he didn't really want to become a soldier and fight for Hitler. He can't pass any information on to anyone even if he wanted to, because we've got censors checking everything that everyone writes. He wanted to stay on the farm. And as for what Hitler is doing to the poor Jews . . .'

Emily sighed. Tommy was such a quick, bright boy and of course children were bound to talk about what they heard their parents discussing. People naturally were horrified by the dreadful stories coming out about the death camps to which Jews were being sent.

Putting her arm round Tommy's shoulders, she drew him closer to her. 'Now you listen to me, Tommy. You know how much I love you, don't you?'

Immediately he nodded.

'And you know too that I'd never let anything bad happen to you?'

Now he said hesitantly, 'Grown-ups say that but sometimes bad things happen that they can't stop happening. They can't promise.'

Emily's heart was wrung with protective love for him. Who knew what terrible dreadful things he had experienced before she had found him? He never talked about his past, and she never asked, but something must have happened to have made him mute like he had been when she had first found him scavenging in the rubbish behind the Royal Court Theatre.

'That's true, Tommy,' she felt obliged to answer him honestly. 'But I can promise you that I will always do my utmost to keep you safe. I love you and there's no one and nothing that will ever mean more to me than you do.' Still holding him to her, she exhaled and told him, 'If Wilhelm coming here bothers you in any kind of way, then you just tell me and I shall tell the farmer not to send him any more.'

'No. I want him to come. I like him. Davey Burrows is daft; everyone knows that.' Tommy's voice was scornful now.

What she had said to him had obviously banished whatever it was that had been preying on his mind, Emily decided, relieved, her relief turning to a rueful smile when he added, 'We aren't having carrots again, are we? Only it's light nights now and I won't need to see in the dark.'

'Well, the thing about carrots is that you need

to keep on eating them to make them work,' Emily informed him, watching as he digested her statement without comment.

'You know what I think?' Tommy asked her sagely, looking pleased with himself, obviously having accepted that he was not going to win the war over the carrots. 'I think that Davey Burrows is only saying those things about Wilhelm because Wilhelm has been teaching me to play football, and I got two goals right past Davey.'

'Well, I'm sure you're right, Tommy, and that could have something to do with it,' Emily agreed, hiding her smile.

It had been lovely having Wilhelm coming round again, but if having him here upset her Tommy in any way, then Wilhelm would have to go, despite the sharp pang the thought of that caused. Tommy wasn't just any boy – he was special, he was hers, given to her by the war. He had filled her empty heart and her equally empty life and there was nothing she wouldn't do for him.

ELEVEN

Lou was tired of having to stay in bed in Halston's medical unit in the grounds of the base, under the stern eye of a medical orderly, who wouldn't so much as let her put a foot down on the floor unless the doc sanctioned it.

She was wearing 'blues', as the regulation pyjamas were known, her hair cut short because it had been so badly singed on one side, the new style giving her face an elfin appeal.

The burns on her hands had healed well, although the skin was tight and tender. The worst of the burns had been on the backs of her hands and her arms, which meant that she was still able to use her fingers properly, and would be able to continue with her training, much to her relief.

The surgeon who had removed the piece of fuselage from the back of her leg had, according to the RAF MO, done an exceptionally neat job of 'sewing her up' so that she would have only a very small scar.

'You were lucky.' The MO had told her. 'A tenth of an inch further in and it would have severed an artery.'

The pilot whose life everyone said she had saved would also make a full recovery, and the men who had bailed out were all also all right, although one of them had a broken leg and another a broken shoulder.

Lou hadn't been informed of any of this officially; that wasn't the RAF's way. Instead she had been told in snippets of information whispered to her during the many visits she had had from the other girls in her hut.

It had been a shock to come round from her operation to find not just the corp standing by her bedside, but, even more astonishingly, Halton's most senior WAAF officer, and the base's C-in-C.

Nauseous from the gas used to anaesthetise her, her head pounding and her recall of what had happened confused and vague, Lou had wondered what on earth they were talking about at first when they had praised her for her quick action and her courage.

'Corp's got her chest puffed out with pride, and you're a real heroine,' Betty had told her when she had managed to sneak a visit to Lou's bedside in the otherwise empty medical ward.

'I didn't mean to be,' Lou had replied. 'I just saw the plane and the pilot, and I just did everything automatically without stopping to think.'

'Well, everyone's saying that if it hadn't been for you being there and your quick thinking the pilot would have been a goner. And he isn't just any old pilot, you know. He's a squadron leader and an honourable,' Betty had informed her.

Lou didn't really care about any of that. She was just glad that he was still alive.

She'd been well and truly spoiled since she'd been in here, she admitted, with special meals sent over to tempt her appetite, and yesterday a parcel had arrived, sent anonymously, but containing thirty bars of Fry's Chocolate Cream – one for each of the girls in the hut, Lou guessed – and, as everyone knew that prior to being sent on an op the Bomber crews were given a special meal that included a bar of Fry's, it hadn't been hard to guess that the chocolate had come from the squadron leader's pals.

Lou had written home, explaining what had happened, but playing everything down so as not to worry her mother, and there'd been a positive flood of letters back, from her parents, from Grace, from Sasha, of course, and even from Cousin Bella, all wishing her well and telling her to hurry up and get better.

She'd been told that once she had been declared medically fit she was being given some special leave so that she could go home and see her family. Lou wasn't sure how she felt about that. Her mother would certainly have something to say about her being too impulsive and taking unnecessary risks.

It was a pity that she was the only occupant of the small ward, Lou reflected. She could have done with some company, although not perhaps the company of Sister Wilson, she acknowledged, as this rather formidable-looking individual came in.

Sister Wilson had been the kindest and most sympathetic person when she had been feeling really poorly, seeming to understand, without Lou needing to say anything, how uncomfortable the sometimes scratchy sheets felt against her burned skin, but now that Lou was well on the way to recovery Sister Wilson had turned into a gaoler, determined that her patient was going to stay within the rigid confines of her bed with its bedding pulled so tight into hospital corners that it was like a strait-jacket, instead of doing what Lou would much have preferred to be doing, which was getting up to go and look out of the window to see what was going on outside on the base, and teasing the nurse on duty to let her friends come in to see her outside visiting times.

Now, summoning a nurse to pull the screens round her bed, Sister Wilson told Lou briskly, 'You're about to have an important visitor. Nurse Allington here will help you into clean pyjamas, and remember, you might be in hospital but you are still in uniform.'

'What was that all about?' Lou asked the nurse when Sister had gone.

'I don't know, I'm sure,' the nurse replied unconvincingly as she buttoned Lou into a clean pyjama jacket and then told her, 'You'll have to put this on,' handing her the red tie that Waafs were supposed to wear with their blue pyjamas when in hospital.

'A tie? What do I need a tie for?' Lou demanded, but the nurse didn't answer her. Instead she was plumping up extra pillows and putting them behind Lou's back so that she was forced to sit up in bed almost bolt upright, before whisking away her old pyjamas and then removing the screens.

Lou didn't have long to wait to discover what all the fuss was about. The nurse had barely disappeared in the direction of the sluice room when

Sister reappeared, standing formally to attention at the entrance to the ward, and then saluting as the doors opened and a several people came in, including the MO, the senior WAAF officer, and the base's C-in-C, along with two other men, one of them in RAF uniform, and the other . . . the other was surely the most immediately recognisable man in the country, his familiar cigar clamped in his mouth, his bald head shining beneath the ward lights, bringing into the ward with him an air of energy and determination. Winston Churchill. The man whose stirring speeches had brought the whole country hope in its darkest moments. Now Lou was glad of the hard pillows stiffening her spine. Automatically as the party approached her bed, she saluted, only dropping her hand and arm when her own commanding officer ordered, 'At ease.'

It was the Prime Minister who spoke next, turning to the C-in-C, speaking in that famous voice, which sent a thrill of disbelief through her that this wonderful man, a hero to the whole nation, should be here at her bedside. If only Sasha could have been with her to share in this moment.

'Well, Commander, this is heart-stirring news indeed to learn that one of the many young women who obeyed the call to serve her country has comported herself with such quick-thinking and bravery, not just saving another's life, but showing that spirit that I have always said will enable us to defeat our enemies.'

Then to Lou's astonishment the Prime Minister held out his hand to her. Lou stared at it, for a second too transfixed with awe and disbelief to do anything,

165

until a timely warning cough from her commanding officer had her extending her own hand so that it could be shaken by the Prime Minister.

'Very well done, young lady. You are a credit to Halton and to the service.'

Lou's 'visitors' had gone, the pillows had been removed, and the nurse, far more ready to talk now than she had been earlier, was agog with what had happened.

'Just fancy, the Prime Minister asking to see you, 'cos of him hearing about what you did, and not just the Prime Minister, but the head of Bomber Command as well.'

So that was Sir Arthur Harris who had been with the Prime Minister, the Head of Bomber Command himself!

Of course Lou couldn't help but bask in the glory of what had happened. A constant stream of visitors, having heard in the way of such things about the august visitation to her bedside, were prepared to brave the wrath of Sister, who astonishingly, and in direct contradiction of her normal *modus operandi*, was nowhere to be seen when these small groups of uniformed Waafs peered eagerly into the ward and then made a concerted dash to Lou's bed. Turning a blind eye to the rules on this scale was unheard of, and Lou, as much as her visitors, made the most of it. Time was hanging heavily on Lou's hands now that she was a convalescent, and the companionship of the other girls was very welcome, although she did begin to tire of saying truthfully, 'There isn't much to tell, honestly.'

'You mean to say that Winnie didn't sit down and discuss strategy with you or confide his plans to you?' Betty, who had taken up an almost permanent post at Lou's bedside, teased, rescuing her from the ever-persistent question when it had been asked for the umpteenth time.

It was only when her own special pals had been there for over an hour, Betty, Ruby and Ellen all sitting on her bed, and just after Ruby had asked her hopefully, 'You haven't had any more parcels of those Fry's Chocolate Cream bars, have you?' that a nurse appeared, warning them all, 'Sister's on her way and there'll be a devil of a fuss if she finds you lot here.'

Watching the swift disappearance of WAAF uniforms and the smiling faces of her friends, Lou felt her own spirits sink a little. It had been such fun having them here. She missed their company, and she missed her training as well, she admitted.

She said as much later when the MO came round to check the wound on her leg whilst the dressing was being removed and a fresh one put in place.

'The sergeant in charge of your workshop isn't going to want you back until you're fully fit and can stand on that leg properly,' was Sister's stern comment after the MO had gone, having announced that Lou was to start exercising in the gym on her return from her compassionate leave, which was to start in two days' time.

'But if I can go in the gym then I could at least go and watch what Sergeant Benson is teaching everyone,' Lou wheedled.

When they had visited her, the other girls on her course had been talking about their progress and the 'practical work' they were about to start doing on real planes in the hangars, and Lou desperately wanted to be a part of that. She wasn't going to say anything in case it made her look soppy, but the Prime Minister's visit and what he had said had doubled her determination to do her bit and to do it well. What she wanted, Lou recognised, was to be the best WAAF mechanic there was, and she couldn't do that stuck here in bed whilst the other girls were getting on with practising what they had learned.

'You'll be no use to Sergeant Benson or anyone else until that leg's been passed fit for duty,' was Sister's unsympathetic response.

The visits from her chums, plus Sister's comments, and of course the heady words of praise from Winnie himself, which were still floating inside her head, fired Lou with determination to get back to her training.

As she was the only 'poorly' occupant of the ward, it was easy enough for her to wait until Sister was doing her regular round on the RAF ward, and the nurse on duty was out of the way, to scramble out of bed and then, using the bed itself and the chair to one side of it, attempt to walk properly.

Normally the only time she had been allowed out of bed had been under Sister's eagle eye, when intially she had been permitted to hop her way to the ablutions with her injured leg bent and a nurse's arm to learn on, and then more latterly to do a turn up and down the ward using crutches.

Being in the WAAF had taught Lou a lot; perhaps

most importantly of all it had taught her to take responsibility for her own actions. Thus whilst the old Lou would have immediately ignored the risk of additional damage to her injured leg, and perhaps even have relished the fuss her recklessness would have caused, much as she wanted to be properly back on her feet, the Lou she had become wasn't going to risk putting her recovery back by being reckless, 'showing off' as Lou herself now thought of it.

Instead, carefully testing her way and holding on to the back of the chair, with the wall behind her she tried to straighten her leg, stopping when pain gripped her weak muscles, and then cautiously trying again.

By the time she had finally got her foot flat on the floor, sweat was dampening her palms and her leg muscles felt as though they were on fire, but a quick look down over her shoulder assured her that her wound hadn't opened up and started to bleed, so using the chair as a support she started to move slowly forward.

The pain in her leg was excruciating and the healing burns on her hands and arms were stinging like mad, but when she finally reached the end of her bed, Lou felt light-headed with triumph and delight.

Her delight, though, quickly vanished when just as she was turning round she heard Sister's voice calling sharply, 'Nurse!'

Of course she was put straight back in bed, and the MO sent for, right in the middle of his tea. Sister left Lou in no doubt that she was in disgrace, as she pointed out severely that if Lou had fallen on the ward's shiny linoleum floor, it wouldn't just be her wound she would have to recover from, it would be a broken bone as well.

Bearing all that in mind, Lou quailed a little as, later, she watched Sister Wilson coming towards her, her cape on, obviously ready to change shifts with the night sister.

No doubt she was going to be in for another drubbing, Lou thought warily, but instead of telling her off, to her astonishment Sister announced crisply, 'From tomorrow morning you are to have two separate one-hour exercise periods a day, during which you will have one of my nurses in attendance and I shall be watching you to make sure that you do not try to run before you can walk.'

A thin smile touched Sister's mouth as though she was pleased with her own joke, emboldening Lou to say humbly, 'Thank you, Sister.'

'It is not me you should thank for the fact that you are able to undertake such exercise with two legs, Campion, it is Alexander Fleming, and the new drug that has resulted from his research.'

When Lou looked blank, Sister explained, 'Without the injections of penicillin you received after the operation to remove the piece of metal from the fuselage from your leg, it is more than likely that you could have succumbed to blood poisoning, which in turn would have meant the amputation of your leg. Now that you are aware of that I trust you will treat the limb that Professor Fleming's research has allowed you to retain with a little more respect.'

'Yes, Sister,' was all that Lou could manage to say.

TWELVE

'Can you see Lou yet, Grace?' Anxiously Jean craned her neck to search the faces of the mass of people on the platform of Lime Street Station.

There must be nearly as many people in uniform as there had been when she and Sam had come here to say goodbye to Luke when he had left for France right at the beginning of the war, Jean felt sure. Only now, of course, it wasn't just young men in army uniform, uncertain of themselves and new to war, but young men and women, in a variety of uniforms – so many, in fact, that Jean was worried that she might not be able to pick her daughter out amongst the sea of faces.

'Lou will find us, I'm sure, Mum,' Grace tried to reassure her. 'We said we'd meet her here, near to the tea stand.' Privately Grace had anxieties of her own for her younger sister. Being a nurse herself she had read between the lines of Lou's nonchalant statement: 'I shall probably still be on crutches, but they don't hold me up very much.' She worried about just how badly Lou had been hurt.

The official letter her parents had received, and

171

which her mother had shown her and Seb this morning when they had arrived in Liverpool ready to welcome Lou home, had not told them much other than that Lou had been injured 'performing an act of bravery' but that her life was not in any danger.

Rather irritatingly, when she had looked at Seb for enlightenment of this military phrasing, instead of returning her look he had exchanged very male glances with her father.

'It's all very well Lou writing to say that we aren't to worry and that she's almost as good as new, I shan't be easy in my mind until I've seen for myself. I just hope that she hasn't been making a bad situation worse by acting daft and taking risks,' Jean sighed, able to confide in her eldest daughter now that Grace herself was grown up and married.

'I don't think she'll be allowed to do that, Mum,' Grace comforted her. 'Not if the WAAF is anything like being a nurse.'

'Well, that's another thing, Grace. Knowing what Lou's like and how she only has to hear the word "no", or be told to do something, for her to do her utmost to do just the opposite, I can't help worrying about her being in uniform. Naturally, me and your dad were against it when we found out that she'd joined up, but we agreed that she'd have to take her medicine and stick with it – well, at least that's what your dad said – but that doesn't mean either of us wants her to be unhappy.'

'As if anyone would ever think you wanted any

of us to be other than happy, Mum,' Grace smiled, slipping her arm though Jean's.

Grace loved every member of her family, but in her opinion her mother was just the best mother in the world.

'I'm surprised that Sasha didn't want to come with us,' Grace continued.

'Well, I think she was afraid she'd be too upset and go and make a fool of herself. She's not said a lot since we heard the news, but you can see in her face how she really feels, and how worried she is. I haven't said too much to her, because the last thing me and your dad want is for her to go blaming herself for Lou joining up and then this happening . . .'

'Mum! Grace hissed, nudging her mother in the ribs. 'There she is with that young RAF chap.'

Jean's heart seemed to turn over as she focused on where Grace was indicating and she saw her daughter.

After the initial shock of seeing Lou on crutches, an unexpected surge of pride overwhelmed Jean, bringing sharp tears to her eyes.

That was her Lou, that surely taller, and definitely more shapely, although still very slender young woman, whose slimmed-down face, with its high cheekbones and delicately shaped jaw, gave her face a beauty Jean had never expected to see in one of the twins, who had inherited what she always thought of as her own rather ordinary looks.

It was plain from the manner in which Lou was chatting to the young man, who seemed to be carrying her case, how relaxed and at ease she was in male company – another change Jean had not been prepared for.

Fresh pride filled her. Watching Lou, Jean saw a young woman in uniform who was attractive and confident, and whose company was apparently courted by young men but whose manner towards them was so free of flirtatiousness and artifice that it would gladden any mother's heart.

As yet Lou hadn't seen them but, as though she was sharing her mother's thoughts, Grace squeezed Jean's arm and said huskily, 'Oh my, doesn't she look grand?' And then before Jean could say anything Grace raised her hand and called out, 'Coooee, Lou, over here.'

Although Jean would never have expected Grace's voice to carry through the crowds thronging the station, somehow or other it must have done, because Lou turned in their direction, a wide smile curling her mouth as she waved back, and then turned to say something to the young man with her.

'Oh, no, look at that. She's telling him that she can manage with her case now.' Grace clicked her tongue, suddenly a nurse before she was a sister. 'Here, Mum, hold my handbag for me, will you, and wait here whilst I go and get her? The last thing we want is Lou being all independent and then coming a cropper.'

And so it was that within a handful of minutes, Grace and Lou were coming towards her, Grace holding Lou's case in one hand, her free arm tucked very firmly and protectively through Lou's as she walked alongside her.

'Honestly, Grace, it's true, I don't really need this. I just thought I'd bring it so that you'd all feel sorry for me,' Lou was laughing as Jean opened her arms and hugged her tightly to her, before pushing her gently away and looking at her.

'You've grown at least another half an inch,' she announced a bit tearfully, 'and you've lost weight.'

'Three-quarters of an inch, and I expect that Sash has done the same. You'll have to measure us back to back like you used to do when we were little, Mum.'

'I remember Mum doing that, and I remember too that you'd always rise up on your heels and make Sasha do the same so that you'd look taller.'

'That was because Mum said Dad wouldn't let us go to the Grafton until we were at least five foot five inches.'

Lou might not have said anything about her twin not being there but Jean, with a mother's eye, had seen the way she had glanced quickly round when she had reached her, as though hoping that Sasha would appear.

'Sasha said she couldn't trust herself not to disgrace you in public by bursting into tears, that's why she isn't here.'

'This is better, like opening Christmas presents slowly,' Lou smiled.

It wasn't just outwardly that Lou had changed, Jean recognised with another surge of shock tinged with pride, and her height obviously wasn't the only way in which she'd grown.

'Do you want a cup of tea?' Jean asked.

Lou shook her head. 'I'd rather wait until we're home.'

'You just be careful with that leg,' Grace was warning, as they made their way through the bustle.

Where once Lou would have teased her elder sister, calling her 'nursie' or some such thing, now she nodded and replied, 'Don't worry, the last thing I want is to slow up my recovery and not be able to get back to my training. Sister's promised me that if I do my walking exercises whilst I'm at home, she'll have a word with the MO when I get back to see if I can be allowed to return to training a couple of hours every day, instead of having to wait until the PT instructor has signed me off as fit. It's been ever such a bind having to miss out on lessons, especially when the other girls are talking about what they're doing and I know that I'm falling behind.'

Jean and Grace exchanged astonished looks. Was this the same Lou who had abhorred school and lessons and done everything within her power to undermine her poor teachers?

'So you're happy in the WAAF then?' Grace asked.

'I love it,' Lou responded immediately, adding quickly, 'Of course I miss home and all of you, but it really makes you think that you're contributing something important towards the war effort, knowing that the work we'll be doing on the planes will help to keep them flying.'

Lou displaying tact and discretion, and actually thinking about how what she was saying might be received? If that was the effect being in the WAAF was having on her then Grace was impressed.

176

Unaware of her elder sister's thoughts, Lou continued, 'So far I've only worked on pieces salvaged from crashed aircraft, and I'm just so envious of the other girls starting working on the real thing soon. Mind you, if I can get my leg passed by the MO then there's no reason why I shouldn't join them. I must have taken in more than I knew, listening to Dad talking about his work, because our sergeant says I've got a natural aptitude for the work.'

Hearing her daughter talking so enthusiastically and confidently about what she was doing filled Jean with relief. But alongside that was a certain sadness. This Lou, the Lou who was walking along arm in arm between her and Grace as they started out towards Edge Hill and home, was not the Lou who had left Liverpool earlier in the year. That Lou had been a young girl, awkward sometimes in adult company, rebellious, stubborn and headstrong, filled with an energy she had not learned how to channel, and unhappy because of that – with herself as well as with others. This Lou was a young woman, poised, determined, confident, but most of all happy.

Pleased as she was for her daughter, Jean still felt cheated that she had not been there to witness the almost magical transformation that turned all young human 'cygnets' into the adult 'swans', who filled their parents' hearts with pride.

'Oh, and you'll probably be interested in this, Grace,' Lou told them. 'The surgeon who oper-ated on my leg instructed that I was to be given a new medicine. Penicillin, it's called. Have you heard of it?'

Indeed Grace had, and Jean listened in silence as her daughters talked enthusiastically about the marvels of modern medicine and what a difference this penicillin would make to treating wounds that might once have turned gangrenous.

'You'll have had the drug by injection,' said Grace knowledgeably.

Lou laughed. 'Yes, I was a bit like a pin cushion, but without it Sister said that I might well have ended up losing my leg.'

Jean's gasp had them both looking at their mother.

'It's all right, Mum,' Lou was quick to reassure her. 'I didn't lose it and I'm not going to now. The MO says it's a lovely clean heal and that I'll only have a small scar.'

'What happened to the pilot you saved?' Grace asked diplomatically after a quick look at Jean's pale face.

'Oh, they shipped him off to another RAF hospital closer to his own base, in Leicestershire. He'd been on a bombing raid, and somehow or other they'd got lost on the way back.'

'He was very lucky, and you were very brave,' Jean told her.

'I didn't do anything that any other WAAF wouldn't have done in the same circumstances, Mum.'

There she was again: the new grown-up Lou, quick to be calm and modest, not at all like the younger Lou, who would have fought passionately with Sasha to claim the glory.

Sasha! What would her twin make of this new Lou, Jean wondered a little anxiously.

It was only when they turned into their own

road, just on the border between Edge Hill and Wavertree, that Jean saw a glimpse of the old Lou when suddenly she held back and looked uncertain, saying with more than a touch of bravado, 'I suppose I'm going to get it from Dad, especially since I joined up without getting his permission. He'll be saying, "I told you so," to me, I expect – and worse.'

'Well, if your dad were to tell you off it would be no more than you deserve,' Jean felt bound to stick up for her husband, 'but, like me, all your dad really wants is your happiness and your safety, Lou, and you have to admit that going behind our backs like that would upset any man.'

'Yes, of course,' Lou agreed. 'It was the wrong thing to do, I admit.'

Again Jean and Grace exchanged astounded looks.

'But I'm ever so glad that I did do it, Mum, because I'm just so happy now.'

'You must miss Sasha, though?' Grace asked.

'Of course. It would have been wonderful if she'd joined up too, although I dare say they'd have been bound to separate us. But the thing is that I don't think that Sash would have enjoyed it as much as I do, so it's better that she's here in the telephone exchange, like she wanted to be.'

There was no truculence or resentment in Lou's voice, only acceptance.

'I had a lovely letter from Luke,' Lou continued. 'He didn't say much about how things are for him, of course, but he did say that he was proud of me. I do wish that he and Katie were still engaged. Do you hear from her at all, Mum?'

179

'No.' Jean tried to smile. 'She felt that it wouldn't be right to keep in touch, on account of Luke, and of course she was right.'

They were home now, Sam and Seb and of course Sasha waiting to greet them and to welcome Lou home, the family filling the small cosy sparkling clean kitchen with its bright yellow walls and its air of being the heart of the house.

Lou hugged Sasha first, not trusting herself to say anything really meaningful to her twin until they were on their own, and having to make do instead with a muttered, 'We can talk properly later,' before releasing Sasha to go and hug her father.

Watching Lou hug Sam, Jean knew that Sam was as aware of and bemused by Lou's changed demeanour as she had been herself.

It was only when Lou took off her cap, though, that Jean finally couldn't control her emotions any longer.

In place of the neat bob with which Lou had gone away, her hair – or what was left of it – was a mass of short feathery curls that somehow, instead of making her look boyish, had just the opposite effect and gave her a gamine femininity instead.

All Jean could say though was, 'Oh, Lou, your hair! What happened?'

'What? Oh, this.' Lou raked her fingers through her curls and looked rueful, giving them all an impish smile, before saying lightly, 'One side of my hair was badly singed when I was dragging

180

the pilot free. I could smell burning hair but I was so busy trying to get him to safety that I didn't stop to think that it might be my crowning glory. Obviously I couldn't go around with a lopsided bob so it had to be cut. Luckily one of the other girls was a hairdresser before she joined up and she offered to cut it for me, otherwise I'd have probably ended up with the RAF barber giving me a short back and sides.

'It's very pretty, isn't it, Seb?' Grace announced, asking for her husband's support.

'Very,' Seb agreed with such relish that Lou promptly blushed and Grace turned on Seb with mock wifely anger, warning him, 'That's quite enough of you noticing that my little sister has turned into a beauty, thank you, Seb.'

Standing on the sidelines, watching everyone gather excitedly about her twin, Sasha wasn't sure just how she felt. She had been desperate to see for herself that Lou was, as she had written to her, recovering well from her injuries, but where there should have been relief Sasha found that what she was actually feeling was closer to anger, as though the changes she could see and sense in Lou – not just in her appearance but in her self – somehow took something away from her.

For instance, their mother was going on about Lou having grown, and making a fuss about it, without making any reference to the fact that she had grown too, Sasha thought crossly, as she justi-fied her feelings to herself. Her mother and Grace were talking about Lou as though being a bit thinner and having had to have her hair cut because she had behaved in her normal reckless, unthinking way had somehow turned Lou not just into a heroine but also into a beauty. *She* was thinner too, but no one seemed to have noticed. It was Lou they were all fussing over, as though being away from home and joining the WAAF and risking her life had turned her into a new person, a Lou whom they admired and wanted to praise, instead of cautioning as they had done in the past.

These were difficult thoughts and feelings for Sasha to digest and understand. She had been longing to see her twin and yet now, instead of being thrilled to see her, she was actually wishing that she wasn't here, and that made her feel dreadful.

'What I don't understand, Lou,' she challenged her twin, 'is why you were the only one around when the plane crashed.

When everyone turned to look at her with varying degrees of astonishment, Sasha realised that she had gone too far. But instead of back-tracking, as she would normally have done, to her own confusion she heard herself saying even more challengingly, 'Bobby says that it was more than likely that you shouldn't have been there at all.'

Now she had done it. Lou was bound to retaliate with a nasty comment about Bobby saying something, like he wasn't a part of the family so he had no right to comment. Sasha had been warned by her mother not to rub Lou up the wrong way by going on to her about Bobby because in Lou's eyes he had come between them.

Poor Sasha couldn't understand her own behaviour. She was saying the kind of things, behaving
in the kind of challenging way that in the past would
have been Lou's chosen role. Now her mother had
a small anxious crease between her eyebrows
and her father was frowning heavily, whilst Grace
was giving Seb one of those stupid married looks
that said quite plainly how much she disapproved
of what Sasha had done.

A horrible feeling was twisting angrily inside
her, a sort of hot miserable pain that was driving
her to be even more cross and outspoken, and yet
at the same time also made her want to burst into
tears and beg Lou to forgive her. What was
happening to her? Sasha wasn't used to Lou getting
so much approval and praise. It had always been
Lou who had been the one who provoked others,
and who always caused the trouble they had both
so often ended up in, not her.

It was Jean who spoke first, not just surprised but
also a little bit cross with Sasha for spoiling the happy
mood of Lou's homecoming, and after everything she
had said to her about not mentioning Bobby as well.
Jean had thought better of Sasha, she really had, and
now because of that, her voice was quite sharp.

'That's quite enough, Sasha.'

Lou could almost feel her twin's misery and
immediately wanted to protect and defend her
but, more than that, she discovered a little to her
own surprise, she didn't want her family making
her out to be something she wasn't, especially
not at Sasha's expense, so she spoke up quickly,
admitting without heat, 'Actually, the truth is,

Mum, Bobby is sort of right. I wasn't doing anything wrong or breaking any rules in being where I was, but the reason that I was up so early in the morning and on my own was because that trouble I'd got into had affected all the other girls in my hut as well.'

Quickly she explained about the points, then turned to Sasha.

'So you can tell Bobby that he was right, but do tell him too that I have well and truly learned my lesson. I felt dreadful knowing that the other girls were being punished because of me. It made me think of how often you'd been punished along with me, Sash, when we were young, and yet you never complained or told on me. I'm so lucky to have such a loyal and wonderful twin.'

There was a moment's emotional silence from the whole room and then Seb said firmly, 'As a fellow member of the RAF, well done, young Lou. I'm proud to share the uniform with you.'

Seb's warm-hearted words broke the dam of startled silence that had gripped them all, but it was her father who said the words that nearly made Lou disgrace herself with silly tears.

'Well, I always knew that you must have at least some of your mother in you, despite everything, but I never thought to see you prove it like you have done now, Louise Campion.'

Taking advantage of the situation, Lou asked Jean, 'Mum, is it all right if me and Sasha go upstairs and have a proper chat? I promise I won't bully her into putting on any records.'

Everyone except Sasha laughed at Lou's reference

184

to her youthful habit of insisting on playing the gramophone records she and Sasha had loved to dance to at maximum volume, as Jean nodded in agreement.

'It seems ever so strange seeing you in uniform,' Sasha said awkwardly once they were upstairs in their shared bedroom.

'Does it? I feel strange now when I'm not wearing it,' Lou responded equably, sitting down on her old bed and then adding warmly, 'I like being in the WAAF but I've missed you ever such a lot, Sash.'

'Well, I hope you aren't going to try to persuade me to join up.'

Sasha's voice was deliberately hostile, but instead of being provoked into a quarrel as the old Lou would have been, Lou merely laughed and answered, 'No. I can see now that it was wrong of me to always want you to do what I wanted to do.' She reached for her twin's hand. 'I know you like working at the exchange and living here at home with Mum and Dad, and going out with Bobby, but—'

Sasha pulled her hand free. 'But you don't approve. Well, I don't care. Bobby means a lot to me. He saved my life, after all, don't forget.'

Lou looked at her twin. She could have pointed out that she too had done her part in saving her twin's life and the old Lou would have done so, oblivious to the fact that her insistence on her role being recognised would only further antagonise her twin.

Her coming home and being treated like a heroine had upset Sasha, she could tell, but her

185

own new-found maturity told her that saying so would only make the situation worse.

'I know I was a difficult about you and Bobby before I went away, Sash, but that was because I felt jealous. I didn't want you to want to be with him more than you wanted to be with me.' Lou smiled at her own immaturity. 'If you like him then that's all that matters, and it's certainly good enough for me.'

Sasha was eyeing her suspiciously. 'You don't mean that,' she accused Lou. 'You wanted me to be in trouble. You always did.'

Lou felt dreadfully guilty that she was the cause of Sasha's angry upset, and sad too – sad for Sash and sad for herself. It was as though in some peculiar way they had changed places, Lou realised, the thought making her frown slightly.

'I always wanted you to be in trouble with me,' she agreed. 'I wanted us to do everything together, but I never wanted to just get you into trouble, Sash. I was always the bad twin, and you were the good one.'

'And now because you're the good one, that means that I'm the bad one.'

'No,' Lou denied. 'I'm still me, Sash, and I expect I'll always be too impatient and too impulsive, and that I'll have to stop and think about what you'd do instead of rushing into things. I love being in the WAAF and doing what I'm doing and I'm determined to make a go of it, and that's going to take discipline, I know, but that doesn't mean that you and I have to change places. We can both be good, can't we?' she appealed, reaching out for Sasha's hand again, adding ruefully, 'Although, of course, you will always be naturally more "good" than me.'

Lou could feel the resistance in Sasha's silence and the stiffness of her hand.

'Sash, we always said that we'd never let what happened to Mum and Auntie Vi happen to us, remember?' Lou appealed to her twin.

'That wasn't Mum's fault. It was Auntie Vi's. She changed, Mum always said, just like you've changed.'

Lou's heart dropped. Sasha was still angry with her, she knew, and, for all her sweetness, Sasha could be determinedly stubborn when she wished. She might be slower to impatience and irritation, but Sasha was also slower to forgive and forget, Lou knew.

'It's all right for you, coming home and having everyone make a fuss of you because you're a heroine, but you'll soon be up to your old tricks, trying to put me off Bobby and make me do what you want. I know you, Lou.'

This time it was Lou who released Sasha's hand, her voice quiet and sad. 'No you don't, Sash. Not any more.'

'So what about you taking me out now for this dinner you keep on promising me?' Eva suggested archly to Con.

She'd come out of her dressing room just as he'd been on his way past and Con could see that he wasn't going to get away with an excuse. She'd been pursuing him very determinedly from the moment she'd arrived, and Con had done his best to keep her sweet, whilst at the same time keeping her at a distance.

'You can come and wait for me in my dressing room. It won't take me long to get changed.'

Eva hooked her arm through his. She'd got a grip like a wrestler, Con decided, as she was more of less dragged him into her dressing room and then closed the door, clasping both her hands to her breast as she stood blocking his exit.

'At last we are alone, just as we have both longed to be,' she told him emotionally. 'I have seen your desire for me in your eyes when you look at me. I have waited a long time for a man like you to come into my life.'

She was no shrinking virgin, Con was just thinking, when, as though she had read his mind, Eva told him, 'I cannot pretend that there have not been occasions when I have allowed myself to believe that other men, lesser men than you, have deceived me with their false promises of love, only for me to discover that they were not worthy of me. I am a woman, after all, the passionate daughter of a very passionate man. He was a knife thrower in a circus and he was so passionate, in fact, that he killed my mother out of his love for her when he believed she had been unfaithful to him.'

Con tried not to shudder. Intense emotions were something he always tried to avoid. The passion and thrill for him in a love affair came from pursuing his prey, and charming them until they succumbed to him.

'I still have the knife with which my father killed

my mother. I carry it with me always. Would you like to see it?'

Con started to shake his head, but Eva obviously wasn't going to let him refuse. She put her foot on the stool in front of her dressing table, which was littered with pots and sticks of stage make-up giving off its familiar smell of greasepaint under the hot lights illuminating the mirror. The robe she was wearing fell back to reveal her surprisingly good legs. She was wearing silk stockings, her suspenders attached to a sturdy-looking corset, around the waist of which she had on a narrow leather belt, with a sheath from which she produced a knife.

Just watching the way she gripped it made Con feel nervous. Despite his height and breadth of shoulder, Con was a physical coward who avoided confrontation and violence whenever he could.

Eva was smiling as she ran her thumb tip down the edge of the knife in a loving gesture.

'This knife reminds me of my father and the passionate nature he passed on to me. Any man who arouses those passions and then deceives me will answer to my father's knife.'

That was the trouble with these artistes, they were always so dramatic, Con thought irritably, but the sight of the knife, which Eva was now returning to its sheath, had made him feel apprehensive, and all the more so because of what Eva was implying.

Con was so worried about the knife that when Eva reached for him he didn't react fast enough and ended up with his hand being placed on her silk stocking-clad ankle and held there.

'You have such wonderful hands, so large and manly.' Her voice a throaty purr, Eva urged Con's hand up her leg.

It wasn't his fault that he was unable to stop himself from automatically stroking her flesh. He was a man, after all, so used to the pleasure of caressing chorus girls' limbs that it just came naturally to do so.

'Ah, your touch is too much for me to resist. You are seducing away my self-control. I cannot deny you.'

The theatrical magnificence of these words, delivered in a voice throbbing with feeling, whilst Eva threw back her head and placed her free hand against her brow, might be lost on Con, but their meaning certainly wasn't.

Another couple of minutes and they'd pass the point of no return, and he'd be far more involved with Eva than he wanted to be. He tried to pull away, but Eva's hand was trapping his against the warmly moist inside of her thigh.

'I know what you are asking me for when you look at me like that. I know what you are compelling me to give you. I confess I cannot refuse such a man as you . . . so very much of a man.'

With one lightning move, Eva had fully opened her robe and was reaching into Con's groin, her hand going straight to his balls, which she proceeded to massage with expertise. The movement of her body caused her breasts, which pouted over the top of her corset, to tremble so much that they reminded Con of the way the pink blanc-manges that his sister Alice made for her brood of children quivered after she had turned them out on a plate.

'Ah, but your little man is so impatient for me. I can feel him pleading for us to release him from his torment. Let us not waste another second in coming together in our love for one another . . .'

Con exhaled in relief as he stepped into the welcome dimness of the theatre, via the stage door.

When he had woken up this morning with a pounding headache, he hadn't even known where he was at first, never mind who he was with, and it had been a shock to turn over in the unfamiliar double bed and find Eva next to him, naked and snoring slightly.

Slowly everything had come back to him. After the inevitable had happened in her dressing room, she had insisted that he took her out for a meal. They'd ended up not in one of the cheap cafés Con favoured, but in a new nightclub that had only recently opened up in the city to cater for the influx of men in uniforms looking for somewhere to spend their money when they were on leave. Its interior had been discreetly dark, its dance floor very small and its prices very high.

Eva had insisted on ordering champagne, which had cost him twenty pounds, so that they could toast their love for one another, and Con had had a fight to get her away from the place before she ordered a second bottle. Then she'd threatened him with hysterics when he'd suggested that she could see herself back to her digs, and he'd had to go with her just to stop her from screeching. Once there, she'd produced a bottle of whisky, and then she'd matched him drink for drink, somehow managing to stay sober whilst he had not. And then . . . She certainly knew what she was doing when it came to the bedroom, Con acknowledged with admiration. He'd been tempted to stay with her and those magnificent breasts of hers this morning, but he didn't want her getting even more of the wrong idea than she already had. All that talk of love made him feel distinctly wary. She'd even been talking about moving in with him. He might not have thanked her for it at the time, but he'd been pretty relieved this morning that he had those billetees his wife, Emily, had let the council fill the house with as an excuse for insisting that Eva stayed where she was. She'd obviously fallen for him, and Con couldn't blame her for that. She wasn't the first woman to have done so and she wouldn't be the last. He hummed under his breath and then stopped as the pain from his aching head increased, wincing as he started to climb the stairs to the cubbyhole that was his office.

'Morning, Con.' Ricky smiled widely at Con.

Con stared in disbelief at the American, who was sprawled in Con's own chair, his feet on Con's own desk, whilst smoking one of Con's cigars.

'What the ruddy hell's going on?' Con demanded.

No one, but no one, was allowed into his office when he wasn't there, and as for sitting in his chair

192

with their feet on his desk, displaying a loucheness that Con had claimed for himself . . .

'You mustn't blame your boys, Con,' Ricky informed him, giving Con the answer to the question he had not yet asked. 'Like you they couldn't resist getting their hands on some of Uncle Sam's money.'

There was a look in the hard, almost black, eyes that sent a sharp thrill of alarm through Con as he made a mental note to deal with Stu and Paul later.

'If you're talking about last night's card game, everything was fair and square, you said so yourself,' Con responded, struggling to look relaxed whilst his hangover pounded.

'Sure I did, but that hasn't stopped Chip bad-mouthing you to the other guys at the camp. You don't mind if I give you a bit of advice, do you, Con?' Without waiting for Con to reply, Ricky leaned back in Con's chair, his hands folded behind his head as he told him, 'The way I see it is that it would have been a better move not to have done the kid twice over. Guys talk, y'know.'

'It isn't my fault that lady luck was with me and not with him,' Con blustered. He was increasingly anxious and eager to get the American out of his office and out of his life.

Ricky laughed and removed his feet from Con's desk, getting up and coming round to stand in front of it.

'Lady luck, eh? Come on, Con, it wasn't lady luck that was responsible for you winning. We both know that.'

'I don't know what you're talking about and I don't have to listen to this,' Con told him.

'Sure you do – if you want to keep on fleecing raw soldiers. I've got to say that I've seen plenty of guys palm cards in my time but you sure do it nicely. Real neat. Hey, Con there's no point in looking at me like that. We both know what's going on. I've been asking around and I reckon you're making twenty-five bucks or so a game. Peanuts. You could be making five times that. What you're doing now is amateur stuff; you need to think professional.'

A hundred and twenty-five pounds? Con couldn't help but feel dizzy with excitement at the prospect of so much money.

'Of course you'd need help – a partner. A guy who can drop a word here and there, and make sure the guys keep on coming, and that any fuss they make afterwards is smoothed over. I like you, Con, and I reckon you and me could work a really good deal here. What d'you say? I reckon a partnership with us splitting the profit sixty-forty is a pretty good offer.'

Sixty-forty?' Con queried, 'Eighty-twenty would be more like it.'

The American laughed. 'OK, if you're willing to give me another twenty per cent, then—'

'Give you another twenty per cent? I'm the one who'll be getting eighty per cent,' Con announced angrily.

Who did Ricky think he was, trying to take over?

'Look, buddy I don't think you quite understand,'

Ricky said softly. 'You've made some big mistakes, and you could find yourself in a hell of a lot of trouble if guys like Chip go complaining about some theatre manager ripping them off in card games. You could find that some of the guys decide to take it into their own hands to come and have a word with you. Be a pity if that handsome face of yours got beat to a pulp.'

Con started to sweat.

'You're a sensible man, Con. I knew that right off from when we met – a clever man, the kind of man who knows which side his bread's buttered, I reckon. The way I see it is that if you and me go into partnership like I've just told you, then we both get to benefit. With me putting the word out in the right ears, you could easily be pulling in a hundred and twenty-five dollars a week instead of only twenty-five. Any man would be a fool to turn down that kind of money, and something tells me that you ain't a fool, Con. So what do you say? Shall we shake on it partner?

What could he say, other than yes?

THIRTEEN

'Well, I don't know, Bella, you used to be such a pretty girl, and now look at you. You look positively gaunt. It's very ageing, you know, to be thin. Young men don't like it at all.'

Bella bore her mother's unkind remarks in stoic silence as she finished drying the crockery and putting it away whilst her mother sat watching her from her kitchen chair.

'It's that place, of course. I never approved of you taking that job in the first place, and if you'd listened to me, like a dutiful daughter, you never would have done. If you'd gone to work for your father he wouldn't have been driven to temptation by that . . . that hussy, and you wouldn't be looking like you do.'

It was true that Bella had lost weight, and that the late May sunshine showed up the shadows under her eyes, but it wasn't her work that was the cause, Bella acknowledged. The truth was that her work at the nursery and the responsibility that it carried was almost the only thing that kept her going. That, and Lena and the baby, of course.

But they were part of their own little family now, and not her responsibility any more.

It was because of Jan that she looked the way she did, and that the pre-war yellow dress with its pattern of white daisies she was wearing, and which had fitted her perfectly last year, was now loose on her, and her face looked pinched and drawn. Because of Jan and because she loved him.

It was nearly a month since she had sent him away and there hadn't been a minute, not a second during that time, when she hadn't thought about him and longed for him, and hoped secretly that he would write to her, even though she had said he must not do so. But he hadn't so much as sent her a single word.

She had told him not to, Bella reminded herself as she set off for work, having first prepared her mother's lunch and seen to it that their neighbour would pop in to see her and that a fellow member of her WVS group would call round to take her with her to their afternoon meeting.

In reality Vi was perfectly capable of doing these things for herself, had she wanted to do so, but since she didn't and preferred instead to cling to her self-pity and insist that she was too filled with despair to do anything, Bella had to organise her life for her.

Most of the trees were now in new leaf. Their differing shades of greens, broken here and there by the newly minted leaves of a copper beech, were a sight that should have lifted the heaviest of hearts, but stubbornly Bella's refused to be uplifted. The distant glimpse of a man with dark hair, wearing an RAF uniform, lifted it, though, sending it so high that it felt as though it was almost in her throat until she was close enough to know that he wasn't Jan.

Jan, Jan, Jan. Why couldn't she behave like a mature woman and not some silly girl? Seeing the gap between some houses where a bomb had dropped in the early stages of the war, the site now cleared of the collapsed building and the ground overgrown with rough grass and weeds, Bella paused, remembering the baby girl who had been removed alive from the wreckage of her home. Bella had held her for a few minutes, the feel of her small body in her arms a painful reminder of the baby she herself had lost.

Well, now she had any number of babies to hold and to fill her life, Bella told herself robustly, since the nursery was filled with them, and of course she had Lena and Baby as well. What kind of example would it have set Lena if she, Bella, had gone rushing into Jan's arms with his poor dead wife's body barely cold? Not, of course, that Lena needed Bella to set her an example these days. After all, Lena herself was a happily married woman now.

The morning air had that May softness and warmth about it, small white clouds drifting lazily across a blue sky. There was birdsong in the air, and the laughter of children from the playground of a nearby school. Normal sounds of normal life, but life wasn't normal and, as though to prove it, a fighter plane suddenly sped through the sky above her – from the Coastal Protection Squadron, based locally, Bella decided as she watched it head out to sea, leaving behind a vapour trail of white against the blue.

She'd left home a bit earlier than normal – more, Bella admitted ruefully, to escape from her mother than because she had any need to be at her desk early, and as she approached the nursery, mothers and sometimes grandmothers were arriving with their children. Several recognised her and stopped to talk to her,

'Ever so well, little Roger's doing, since he's been coming here,' one mother told Bella gratefully. 'I must say that when we first learned that Mr Churchill was bringing out a law that would mean that we had to go to work, I was worried about leaving Roger, but he's come on a treat.'

'We can't take all the credit, Mrs Hunter,' Bella responded diplomatically. 'The nurses tell me that they can always tell which little ones have a mother with the right attitude, because their babies are so much happier and more responsive.'

Roger's mother's chest swelled with pride, enabling Bella to excuse herself, but she didn't get much further before she was stopped again. Not by a mother this time, but by a sister. Jan's sister, Bettina.

'Bettina,' Bella began uncertainly.

But Jan's sister stopped her, saying quickly and fiercely, 'There's something I have to tell you, and I can't stay long. I have to get back to Mother and then go to work. It's about Jan, Bella.'

About Jan? Although neither of them had spoken openly about things, Bella knew from the light hints that had been dropped by Bettina after Jan had first revealed to Bella his love for her, that Jan's mother and sister were aware of the situation and were grateful to her for the moral stance she had taken. The fact that they had wanted her to know about Magda's death had confirmed Bella's feelings in this regard.

'I can't see him, Bettina, no matter how much I might want to. It wouldn't be right and one day he'll think that himself. The last thing I want is for him to end up despising me like he did before, and . . .' Perhaps she shouldn't speak so openly, but it was impossible for her not to do so, Bella knew, given how she felt.

'Bella!' There was a desperate urgency and pain in Bettina's voice that suspended her own. 'Jan's been posted as "missing in action, believed dead".'

'No, no . . .' Bella was shaking Bettina's arm. 'Tell me that isn't true?' she begged her.

'Because of the Baedeker raids from the Luftwaffe, 307 Squadron's been on night coastal protection duty. Jan had already intercepted and shot down one of the attackers over the Channel and then he started to pursue another. One of the other pilots in the squadron saw him. He told me all this when Mother and I went down . . . Well, Jan's CO wanted to tell us in person. Pieter was a friend of Jan's; they were both in the same squadron in Poland. He told us that he saw two German fighters go up on either side of Jan just after he'd shot down his own target. Pieter said that Jan didn't stand a chance, although he tried hard to shake them off.'

'He could have bailed out, into the Channel.' Bella's own voice was wild with despair and a refusal to accept what she was being told.

Bettina shook her head. 'No. Pieter said that Jan was already over the French coast. No, Bella, I'm afraid he's gone. I must get back. As you can imagine, Mother is . . . dreadfully upset.'

'Yes, yes, of course . . .'

'Here.' Bettina held out an envelope to her. 'Jan asked me to give you this if he ever . . . when I knew that he wouldn't be coming back.'

Bella's hand shook as she took the letter from him.

'You're sure that there's no chance? No hope that—'

'Yes.'

'Oh, Bettina.'

They were in one another's arms, two women who had at the beginning of their relationship shared a dislike for one another, united now in their grief for the man they had both loved.

'I sent him away,' Bella wept. 'It was for his own sake.'

'You did the right thing. Your love guarded his honour, Bella. It was the right thing to do.'

'No,' Bella denied. 'If I hadn't then now I would have known . . . we would have shared . . . there might even have been the promise of a child.'

They looked at one another in mutual understanding, knowing that the war had changed them for ever.

'I must go,' Bettina repeated, adding as she released Bella, 'Don't forget us, please, Bella. Come and see us. It is what Jan would have wanted.'

Bella nodded.

She couldn't go to her office now, but she must, she had to. She looked towards the nursery, and then at the envelope containing Jan's letter to her. Such a mundane thing, a letter, and yet so very important when it was all that she would ever have of the man she loved.

She wanted to go somewhere where she could be alone to read it, to hide away somewhere and feel that when she read it that he was there with her, but where was there? Not her mother's house, which never felt like a proper home in the way her own house had for those few short months during which she had shared it with Lena. It would have to be her office, although reading personal correspondence in working hours was against the rules she had set for herself. Bella looked back down the way she had just walked. She could retrace her steps and read Jan's letter in the privacy of the overgrown garden of the bombed-out house where she had held the baby who miraculously had survived so much devastation. There she would be alone with the letter, but she had a duty here at the nursery, and if she should be needed . . .

Bella walked towards the nursery.

'My, you're early this morning, Miss Bella,' Mary, who helped Cook, smiled. 'I'll bring you in a cup of tea as usual, shall I?'

'No, thank you, Mary, not this morning. At least not just yet. I had a second cup with my mother before setting out,' Bella fibbed.

Once in her office she closed the door and then removed her white gloves and unpinned her straw hat with its trimming of white daisies before sitting down at her desk and starting to open the letter, only to stop and lift the envelope to her nose, closing her eyes as she tried to find Jan's scent on it – that special unique mix of cigarettes, soap, Brycreem and, most of all, Jan himself, but it wasn't there.

Her fingers shook as she went back to opening the letter, the paperknife slipping from them and clattering onto her desk. Her hear thudding, she picked it up and tried again.

There were three sheets of paper inside the envelope, both sides filled with strong masculine writing in black ink. Tears blurred her eyes. Fiercely she blinked them away and concentrated on Jan's writing.

Bella, my dearest heart, my darling, my true love now and for always, should you receive this letter it will be because I am no longer here on this earth with you to say these words in person. Not on this earth, Bella, but never doubt that I shall be with you always, loving you and watching over you.

You sent me away and I was resentful and angry, where you were forgiving and loving. I was foolish where you were wise. I was selfish where you were compassionate. I was wrong where you were right.

These are things I wanted to say to you in person when I thanked you for your strength and your love on my behalf, but I have written this letter in case this war deprives me of the opportunity to do so. I would not want you to be left thinking that you loved a man who was too much of a fool to recognise how much he owed you. You were right to say that I was asking for too much too soon, right too to remind me that I was lacking in respect – even if my marriage was no marriage at all. What I have shared and known with you was a thousand times more what a true marriage of hearts and minds should be. To me, my Bella, you are my other half, the person who completes me, the perfection in every way that wipes out my own imperfection. We have had so little time together, and yet a thousand lifetimes could not make me love you more, and that love will be with you for ever.

However, I do not want you to grieve for me or spend your life mourning me. Your fulfilment, your happiness, the sound of your laughter, the children who will bring you that laughter, these are what I wish for you and I want you to promise me when the time is right you will welcome into your life the man who will provide you with them. When you say your prayers at night, and you speak to me in your heart, I will be there to listen and I shall want to hear you say that you will not close your heart to your own future happiness because of me.

Think instead of what you would want for me if our positions were reversed and this letter had been written from you to me.

My dearest and only love – for that is what you will always be – know that my last and my first thoughts as death takes me will be of you, the last image seen by my dying eyes as I conjured your memory to me will be yours, and your arms, and your kiss my last earthly touch.

My darling, forgive me.

Your Jan

When she had finished reading it, Bella pressed the letter to her trembling lips and wept. It should have comforted her that Jan had understood why she had sent him away – one day maybe it would – but right now she would have sacrificed every bit of comfort she had derived from his letter for Jan himself to be alive, even if that had meant that he no longer loved her.

It was so cruel that he should have died. He had so much to give to other people, such gifts and strengths. When this war was finally over the country would need men like Jan. Why must it be that the brave and the good should die whilst men like her father and her brother were allowed to live?

'Are you planning to go to Hampstead to see your parents this weekend, Katie, only if you aren't I thought the two of us might do something together, seeing as the weather is so nice – perhaps go to Richmond on a pleasure boat, and then maybe the cinema in the evening?'

'What a lovely idea. And, no, I'm not going to Hampstead,' Katie told Gina.

'Good. I'll make some enquiries about what pleasure boats are running.'

The two girls exchanged warm smiles.

'I can't think of anyone I'd rather have as a pal than you, Katie,' Gina told her. 'I bumped into one of the girls I was at school with the other day. She's married now and living in the country, not really doing any kind of war work at all, and talking to her made me realise how little we now have in common. Not like you and I.'

'It's the war,' Katie agreed knowledgeably. 'It's changed things so much. If it hadn't happened and we'd met I'd have heard you speaking and decided you were too posh to want to know me, without even thinking about what you might be like as a person. Before the war, we all knew our place and we stuck to it, but now the war has put so many of us into a different place and with different people that we have to get on with. We all have to pull together, and out of that friend-ships are being made that never would have before. It's divided us all in a different kind of way – those of us who get stuck in and get on with things, and those who try to cling to the old ways.'

'Well said, Katie, and we're all the better for that,' Gina applauded Katie's speech. 'I'm glad to see that you're putting the hurt that chap of yours caused you behind you as well. Good for you. You've got such a kind heart, Katie, and I'm not surprised that the powers that be have promoted you. Now the other girls can turn to you for advice on whether or not they need to refer letters they have concerns about to their table leaders. You have a natural ability to draw people to you that makes them feel comfortable confiding in you.'

Katie blushed a little. 'I am pleased with my promotion. I just hope that I do a good job.'

'You will,' Gina assured her confidently.

They had the discussion about the coming weekend in the canteen over lunch. When they got back to their desks, to find their head of table waiting for them, they exchanged silent looks.

'It's nothing to worry about,' she told them both promptly. 'It's just that you've had a pair of visitors, male, and in uniform and with official permission to call and see you. If you go to reception you'll find them waiting there for you.'

'Who?'

'Who?'

When they both spoke at once, they exchanged another look.

'I can't tell you any more, because I don't have that information. All I do know is that they have official authority to speak to you, so if I were you I'd look lively and go and see them.'

'Who on earth can it be, do you suppose?' Gina asked Katie as they hurried to obey their superior.

'And why do they want to see us?' Katie's question was more anxious and less curious than Gina's, but then Katie had not forgotten the disquiet and discomfort she had felt over the whole issue of her Liverpool colleague and friend's insistence on getting too pally with the young Irishmen they had met at the Grafton Dance Hall. Katie wasn't aware now of having done anything 'wrong' that might be damaging to national security, but she still felt worried.

However, when they reached the reception area and she saw exactly who was waiting for them, looking so very smart in their naval uniforms and attracting admiring glances from the women toing and froing through the reception area, her anxiety vanished.

'It's those naval men from Bath,' she whispered unnecessarily to Gina. 'Captain Towers and Lieutenant Spencer.'

Although he had the more junior ranking, it was the lieutenant who stepped forward to greet them and to explain the purpose of their visit.

'The Royal Navy is so grateful to you for saving my life, my services to them being, of course, irreplaceable,' he paused with a mischievous look in his eyes, 'that they have sent us here to pass on their thanks in person via a dinner date at—'

The captain, who had so far stood back, now shook his head and told him drily, 'Somehow I don't think they're going to fall for that line, Eddie – they're far too intelligent.'

He turned to the girls. 'We do want to thank you. As I mentioned in Bath, Eddie here is my cousin, and I'd have had to face a real telling-off from our shared grandmother if anything had happened to him.'

'I'm her favourite,' the lieutenant announced smugly.

Katie couldn't help but laugh. The lieutenant, although quite obviously an accomplished flirt and used to getting away with the most outrageous behaviour, was nevertheless good fun.

'Eddie here has just been pronounced fit to return to active service, and as we are both on leave at the moment, we would appreciate it very much if you would allow us to take you both out to dinner as a thank you for what you did for him.'

Gina looked at Katie. 'What do you think? On the one hand we would probably get a decent dinner, but on the other we'd have to put up with the company of these two to get it.'

Gina was so clever knowing just the right note to strike, Katie thought admiringly as she guessed from her friend's manner that she was happy to accept the invitation as long as she herself felt the same.

'A decent dinner sounds very tempting,' Katie answered, echoing Gina's own tone.

Gina's small nod of the head told Katie that she had given the right answer, and Gina was smiling when she turned to the captain and told him, 'Dinner it is.'

'Excellent.' The lieutenant looked buoyant. 'How does the Savoy sound? We can pick you up and—'

'The Savoy would be very acceptable, but we will meet you there,' Gina told him firmly.

Within ten minutes it was all arranged. Katie and Gina would meet the captain and the lieutenant at seven o'clock on Saturday evening at the Savoy, to be their guests for the hotel's Saturday evening dinner dance.

'I hope they realise that they may not be able to get tickets,' Katie told Gina, as they made their way back to their desks.

'Something tells me that they will get them by hook or by crook,' was Gina's answer.

Katie wasn't the least bit romantically interested in either of the naval men but it had been fun to banter with the lieutenant. A little bit guiltily she recognised that the few minutes of fun they had shared with the men had lifted her spirits and that she was looking forward to Saturday evening. Even so . . .

'You don't think we've given them the wrong impression, do you?' she asked Gina, her hand on the door to their workroom.

'Not for a minute,' Gina reassured her, adding wryly, 'Mind you, if you want my opinion I reckon that the lieutenant's the sort who doesn't need any kind of encouragement – not that either of us gave him any, but my guess is that the captain is cut from a different sort of cloth, even though they are cousins, and that he will make sure that the lieutenant toes the line and behaves as he ought. Of course, if you're having second thoughts . . .'

'No,' Katie admitted a bit self-consciously. 'To be honest, I'm rather looking forward to it, although . . .' She looked uncertainly at Gina. Katie knew that whilst she liked the idea of having fun, she certainly didn't want that 'fun' to include anything 'romantic' or, even worse, having to deal with a man who behaved like an octopus, with his hands everywhere and one purpose on his mind, but she wasn't sure how to say as much to Gina, and felt able only to add rather weakly, 'I wouldn't have wanted to go out with one of them on my own, but seeing as we're both going it should be fun.'

'I think we pretty much share the same opinion,' Gina smiled. 'One hint of any funny business and we're leaving, right?'

'Right!' Katie agreed with real relief and gratitude that Gina had been confident enough to speak so frankly.

'Bella?'

Bella tensed as the door to her office opened and Lena peered round it.

'It's such a lovely sunny day I was wondering if you and your mum would like to come round and have tea with us today. It would save you cooking.'

With every word Lena said Bella could feel her tension growing.

'I can't,' she told her abruptly. 'I'm far too busy.' Bella bent her head over the papers on her desk, hoping that Lena would take the hint and go away.

Instead Lena protested, 'But, Bella, you worked all weekend, and . . .'

Bella had had enough. Her teeth were gritted, the knuckles showing white where she had gripped her hands into tight fists in an attempt to control her emotions. Her nails bit into her palms, but she didn't care. She deserved that pain; she wanted it and welcomed it even though it could nowhere near mirror the depth of pain that Jan must have known in his last precious minutes of life, his plane shot down, burning as it screamed towards the sea, Jan himself probably on fire as well. A shudder of anguish shook her whole body.

Lena rushed to her side to a protective arm around her shoulders, as she whispered, 'Bella . . .'

Bella tensed her body against Lena's sympathy. It wasn't what she wanted. Lena wasn't who she wanted.

'I've got work to do, Lena,' she repeated fiercely, 'and so have you.'

This time Lena took the hint, closing the door quietly behind her as she left Bella's office.

It was June. Outside the sun was shining. From the nursery she could hear the children's voices mingling with those of her nursing staff. A bee was droning dizzily, no doubt heavy with pollen, as it worked the yellow flowers of the laburnum tree outside her office window. Despite the war, people were trying to make the best of things and look forward to the summer. Government notices urging people to 'Holiday at Home' seemed to be posted everywhere, alongside posters from local councils advertising the events they were planning to entertain people, the business of everyday life humming as busily around her as the bee was humming around the laburnum racemes, but Bella felt completely removed from it all, as though it was happening in a different world, a world she no longer wanted to inhabit. Her world was different: a wasteland of might-have-beens, of wasted opportunities and dead dreams; a world of coldness so icy that it burned her heart, a world in which she was frozen for perpetuity.

She had lost Jan, and not just lost him but failed him and their love. He might have written to her that he understood, he might have tried to spare her with his gentle and loving words, telling her that he believed she had done the right thing, but she knew better, she knew the truth. She had betrayed him and their love.

How different things would have been, how differently she could have felt if only she had had the strength to put their love first; if only she had gone to him, with him, given herself wholly and completely to him, and shared with him that most precious gift of love and intimacy. But instead she had behaved like a coward, putting the views of others – of society, of her employers – putting herself and her status, her respectability within that society before Jan's need of her, and now she was having to pay the price for that selfishness. That was why she couldn't accept the sympathy Lena was trying to offer her, why she couldn't allow herself the relief of tears; because she did not deserve either of those things.

Instead she must suffer. She deserved to suffer because of what she had made Jan suffer, because of what she had denied him and let him die without. How could she claim to love him and yet not have known that his need must come first? Wherever he was now he must be looking at her in sorrow and reproach, perhaps even in contempt too, for her lack of courage and for the way in which she had failed him and their love. And because of what? Because she had wanted to be seen as moral and respectable, because her pride could not bear for her to be dragged back down to what she had seen as her old unworthy self, her old selfish, self-obsessed self. How blinded she had been by that pride. How cruel and thoughtless, and yes, how selfish she had been in not putting Jan first. Instead she had cloaked that selfishness in 'moral right', and in doing so she had lost the opportunity to give him the gift of her love, to cherish him and perhaps, in doing so, to keep him safe.

Pain gripped her, shuddering through her body. That was the hardest guilt of all to bear, torturing herself with the belief that, had she put her hand in his, had they gone to bed together, then he would not have died, because his sense of duty to her, and to the child they might have created together might have made him more cautious.

His letter to her, so loving and forgiving, held in its words the true essence of the man he had been, compassionate, strong, heroic, a man of the type this country would need so desperately once the war was over, a man who now, thanks to her, was lost to them all.

She could never forgive herself. She must never forgive herself.

FOURTEEN

Katie and Gina had had a lovely afternoon in Hyde Park, having decided, in view of the fact that they had agreed to go out with the captain and the lieutenant, to put off their river boat trip until another weekend, just in case they couldn't get back in time.

Now, at five o'clock, having enjoyed a cup of tea, they were walking arm in arm down Sloane Street, towards Katie's billet, Gina having disclosed that she lived not very far away from Cadogan Place herself, 'in a small flat that actually belongs to an aunt of my father's, but which she's allowing me to use. It was her *pied-à-terre* for when she visited London. She's widowed now, and she finds the damage the German bombs have done to the city too upsetting to want to visit very often. Her husband was an architect, and she's rather passionate about buildings.'

Katie noted this information, recognising that it confirmed what she had already guessed, namely that Gina's family was rather well-to-do. Not that Gina gave herself any airs and graces – far from it.

215

As they said 'goodbye' to one another on Sloane Street, standing by the private garden that belonged to Cadogan Place, Gina told Katie, 'I'll get a taxi and call to pick you up at a quarter to seven. If we get to the Savoy and they aren't there waiting for us then we can ask the cabby to drive up to Green Park and then turn round and take us back.'

Katie agreed, then turned to leave, only to hear Gina saying almost awkwardly, 'Oh . . . I expect you know that the Saturday night dinner dance at the Savoy is rather dressy, only there's nothing worse than arriving somewhere and feeling one is wearing the wrong thing.'

Once Gina's comment would have reduced her to a silence of tongue-tied hot-faced self-conscious embarrassment, Katie acknowledged, but now she was able to say easily and comfortably, 'I remember how elegantly dressed the women always were when I used to accompany my father to the Savoy. He's a musician and a conductor. I haven't been since I came back to London but I dare say, if anything, people are making even more of an effort.'

There! In a couple of sentences she had acquainted Gina with her parents' and her own status, and assured her that she wasn't going to embarrass herself.

'Oh, yes, absolutely,' Gina agreed, looking relieved. 'Of course the American women – the diplomatic and high-ranking military wives – are incredibly well dressed. No rationing for them, although our lot do their best to hold their end up. The last time I was there an awful lot of old family jewellery was on show, even if it was being worn with pre-war evening gowns.'

There was no real question over what she would have to wear, Katie admitted once she was back in her room in her billet. After what Gina had said, there was only one dress that could be worn, and yet it was with great reluctance that she removed it from her suitcase where it was carefully packed away in layers of tissue paper. Tissue paper that had been smoothed down by Jean's maternal hands, the dress itself a gift of love from Luke's aunt Francine and from Jean herself.

Tears trembled on Katie's eyelashes when she lifted it from its resting place. It was so beautiful, the most beautiful dress she had ever worn, the memories that went with it so precious to her, each one folded every bit as carefully into her heart as Jean had folded the dress.

The pale grey silk taffeta shimmered in the still-bright sunlight, causing more tears to blur Katie's vision. She had been wearing this dress the night she had first met Luke, not knowing who he was then other than the grim, hostile but oh so handsome dark-haired young corporal who had done so much to protect the Grafton Dance Hall from catching fire after a bomb had been dropped on the building next door to it. She had had no idea then that he would turn out to be the son of the couple with whom she was billeted, the 'Luke' his mother spoke of with such love and pride.

Luke. Katie sank down on to her bed, letting the dress slip to the floor as she covered her face with her hands and let the tears flow. She had tried so hard not to give in to her emotions, to remember how much others were called upon to bear because of this war, to tell herself that whilst Luke was safe and well, she had nothing to cry for other than her own foolish broken heart, and that truly loving someone sometimes meant putting them first and being hurt when your love was not returned. She knew she could no more have held Luke to an engagement he no longer wanted than she could have lied that she no longer loved him. He had wanted his freedom and, much though that hurt her, she had to accept that. He had claimed that he was breaking their engagement because he couldn't trust her, but Katie felt there was more to it than that and that at some stage whilst he had been away from her he had either stopped loving her or realised that he had never loved her at all.

By the time she was bathed and dressed, her dark gold hair brushed, and the neat little matching bolero that went with her gown nestling against the wide white sash emphasising her slender waist, Katie had a brave smile pinned to her lips, but her heart still felt sore.

Peggy Groves, who was coming into the house as Katie was leaving, having seen the taxi pull up outside from her bedroom window, paused to say admiringly, 'Oh, I say, don't you look glam. I hope you're going somewhere nice.'

'The Savoy,' Katie told her, before darting outside and hurrying over to the cab just as Gina was about to get out of it.

'You're prompt,' Gina smiled approvingly, her eyes widening slightly when she saw Katie's gown. 'What a beautiful dress, and how perfectly it suits you, Katie.'

'It isn't actually mine. It belongs to . . . to my ex-fiancé's aunt. She is, or rather she was, a singer – she's married now. She's the most generous person. Even though Luke and I broke up, she insisted that I was to have this dress, which she'd loaned to me whilst I was billeted with Luke's parents, and Luke's mother sent it on to me.'

'They obviously thought a lot of you, Katie, and with good reason.'

'I loved Luke's family,' Katie told Gina truthfully. 'I still miss them and I think I always will. Your own dress is lovely too.'

'Well, it's pre-war, I'm afraid, although I've always loved it. I wore it for my twenty-first birthday party.'

The burgundy silk was perfect with Gina's dark hair and eyes, and Katie saw that Gina was wearing a very pretty pair of pearl and diamond ear clips, which matched the pearl necklace she always wore.

'Well, at least we shan't have to ask the cabby to drive past and then bring us back,' Gina announced when the cab turned into the Savoy. 'The boys are already here waiting for us.'

Indeed they were, and looking very handsome and masculine in their Royal Navy uniforms, Katie had to admit as the doorman came forward to open the taxi door for the girls, prompting the captain to step towards the cabby, obviously intent on settling the bill.

Katie looked at Gina, who gave a small nod of her head, obviously approving his good manners.

Katie could see that both men were impressed by the girls' appearance, their approval giving her confidence a boost as she thanked Eddie for the corsage he presented her with, whilst the captain did the same to Gina.

Of course, they had to retire to the cloakroom to pin the corsages to one another.

'So sensible of them to choose white so that they wouldn't clash with what we are wearing,' Gina smiled.

To Katie the Savoy was almost a home from home. She had come here regularly with her father when he had worked here, although in those days she had been dressed very plainly in something businesslike, not a beautiful evening gown. So many times on those evenings her feet had tapped eagerly as she longed to dance. Luke had been a very good dancer. It was a family gift the Campions, including Jean shared, although Sam had always claimed that he had two left feet.

'Cocktails first, don't you agree?' Eddie was suggesting, as he led the way to the already busy cocktail bar.

The captain, Leonard, might be quieter than his more outgoing cousin, but he still had an air of authority about him that others plainly recognised, falling back a little to make room for the naval officers

Not that Leonard and Eddie were the only two men in the room in uniform – far from it. Katie had become used now to the sight of so many different uniforms in the capital, but tonight somehow it seemed that rather more of them were American than had previously been the case.

Not to be outdone by the men's smart uniforms, the women were all wearing elegant dresses, many of them, as Gina had already said, looking a little pre-war in style, but very elegant none the less, reminding Katie of pictures she had seen in her mother's copies of *Vogue* as a young girl. A woman in her forties, walking past proudly on the arm of her partner – a colonel in the army – was wearing a beautiful dull yellow silk satin gown that was very 1930s in style, its colour perfectly complimenting her diamond-set topaz jewellery.

Sequins were very much in style, brightening up the plainness of the otherwise very simple black evening gowns worn by many of the older women, whilst Katie heard one young girl still in her teens confiding to her friend as they walked past them that her dress – a lovely pale pink embossed silk over net petticoats, had been made from 'Granny's coming-out frock'.

As she sat and watched the other diners, Katie was relieved to see that, like her, Gina was quite content with one cocktail, and she suspected that the captain rather approved of this, although Eddie tried to persuade each of them to have another.

Over their cocktails they talked generally about Bath and how sad it was that Hitler's Luftwaffe had bombed such a historical city. Leonard and Gina quickly discovered a mutual interest in Georgian architecture and the books of Jane Austen, and were soon chatting animatedly. Watching them, it struck

Katie that Gina's natural confidence and warmth were bringing the captain out of his shell, whilst the captain's knowledge on a subject so dear to Gina's heart plainly had her warming to him and enjoying his company.

Eddie, though, obviously bored with their discussion, livened up the conversation when he remarked drolly that he felt honoured that Katie had sacrificed her petticoat on his behalf.

'I would have returned it to you if I'd been able to, of course, but unfortunately the nurses whisked it away. I don't think they approved of me sleeping with it under my pillow,' he added teasingly.

Katie couldn't quite stop herself blushing.

'Ignore my little cousin, Katie,' the captain told her. 'He's been at sea too long and has forgotten how to behave.'

It was obvious from the way they spoke to one another that the two men were close, and that couldn't help but soften Katie's heart towards them. There was nothing that warmed Katie's heart more than family closeness and shared love, and soon she felt relaxed enough not to be at all self-conscious when Eddie continued to tease her.

Eventually they were shown through for their dinner and, as both girls had expected, virtually every table was taken. It touched Katie's heart a second time to see so many Americans in military uniform eating their dinner, with its somewhat meagre portion of meat, with every evidence of enjoyment, when she knew that in their own country there was no rationing. Their good manners couldn't be faulted, even if Luke had been antagonistic towards the American soldiers he had come across in Liverpool.

As fish wasn't rationed Katie opted to have Dover sole, a mouthwatering treat, and one of her favourite dishes, which was every bit as good as she had anticipated it would be.

The Peach Melba she ordered for dessert might have been made with tinned peaches rather than fresh, but it was still a deliciously sweet treat at a time when anything containing sugar, which had to be imported, was on ration.

Katie wasn't entirely surprised when Leonard and Gina, who had been conversing together for several minutes, leaving her to be entertained by Eddie's jokes and flattery, announced that they had discovered a connection between their families, a third cousin of a second cousin twice removed sort of thing. It struck Katie that Gina and Leonard would be very well suited to one another. Eddie, of course, was much more lightweight. Fun to be with, but Katie suspected that it would be a foolish girl indeed who lost her heart to him.

However, her impression of Leonard as a kind quiet man of great moral strength and devotion to those he loved was shattered later on in the evening when she and Eddie were dancing and he made a casual reference to Leonard's children. Indeed, Katie was so shocked that she almost missed a step.

Eddie, who had earlier praised her for her dancing, asked, 'Are you all right?'

'I was until you mentioned Leonard's children. I had no idea he was married and neither has Gina.

I hadn't thought of him at all as the kind of man who would ask a girl out to dinner when he already has a wife.'

Normally she would never have been so outspoken, but her concern for her friend and her indignation on her behalf had overrun her normal reticence.

When Eddie's reaction to her outburst was to start laughing, she felt even more protectively angry on Gina's behalf until Eddie told her ruefully, 'I'm sorry, but the very idea of Leonard doing anything remotely improper is just so ridiculous.'

'But you said he has children,' Katie defended herself.

'Yes, he does: a boy of three and a little girl of two, but as for their mother . . .' Eddie paused. 'The whole family was rather surprised when Leonard announced that he was marrying Odile, a French girl he'd met when his ship was deployed to St-Nazaire in 1938. Of course, when war broke out Leonard brought Odile to England, but she never really settled here, and shortly after little Amy's birth she sent Leonard a "Dear John" letter, telling him that she'd met someone else and that she was leaving him. However, before he received that letter, she was killed in a road accident in this other chap's car. They were both killed, in fact.'

'Oh, how dreadful.'

'Yes it was,' Eddie agreed, for once sounding and looking serious. 'Leonard was never a life-and-soul-of-the-party type, but after that he withdrew even more into himself. Your friend is the first girl he has been out with since, and I only managed to persuade him to come to London with me and take you both out because he agreed that we must repay your kindness to me.'

Katie's eyes widened as a new thought struck her. 'You're matchmaking,' she accused him.

'Just call me Cupid,' Eddie grinned, adding, 'To be honest, when I came to in that gutter and heard the two of you talking the way you were, I knew immediately that you were just the kind of girls Leonard needed to meet, although I had a devil of a job persuading him to agree.'

Now it was Katie's turn to be amused. Eddie was surely a very unlikely matchmaker, but on the other hand there was no doubting his affection and loyalty for his cousin.

'What a risk to take,' she laughed. 'How could you know that Gina and Leonard would get on so well together?'

'I didn't,' he confessed. 'I just hoped that one of you would be able to get him to come out of his shell, enough for him to recognise that there are far more decent girls around than there are girls like Odile. I must say, though,' he added, smiling down into Katie's eyes, 'I am rather pleased that it is Gina with whom he's hitting it off so well, and I hope that you agree with me that such a promising romance deserves all the help it can get.'

'Well, yes, of course . . .' Katie began, and then stopped as she saw the gleam in his eyes. 'You're up to something, I know.'

'Not at all.' Eddie was all injured innocence. 'I simply meant that for Leonard and Gina's sake you and I might find ourselves in the position of having to double-date with them.'

It was impossible not to laugh and at the same time not to be just that little bit flattered by Eddie making it so plain that he was keen to see her again, Katie admitted as he led her back to their table.

The Savoy Orpheans was justifiably famous and, of course, through her father Katie was acquainted with several of the members of the band, but tonight she was enjoying their skill simply as a guest rather than studying it through her father's professional eyes.

If Eddie was not as good a dancer as Luke, then she was glad of it. Her foolish heart could not allow anyone to be as good a dance partner for her as Luke had been, and her own natural caution would certainly not permit Eddie to hold her as closely as Luke had done.

Most of the couples on the dance floor quite obviously did want to hold one another close, especially those in uniform, several of whom, Katie suspected, would be newly married and snatching a few precious hours together before returning to their duties.

The sight of a tall dark-haired man, his back towards her as he held his partner close, brought a lump to her throat and pain to her heart.

When the time came for them to leave, Gina made no objection when Leonard insisted on the four of them sharing a taxi, so that he and Eddie could, as he put it, 'see you girls safely home', before the cab took them on to their hotel.

Katie was dropped off first, much to her private relief. Eddie had been a good companion and fun to be with, nothing he had done had suggested that he might try to overstep the mark in the privacy of a taxi in any kind of way, and of course had he planned to do so, Leonard's presence must have deterred him. Nevertheless, Katie was glad to share a communal 'goodbye' to the other three, having assured Leonard that she did not need an escort from the kerbside to her door when she thanked the men for her evening out.

It was only when she was finally alone in her room, the dim light throwing back to her the reflection in her silver gown, that she permitted herself a few silent self-indulgent tears for the love she had lost with Luke.

She was being silly really, she knew. There had, after all, been many times when Luke had hurt her with his jealousy and his inability to trust her. The Luke and the love she was mourning were her own creations, made 'perfect' by her loss and not really a true reflection of what their relationship had been, any more than the image in the mirror of her in her beautiful gown, softened and shadowed by the dim light, was a true reflection of her. Eddie had in fact been much easier to be with tonight than Luke had sometimes been. There had been none of the anxiety she had sometimes felt with Luke, none of that sinking feeling that she had somehow done something wrong, no worry cramping her insides in case things went wrong and they ended up quarrelling. She mustn't fall into the trap of putting Luke on a pedestal, Katie warned herself. But even though she knew that her advice to herself sensible, her vulnerable heart still ached for what was lost.

Lou was finally back on her course, and if her leg sometimes ached more than she had admitted to the MO, then she gritted her teeth and pretended that it didn't, because the last thing she wanted was to be sent back to the sickbay.

On Seb's advice, when she had first returned from her visit home she had asked if it was possible for her to have some technical books to read to keep her up to date with her course, even if she wasn't able to do any of the practical work, and as a result she had received a visit from the tutor himself, armed not with books but with printed diagrams and technical data from the makers, relating to every aspect of the planes' designs and working parts.

Lou hadn't been sure whether her tutor had heaped this avalanche of information on her bed because he was impressed by her determination and wanted to encourage her, or because he disapproved of it and wanted to dampen her enthusiasm. If Sasha had been with her she would have been able to point out to her that her resolution not to be discouraged but to prove herself instead showed that inside she hadn't really changed at all, and was still that same determined rebel she had always been.

Lou had been so concerned about the accusations her twin had levelled at her, and for Sasha herself, that she had taken Grace on one side before leaving Liverpool to confide her anxiety.

'I don't want to worry Mum,' she had told Grace, adding ruefully, 'although I dare say she would say that she's used to me worrying her. But I am worried about Sash. We used to be so close and now it's almost as though she doesn't even like me any more.'

Grace had hugged her and assured her that she would keep an eye on Sasha for her.

In an effort to make things right between them Lou had written to her twin telling her how much she loved her, and how she had always thought that Sasha was the 'wiser' of the two of them, and that she had looked up to her for that.

Now that she was back on her course and determined to catch up with everything she had missed, there was almost no time to brood on the change in Sasha's attitude towards her. The WAAF kept them all busy, what with twice daily flag parades, weekly kit and 'housekeeping' inspections, obligatory PT training, in addition to their chosen course work. There was hardly time to breathe, never mind anything else, especially now that they were nearing the end of their eighteen-week course and about to sit their exams. Somehow, though, they did manage to make time for some fun. Halton had some excellent recreational facilities, and the girls did their best to take advantage of them.

The regular onsite dances were particularly popular, although there was no opportunity for any discreet 'smooching' for a Waaf being walked 'home' to her hut by a man. A white line painted on the ground a few feet off the huts and all the way around them denoted the limit beyond which no escort was allowed to step, and woe betide any Waaf who allowed him to do so. Not that Lou was in any way interested in getting involved in a romance; she had decided she had far more important things to do, like passing her flight engineer's exams.

Although she would never have admitted it, even to herself, Lou had been badly hurt by what had happened with Kieran Mallory. Of course, she derided herself that her feelings for him had been nothing more than kid's stuff, a silly girlish pash, which she was far too grown up and sensible to allow to affect her. But underneath this common-sense approach she had determinedly developed, a part of her still felt raw and humiliated by her own knowledge of now naïve and silly she had been. Her own common sense should have told her what Kieran was, and that he was playing her and Sasha off against one another. And she should have been able to work out for herself that a young man of nineteen, as good-looking as Kieran was, was hardly likely to be genuinely romantically interested in girls as young and immature as she and Sasha had both been. He had flattered and fooled them for his own purposes and they had fallen for it.

Now, because she couldn't forgive herself for her own silliness, Lou just wasn't prepared to get involved with any young man. Not like some of the other girls who were already coupling up with young airmen they had met since coming to Halton. Lou didn't envy them their romances, not one little bit.

They had finished their lessons for the day, and Betty, who was now on a different course from Lou, was waiting for her when Lou emerged from the hangar where she'd spent the afternoon taking her turn at changing the spark plugs on a Lancaster engine, recovered from a written-off plane that was now used for their practice.

Lou's slender fingers had soon adapted to the task and it had given her a quiet sense of satisfaction when she had completed it more speedily than the others.

As Betty came hurrying over to her she was mentally repeating the order in which the first service check on Lancaster had to be done.

'Do you fancy a game of tennis after tea?' Betty asked. 'It seems a shame to waste such a glorious evening.'

'I'd love to, but I've got my written exam tomorrow morning and then my practical in the afternoon, and with missing so much time I want to do some reading-up tonight.'

'Of course you'll pass,' Betty assured her loyally. 'You're far and away the best of all of us.'

Her praise pleased Lou but she didn't want to make a thing about it – that wasn't the service way, as the girls had now learned. However, the pleasure Betty's praise had given her disappeared when she reached the hut, Betty having left to go and find someone else to partner her, to find their corporal waiting.

'Good. I'm glad you came straight back here after your lesson. You're to report to the office on the double. The CO wants to see you.'

Lou felt her stomach plunge, anxiety coiling through her as she set off to the admin block, trying to work out what she had done wrong and what her punishment was likely to be.

A grim-faced duty sergeant took her name when she presented herself at the admin block, ordering her curtly to 'Wait here' and leaving her standing stiffly, not daring to relax a muscle whilst the sergeant disappeared through a door at the back of her office.

When the duty sergeant returned a few minutes later she had Lou's captain with her, and when Captain Hart and the duty sergeant stood either side of her and marched her towards the door Lou felt as though her knees were knocking together so loudly with fear that they must be able to hear them. What on earth had she done? No matter how hard she searched her conscience she couldn't think of anything, but she must have done something, and something extremely serious if she was being hauled up in front of the CO – marched into her office, in fact, by a pair of gaolers.

It was the captain who knocked on the CO's door, obeying the order immediately: 'Come.' The three of them saluted and had their salute returned when the CO stood up to greet them.

'You are due to sit your flight engineer's examination tomorrow, I believe, Campion?' was the CO's first question.

Lou nodded, her mouth too dry to speak, and then managed a strangled, 'Yes, ma'am.'

Was her crime so serious that she was going to be sent away before she had had a chance to prove herself? Despair filled her.

'Hmm . . .' The CO looked down at some papers on her desk.

'Well, it seems that the War Office is determined to give you at least one reason to celebrate. At ease.' She commanded them all, although poor Lou was in so much dread that she simply couldn't relax her tense ribcage and stomach.

'With regard to Wellington the matter of the incident in May with the Lancaster and its pilot, it has been decided that you should be awarded the George Cross for bravery. I may tell you that the Prime Minister recommended that you be put forward for this award.'

There was a funny buzzing in Lou's ears and she was beginning to feel decidedly odd. A hand, the duty sergeant's, she thought, was somehow or other on her back keeping her upright, giving her time to get over her disbelief and her shock and to salute her CO. And then a thought struck her.

Before she could stop herself Lou heard herself asking recklessly, 'I am honoured, of course, ma'am, but . . .'

The CO was frowning. 'But what, Campion?'

Lou took a deep breath. 'But if it could be arranged, ma'am . . . that is to say, I wonder if it would be possible instead of me having the award for my Hut to be given back the points I lost them?'

The silence that followed her request seemed to go on for ever. Now she had gone and done it and if she hadn't been in trouble before then, she certainly was about to be now, Lou decided, her realisation that she shouldn't have spoken confirmed by the CO's crisp reply.

'The awarding of an honour is not a matter for discussion or barter with its recipient, Campion. Therefore I intend to forget that such a discussion took place and I advise you to do the same.

'Now, you will be informed in writing in due course of the formal award to you of this honour, with instructions as to when you must present yourself before King George in order to receive it. In the meantime, until official notice of the award is posted, it is not to be mentioned to anyone. You may inform your family once you receive official notice but not until then. They may join you for the investiture ceremony if they wish and are able to do so. You have a brother serving overseas, I understand?'

'Yes, ma'am.'

'If you wish him to be advised then this can be arranged via official channels in order to avoid any conflict with the censorship rules.'

'Yes, ma'am.'

'Good. Dismissed.'

She was in such a state of shock about the award, and dread about what she had said, that Lou almost changed step on the wrong foot, and she was glad of the sergeant and the captain on either side of her to force her into the right march.

Once they were back in the main office Lou braced herself for the telling-off she was sure she was about to receive, but instead the captain merely dismissed her with a, 'Jolly good show, Campion,' and an unexpected, 'Good luck with your exam

234

tomorrow,' before she was being dismissed with a further warning not to discuss what she had been told with anyone.

She was certainly lucky to have got away so lightly with saying what she had, Lou admitted, but the truth was that she would far rather have had her Hut's points returned than receive the George Cross. After all, she had done nothing that any other Waaf wouldn't have done in the same circumstances.

'Got a minute, Con?'

Con exhaled noisily, and then chomped impatiently on his cigar as Joe, the landlord of the Pig and Whistle, stood in front of him blocking Con's access to the side door he had just opened. Con had called at the pub on his way to the theatre to replace one of the light bulbs that had gone the previous night. He'd managed to get hold of some that were stamped 100 watt, but gave off only the same amount of light as a 40 watt bulb. They should stop any complaints about the lack of light whilst continuing to ensure that the room remained dimly lit.

Con was wearing a new suit, his camel-hair coat resting on his shoulders and his trilby tipped at a rakish angle. The suit was one of two he'd recently had made up by a tailor who'd been recommended to him by the same flash Harry who'd sold him the suit lengths, one brown with a cream stripe in it, the other navy with a chalk stripe. Top-quality goods and no questions asked or answered. Not that the stuff had come cheap. The suits had cost him the best part of fifty quid, but he could afford it, Con admitted, thanks to Ricky's constant supply of still wet-behind-the-ears young soldiers, and Con's own cleverness with the cards.

Eva, mind, was costing him an arm and a leg, as well. He'd made a big mistake buying her that necklace she'd been going on about. Of course, then he'd thought that she'd be moving on, since she'd been going on about ENSA keeping asking her to work for them, and he hadn't bargained for the owners of the Royal Court Theatre deciding to extend her contract with them, which had meant that she was staying on in Liverpool.

'It better be only a minute, Joe, I'm a busy man,' Con told him.

'Just thought I'd warn you I've had one of Ed Mulligan's boys round asking a lot of questions about your bit of business upstairs.'

Con tensed. Ed Mulligan ran a local protection racket, backed up by a gang of thugs whom he sent round to deal with anyone who refused to pay him.

'What did you tell him?' Con demanded.

The landlord spat the wad of tobacco he had been chewing into the narrow alleyway through the open side door.

'Told him he'd be better off speaking direct to you.'

Con shrugged, dismissing his own earlier concern along with Joe's warning. So what if Ed Mulligan did demand a bit of protection money from him? With what he was making he could afford it easily enough. Ed might even be able to recommend some better premises. Ricky had been saying for a while that they should think about expanding into providing the boys with something to keep their minds off the money they were losing. He'd talked about them not just having a bar but also getting a few of the Royal Court's chorus girls to act as 'hostesses'.

'A pretty girl and a shot of bourbon go a long way to soothing a loser's feelings,' had been Ricky's comment.

Eva had talked him into taking her to Blackpool for a night when she had her day off later in the week. Con hadn't objected. It would give him an opportunity to try out the Jaguar roadster he'd picked up at a bargain price, via one of his new black market contacts.

Whistling confidently, Con headed for the Royal Court. If he was lucky – and he certainly had every reason to think that he was lucky these days – he might be able to snatch five minutes to flirt with that new singer who was understudying Eva, whilst Eva herself was on stage for the matinée performance.

FIFTEEN

Bella knew that Lena was worried about her, and she knew that Lena must wonder why she had rejected her attempts to comfort her. But if she hadn't, then she would have broken down and then . . . The truth was, Bella knew, that she just didn't deserve Lena's sympathy. She had let Jan down. If she had behaved as a woman in love should behave, then he might even still be here. She had let him down and she deserved to be punished, not given sympathy.

It was late in the afternoon. She had waited until everyone else had left the nursery before leaving herself, and now she was reluctant to go home, knowing that her mother would be full of a hundred small complaints when all Bella wanted to do was shut herself in her bedroom and think about Jan and how she had betrayed him.

It had been a hot day and that heat still lingered, the sky a cloudless deep blue, the warmth coming up from the pavement, and scenting the still air. The knowledge slid into Bella's heart that the weather was perfect for lovers, with its heat there to stroke bare limbs, and its stillness engendering a lazy sensuality made for walking hand in hand, for kissing and touching and for . . .

Gritting her teeth, she started to walk faster, her heart thudding with a mixture of anger and pain. She hadn't been sleeping, and whilst her body felt drained of energy the turmoil of her thoughts would not allow her any rest. If she had not sent Jan away then the two off them might have been enjoying the balmy warmth of this late afternoon. Jan could have been home on leave, he could have been waiting outside the nursery for her, ready to whisk her off in his car to a romantic hotel near a secluded cove where they could have . . .

Stop it, stop. Stop tormenting me, Bella wanted to cry out to her own thoughts, but why should she have any relief from them? She deserved this pain.

Wrapped in the punishing agony of her own thoughts she was walking up the drive to the house before she realised that there was someone waiting by the front door for her.

The colour left her face, as she demanded, 'Bettina, what are you doing here?'

'I've come to talk to you. But let's go inside first, shall we?'

'My mother will be waiting for her tea. She's—'

'Lena has arranged for your neighbour to take your mother out for tea so that we can talk undisturbed.'

'Lena? What has she got to do with you being here?'

'Everything,' Bettina answered her succinctly,

picking up the key that had fallen from Bella's grip and putting it in the lock herself. Once they were inside the hall she continued, 'Lena came to see me to tell me how worried she is about you.'

'Lena doesn't understand,' Bella told Bettina flatly. 'She thinks I deserve sympathy because I've lost Jan, when the truth is . . .'

'The truth is what?' Bettina pressed her. 'Let's go into the kitchen. Mama has sent you one of her special carrot cakes, and I'm desperate for a cup of tea.'

Bella pushed her hair off her forehead. She felt slightly sick and somehow very weak. She hadn't been able to face eating since she'd read Jan's letter. Why was everyone trying to be so nice and kind to her when she didn't deserve it?

Bettina pushed her down into a chair and filled the kettle, a job that should have been hers, Bella recognised, but somehow she felt too weary to do anything other than punish herself as she deserved to be punished.

'What is this truth that is making you so wretched, Bella? And don't tell me that you aren't because I can see for myself that you are. No wonder Lena is so worried about you.'

'I don't deserve her worry. Not after the way I treated Jan. If it wasn't for me he might still be alive, do you realise, Bettina?'

Bella couldn't sit still. She got up out of the chair and paced the kitchen floor in her agitation. 'Your mother has sent me a gift. She wouldn't feel like doing that if she knew how cruelly I treated

Jan. I was so wrapped up in my own pride, my own moral "rightness", thinking about myself when I should have been thinking about Jan.'

Covering her face with her hands, Bella sank back into the chair she had vacated.

The kettle was almost boiling. Bettina lifted it from the ring to pour a little of the water into the teapot, returning the kettle to the ring to boil, and then turning to Bella, eyeing her with sympathetic concern.

'Bella, I know that you loved my brother and that he loved you.'

The kettle was boiling. Bettina poured the hot water from the teapot into the sink, then spooned tea into the pot – three very small teaspoons of it just to pay lip service to the adage of 'one spoonful per person and one for the pot'; tea, like so much else, was rationed – before switching off the gas and then lifting the kettle from the ring to pour the boiling water onto the tea.

Even the smell of freshly made tea was comforting, Bettina recognised, although she doubted that poor Bella was taking much comfort from the rich aroma.

'I loved him, yes, but I refused to show my love for him, to give my love to him as he wanted me to, to give myself to him,' Bella emphasised deliberately to Bettina, folding her arms tightly around herself as though to contain and control her emotions. 'Jan wanted me to go with him, to go to him. He asked me to when . . . when he came to tell me about his wife's death. I refused him, Bettina,' Bella announced bitterly. 'I sent him away.

241

I told him it would be wrong and that if I agreed there'd come a time when he'd resent me for not protecting his honour as a married man. But it was all a lie, I can see that now. It was myself I was protecting even though I pretended to myself that it was him.'

'Bella, you're being far too hard on yourself,' Bettina told her, pouring tea into the two cups she had removed from their hooks and put on their matching saucers before going to the pantry to find the milk.

'Here, drink this.' She handed Bella the cup of tea she had poured for her, and then sat down with her own cup to start cutting the cake.

'Please,' Bella begged her, distraught, 'please don't sympathise with me. That's what Lena wanted to do and I can't let her. She thinks far more highly of me than I deserve, but if she knew the truth, she wouldn't. I let Jan down.'

'No, Bella.' Putting a slice of the cake onto a plate and pushing it towards her, Bettina got up and went to kneel beside Bella's chair, putting her arm around her shoulders.

'Jan loved you. He told me a little of what was said between you—'

'There, you see. I let him down, and he was so upset that—'

'No, Bella. He was not upset, quite the contrary. He told me what you'd said to him and he said that he admired you for it; that he agreed with you and that he believed you had saved him from doing something that would have shamed him and caused him to shame you.'

Bella's hand was trembling so much that she had to put her cup down, her tea untouched, her gaze fixed on Bettina's face.

'He really said that?'

'Yes,' Bettina assured her. 'He praised you to me and said how much he felt he owed you, how you had encouraged him to stand by his marriage and how you had put your own feelings to one side for that marriage. Now, Bella, please do drink your tea before it goes cold.'

Bella picked up her cup and took a sip of the hot, reviving liquid.

'Jan understood that you had done that, not because of convention but for him, so that he would never have any cause to reproach himself,' Bettina told her gently. 'He admired you so much for that, Bella, and so do I. You could not have given my brother a better gift nor a better memorial than the one you did give him when you gave him his honour through your own sacrifice.'

Bella, who had been about to take another sip of her tea, put her cup down again, her suspicions suddenly aroused by Bettina's words

'Lena begged you to say that to me, didn't she?' she accused her. 'She's always thought I'm a far better person than I really am. I let Jan go to his death without . . .' Bella bit her lip, and reached for her tea cup again, this time taking a deep gulp from it as though seeking courage from it, before putting it down again. 'It didn't have to be like that. It's not as though I haven't been married and had a husband. I could have gone with him, shared that intimacy with him.'

'If you had then don't you think that now, instead of blaming yourself for what you didn't do, you'd be blaming yourself even more for what you did do?' Bettina demanded.

Bella shook her head. 'If I had then there might have been the promise of a child – Jan's son.'

Bettina kneeled down at her side again and put her arms around her, holding her tightly so that Bella's downbent head was on her shoulder as she said softly, 'Oh, Bella . . .'

Now the tears that Bella hadn't been able to shed before came, torn from her with the words that revealed the deep-rooted source of her pain, the child she could have had.

'We would have had Jan's son,' she told Bettina, the words muffled against Bettina's shoulder. 'Me and you and your mother. We would have had him to love and to cherish, and somehow Jan would have known that something of him remained with us.'

'We would have had all those things, yes,' Bettina agreed, lifting her hand to stroke Bella's curls gently. 'We would have had joy and delight in such a child, Bella, but what of the child, the son that would have been Jan's? What of him and his happiness?'

'What do you mean?' Bella asked her, lifting her head to meet Bettina's gaze.

'What I mean is, what of his happiness?'

'His happiness would have been my first concern. I would have loved him beyond anything or anyone because he was Jan's, a living memory of our love. I would have told him about Jan, brought him up to understand what a wonderful man his father was and how much we all loved him.'

Bettina's own eyes were filling with tears now but she still shook her head and said, 'Bella, can't you see what a terrible burden that would be for any child to bear? To grow up without his father, and in the shadow of all that that father had been, to all three of us? He would have to carry the weight of our love for Jan and our expectations for him. He would perhaps even feel that he had to be his father and become the same kind of man that his father had been. Jan would never have wanted that for his child and I know that in your heart you wouldn't want it either. I could be selfish and say that there is nothing I would like more than to hear that you are to have Jan's child, but it would be selfish. We both know that. You're a strong person, Bella, not a selfish one. You've already proved that.'

Their tea forgotten now, each woman looked at the other.

'No,' Bella denied, weeping because she knew that what Bettina had said to her was true.

'Yes, you are,' Bettina countered, 'and Jan loved you for that strength. He depended on you for it and he depended too on it to guard him from damaging you both in the eyes of the world. You were the foundation stone on which Jan built his own ability to endure his marriage. He had the most profound love and respect for you, Bella, more profound than any mere feverish passion of desire. Jan considered you to be his soul mate. He had seen that, felt it in you right from the first, I know that. He believed that it was your fate to meet. It would grieve him dreadfully to see you like this, and all the more so if he knew that you were punishing yourself out of a foolish belief that you had let him down in any way. You did not. On the contrary, you held Jan up, Bella. You held him up to be the very best that he could be.'

'That's not true,' Bella protested shakily.

'Yes it is,' Bettina insisted, giving Bella a small shake to underline her point. 'Mama and I have both said so to one another. We have both seen you grow through so much, Bella, and we have marvelled at the transformation in you, and been humbled by your own humility over that growth. To us you are a part of Jan as truly as though you had been married, and as precious to us as though we shared the same blood. Mama is dreadfully concerned about you. She wanted to come with me, but I felt we could talk more easily together as sisters.'

Bettina gave Bella a fierce hug and then kneeled back from her, taking hold of her hand and holding it in her own, as she told her, 'You must not punish yourself like this, Bella. Truly, there is no need. It is not what Jan would have wanted.' She reached into the pocket of her cotton skirt, her hand closed. Then she removed it again to open Bella's palm and place something into it, curling Bella's fingers over it and keeping them closed.

'Mama wanted you to have this.'

Bella knew what it was before she opened her hand, tears rolling down her face as she focused on the thin gold chain with its small St Christopher medallion. Maria's St Christopher medallion, which Jan had once told her he had given his mother before they had left Poland.

'No, I can't take it,' she wept.

'No, you can't "take it",' Bettina agreed. 'But Mama can gift it to you, Bella, as a token of our love. Please don't reject our love, Bella.'

She was in Bettina's arms again, both of them crying and holding one another tight.

The pain wasn't over – it would never be over, Bella knew – but the poison of her guilt had been cleansed away.

'I shall have something to say to Lena about all of this,' she told Bettina once they were both sitting down again, their emotions back under control, drinking the freshly poured second cups of tea Bella had managed to wring from the pot with the addition of some more boiling water, restored to her rightful position as 'hostess.'

'I shall have something to say to her as well,' Bettina agreed, 'and it will be a very big "thank you".'

'She really is the most darling girl,' Bella acknowledged, her pride in Lena and all that she had achieved warming her voice.

She had lost Jan but unexpectedly she had been given something that would offer her some comfort. The tentative bond she and Bettina had forged together could, if they both cherished it in Jan's name, grow stronger.

The sun pouring in through the window was making Lou's scalp prickle with heat, or was it her nervousness that was doing that? All around her in the room, Waafs were bent over their exam papers, some poring over the questions, others diligently writing.

She wanted to pass her exam so much; the questions seemed straightforward and Lou thought she knew the answers, but she wanted to read them again to make sure that she wasn't missing anything. Sarge had warned them during their training that with aircraft it was vitally important to be a hundred and ten per cent sure you knew what you were doing before you did it, and that just thinking you knew wasn't good enough.

Her pen felt sticky in her palm, and every now and again when she remembered about the previous evening and her interview with the CO, a sense of disbelief and wonder gripped her. Her being awarded a George Cross. Who would have thought it? Not her family, that was for sure. But she mustn't think about that now; she must concentrate on her exam. Determinedly she started to write, the tension within the room fading as Lou focused on the questions, her forehead pleated into a frown of concentration.

'Oh, thank heavens for that,' Betty announced, falling into step beside Lou as they made their way toward the Naafi, when they had both finally been released from their practical exams. 'I swear I thought I was going to melt in the workshop when I had to start riveting a joint. All I could think of was, when we first started the sarge yelling at us when he asked us if we knew what a file was and

Jenny put her hand up and said they were for putting letters in.'

'It could have been worse. She could have said they were for doing her nails with,' Lou laughed.

'How did you get on? What did you have to do?' Betty demanded.

'I had to plug in one of the batteries and start up an engine, and then when it wouldn't start I had to find out why. Luckily it was the spark plugs and I'd remembered how to do that. Then I to run through a check list and tell them what was missing from it and what would happen if it was missed off – and then I had to find the fault in an altimeter, and repair it.'

'Phew, I'm glad I decided to train as a welder and not a flight engineer,' Betty told her. 'Do you fancy going to the dance in the mess on Saturday? We should have our results by then and we can either celebrate or commiserate with one another – not that it feels right dancing in uniform. I'd love to go out dancing in civvies again. Do you think—'

'No,' Lou stopped her, 'not unless you want to be hauled up before the CO.'

'Well, I never. I told you as how you should go and see Phoebe Evans, seeing as you've lost so much weight, and get her to alter your clothes for you. Stands to reason when I dare say there will have been enough cloth left to make something else, but I must say that I never expected to see such a difference in you, Emily. I hardly recognise you.'

The genuine kindness and approval in her

neighbour, Ivy's, voice made Emily feel all the more self-conscious in this, her first public outing in her remade clothes.

'I hardly recognise myself,' she admitted.

'And your hair looks better like that as well,' Ivy continued. 'When you first came here I thought you looked more like little Tommy's grandmother than anything else, from the way you dressed and that. You look much better now.'

Ivy was inclined to be outspoken but Emily didn't feel offended. What she said was true, after all. Even Tommy had commented on her 'new' appearance, telling her approvingly, 'You look really pretty now, Mum.'

Of course she hadn't lost weight deliberately – it was the war that had done that – but there was no point in looking a gift horse in the mouth, as the saying went, and Emily reckoned she owed it to Tommy to do what she could to make him feel proud of her.

There was no getting away from the fact, though, that it had been a real shock to look at her own reflection in the slightly spotted pier glass in the spare room that Phoebe Evans, the local dressmaker, whose husband was related to Brenda Evans at the Post Office, used for her customers.

Emily had known that she'd lost weight, of course, but what with her keeping on wearing the same clothes – albeit now very loose on her, she hadn't realised just what a transformation had taken place until she'd been standing there looking at a slender woman wearing a shirtwaister dress in a multicoloured floral print cotton that she had recognised as formerly the much larger sacklike garment she had been wearing. The shirtwaister buttoned all the way down the front and went in at the waist with a neat A-line skirt. Her with a waist, a proper waist, which she now needed a belt for.

Emily had been so overcome that she hadn't been able to speak, but thankfully Phoebe Evans had understood, patting Emily gently on the arm and smiling at her.

Now Emily had a wardrobe full of pretty summer dresses and skirts, and her winter clothes were now with Phoebe Evans, being made over. Phoebe had offered to make her up some extra things out of the spare fabric but Emily had shaken her head and said that instead she wanted to donate it for those children whose mothers could not afford to replace the clothes they had outgrown.

It had been Phoebe who had suggested that Emily might like to think about visiting her cousin, who was a hairdresser, to get a new hairstyle to go with her 'new' clothes.

Naturally, Phoebe wanted to put business her cousin's way – Emily wasn't daft – but there had been no harm in going to see what could be done.

As a result, Emily now had a pretty, much shorter haircut, which somehow made her look as though she had more hair, not less, since it allowed the natural wave in her hair to be shown off instead of being dragged back into a bun.

And thinking of buns, Emily had been thrilled to bits to discover when she looked in her own mirror that what Con had always described as her 'little currant eyes in a bun-shaped face' looked so much larger now even the shape of her face had changed.

It had been one thing, though, to note all these changes in the privacy of her own bedroom – she had hurried home from the hairdresser's with a scarf over her head – but quite another to go out in public with her hair newly styled and wearing one of her altered frocks.

She had deliberately chosen half-day closing but, as luck would have it, her neighbour had spotted her, and now the revealed curves of her cheek-bones were pink with all that she was feeling as she hurried home.

'Fran, there's something I want to talk to you about.' Brandon's voice was thin but firm. His health was deteriorating and they both knew it, but they didn't discuss it. There was no need and no point. His doctor visited regularly, and was on hand should they need to call him, although Francine had put her foot down and refused the assistance of a live-in nurse. She wanted to keep things as normal as she could for Brandon for as long as she could.

It amazed and bemused her that she had come to feel so much love for the young American she had married more out of pity than anything else – not the love of a woman for a man, not the foolish youthful passion she had felt for Con, nor the deep intense woman's love and desire she had felt for Marcus, but the love of one human being for another, which was, she thought, perhaps the purest form of love of all.

After Brandon's collapse at the embassy, the American Ambassador had visited them, naturally concerned for Brandon, and had had to be taken into their confidence. Since then Brandon had seen the Ambassador twice without her – at his own request. Francine had assumed that he had wanted to talk to the Ambassador about the situation with his parents: the father who, according to Brandon, was terrified of the idea of ill health and death and who would refuse to accept that his son could carry a condition inherited from him that was going to kill him; and the mother so acutely 'sensitive' that hysteria would be her response to Brandon's illness.

Poor Brandon, to be born to parents so rich in material assets, and yet with so little real love to give to their son.

Now Francine smiled at Brandon and reminded him gently, 'If you are going to try yet again to get me to agree to be a beneficiary to the trust funds your grandfather left to you, then you already know my answer. I don't want your money, Brandon.'

'No, I know you don't, but please try to see things from my point of view, Fran. I love you and more than anything else I want to do whatever I can, whilst I can, to make your future as happy and secure as you deserve it to be, so I want you to promise me something.'

Francine's heart ached for him. He was so young and he had had so much potential to do good things. To have all that he could have been taken from him in such a cruel way was hard enough for her to have to witness, so how hard must it be for Brandon himself to have to bear?

He was half lying and half sitting in a day bed in the living room of their apartment, his poor wasted body covered by a blanket and the electric fire on to keep him warm, even though it was summer.

Francine had been sitting beside him on a stool reading to him from the *Illustrated London News*, which she now put down to reach for his hand and hold it in her own.

'You mustn't worry about me,' she told him gently.

'Of course I must,' Brandon insisted. 'You are my wife, and it's my right as well as my duty to do so, and to worry about your future when I am no longer here. I want your promise, Fran, that when I am gone you will remember now, and that whatever decisions you choose to make you make them in the knowledge that I want you to be happy.'

A lump in her throat prevented her from speaking, so instead she had to nod her head.

A small squeeze of her hand signified that Brandon was satisfied with her response.

His voice thinner, he continued, 'I've seen what money can do to people, both too much of it and too little. I have left you an allowance that will provide for you but not too much nor too little, and I have left a lump sum for medical research into the causes of this wretched disease that is destroying me, but it is about the rest of the money that I want to talk to you now.'

'Brandon—'

'No, please let me say what I need to say, Fran, whilst I still can. The legal details have all been dealt with but I want to tell you what I've done. The money that will come to my estate from the trust fund left to me by my grandfather is to go into a foundation, the income from which is to be used to help children and young people, those who are orphaned or abandoned, or treated cruelly by those who should love them. I have appointed you to act as a trustee of this foundation on my behalf and to sit on its board. It is a lot to ask of you, I know; when this war ends, as it eventually will, there will be many children in need of our foundation's help. You will be called upon to travel, to judge, to give to them the same compassion you have already given to me. You will be doing this in my name, so that I will have the glory and you will have the heartache, but there is no one that I trust more than you to do in my name what I won't be here to do myself. Will you do it? Could you, would you, make the sacrifices you will have to make, and which I have no right to ask you to make, given those you have already made to be here with me now?'

Francine's heart was thudding against her ribs. She had known that Brandon wanted to do something charitable with his wealth – he had talked about it with increasing intensity as his health had deteriorated – but she had had no idea that he intended her to be a part of it.

'Your foundation is a magnificent idea, Brandon, and typical of you. As you say, it would be a heavy responsibility for me, with many demands on my time. I take it I won't be the only trustee?'

'No, but the other trustees are still to be approached. I wanted to ask you first.'

Francine could feel his tension. This was so important to him. It would be his gift and his memorial, a testament to all that he was and all that he could have been. He wouldn't pressure her to take it on, she knew, but if she did it would take over and dominate her life. Take over and dominate? Or give her a purpose, a cause, a role that she already knew would suit her?

'You speak of sacrifices, Brandon, but there is no sacrifice for me. Rather it will be an act of joy and love, and a very special bond between us, which I shall treasure and do my best to honour, as trustee, as your wife, and as someone who loves you very dearly, and is grateful to know you and to have this precious time with you.'

'I think this calls for champagne,' was Brandon's valiant response.

SIXTEEN

'I daren't look, I really daren't,' Betty groaned as she and Lou joined the anxious crowd of Waafs, waiting to read their exam results, just posted up in the admin block.

From the front of the group crowding round the notice board, cries of relief interspersed with the occasional groan were reaching back to them. Lou's tummy was a mass of squiggly wriggling nervousness. So much depended on their passing, and she was doubly apprehensive about her own results because of the time she had lost.

'Come on,' Betty urged her, grabbing hold of her arm. 'We might as well know the worse.'

'No, I can't,' Lou admitted. 'You go and look for me.'

The way she felt reminded her of her anxiety when she and Sasha had sat their entrance exam for the telephone exchange, only then she had been hoping that she wouldn't pass. Now, remembering how anxious Sasha had been that they both passed, Lou felt very guilty. Poor Sasha, she had behaved selfishly towards her. She was older and wiser, though, now

257

and she would treat her twin and their relationship far better in the future, Lou promised herself.

Betty had reached the board. Lou kept her gaze trained on her friend's red curls, her fingers mentally crossed.

A taller, dark-haired girl from another hut, who Lou didn't know, was standing behind Betty, obscuring Lou's view as she leaned over her, the better to get a look at the board.

Girls who had seen their own results were streaming past Lou, either commiserating with one another or filled with excited relief.

'I can't believe it,' Lou heard one of them say. 'I had to look three times when I saw Leading Aircraftwoman First Class opposite my name. First Class not just Second. Oh, bliss and heaven, and more bliss.'

Getting upgraded straight to LACW 1 meant that one's results were exceptional. Only a handful of trainees were ever considered good enough for such an accolade.

Betty had extricated herself from the crowd in front of the board and was making her way back to her, her expression concealed by the peak of her cap.

'I've failed, haven't I?' Lou guessed miserably when Betty reached her.

'No, we've both passed.' Betty assured her, but just as Lou was exhaling with relief, she added triumphantly, 'Leading Aircraftwoman First Class.'

'First Class. But . . . you're making it up,' Lou accused her friend, knowing what a tease she was.

'No, I'm not,' Betty assured her. 'It's true. Come and see for yourself if you don't believe me.'

Taking hold of Lou's arm she almost dragged

her over to the board, pointing out triumphantly, 'Look, there it is, see!' much to Lou's embarrassment when several other girls turned to look.

It was typical of her friend's jolly generous nature that she wasn't the least bit upset or envious about Lou's success and was instead happy with her own more modest pass, although she did insist, 'Well, we jolly well *are* going to celebrate now at tonight's dance.'

How could Lou refuse? Especially when it turned out that everyone in their hut had passed their examination, although she was the only one to be upgraded to Leading Aircraftwoman First Class.

'I suppose it must have been all that swotting up I did when I was in hospital,' Lou modestly answered the other girls' demands to know how she had done it.

As always on a dance night there were queues for the showers from girls wanting to look their best, even though they had to wear their uniforms.

'It's all right for the men,' Betty complained. 'They look fine in their uniforms, but just look at me. I look like a sack of potatoes in mine.

Lou grinned at her. 'No, you don't,' she assured her, 'especially not now you've taken in your jacket and the waist of your skirt.'

Betty was very curvy and blessed with a tiny waist, and she had the grace to laugh.

'OK, I admit I did alter my uniform, but don't you dare tell anyone else. It's all right for you, Lou. You're taller than me and lovely and slender, and the uniform suits you.'

All too soon it was seven o'clock, and Lou hadn't even had time to sit down and write to her parents to tell them about her results, although Sunday afternoon after church was normally when she did her letter writing.

She'd just pulled her brush through her curls when their corporal came into the hut, commanding briskly, 'Attention.'

Immediately all the girls obeyed. Mavis Carter, their corporal, was a decent sort, they thought now they knew her, and fair-minded. However, she took her authority seriously and she made sure that those under that authority did so as well. Lou avoided her as much as she could. She still felt dreadfully guilty about the points she had cost the Hut.

'You've all had your exam results today. I won't congratulate you on a full pass rate for the Hut – we don't expect anything else. You'll soon be posted to your new bases to take up the duties for which you've been trained here at Halton, but until you do I would just remind you that it is still possible to win – and lose – points for this Hut up until the time you actually leave here. I imagine that tonight you'll be anticipating celebrating your exam success, so let me just remind you first that base and WAAF rules still apply. Dismissed. Except you, Campion.'

Oh, no, here it comes, Lou thought grimly. She was going to get a private telling-off for the points she had lost them.

The other girls were filing out of the hut, anxious to make the most of their Saturday night off, Betty giving Lou a sympathetic look as she marched past her, saying out of the side of her mouth in a hissed whisper, 'I'll wait for you at the Naafi.

With the corporal's steely gaze on her, Lou didn't dare so much as nod in response.

The door banged closed after the last girl to leave, dust motes from the evening sun dancing in the disturbed air, which smelled of scent and excitement.

'Congratulations on your results, Campion. Very well done indeed.'

'Thank you.' Lou didn't dare relax and add the word 'Corp', remaining standing stiffly to attention.

'At ease.'

At ease – she wished she could be, Lou reflected as she did her best to obey the command given with a body that felt as tightly coiled as a steel spring inside, with limbs attached to it as stiff as her mother's wooden dolly pegs.

'A pass rate of ninety-eight per cent, which yours was,' the corporal announced, 'is considered by the officers here to denote the skill of both a trainee and their tutor.'

Her pass mark has been ninety-eighty per cent? Lou's knees had gone all weak, her wooden dolly peg legs suddenly turned to jelly. Surely there must be some mistake? But of course the RAF did not make mistakes.

'The CO feels that something which reflects so well on WAAF Halton should be rewarded,' Corporal Carter continued. 'As a result I have been informed that twenty good conduct points will be given to this Hut as a mark of recognition of the achievement.'

'Twenty points?' Lou croaked. 'But that's—'

'This puts our Hut at the top of the league table,' the corporal went on, ignoring her, 'where I trust it will now remain. Dismissed, Campion, and jolly good show.'

'Eva, no, I can explain,' Con protested, expertly dodging the tin of Spam his enraged mistress hurled at his head, followed by a tin of peaches, both taken from the pile of tinned food on Con's desk.

'Those tins you've just been chucking at me will be dented now,' he protested. 'Cost me good money, they did, and I know plenty who would be grateful for them.'

It was unfortunate that Eva had caught him being kissed by little Jenny, the understudy, as a 'thank you' for the tinned stuff he'd just given her, and which she'd had to leave on his desk when Eva had burst in on them. But there was no call for her to carry on like she was doing, Con thought defensively, especially not after the way he'd been so generous to her. The trouble with Eva, though, was there was no satisfying her, in bed or out of it. Con grimaced to himself. It would suit him very nicely if Eva took the huff good and proper. And slung her hook, taking herself off to another theatre.

'Like that harlot who is trying to steal you from me, you mean?' Eva demanded.

'You've got it all wrong,' Con tried to defend himself. 'All I was doing was having a word with her about her singing at the nightclub. She's only a kid, Eva; she means nothing to me. How could she when I've got you?' Con tried to soft-soap her.

Eva had been keen enough to encourage him to

go ahead when he had told her that he'd been invited 'by a business associate' to help him set up a new private membership-only nightclub. Joe's idea, since that was the best way for them to get round the strict antigaming laws, and at the same time to do as Ricky had suggested and have a bit more than a card game to tempt the American troops to gamble away their money.

'Do you want to break my heart?' Eva demanded, only partially mollified. 'Can you not see that that harlot is trying to steal you from me? Well, she shall not. I shall kill her first with my father's knife. I shall kill you both and then I shall kill myself.'

'Eva, there's no need for you to talk like that,' Con tried to soothe her.

'Hold me, then; kiss me and tell me that you love me and only me.'

Eva was holding out her arms to him, and the thought of her threat and her father's knife was enough to have Con giving in to her.

She didn't know what she'd have done without Wilhelm being here to keep Tommy occupied during the summer holidays, Emily admitted, as she washed the fresh lettuce Tommy had just brought up to the kitchen for her, showing her how neatly he had cut it, under Wilhelm careful eye, and telling her that he and Wilhelm had counted twenty-three slugs in the jar of beer they had put out to trap them in.

Emily had shuddered at the thought of the slugs – there were some things that, no matter how much she loved Tommy, did not have the interest or appeal for her that they did for him, and slugs were one of them. She'd have their lunch ready soon. Wilhelm had repaired an old wooden table he'd found in the shed and Tommy enjoyed having his lunch there with Wilhelm out in the summer sunshine. Emily didn't join them; she didn't consider that it was her place, or fitting. Wilhelm did more than enough for them already without him having to put up with her company as well. She might sit out on the back step after lunch, with it being so warm and sunny. She could leave the door open so that she could hear the wireless, and she could get on with her knitting. She was making Tommy a new pullover for when he went back to school, from wool she'd unwound from an old jumper of her father's. Her father would have liked Wilhelm, Emily reckoned. A fierce blush burned her face. What on earth was she thinking now!

'Why don't you have your lunch here with us?' Tommy questioned, after Emily had put down their plates and was preparing to go back to the house.

'It is because your *Mutter*, she is the lady of the house and we here we are the men,' Wilhelm explained to Tommy.

She really ought to explain to Wilhelm that Tommy wasn't her son, Emily thought, but now with Tommy himself calling her 'Mum' of his own accord, and her never thinking to say something because it meant so much to her to have him do that, it made things a bit difficult.

'I'm knitting you that pullover for when you back to school, remember,' she told Tommy now, 'and I don't want those nasty slugs near my nice clean wool.'

She'd turned to walk back up the garden as she spoke, but the strong sunlight blinded her for a moment so that she didn't see the wheelbarrow and stumbled against it.

Immediately Wilhelm was on his feet, taking hold of her as she fell.

It must be the shock of nearly falling that was making her feel so weak and dizzy, Emily told herself as she leaned gratefully against Wilhelm's supporting arm, just as it also must be that same shock that was making her heart beat so rapidly. It could not and must not be the fact that Wilhelm was holding her so carefully and so comfortingly whilst he asked anxiously if she was all right.

Wilhelm smelled of earth and sunshine and fresh air. His concern for her underlined what a genuinely kind man he was.

'I am so sorry. I should have moved the wheelbarrow. If you had been hurt, I should never have forgiven myself.'

'No, it was my fault for not looking where I was going,' Emily insisted.

'You are sure you have not hurt yourself? You are able to walk?'

'Yes. I'm all right.'

Wilhelm still hadn't released her and although she knew she should move away from him, Emily felt strangely reluctant to do so.

'You say that, but with your permission I shall walk back to the house with you, just to be sure.'

She could, Emily knew, have told Wilhelm that Tommy would walk back with her, but there was something about the way the warmth and protection of Wilhelm's arm around her, and the concern in his eyes made her feel, which kept her silent, so that it was Wilhelm who guided her gently back towards the open back door whilst Tommy continued to enjoy his lunch.

'You really needn't have bothered,' Emily told Wilhelm once they had reached the house. 'It was my own silly fault for not looking where I was going, and it would have served me right if I had hurt myself.'

'I am glad you did not. It would not have been your fault.

'If you want to wait I'll put the kettle on and then you can take a tray of tea back down for you and Tommy,' Emily suggested.

Wilhelm had been in the kitchen before so there was no reason for her feel like she was doing, all breathless and giddy, as though something important had happened.

As she bustled about the kitchen Emily took very great care not to look at Wilhelm or to behave as though there was anything out of the ordinary, but inside she knew that once she was on her own it wouldn't be Tommy's new pullover that occupied her thoughts but the lovely comforting warmth of Wilhelm's arm around her, holding her as though she was fragile and precious and all those things that, as a girl, she had so longed to be.

'Emily.'

The sound of Wilhelm's voice so close to her ear as she stood in front of the cupboard about to lift the cups from it had Emily's heart pounding.

'I have wanted to say to you for a very long

time how much I admire you and how beautiful I find you.'

Unable to stop herself, Emily turned round, her chest lifting with her gulped breath as she saw how close to her Wilhelm was standing.

'Beautiful in here.' Wilhelm told her, touching his own chest over his heart. 'The true beauty that comes from true goodness inside. But now you are very beautiful outside as well.'

Her, beautiful? Emily was about to deny that she was any such thing when she saw how sad Wilhelm looked.

'Such a beautiful and good woman will have many men who admire her and who want to offer her their hearts. She would never want the heart of a man such as me, a prisoner of war, who is not worthy of her. I should not speak but my heart demands that I do.'

'Oh, Wilhelm, how could you ever think you aren't worthy of any woman?' Emily protested with heartfelt emotion. 'You are the most worthy man I have ever met. A good man, a kind man.'

They looked at one another, both of them hesitant and uncertain, and then Wilhelm stepped forward purposefully and Emily's heart threw itself valiantly across the chasm that separated her from the happiness she longed for, forcing her body to follow suit, so that she was stepping into Wilhelm's arms and he was kissing her gently and respectfully.

The boiling kettle whistled, and, startled, they separated and looked self-conscious, whilst smiling happily at one another.

SEVENTEEN

'Truthfully, Grace, I could hardly believe it, and nor could your dad. Both of us had to read the letter twice. Of course, your dad's chest is swelled to twice its normal size, and I don't think there's a soul that works for the Salvage Corp that doesn't know about Lou getting the George Cross. If your dad's like this now, I don't know what he's going to be like after he's seen King George giving Lou her medal at the investiture.'

'Well, you've got to admit that it is exciting, Mum,' Grace laughed. 'And Lou, of all people.'

'We said, didn't we, when she came home how much being in the WAAF had done to help her grow up? Oh, and I've had a letter from your auntie Francine saying that we're not to worry about hotel rooms or anything because that's going to be her treat. You and Seb will be able to come, won't you?'

'We wouldn't miss it for the world,' Grace assured her mother as they stood together in Jean's kitchen, drinking the tea she had just poured.

'Sasha will be going, of course, but what about Bobby? I know that Lou wasn't keen on him.'

'Lou said in her letter that she's got tickets for all of us, including Bobby, but that she doesn't know if she'll be allowed to have much time with us. The George Cross isn't a purely military award, of course, but she'll be in uniform and I dare say there'll be things she'll have to do, although she did say that she'll be able to stay at the Savoy with us.

'I don't know what I'm going to wear, mind, although again your auntie Francine has said not to worry. It's not until late October, and I've been thinking that I could wear the outfit I had for your wedding. I was going to save it for . . . well, it seems silly not to wear it.'

Grace knew perfectly well what her mother had been about to say before she had stopped herself: she had been intending to save the lovely outfit her sister Francine had brought home for her from Cairo for Katie and Luke's wedding. But now, of course, Katie and Luke weren't going to be married, and Grace knew how very disappointed and sad that had made her mother.

However, since 25 October was the date when Lou was to be presented with her medal by the King at the investiture ceremony in London, it did make sense for her mother to wear the outfit. Grace had already decided that she was going to wear her own going away suit for the occasion.

Grace had been as thrilled as Jean when she'd learned about Lou's George Cross, and Seb had been the first to insist that they must make every effort they could to be at the investiture. He couldn't have been more proud of Lou if she had been his own sister, but then of course they were both in the same service, although very different parts of it.

'I'd have liked to have taken Bella with us,' Jean continued. 'It's such a shame that Vi treats her the way she does, and Bella with all the responsibility for that nursery on her shoulders . . .

'Lou put in her letter that the RAF is making arrangements for Luke to get to know.' A shadow crossed Jean's face, and Grace knew why. It wasn't just Luke's broken engagement that caused her mother concern.

Everyone knew how vitally important it was that the British troops stopped Rommel from over-running the Middle East, taking control of the Suez Canal and the vital supply of oil. The Afrika Korps Radio had already warned the ladies of Cairo to 'make ready for us tonight' and naturally, with Luke fighting with the British Eighth Army and the previous month's fall of Tobruk, Jean was concerned for her son's safety.

Later, after she had seen Grace off on the train back to Whitchurch, Jean thought over her one plan for their trip to London that she had not revealed to her daughter. It wasn't that she would be meddling or anything, she assured herself. She had liked Katie for herself, after all, and it was only natural that if she was going to be in London she should try to see her ex-billetee. The trouble was that her ex-billetee was also Luke's ex-fiancée, and Sam would not approve of Jean making contact with her for that reason. But Jean wanted to see Katie; she missed her and she wanted to reassure herself that Katie was all right. It wasn't as though she was actually going to lie to Sam; she would never do that. No, it was simply that she wasn't actually going to tell him that she had written to Katie's parents telling them what was happening, and enclosing a letter for Katie, suggesting that if Katie was willing, they could meet at the Savoy for a cup of tea. There was no harm in that, was there? No, there wasn't. And she wouldn't even mention Luke – well, at least not unless Katie mentioned him first and wanted to talk about him and perhaps have news of him.

It had been such a relief when he had written to them after the fall of Tobruk to reassure them that he was safe and well. Not, of course, that he'd been able to write anything specific, not with the censorship rules that forbade people refering to anything that might help the enemy if it should fall into their hands. Families soon learned to put two and two together, though, listening to the news on the wireless, reading the papers and knowing where those members of their family were serving abroad.

Luke was still in the desert, but now the news-papers were full of the progress the British Eighth Army was making under its newly appointed generals – Alexander and Montgomery – against Rommel, saying how Rommel's tanks had become embedded in the sand.

Jean couldn't bear to think of her Luke having to face those tanks. Every night she prayed for all those she loved but she always said an extra special prayer that Luke would return home unharmed.

Sam was worrying too, she knew, even though

he didn't say so. The anxious frown with which he read the evening paper told its own story. Not even his allotment could keep him from coming in in time to sit down with her to the nine o'clock news.

Jean couldn't imagine what being in the desert must be like. All that sand. The most sand she had ever seen had been at Southport when the tide was out, but according to Francine the sand in the desert wasn't flat like it was in Southport. Instead it formed hills and valleys, which could change overnight with the wind, burying whole villages, never mind brave English soldiers whose mothers were worrying themselves sick about them.

'I wish we didn't have to go to London, Bobby.'

'Aww, come on, Sash, don't be like that. You'll enjoy it.' When Sasha hunched a shoulder and turned away from him on the bench in Wavertree Park, where they'd been sitting together in the warm evening sunshine, Bobby reached for her hand and, holding it tightly, added, 'And don't forget that we'll be there in London together, and won't that be something? And seeing King George, and all.'

Sasha managed a small smile. 'Well, if you want to go, Bobby, but I don't want Lou treating you like she normally does, as if you and me aren't together.'

'I don't reckon she'll do that. I know me and your Lou haven't always seen eye to eye, and that she took against me when you and I first got together, but that's all in the past now.'

'All everyone seems to be able to talk about at home these days is Lou and her medal,' Sasha complained. 'Even Dad seems to have forgotten how angry he was when he found out that Lou had gone behind his and Mum's back and joined up.'

'It's only natural that they're proud of her, and I bet you are too really. After all, she is your twin.'

'Well, yes, of course I am, but I know Lou, and when we get to London it will be all "I've done this" and "I've seen that". It makes me feel as though I just don't matter any more.'

Sasha had to squeeze her eyes tightly together to prevent them from filling with tears.

'Of course you matter.' Bobby's hand tightened comfortingly round hers. 'You matter to me. You matter to me more than anyone else in the world, Sasha,' he told her gruffly. 'And if I had my way . . . well, let's just say if I thought for one minute that your mum and dad would let me put it there, you'd be wearing my ring when we go to London.'

Her unhappiness forgotten, Sasha turned towards him.

'Oh, Bobby . . .' Her eyes were shining now, her cheeks flushed as soft a pink as the evening sky at sunset.

'One day, Sasha, when this war is over, if you'll have me, you and me are going to be married.'

'Oh, yes, Bobby,' Sasha breathed happily, her earlier misery forgotten in the delight and excitement Bobby's words had brought.

Lou could have her medal; she had Bobby, and his love.

*   *   *

'So you're to get the George Cross then?'

'Yes, not that I deserve it, not really.'

'You can't expect me to agree with that. You saved my life, after all.'

It was silly to feel so shy and self-conscious, Lou knew. After all, this was the man she had virtually dragged bodily from the cockpit of his burning plane.

But of course that had been then in the heat of a few dangerous minutes; this was now, and the company and the attention of the tall, handsome squadron leader walking beside her in the gardens outside the officers' mess, the only visible signs of what he had been through a few telltale marks on his hands and the sling still supporting his broken arm, was making Lou feel rather shy.

'It's very kind of you to come and see me like this,' Lou told him politely, feeling awkward as well as self-conscious. It had been such a surprise when she had been told that Squadron Leader Maitland was coming to see her to thank her personally for what she had done.

'He's terrifically well-connected, you know,' one of the other girls had told Lou knowledgably. 'Posh family and that kind of thing.'

'Not at all. I owe you my life, and I wanted to thank you personally for what you did, at such a risk to yourself. If there's anything I can do to show my thanks . . .'

'Thank you, but I've already benefited enough. I've passed my exams and I'm being posted to RAF Lyneham in Wiltshire next week. I'm getting a medal I don't really deserve. The only thing that could make things any better would be going up in a plane, but of course that's forbidden.'

Lou had only been speaking in an effort to pass the time and for something to say, but instead of agreeing with her, Squadron Leader Maitland stopped walking so that she had no choice other than to do the same.

'If you're serious about that and it's really what you want, then I dare say it can be arranged.'

Lou shielded her eyes from the sun to look uncertainly at him. He had thick brown hair, bleached by the sun at the ends, and very blue eyes, and that air about him that flying men just did seem to have. Cockiness, Luke would no doubt have called it, but it wasn't, not really. It was, though, a very special sort of confidence, and it made the RAF men so attractive to the opposite sex.

'But it's not allowed,' she protested.

'Well, yes,' he agreed with a smile, 'but I think there is something I can arrange. Leave it with me. You're being posted to Lyneham, you say?'

Lou nodded.

'I'll be in touch there then, but in the meantime, mum's the word, eh?'

'Bella, the doorbell's ringing. Fancy anyone being thoughtless enough to come calling at this time on a Saturday morning. Whoever it is, send them away. I'm still in my dressing gown.'

Bella tried not to feel irritated by or impatient with her mother but it was difficult at times. There was, after all, no reason why her mother shouldn't go the door herself. It was half-past nine and the only reason she was still in her dressing gown was that she had come down to complain that Bella was late in taking her cup of tea up to her. Since Bella had been up since seven o'clock trying to catch up with some paperwork from the nursery, and hadn't had time to have a drink herself, she had had to bite on her lip and not say anything.

It wasn't that she actually minded being the one to answer the door, it was just her mother's attitude that jarred on her. Indeed, there were occasions on which she actually found herself understanding why her mother's selfishness might have driven her father into the arms of a man-eater like Pauline – not that he was any less selfish than her mother, although Bella suspected that Pauline would soon put an end to that.

She shouldn't be critical of her mother, she told herself. It had been dreadfully hard on her, having everyone know that her husband had left her, and had led to her mother seeking solace in drink, something Bella would never ever have expected from her oh-so-correct and proper parent. That had been a truly terrible time and Bella was thankful that it was over and that her mother had reverted to her old self, even if that did mean that she never seemed to stop complaining and expected Bella to be at her beck and call. Bella was grateful to her mother's WVS colleagues for their forbearance in welcoming her back in their midst and treating her as though nothing untoward had ever taken place.

It was a beautiful bright sunny morning and Bella had promised herself that once she had finished her paperwork she was going to go into the garden. Since her father had left there was no one to keep the lawn in its once pristine state and Bella had come to an arrangement with the people whose garden backed onto their own that the husband could extend his vegetable plot into their garden, if in return he would give a share of his produce to Bella and her mother. It was an arrangement that was working extremely well, keeping them supplied in fresh vegetables and salad ingredients, as well as eggs from his hens.

Bella unlocked and then opened the door, her lips forming a polite smile, only for her eyes to widen when she saw both Bettina and Maria standing on the doorstep, their faces shadowed by the brims of their hats. She might not be able to see their expressions but Bella knew what must have brought them.

'Jan? You've had news?' she guessed as she ushered them inside.

There was only one kind of news it could be. The authorities must have found Jan's body. Pain seized Bella's heart, wringing it with the agony of her loss.

'Who is it, Bella?' her mother was demanding querulously from the kitchen.

'We can talk in here,' Bella told her visitors, pushing open the door to her mother's precious front room and gesturing for them to go inside. 'Let me take your hats and coats and then I'll go and make us a cup of tea.'

'Bella, please, wait a minute,' Bettina begged her.

'Bella, who is it?'

Bella looked down the hallway towards the kitchen, but Bettina's hand was on her arm, her expression determined, and Bella's heart overruled her head. Ignoring her mother's demand Bella nodded to Bettina and then went to the door, closing it, blocking out the sound of her mother's voice.

'We've had news,' Bettina told her unnecessarily. 'It came this morning.' Mother and daughter looked at one another.

'We . . . wanted to come and tell you straight away.'

As though she couldn't wait any longer, Maria burst out, 'Jan's alive, Bella.'

Alive?

Bella felt her legs buckle with the shock. As though she knew what she was feeling, Maria reached for her, putting her arm around her, her voice tender as she told her, 'It is true, Bella. Jan is alive.'

It was left to Bettina to continue the story.

'He's a prisoner of war, Bella. Apparently his plane crashed in France, not over the Channel. He bailed out and was captured by the Germans. Fortunately it seems that he wasn't injured.'

'A prisoner of war?' Bella didn't know what to think. First had come the joy of knowing that he was alive, but now she was afraid for him, her spirits plummeting. 'He's all right, though, isn't he?' she demanded. 'He's well, and . . . the Germans have to abide by the Geneva Convention.'

Once again Bettina and Maria exchanged looks.

'They do, but Jan is, of course, Polish, not British.'

'That doesn't make any difference surely? The Geneva Convention applies to all prisoners of war.'

None of them wanted to say what they were all thinking, namely that they had all read of the terribly suffering endured by the POWs taken by the Japanese. Not everyone obeyed the rules. Who could you trust to do so?

'All we know is that the Red Cross have confirmed that he's a prisoner of war,' Bettina told her. 'But we can write to him and send him parcels. We've brought the address for you.'

Tears brimmed in Bella's eyes as she took the piece of paper Bettina was holding out to her.

Jan was alive. It was a miracle.

Maria hugged her fiercely and then so did Bettina.

'I'm afraid to let myself believe it, in case it isn't true,' Bella told them.

'It is true,' Bettina assured her firmly. 'Jan is alive, Bella.'

Alive but a prisoner of war. A Polish prisoner of war. Would that make any difference? Would it mean he would be in more danger than British POWs? As a prisoner of war he would be protected by the Geneva Convention, Bella repeated inwardly to herself after Bettina and Maria had gone, as though somehow those words alone had the power to protect Jan and keep him safe.

EIGHTEEN

It was over. Brandon was gone, his life slipping slowly away from him as the August afternoon had given way to evening and sunset, but Francine was still holding Brandon's hand – cold and waxen now within her own – as she had done throughout this long sad day.

Tears filled her eyes and ran slowly down her face – not for herself but for him, for Brandon, who had had so little of the life he should have had and who surely had deserved more. He had been a good person, a kind, loving, generous person, a person who would have made a good husband and a good father.

Life could be so cruel.

She used her free hand to wipe away her tears before leaning over to kiss his forehead.

Already death was making its mark on his features, softening and blurring them.

The nurse – one of two who had been with them for the last three days, providing twenty-four-hour care for Brandon – came back into the room.

'There'll be things you'll need to do,' Francine acknowledged, gently slipping her hand from Brandon's and then folding his against his chest on top of the bedcover.

There were things she had to do as well, things she and Brandon had been through together so that she would know exactly what his wishes were.

He had wanted to be buried here in London but Francine had spoken to the Ambassador and between them they had persuaded him to agree that his body should be sent home for burial at Arlington Cemetery.

'I'm no fallen hero,' he had objected.

But Francine had pushed aside his objection, telling him tenderly, 'You will be with others there, Brandon, with your own people.' And she had seen that he knew what she meant, and that she had not wanted him to lie perhaps one day forgotten in an unloved grave in a foreign land. At Arlington he would be with the young and the brave, young men like himself whose lives had been cut short by war. The only difference was that their war would be a war against other men whilst Brandon's had been against an enemy mightier than any mere flesh, blood and bone.

There was to be no formal funeral service – Brandon hadn't wanted that, and nor, he had told her, did he want her wearing black.

'I want to think about you singing and looking beautiful, just like when I first saw you.'

Francine had to bite down hard on her bottom lip to stop herself from crying again.

*   *   *

281

'Anyone in here by the name of Campion?'

Lou looked up from the service she was doing on one of the planes that were used to train new flying instructors. The pilots attending the school had all finished their tour of operations and were now being retrained as flying instructors. Lou loved the work she was now doing even more than she had expected to do. It was wonderful to think that she was finally part of the war effort.

The plane she had been working on was the very first one she had been set to work on when she had first arrived at the base at the beginning of August, and was one of her favourites because of the way it had made it easy for her to pass the eagle-eyed inspection of her new sergeant. Every plane had its own idiosyncrasies and some of them were hell to work on, but not this one. She was sweet and sunny-natured, no matter what indignities raw new pilots heaped on her.

Pushing her cap back on her curls, Lou reached for a rag to wipe her oily hands as she looked towards the open doors to the hangar where the young woman who had made the enquiry was standing, her hands on her hips in a stance of care-less arrogance.

'Watch out, she's one of those posh ATA girls,' Hilary, the girl Lou was working with, who had been at base for longer than she, warned her. 'You know, the ones that fly the new planes in and that sort of thing.' Hilary gave a disparaging sniff. 'Think they're the bee's knees, that lot do.'

Acknowledging Hilary's advice, Lou made her way to the front of the hangar.

The woman waiting for her was wearing flying kit but had removed her helmet so that her sun-streaked hair was catching the light. There was something vaguely familiar about her, but Lou knew that she had never met her before. She was older than Lou – in her late twenties, Lou guessed – and her voice when she asked, 'You're Campion?' as Lou approached was very definitely, as Hilary had warned Lou, 'posh'.

'Yes.'

'Good-oh. I'm Verity Maitland,' she announced, extending her hand for Lou to shake. M'brother, George, asked me to look you up. To look you up and take you up, in fact.' She laughed at her own joke. 'Don't have much time right now, I'm afraid. I've got to get back up to a certain factory ready to start transporting some new planes down, along with some of the other gals, but since I'm here I thought I might as well introduce myself.'

Lou's eyes widened. So this was the 'something' the squadron leader had said he thought he could do, Lou guessed.

They were outside the hangar now, and Verity Maitland was opening a packet of cigarettes and offering Lou one.

Lou shook her head, too bemused to say anything. Lighting a cigarette, Verity inhaled, arching her throat and tossing her hair before exhaling again. Her nails were painted a bright glossy red, and Lou remembered reading somewhere that the ATA girls prided themselves on being 'glamorous' whilst also being first-rate pilots.

'It's just too bloody, all this fuss about not

wanting women to fly. Daddy thinks it's frightfully funny. He taught both Georgie and me years ago. Look, when's your next off-duty?'

Lou thought quickly and then told her.

'Well, if you haven't already made some plans why don't I pop down here with my own plane then and take you up for a spin? What do you say?'

Somehow Lou managed to stammer a disbelieving, 'Yes.'

'Good-oh. Must go. See you next week.'

'That was quick,' Hilary commented, when Lou returned to the hangar. 'What did she want? A fuel refill?'

Lou thought it best to nod.

'Thought so,' Hilary sniffed again, as Lou went back to working on the engine of her plane.

Later on in the day, Lou and Hilary did genuinely have fuel refills to do, when six planes from a Coastal Defence squadron came in for refuelling, and Lou and Hilary were called on to assist the regular refuelling team.

The first task was to cycle out to where the planes were refuelled, and then help to get the aviation bowsers in place, before climbing up onto the wing to uncap the fuel tank, ready to start refilling the planes' tanks. Naturally the girls all wore their uniform trousers or overalls for this kind of work. It still made Lou smile when she remembered how, when she had first been given her kit, one of the other girls had told her that the reason their greatcoats were lined with white wool was so that aircrews could place these coats lining up on the ground after a forced landing so that the white lining could be picked up at night by those looking for them.

Not that Lou needed her greatcoat on a hot August day like today, with the heat of the sun being reflected back from the hot metal of the wing, as she kneeled on it to unscrew the fuel tank cap, screwing her eyes up against the bright light as she did so. The pilot, who was climbing out of the cockpit, probably, Lou imagined, intending to use the break to make a call of nature and grab a cup of tea from the Naafi if he was quick, removed his flying helmet.

Lou froze in shocked recognition.

Kieran Mallory. She rubbed her eyes and looked again. It couldn't be, surely? But a swift second glance confirmed that it was.

Her face on fire and her heart thudding with panic and dread in case he recognised her, Lou's normally deft fingers became awkward and stiff, the cap clattering onto the wing and rolling away from her as it finally came free and she dropped it.

She knew that the noise had Kieran looking at her because she could see the movement of his shadow on the wing. Desperate not to be recognised, Lou huddled over, tucking her chin into her, praying that he could go away so that she could get on with the refuelling and retrieve the cap, but instead to her dismay she saw his shadow leaning over the cap, his lean fingers closing round it.

His command to her to 'Catch' was delivered with an amused and teasing nonchalant mockery that left her with a split-second decision to make and two equally unwanted options – either to catch it and risk exposing herself or to let it fall and risk the humiliation of missing it.

Luck was on her side, though, because another pilot coming past caught it for her, placing it down on the wing as he went by, calling out to Kieran as he hurried to join him, 'That was a good kill of yours the other night, Mall . . .'

It was safe for her to turn round now, Lou knew, but she had better things to do than gaze after Kieran Mallory like some stage-struck girl mooning over a handsome matinée idol, even if Kieran did have matinée idol good looks; better things like filling the fuel tank of his plane so that she didn't have to be around when he came back.

The shock of seeing him wiped out the excitement she had felt earlier, leaving her anxious and vulnerable. What was the matter with her? She wasn't a silly young girl any more, taken in by an experienced flirt's cold-blooded decision to use her foolish adoration for his own ends. No, she was a fully qualified flight mechanic, a Leading Aircraftwoman First Class; a girl in uniform who had won the respect of her peers and her superiors, and who enjoyed the pride that that respect gave her.

But all that could be taken from her if Kieran Mallory saw her and recognised her, and starting telling tales in the mess about her silly naïvety when she and Sasha had first met him. She would be ragged unmercifully, she knew, by the RAF aircrews, some of whom cloaked their dislike and disapproval of WAAF girls doing what they considered to be 'men's' work with often deliberately unkind and even cruel 'joking'.

It needn't be as bad as that, and she mustn't let her imagination run away with her, Lou tried to reason when she went back to the hangar. She wasn't, after all, on regular refuelling duty – she had only been standing in. The chances of her seeing Mallory again, never mind of him seeing her and recognising her, were so slight, surely, as to be negligible.

If there was one thing being in uniform taught you it was not to worry about the 'what ifs' of life but to concentrate on the here and now.

Even so, it was with great relief that Lou watched the Coastal Defence fighters take off again half an hour later, before giving her full attention to the engine she was checking.

NINETEEN

Francine put down the letter she had been rereading: Brandon's last to her, given to her at his funeral by his solicitor.

In it he had repeated what he had already said to her.

What I have done I have done for you, and because of you, because of the love I have for you and the love and care you have given to me. What I have done is, I believe, the best gift that I can give you. You may disagree. I may have made a misjudgement and if I have then I apologise, but if I haven't then know that if there is a hereafter, then from it I shall be up there with the good guys, praying for your happiness.

You have given me more than you will ever know, Francine. You have made it possible for me to travel a road I feared as a man and not as a coward, in love and not in fear.

Forgive me if you feel I have not done 'right' by you, Francine, and believe me when

I say that my intentions were not to do that but the opposite. Forgive me too if you think I have concealed things from you or deceived you. My motives were always 'for you' and not 'against you', my decisions made out of love and my desire to repay you for all that you have given me.

Be happy, Francine.

Mr Haines, Brandon's solicitor, had told her that Brandon had asked specifically that she reread his letter prior to the first meeting with Mr Haines to discuss the practicalities of the foundation Brandon had set up prior to his death, and to remember it during that meeting.

When Francine had tried to question the solicitor in more detail he had said that there was no more he could tell her.

It had been at Mr Haines' suggestion that the meeting was held in the apartment Francine had shared with Brandon. Francine had agreed with him that it would be more convenient and more comfortable for her. What she hadn't said to the solicitor was that she would also feel that Brandon was a part of what was happening because the apartment still held so many memories of Brandon for her.

Since it was to be a formal business meeting, Francine had asked the Dorchester to send her a waiter to serve the afternoon tea she had ordered. In accordance with Brandon's wishes she wasn't wearing mourning but instead was dressed in a plain cream linen suit she had had made in Cairo, its jacket lined with the same delicate rosebud print on a cream background as her blouse. She had lost weight during the last sad weeks of Brandon's life, and in her own opinion now looked unflatteringly gaunt, despite the attempt she had made to conceal this with lipstick and rouge.

The dull buzz of the bell announced the arrival of the solicitor.

The waiter, who had already arrived, went to open the door for her but when he returned to the drawing room, he wasn't accompanied merely by one man but by two, one of whom naturally was Mr Haines, whilst to her shock and disbelief the other was Marcus Linton, the army major she had met and fallen in love with in Cairo, but who had then ended their relationship, thanks to the malicious lies of one of the other ENSA singers.

Of course, Francine did her best to cover what she was feeling, summoning a professional smile for Mr Haines' benefit as she shook his hand, keeping her back to Marcus whilst she invited them both to sit down.

Thankfully the small ceremonial bustle of the waiter offering and then pouring tea provided Francine with some camouflage behind which to attempt to gather her composure, so that by the time they had all been served and the waiter had left, she had in place a polite social mask to hide her real feelings of shock and dismay.

That Brandon was responsible for the presence of Marcus, Francine had no doubt. Brandon had known that she loved the major and that he had walked away from her, and her terrible fear now was that Brandon had actually informed the major of her feelings in some kind of loving attempt to 'help' her.

Francine, though, was too sensible to rush into the kind of questions that might betray her to even more humiliation than she suspected already awaited her. Instead she waited until Mr Haines had sipped his tea and enjoyed the bloater paste sandwiches that now passed as 'afternoon tea', for the solicitor to explain to her the purpose of their visit.

The solicitor's explanation was long and windy but could be summed up essentially, Francine recognised after she had listened patiently to it, as Brandon's decision to appoint Marcus as her co-trustee on the foundation's board.

'As you both know, the position as trustee of the foundation is one without remuneration, which you have both taken on for the benefit of the foundation. The income the foundation will derive from its assets will be yours to distribute to those who you best judge to be worthy recipients of the money within the criteria that Brandon laid down. It was his wish, expressed to me and I understand discussed with both of you prior to his death, that you will work together to this end. However, there is a clause in the charter for the foundation that allows for either or both of you to withdraw from the agreement you have already given – and signed – should you wish to do so.'

Thanks heavens for that, Francine thought weakly. She didn't trust herself to speak, though.

'Forgive me,' Brandon had written, and now she knew why. There was no point blaming him or accusing him; the fault was hers. She was the one who had allowed Brandon to see how much Marcus had hurt her and how much she still loved him. She had no idea what method of persuasion Brandon might have used to get Marcus to agree, as he obviously had, to be her co-trustee, other than to acknowledge that Marcus was an extremely honourable man. It could be that Brandon might have compelled him to agree by insisting that the foundation and those who would benefit from it needed Marcus. He too, after all, knew what it was to lose a child and he, like her, would not have been able to withstand the obvious need of all those children rendered lost and vulnerable by the war.

However, there the similarity between them ended, for whilst Marcus would put his duty to be honourable first, and refuse to be daunted by the thought of working closely with her, as he had plainly known he must do, Francine knew that had Brandon told her that he intended to appoint Marcus as her co-trustee, she would have refused to take on the role, knowing that she could not work effectively alongside the man she loved so much and who had hurt her so badly.

Brandon had deceived her. He had lied to her by omission, by default, because he had known what her reaction would have been if he had told her what he planned to do. Francine knew that. She knew too that he must have said some of this to Marcus, so betraying her twice.

'What I have done, I have done for you,' he had written.

'There are, of course, necessary formalities that will need to be dealt with: the setting up of a bank account, that kind of thing.' Mr Haines' voice intruded into her very private and even more painful thoughts. Francine forced herself to listen to him and concentrate on what he was saying.

'I have already written to Brandon's trustees,' he told them both, 'and they have written back to me to confirm that the assets from Brandon's trusts will now be transferred into the name of the foundation, with the exception of the monies Brandon left directly to you, Francine.'

Francine nodded. She and Brandon had argued more than once over her insistence that he was not to leave her anything more than a relatively modest income, but right now she had more important things on her mind than her own finances.

'I will leave you now, as I know from Major Linton that you will wish to take advantage of the opportunity provided by his leave to discuss your plans for the foundation, but as soon as I have the necessary bank mandates and so on I shall be in touch again.'

Francine couldn't do any more than incline her head and give the solicitor a forced polite smile. Objecting to either Marcus's presence or his decision to remain wasn't really an option. Apart from anything else, and as little as she relished the prospect, the future working of the foundation had to be discussed, even if that meant that she herself had to step down from her own role as trustee in order for Brandon's wishes for it to be put into action.

Naturally Francine was the one to escort the solicitor to the door, where she thanked him for all that he had done as he shook her hand and replaced the hat he had removed on his arrival. Francine refused to look at the coat rack and the shelf above it by the door where Marcus's peaked cap lay.

Her heart heavy with all that she felt, she returned to the drawing room, where Marcus was standing by the window, his bearing soldierly, his hands folded behind his back.

The war had touched him physically as it had done all of them, Francine recognised. There were touches of silver in his hair, highlighted by the August sun slanting in through the windows, new lines fanning out from the corners of his eyes and no doubt put there by the desert sun. But the grimness to his mouth owed its presence not to the war but rather to her, she suspected.

Dispensing with any preliminaries, as she closed the drawing room door, she told him emotionlessly, 'Obviously we aren't going to be able to work together on the foundation. Equally obviously Brandon's actions were well intentioned. Even if I didn't know that for myself, the letter he left me proves it. I am willing to take all the blame. I should never have given in to self-pity and spoken to him about you. I shouldn't have told him—'

'Anything', she had been about to say but before she could do so, Marcus interrupted her.

'You shouldn't have told him what a fool I was or how I let you down out of pride and cowardice?' he asked harshly. 'Why not, when it is the truth? Brandon applauded your honesty. He told me so himself.'

When Francine couldn't stop herself from making

a small sound that was a mixture of pain and protest, Marcus seemed to understand its cause.

'When he originally wrote to me asking to meet me I admit that I didn't want to do so.'

'Then why did you?' Francine's tone was hostile.

Marcus removed his cigarettes from his tunic pocket and offered her one. Francine hesitated. She had stopped smoking when Brandon had had to stop, and although she hadn't missed them, now suddenly she felt she needed their calming effect. She regretted her decision, though, when she automatically reached for the table lighter to light up her own cigarette and was then obliged to offer it to Marcus. Instead of taking it from her to light his own cigarette he leaned forward, his cigarette between his lips, replacing the packet in his pocket as he did so, so that she had no alternative but to ignite the flame and hold it against his cigarette for him. This close she could see the dense darkness of his thick eyelashes as he looked down at the cigarette. Her hand started to tremble. Marcus reached out to cup his own round it to steady the flame – a simple, automatic gesture that meant nothing and yet at the same time was so intensely intimate that she felt its effect all through her body.

'Do you mind if I sit down?'

Francine shook her head, replacing the lighter on the side table as she took a seat on the sofa opposite the one Marcus had chosen.

'When Brandon wrote to me, he enclosed with his letter a sealed envelope with another letter in it, which he said I must read only if you were truly important to me, as he believed you to be. If he was wrong then he directed me to destroy the letter unread.'

Francine felt so nauseous and light-headed that she had to stub out her cigarette.

'I should imagine that anyone's natural curiosity would incline them to open it.' Her voice was brittle with tension.

'Only those who have never felt the agony of a flame's burn are curious to see what effect it might have,' was Marcus's grim response. 'The truth is that Brandon's warning inclined me more to destroy the letter unread than to risk a return of the pain I thought I had already overcome. In fact, I did put the letter to one side but then later – much later, in fact, in that dark hour when everything is stripped away from the human heart apart from its greatest yearning – unable to sleep I retrieved the letter and read it.'

Francine bowed her head.

'Brandon's opening lines stressed that you knew nothing of what he was doing, or of what he was writing. He told me that had you known you would have stopped him. He told me that he risked angering you and, even worse, hurting you, but that he believed the risk was worth taking for the sake of your ultimate happiness.'

Francine couldn't bear any more. 'It's not Brandon's fault, it's mine. I should never have told him. He was so . . . so grateful to me for what he saw as my compassion that he couldn't believe that it was possible for someone else not to . . . not to . . .'

'Love you as he believed you deserved to be loved.'

'Brandon felt that all the giving in our marriage

was on my side, but it wasn't. I needed him just as much as he needed me, albeit in a different way. Whilst I was there with him when he needed someone, he gave me the purpose that I needed to . . . to go on.' Francine stood up, unable to keep still any more, pacing the floor in her tension and her dread of the humiliation she knew awaited her.

'There's no need for you to say any more, Marcus. I can guess what Brandon told you. I can't deny that I did tell him about . . . about my feelings for you, but that was because I wanted to be honest with him, not because I wanted him to approach you on my behalf. Whatever once existed between us is over. It ended when we parted in Alexandria. This attempt of Brandon's to bring us together again, however well-meaning, has to be intolerable for both of us.'

'What is intolerable for me is that out of fear and mistrust I allowed myself to be persuaded that you didn't really love me.'

Marcus's words, so grave and so unexpected, brought Francine's pacing to an unsteady halt.

'Then I compounded that lack of judgement and miscarriage of justice against you by covering my guilt with the erroneous belief that your reasons for marrying Brandon were mercenary rather than the charitable act of compassion Brandon himself wrote in his letter to me that they actually were. You have much to blame me for, Francine, and little reason to forgive me.'

Francine didn't want to hark back to the past or to risk being overwhelmed by her own emotions, but she couldn't stop herself from saying, 'I suppose it is something that exists between men and from which women are excluded that you seem to have been able to accept Brandon's defence of me when you were not able to give me the opportunity to put to you myself my side of the story you were spun in Egypt. I didn't know until I was actually on the ship how we'd both been tricked by Lily. I tried to get off to tell you but the gangplank had already seen raised.'

Francine's voice betrayed the emotion she remembering feeling as she had tried so desperately to attract his attention as he walked away from her – but had failed.

'Not that it matters now,' she added quickly. 'We're both old enough to know that the intensity of war fosters a false intimacy in relationships that were never meant to last. I'm just sorry that Brandon didn't tell me what he planned to do. If he had I could have saved us both the embarrassment of this situation. When I told Brandon that I . . . that I still loved you it was simply as a deterrent to his own proposal.'

Francine had started pacing again, her back to Marcus as she spoke, which was why she didn't realise he had moved until she felt his hand on her arm. When she turned automatically to face him he reached for her. His arms tightening around her, he bent his head to kiss her, fiercely, hungrily, as though he had missed her and ached for her every single minute they had been apart, just as she had for him.

For several precious heartbeats Francine gave herself up to his passion, sharing it, wanting it, registering that he was trembling beneath the force of it as much as she was herself, but then reality cut in, forcing her to step back from him.

'What is it?' he asked.

'We can't do this. It isn't right.'

'Because of Brandon? He wanted us to be together, he said so in his letter to me.'

'Exactly. Brandon wanted us to be together, but what about what you want? What I want?'

'I want you. I love you, Francine. I've never stopped loving you.'

'But you walked away from me. I called out to you but you ignored me.' The words were like sharp thorns stuck in her heart, a constant source of pain that had festered, poisoning her love for him. A private pain that she couldn't admit to him because doing so would make her so vulnerable to being hurt all over again. 'I believe you think that you do, but . . .'

'But you don't think I do?'

'You are an honourable man, Marcus. In making you a trustee of the foundation, Brandon has laid a claim that will make heavy demands on you. I can't influence any decisions you may make now or in the future about those demands, but I will not allow you to carry the additional burden of the responsibility for me and my happiness. I know that Brandon meant well, but I'm a woman, not a girl; an adult, not a child. I am the one who is responsible for my happiness. The last thing I want is for you to feel honour-bound to resurrect what you once felt for me for my sake.'

'There is no question of that. I've never stopped loving you.'

'You can say that, Marcus, but how can I know it? I can't, and I can't either spend the rest of my life wondering if you are with me out of pity and duty, or because you do genuinely love me. If Brandon has taught me one thing, it is the importance of integrity.'

'Very well then, tell me honestly what your feelings are for me.'

She should have anticipated that he would use her own weapon against her, Francine realised.

'I've changed from the person I was in Cairo,' she sidestepped the question. 'For me now love is only worthwhile, worth having, when it is mutual and shared, when it is given freely out of itself, not out of duty or as the payment for an imagined debt, and when I know beyond any doubt that it is all of those things. You say you love me, Marcus, but the truth is that what lies behind us has left me too afraid to believe you. Call me a coward if you wish but I would rather not have what you call your love than risk finding out when it is too late that it is not love at all.'

Her words, spiked with her pain, seemed to hang on the air between them. Marcus frowned and looked away from her. He was going to admit that she was right and that his claim to still love her was motivated by guilt and duty. What she was feeling wasn't pain; she wasn't going to allow herself to feel any more of that. It was—

'No!'

The harshness of Marcus's denial caught her off guard drawing her gaze to him.

'I'm not giving you up, Francine,' he told her fiercely. 'Not this time. Somehow, no matter what it takes, or how long it takes, I shall find a way to convince you that I do love you.'

TWENTY

'All set, then?'

Lou nodded, her mouth too dry to allow her to speak as she gazed at the small two-seater plane on the runway. She'd been so excited that she'd hardly slept last night, in a fever of impatience and dread in case Verity changed her mind or couldn't make it, but now that she was here, dressed in her WAAF trousers, the flying jacket they were all issued with for once coming into its own, the helmet and goggles Verity had handed to her firmly in place, along with her parachute, Lou acknowledged that she felt almost as apprehensive as she was excited.

'Let's start her up and get going then, shall we?' Verity invited. Lou had sat in planes before, and not just sat in them but contorted herself to work on various bits of them, so she should have felt perfectly at home in the passenger seat of the small machine, but somehow it was different sitting here knowing that she was actually going to be flying from how it was working in the cockpit when the plane was on the ground.

'Ready?' Verity yelled above the noise of the

engine, starting to taxi down the runway without waiting for Lou to respond.

It was the most peculiar sensation Lou thought, as suddenly, without warning, the plane started to lift off the ground, the runway falling away beneath them. A feeling of exhilaration danced through her veins as she looked down at the countryside spread out beneath then, the base buildings, like models on a child's toy farm, set amongst higgledy-piggledy hedged fields of all shapes and sizes.

They were climbing higher, the sound of the engine changing, the pressure on Lou's ears reminding her to swallow.

Verity's 'You OK?' had Lou nodding in delighted response, although she clutched at the side of her seat when Verity dipped to one side, after levelling off at a thousand feet, taking them in a westerly direction.

'Look, there's the Atlantic,' she shouted to Lou above the engine noise.

The sea! How blue and pretty it looked beneath the sunny sky, the waves small dancing white crests.

'Pa gave me *Boadicea* here for my twenty-first birthday, and I adore her, but it is fun flying Lancasters and the like from the factories to their bases. Some of those poor RAF boys get so het up when they see a woman getting out of the cockpit. The girls in ATA, though, know what they're doing. We've even had some American fly girls joining us. I've filed our flight path as being to the aviation factory near Bristol and back, strictly speaking half an hour each way, and a straight flight, but how do you feel about a couple of victory rolls? Shall we give it a go?'

Lou dared to agree.

'Hold on then, here we go.'

The sensation of the plane rolling over whilst she hung upside down reminded Lou of childhood rides on a funfair, only, of course, this was far, far more exciting.

'Did you like that?' Verity asked, and when Lou gave her a thumbs-up she laughed and yelled, 'Good show. Let's do it again, shall we?'

Lou had never known an hour pass so quickly or so exhilaratingly. By the time Verity brought the little plane to a halt back at the base, Lou was so dizzy with excitement and victory rolls that she could hardly speak.

'Thank you. That was wonderful,' she said to Verity when they were both back on the ground beside the plane and Lou had handed the other girl her borrowed helmet and goggles.

'It was my pleasure,' Verity assured her. 'You're a natural, and if I was based here I wouldn't mind betting that I'd pretty soon be able to teach you to fly yourself. Pity you can't get one of the chaps to let you have a go.'

'There's no chance of that,' Lou sighed. 'It's a court-martialling offence for a Waaf if she tries.'

'Only if she gets found out,' was Verity's spirited response.

It was all very well for Verity to shrug off the thought of a court martial and to willingly break the rules, but it was different for girls like her, Lou acknowledged ruefully.

*   *   *

Bella's hands were shaking as she signed her name and then read carefully through what she had just written. It had been so hard to stop herself from saying all that she wanted to say, and she had had to stop several times to remind herself that her letter would pass through many hands and be seen by many pairs of eyes before it reached Jan in his German prison, via the Red Cross.

In the end she had simply written that she loved him and was thinking of him and that she would wait for him.

Dear heaven, but it was still so hard for her to let herself believe that he was actually alive. Bella didn't think she would believe it properly until she had had her first letter from him. Now more than ever she longed for the war to end. It was hard not to let her imagination run away with her, encouraging her to conjure up all manner of dreadful fates overtaking Jan, and to think instead of the war being over and him coming back to her. It was hard, but for Jan's sake she must do it.

'I'm sorry, Gina, but I can't make up a foursome this weekend. I've already arranged to meet someone – Luke's mother. Luke's sister is to receive a George Cross and the whole family are coming to London. Mind you, I don't think that Leonard will be in the least bit disappointed at the thought of having you to himself,' Katie told her friend with a smile.

'Well, perhaps not,' Gina agreed. 'I take it that there's nothing doing with you and Eddie?'

'No,' Katie confirmed. 'I like him as a friend.

He's good fun, but there's nothing more to it than that. To be honest I feel rather guilty about him spending his leave on me when he could be taking out girls whose company would probably be more to his taste.'

'Hmm, girls who don't know where to draw the line, I suppose you mean? Do you want me to tell Leonard and ask him to let him know?'

'If you wouldn't mind.'

Jean's letter had come as a bit of a shock to Katie, but it hadn't even for one minute occurred to her to refuse to see Luke's mother – quite the opposite. And somehow, even though Jean had written in her letter that she was sure 'that you will be as surprised as we were to learn that Lou is to be decorated,' Katie had not been totally surprised. There had always been that something about Lou that had made Katie feel that she was very courageous, and that she shared Luke's strength of character.

Jean had put in her letter that they would all be staying at the Savoy, thanks to Francine, and had suggested that Katie meet her there on Saturday 24 October, which was the day before the investiture.

Katie's heart had given a silly little leap of hope when she had first opened her mother's letter to find Jean's letter inside it. And of course it had been a foolish hope because if Luke had really wanted to tell her that he still loved her he would have written to tell her so himself, not asked his mother to write on his behalf.

Now, as much as she was looking forward to

seeing Jean and as delighted as she was for Lou, Katie was also painfully aware that being with Luke's mother could only remind her of everything that had happened and how much Luke had hurt her.

It would have been much better for her if she had been the kind of girl who could have got over her heartache with a fling with someone like Eddie, Katie admitted. Eddie was the perfect antidote for a broken heart, provided one was the kind of girl who believed that having fun was more important than sharing love. Sometimes Katie wished that she were that kind of girl, because London certainly abounded with opportunities to have that kind of fun, with so many young men in uniform heading for the capital to let off steam when they were on leave.

Con was in trouble. A hell of a lot of trouble. He paced his small office moodily. It had all started when Ricky had told him that his unit was being posted to Lincolnshire to work on a new American airbase that was being built there.

'So who's going to take over from you here in our partnership?' Con had asked him.

'No one.'

Con was taken aback, but before he had been able to say anything Ricky had informed him, 'Word's gone out round the camp that there's a rigged card game outfit in town, and the boys are being warned to keep away from you unless they want to lose their money. See, the thing is, Con, some of the boys are starting getting a bit hot under the collar about the fact that you always win and they always lose. I did warn you that you'd have to lose a few games and find a new face to teach your tricks to if we were going to keep the boys sweet.'

Ricky had said something to that effect but Con hadn't been about to share his forty per cent, or his sleight of hand expertise with anyone else, so he had ignored Ricky's warning.

After Ricky had gone Con had soon convinced himself that the American had been exaggerating, no doubt suffering from jealousy because he was being posted away from Liverpool and the gold mine he and Con had created together. Of course the Americans would still come. How could they not when he, Con, was going to the trouble of setting up a private members' club for them, not to mention the amount of money it had already cost him? Money that he could only recoup from future gambling wins.

Only they hadn't come, and now, several weeks down the line, Con was being pressed for money: first of all by the landlord of the run-down property just off Hope Street that Con had been having fitted out as a club when Ricky had given him his news; next, by the spivs he'd been dealing with. The one who'd supplied him with the Jaguar he'd been paying for in instalments had repossessed it, and another, whom he'd asked to source him the fabric for another new suit, had come over quite ugly when Con had told him that he hadn't got the money. Even worse, Con had got Ed Mulligan, who'd been as friendly as anything with him the last time Con had seen him, claiming that Con was in arrears with his protection money.

And if all that wasn't bad enough he'd even got Eva insisting that he'd promised to marry her, and throwing jealous tantrums every time he so much as looked at any of the girls, fingering that knife of hers, and telling him how she was going to stab him with it if she ever found him with another woman again. Looking at pretty girls had always been Con's major source of solace when times were bad, and now, thanks to Eva's jealousy – and his fear of her father's knife – he was even being deprived of that. God knows what Eva would do if she ever found out that he was already married.

He had to get his hands on some money, and fast, but how?

Abruptly Con stopped pacing. The answer to his problems had been staring him in the face! Emily. His wife. She had money and plenty of it. It was all wrong the way she'd taken herself off with that ruddy kid she'd taken in, leaving him, her husband, to fend for himself. Conveniently Con forgot how much having an absent wife had suited him.

Knowing Emily had the money he needed was one thing. Getting it out of her was another. He'd have to go and see her. Where was it she'd gone? Some place in Cheshire; he'd got the address she'd given him somewhere.

It wasn't in Con's nature to worry about anything for very long. Except perhaps now Eva's temper and her constant threats that she would use her father's knife against him.

TWENTY-ONE

They'd all known when Monty had arrived, and then Churchill, that something was brewing. Then the word had gone round that there was no way British soldiers were going to surrender or cross the Suez Canal. Then had come the preparation for a big offensive, using dummy models of tanks and trucks to deceive the enemy and move the men. Last night their battalion, like all the others, had received its full briefing and told what positions it had to take. As experienced desert fighters they had been given command of a strategic position – and the danger that went with it.

Now they'd got a ruddy full moon to deal with on top of ruddy Rommel and his tanks, Luke thought grimly as he went round speaking to his men, checking as he did so that they were well dug in to their positions, ready for what was to come. El Alamein it was called, this train stop in the desert that they'd been pushed back to and somehow hung on to, and from which they were now to mount a huge all-out assault on Rommel's forces.

The Royal Engineers had cleared the mines the

Germans had laid to allow the units to pass through and now all they had to do was wait.

Once he'd checked up on his men Luke crawled back to his own position, next to Andy.

'Gawd, I'd give anything for a fag,' Andy said.

'A fag, did you say, and or a shag?' one of the other men demanded with the bawdy licence of men at war.

'Doesn't matter much either way,' someone else chimed in, ''cos he won't be getting either.'

No sooner had he finished speaking than a huge barrage began lighting up the night sky with the flames from the specially placed burning petrol dumps littering the desert.

A lone Stuka dropped its bombs, clearly visible in the moonlit sky. And then it began: the work they had trained for. A skirl of bagpipes from the 51st Highland Division announced the commencement of the infantry's advance.

'Come on, men,' Luke ordered, and soon they too were moving forward at a steady seventy-five strides a minute, bayonets fixed, their task to clear the way for the waiting armoured divisions.

'The ruddy pipe's stopped playing,' Andy yelled in Luke's ear above the cacophony of war.

'Keep going,' Luke told him. He too had registered the burst of machine-gun fire that had silenced the piper's 'The Road to the Isles', but it didn't do to think of such things.

Katie spotted Jean the minute she walked into the elegant room where the Savoy served its afternoon teas. Her ex-landlady was sitting at a table on her own on the velvet-covered banquette facing the doorway. She was wearing what Katie knew to be her 'best' coat and she was sitting bolt upright, her 'good' leather handbag clasped tightly on her lap. She had obviously had her hair newly done for the trip to London and, standing observing Jean, a wave of love for her filled Katie, drowning out the discomfort she had been feeling on her way here.

Far more familiar with the Savoy than Jean could ever be, Katie felt no self-consciousness about being here. She had, after all, virtually grown up in the hotel, she had accompanied her father there so often. The refined upper-class voices of some of the women taking tea, the obviously expensive if somewhat war-worn clothes many of them were wearing, the preponderance of uniforms bristling with gold braid, high-status-officer pips and the like, couldn't daunt her or make her feel out of place. To Katie the Savoy was familiar territory, somewhere that she felt completely at home.

Unlike Jean, who Katie could see was looking uncomfortable and ill at ease. Another surge of emotion swept through her: tenderness, this time, for this woman who had welcomed her into her home and been so kind to her. Smiling, Katie hurried over to the table, her smile widening when she saw Jean's look of relief when she spotted her.

The two women hugged one another, and then Jean held Katie at arm's length as she looked at her for a moment before she released her so that they could both sit down.

'Grace and Seb have taken the others to Madame Tussauds. Lou and Bobby both wanted to go, although Sasha wasn't so keen. I said that I wanted to have a bit of a rest. We've done that much sight-seeing since we got here last night that I feel as though I've been walked off me feet. It's ever such a big place this, Katie. A boarding house would have suited us fine just as long as it was clean, but Francine said that she wanted to give us a bit of a treat. She's lost Brandon . . . not that it wasn't expected,' Jean added after Katie had immediately offered her sympathy.

'I'm ever so glad to see you, Katie. I think about you a lot.'

'I think about you too,' Katie told her truthfully.

They looked at one another.

'Have you ordered tea?' Katie asked her.

'No. There's that many people here, and the waiters seem that busy.'

Katie signalled to a passing waiter, who immediately came over to them.

'We'll have afternoon tea for two,' Katie told him, waiting until he had gone to tell Jean, 'And it's my treat.'

'Oh, Katie, I couldn't possibly let you pay, not at the prices they charge here.'

'Yes you can,' Katie told her firmly. 'Now tell me about Lou and her medal. I'm dying to hear all about it.'

Jean looked at her. 'Well, of course, I will tell you, but first there's something I want to say to you, Katie, and that's how sorry I am about you and our Luke. I couldn't imagine a girl better suited to him than you. There's certainly no girl I'd sooner welcome as my daughter-in-law.'

'Nor any family I'd more want to be a part of,' Katie admitted to her, 'but maybe that was part of what went wrong. Maybe I should have thought more about me and Luke getting on together and being a good match, and less about how much I wanted to be part of his family.'

Katie's admission had been hard for her to make. It had been only recently that she had started to question her motives in wanting to marry Luke, after Gina had been talking to her about her own relationship with Captain Towers, and saying how comfortable she felt with his family, and now important that was, but how easy it was to fall into the trap of loving a man because one loved his family.

Gina's comments had made Katie think more deeply about her feelings for Luke and his family, and to question whether she would have loved Luke so easily if she had not loved his family so much. And yet there were other times when she missed and ached for Luke himself so much that she could have sworn that she would have loved him for himself, no matter what his family were like.

'I dare say you've met plenty of good-looking young men here in London,' Jean probed.

Katie wasn't offended by Jean's question. She knew that it sprang from love – love for Luke her son, and love for Katie herself.

'Not really.'

'So you've not been seeing anyone then?'

'Well, there is someone,' Katie admitted, 'but he's just a pal really. My friend Gina is going out with his cousin so we double date when the men are on leave, from the navy.

'You must have been anxious about Luke, with him being out in the desert. I hope he's all right.'

'As far as we know. Although with all that you read in the papers about Rommel we can't help worrying. He hasn't written to you or anything then, since . . . well, since . . . ?'

'No, there hasn't been any reason for him to. Not really. I've wanted to write to you to ask how he is, but I didn't want anyone thinking . . . well, I didn't want Luke thinking, that I was making a nuisance of myself or anything.'

'Oh, Katie, you could never do that. I wanted to write to you but Sam didn't think that I should.'

'No . . . he's right. It wouldn't be fair to Luke. Tell me about Sasha. You haven't mentioned her yet. Is she still at the telephone exchange?'

'Yes, and Grace and Seb are still in Whitchurch.'

Jean picked up her cup and sipped at her tea, and then put it down again, her voice filled with emotion as she said, 'Oh, Katie love, I do so wish things had worked out better than this, and you and Luke were still engaged.'

Katie couldn't help it; her own eyes filled with tears as she shook her head and said quietly, 'So do I, but it isn't what Luke wishes or wants, and . . .'

'Oh, there now, I've gone and upset you.'

Jean looked and sounded so upset herself that Katie felt obliged to forced a smile and insist that she was all right.

*　　*　　*

314

It wasn't true, though. She wasn't all right, Katie admitted to herself later, after she and Jean had said goodbye and Katie was on her way back to Cadogan Place. She would have to find a way to make herself be, though, otherwise she was going to end up filled with self-pity, and be pitied by others as well, as a girl who hadn't got the backbone to get over a man who didn't want her. That certainly wasn't a picture of herself that Katie wanted to contemplate. Other girls went through the same kind of heartache, after all, and survived it. Some had to survive much worse, with the death of loved ones. Her heartache was nothing when compared with theirs.

What she ought to do was forget that Luke had ever existed or been a part of her life. And what was more, she should start doing it right from this minute. And she should start making a new life for herself as the Katie she now was, not the Katie who had been the fiancée of Luke Campion. She had both dreaded and wanted to see Jean, but now that she had done Katie realised that seeing herself through Jean's eyes, as someone to feel sorry for – and that was how Jean felt about her, no matter how much she genuinely cared about her – had given her a much-needed jolt. She hadn't liked knowing that Jean, and no doubt the rest of the Campion family, felt sorry for her; she hadn't liked it one little bit. If she wanted others to stop feeling sorry for her then the first thing she had to do was stop feeling sorry for herself, Katie told herself firmly.

TWENTY-TWO

Lou felt dreadfully nervous. She was sure her hands were sweating, but she didn't dare try even surreptitiously to wipe her palms on the side of her uniform skirt, not with so many steely official gazes fixed on the line-up of those King George was going to honour.

She was well forward in the queue, which was something of a relief. She would have hated to have been the first, but neither would she have wanted the long wait that would come with being at the tail end.

She had hardly slept, despite the wonderful comfort of the bed in the Savoy's bedroom she had shared with Sasha, and it hadn't really helped when both her mother and her sister Grace had told her over breakfast that they hadn't slept either.

She was glad that her family were here to see her receive her medal from the King, of course, but at the same time she also felt worried in case she muffed something and let them down.

She had said as much to Sasha this morning when they had been alone together in their room,

316

but Sasha hadn't seemed to understand. Instead she had shrugged and told Lou sharply, 'Well, I don't see why you're worrying. After all, all you have to do is walk up to the King when you're told to, and then walk away when he's given you the medal.'

It wasn't quite as simple as that, though. For one thing, she had to bob a curtsy and then salute, even though she wasn't receiving an exclusively military medal, because she would still be in uniform.

It had been Grace who had understood and helped her the most, taking her back to her and Seb's room after breakfast, so that Seb, a flight lieutenant now in the RAF, could run a military eye over her uniform and generally put her through her paces, whilst Grace's calm presence had helped to steady her.

Even though she had been told what to expect, nothing had really prepared her for the way she had felt when they had arrived at Buckingham Palace. Whilst her family had been taken to join the other guests, Lou had been escorted to a vast room with a high ceiling, all ornately plastered, the room filled with officials and also people who were going to receive medals, most of them wearing the uniforms of the mainly non-military war service they were with. There were nurses and firemen, WVS, ARP officials, and even a young messenger, along with a handful of people, like her, from the armed forces. A smart-looking Wren of around her own age was standing on her own, but when Lou looked across at her she lifted her nose in the air and turned away. Lou sighed. Everyone knew that the Wrens considered themselves to be a cut above everyone else. They certainly had the smartest uniform.

Not that any of the uniforms worn by those there to receive their medals could compare to the magnificence of the dress uniforms worn by those members of the Household Cavalry, who had been on duty when they had arrived, or the guards outside the palace, in their red jackets and their bearskin helmets.

Young Guards officers, in scarlet jackets heavily laden with gold braid, dress swords at their side, looking vastly different from the men Lou was used to seeing in their army khaki, or their RAF or navy blues, stood out from everyone else.

The closed double doors opened to admit what Lou heard someone close to her saying was an 'equerry'. Excitement and anxiety fizzed inside her tummy. Seb had told her that the equerries were sort of like sergeants looking after the King. A buzz of expectation followed by the silence of tension gripped the room.

Busy officials started to organise the formal presentation line. Lou's throat went dry.

'It shouldn't be long now,' Seb told Sam quietly. Sam was very much the head of his family and Seb certainly didn't want to seem to be usurping his authority, but as he and Grace had agreed last night in the privacy of their bedroom, her parents weren't accustomed to either London or the formality of this kind of occasion, so it made sense for Seb tactfully to do what he could to make the day go smoothly for them all.

He had certainly succeeded in getting them a front-line view of the proceedings, but that, as he had told Sam, was merely down to his uniform and the fact that he and Lou were both RAF.

They'd been entertained by a military band whilst they waited outside for the King to arrive and the presentation to begin, but Seb suspected that neither of Lou's parents had been able to give much attention to the jolly martial music being played.

Grace felt so proud. Doubly proud, in fact: proud of her sister Lou, who was here to receive her medal, and proud too of Seb, who had so calmly stepped in and taken charge after their arrival in London, when it had become obvious how out of their depth her parents felt.

Of course she'd done her bit as well. After all, she'd been to London before. She and Seb had spent their short honeymoon in the city, and so when she'd seen that her mother was looking a bit overwhelmed by the luxury of the Savoy, the size of the city, and the realisation of just what an honour Lou was receiving and how grand the investiture was going to be, she'd suggested that she and Seb took everyone to see some of the city's most famous sights.

What she hadn't expected was that both Bobby and her father would want to visit Madame Tussauds Waxworks more than they wanted to see anything else. However, when Sasha had insisted that she wanted to go as well, Grace had given in and agreed that she and Seb would go with them, even though in reality Grace would much rather have stayed with her mother, who had flatly refused to go.

It was like she'd said to Seb once they were on their own, she loved her parents dearly, but they had never been out of Liverpool in their lives. It was different for her and Seb. The war was sending people all over the place, and Grace had felt both protective of her parents and just a little bit superior to them with her own knowledge of the capital and the confidence that being a nurse had given her. She and Seb had agreed that they must quietly and tactfully take charge of the family whilst they were here in London. She was so proud of Seb for the way he had managed things without in any way taking anything away from her father. She had seen too the grateful look her dad had given Seb when he had explained one or two things to him about how the investiture was likely to be organised.

'If anyone should be getting a medal it should be people like you,' Sasha hissed indignantly to Bobby as they stood together, Sasha at her mother's side, and Bobby next to her, whilst her father stood next to her mother, with Seb and Grace next to him. 'You're in danger all the time, and you saved my life.'

'Most bomb disposal sappers don't live long enough to get medals,' Bobby responded flippantly, and then wished he hadn't when he saw how upset Sasha looked.

'Well, it's more like some of them,' he amended

quickly, 'and only them as get a bit too cocky, I reckon, and don't watch what they're doing.'

'Bobby, I do wish you were doing something else. Bomb disposal is so dangerous.' Sasha forgot how irritated she had felt this morning with Lou, and all the fuss that was being made of her, in her anxiety for Bobby. She was proud of the work Bobby did, of course she was, and that was how she'd met him, after all, when he'd saved her life, but she hadn't realised then how dangerous that work was and how many men died doing it.

'You could ask for a transfer, couldn't you?'

'Not really. It's only the married men that generally get transferred out, and then there's often a long waiting list. And anyway, I like what I do, Sasha. Digging out bombs and making them safe, it makes me feel good inside, like every bomb is a bit of Hitler lying there waiting to hurt people, and when we stop it from doing that, it's like we've given old Hitler a poke in the eye.'

'I thought you said you loved me,' Sasha told him emotionally.

'I do.'

'Then you should want to be safe so that I don't have to worry about you.' Sasha was close to tears.

'See here, Sasha,' he told her lovingly. 'You don't have to worry about me, 'cos I was born lucky, I was. Look at how I met you. The best bit of luck I've ever had, that was, and no mistake. We've all got to do our bit, you know, and I dare say you wouldn't think much of me as a man if I refused to put myself in a bit of danger every now and again.'

Sasha wanted to continue their discussion but Grace was leaning across their parents towards her, saying warningly, 'Seb says that the ceremony's about to start any minute now.'

'Oh, look, Sam, there's our Lou, third from the front,' Jean whispered tearfully to her husband as those who were to receive medals came marching out of the palace to form neat lines under the eagle eye of what Seb told them was a regimental sergeant major.

'Oh, Seb, it really is the King,' Grace gasped, her eyes bright with pride and excitement as all those present in uniform, including Seb himself, stood to attention to salute King George as he and the Queen took their places ready to receive those about to be medalled.

It was a cool October day with a brisk wind, but no one in the courtyard seemed in the least bit concerned about the weather.

When the first two recipients had been called up to receive their honours, their medals pinned on and their hands shaken by the King, it was Lou's turn.

'Leading Aircraftwoman Campion.' The stentorian voice of the official bounced round the courtyard.

She mustn't think about anything else other than remembering she was a Waaf, and that she mustn't let the side down, Lou told herself as she began to march toward the dais, shoulders straight, gaze fixed, her head turned toward the dais as she drew level with it, ready to salute and then stand firmly to attention in front of the King and Queen, and the Princess Elizabeth, who smiled directly at her.

There was just time for Lou to manage the small half-bobbed curtsy she had been taught and then the King was taking the Cross from the velvet cushion held by the official standing next to it, and saying in a kind voice to her, 'Very well done indeed,' as he handed the medal to her.

Then she was saluting again and stepping back before executing a neat turn and marching off to join the two who had been medalled ahead of her.

No sooner had she joined them than. Lou's tummy began to rumble with hunger, reminding her that she had not been able to eat any breakfast. Such a waste, as well, when they were staying at the Savoy.

At last all the formalities were over and those who had been medalled were mingling with their families, whilst a military band played rousing music.

As Jean said to Sam later, when they were in their room getting ready to go to see the show Francine had got them tickets for, the best bit of the whole day for her – apart, of course, from seeing her daughter being presented with her medal by the King himself – had been when an RAF officer, a general, no less, Seb had told them, had come over to shake Lou's hand. Lou had saluted him ever so smartly and quickly, and the general had said to Jean and Sam that they must be very proud of her and that the RAF certainly were.

Then, as though that hadn't been enough, it had only turned out that the general was related to the pilot whose life Lou had saved.

TWENTY-THREE

The thing is, well, there's just no easy way to tell you this, but the truth is that I've met someone else. I know you'll think badly of me for telling you whilst you're so far away, in the desert, but I couldn't live with myself if I wasn't honest with you. Anyway, I dare say you'll soon find someone else. From what I've heard there's plenty of girls only too ready to throw themselves at a chap in uniform.

Katie put down the letter she was reading, her heart heavy with a mixture of discomfort and sadness. She knew that censoring the mail was important and necessary, but sometimes when she had to read letters like this one from a girl to her young man telling him that she'd found someone else, Katie's own tender heart ached for the recipient.

Perhaps it was those words 'in the desert' that had made this letter touch home so much for her, but hadn't she vowed that she would forget about her own past, she reminded herself as she neatly crossed out the reference to the desert.

'Katie, might I have a word?' The voice of her supervisor brought Katie's head up.

'It's a private matter really,' her supervisor told her as she drew Katie to one side of the space between aisles of desks.

'In my role as the Chair of my local WVS Committee I've been approached by the American Red Cross to see if I can help find them some suitable young women to work as volunteers in various clubs they are setting up here in London to provide suitable recreational facilities for American servicemen.

'They have made it clear that they only want young women who can be vouched for as both capable of doing the work they will be called upon to do, and who can be trusted to behave sensibly in the company of young men.' She paused and looked at Katie, giving her a small smile.

'I must confess that I thought immediately of you, Katie, and if you would be prepared to take on this voluntary work you would be such a credit to me, I know. However, if you feel that you would rather not then of course I understand. It is a lot to ask, especially if you have a special young man in your life who might not approve of his girl mingling with so many young men, however properly chaperoned and respectable those meetings might be.'

Katie's initial response, which had been to shrink from what her supervisor was asking – she had never been very much of a party girl – had given way to a certain curiosity as her supervisor continued to explain.

'I'm not involved with anyone,' Katie admitted, 'but I'm not sure . . .'

'Quite naturally, you're worried about the respectability of the situation,' her supervisor guessed. 'My dear, I promise you you need not be. My contact in the American Red Cross was at great pains to tell me that they only intend to take on British girls who have been recommended and then thoroughly vetted. The club you'd be based at would be what is going to be called the Rainbow Corner. It's where the Del Monico restaurant was on the corner of Shaftesbury Avenue and Piccadilly. The British Government has commandeered the Del Monico and part of Lyons Corner House, and the American Red Cross is planning to create a 'little America' there for homesick GIs. It's due to open in November, and only a very high calibre of young woman will be allowed to work there. The American Red Cross will run the club, of course, but they will need to take on some British staff and they do want some volunteers as well.'

'Well, I'd like to help,' Katie heard herself say, 'but I'm not sure that I'll be suitable. What will I have to do?'

'You'll receive all the training you'll need from the American Red Cross ladies in charge of the club. As I understand it, it will be a matter of filling various voluntary roles, such as answering questions about this country, helping American GIs to find their way around the city, perhaps offering a feminine ear to listen to their concerns about loved ones left at home. If you would agree you would be doing me an enormous favour.'

'Well, I'm not sure that they will want me, but I'm willing to offer to help,' Katie told her supervisor.

'Bless you, my dear. I knew I could rely on you.' Her supervisor beamed. 'I shall take you along and introduce you myself. Would tomorrow evening be convenient for you? We could have a bite at Joe Lyons after work first and then go along to the club?'

Katie agreed.

The battle had been raging for ten days, relentless and bloody, and now the infantry were attacking the German lines inland under cover of darkness.

'Come on,' Luke ordered his men when he saw the signal from their officer to crawl to their forward positions.

No sooner had they got there than a burst of gunfire from a German position had Luke cursing and telling his men to keep their heads down, as they positioned their Vickers water-cooled machine gun so that they could return the German fire.

All around them were the sounds and sights of bloody warfare, but Luke was too busy watching his men and the German gunfire to have time to be aware of anything else.

Bursts of gun shots from the German position, from what Luke guessed was an 8mm gun, had him focusing on directing their own fire in retallation.

'I think we got them this time, Corp,' one of the men sang out, as he raised his head when the German gun remained silent.

'Get down, you bloody fool, he's probably holding his fire,' Luke warned him, flinging himself down bodily on top of the younger man when his warning was proved correct and a burst of machine-gun fire exploded over them.

Luke felt the pain rip into his leg, a red-hot black hell of agony, accompanied by the sound of Andy yelling and cursing and then silence, a thick dark blank nothing.

'The corp's been wounded,' Andy yelled. 'We need to get him to a field hospital.'

The pain was everywhere: inside him, outside him, all around him, gripping him, tightening its hold on him, searing and savaging him.

Someone was looming over him – a nurse. His sister Grace was a nurse. He tried to say her name but inexplicably instead he said someone else's.

'Katie.'

'He's trying to say something,' the nurse at the casualty clearing station told the sister.

The sister gave Luke a quick glance. The field hospital was filled with wounded men, some on their own two feet or supported by a comrade, others – the worst cases, like Luke – on stretchers.

'Probably the name of his girl,' the sister responded. 'It's either that, or their mother, or God.' She looked up as the doctor reached Luke.

'Sharpnel wounds, right hip and buttock,' the doctor announced. 'He'll need operating on as soon as possible.' Nodding her head, the sister waited for the doctor to write a docket to attach to Luke.

*   *   *

'So who is this Katie you keep asking for then? Your girl, is she?' the nurse whose job it was to try to keep Luke conscious, the better to preserve his chances of survival, asked persistently, as she checked Luke's wounds, a really bad one to his hip that would mean it would be touch and go whether or not he would live.

All Luke wanted was to be left alone so that he could escape to that deep dark place of nothing, but the nurse wouldn't let him. She kept on asking him questions about Katie. Katie, who he didn't want to think about.

'She was my girl but she isn't any more,' he answered the nurse.

'Broke things off, did she? Well, more fool her,' the nurse offered comfortingly. It was an automatic response. She'd long ago lost count of the number of wounded men whose girls had let them down. It made her feel ashamed of her own sex at times, it really did.

'No. It was me that broke off our engagement,' Luke told her, his voice strengthening with harshness.

The nurse looked down the line of injured men. The doctor was still some distance away. Luke's pulse, which had begun to grow fainter and too fast as the shock from his wound set in, had steadied and strengthened as he talked. Best keep him talking then, the nurse decided.

'So why did you do that then?' she asked Luke, keeping one eye on him and the other on the doctor working his way along the line of waiting wounded.

'I had a letter, sent anonymously to me, telling me that she'd been cheating on me.'

The nurse's concentration flickered briefly from Luke's pulse to what he was telling her.

'And she said it was true, did she, your girl?'

'I didn't ask her,' Luke said curtly.

The doctor was taking a long time. Blood from Luke's wound was seeping through his bandage. The nurse wondered whether she ought to leave him and go and get Sister, but she'd been told to stay with him and to keep him alert until the doctor had seen him.

'Well, I wouldn't have thought much of that kind of behaviour if I'd been your girl,' she told Luke frankly. 'Breaking an engagement without even giving me a chance to defend myself, and all on account of an anonymous letter. That's not very fair, is it? I reckon if someone was to write to me and tell me that my chap was seeing another girl, and without telling me who the writer was, the first thing I'd want to do was find out the truth from my chap. Sending anonymous letters is what troublemakers do, not real friends. At least that's how I see it.'

The doctor was still three beds away and her patient had gone worryingly quiet and still. She must not let him slip into unconsciousness. That was one of the hardest things to stop the badly wounded from doing, and from unconsciousness it was a much smaller step to death.

His eyes were still open, though, and he was listening to her even if he wasn't speaking. She had to keep him listening and concentrating. The truth was, though, that her sympathy now lay with his girl and not with him. You wouldn't catch her letting someone else tell tales to her about her own chap and her not bothering to find out if they were true. The blood stain on the bandage was still spreading, and his eyelids were dropping over his eyes.

The nurse sucked in her breath and, ignoring her conscience, announced sharply, 'Mind you, it strikes me that you couldn't have loved her very much in the first place.'

Ah, that had done it. The eyelids lifted, the blue eyes blazing with emotion.

'Of course I loved her.'

'Well, you've a funny way of showing it, that's all I can say, 'cos it seems to me that you were pretty keen to believe she'd done wrong, and that's not loving someone, is it?'

All Luke wanted to do was close his eyes and escape – from all his pain, both physical and emotional, but the nurse wouldn't let him. She kept going on about Katie, like sticking something sharp into an open wound and causing the same grinding throbbing pain in his heart that he could feel in his body. And yet despite his righteous anger there was something nagging at him, and, like desert sand on the skin, it was rubbing a sore place on his conscience, and worse, causing him to suffer a savage stab of regret. He had done the right thing, he told himself stubbornly, the only thing a man could do if he wanted to respect himself. Better by far to have ended it when he had than to have gone home and found that the whole of Liverpool knew that Katie was playing him false.

Not much longer, the nurse recognised with relief. The doctor was only a bed away now, examining a man whose face was heavily bandaged. Poor soul, head wounds were often the hardest to deal with.

She looked at Luke, about to tell him that he was next, when he surprised her by bursting out, 'I had to do it. Katie might have sworn that she loved me and she always would, but how could I believe that? How could I trust her when I'm not there with her?'

The nurse frowned. 'Same way as she has to trust you, of course. When you love someone you give them your trust, don't you? Just as they give you theirs. That's what loving someone is all about, I reckon. That and not letting other people meddle in what should be just between the two of you. You know what I reckon? I reckon this letter you got was written by someone who's got it in for your girl. Either that or it's a woman who's got her own eye on you. Either way, if I was your Katie I'd be thinking I'd had a good escape, 'cos no girl wants a chap who thinks more of his own pride than he does of loving her.'

'Right, Nurse, what have we got here then?'

The doctor had finally arrived. He might have been on duty since before the battle for El Alamein had started, but there was no sign of that as he started to examine Luke.

TWENTY-FOUR

Christmas Eve, and Emily hummed happily under her breath as she walked home after delivering the last of the Christmas cards she and Tommy had made together.

She left Tommy at home under Wilhelm's watchful eye. She didn't want Tommy going and finding those binoculars she had managed to buy second-hand and that she'd got hidden away in Wilhelm's shed. She'd had to do a fair bit of hard bartering to get them, and no mistake, but she'd managed in the end. Mad at discovering more about nature and birds and that, Tommy was, and learning the names of everything.

It was going to be a lovely Christmas, it really was. Emily's breath turned to white vapour in the cold air as she exhaled in happy excitement.

When she'd heard the vicar saying during his sermon a few weeks back about it being Christian for people to befriend POWs and invite them into their homes for Christmas, she hadn't wasted any time in having a word with Wilhelm, first to see if he wanted to have his Christmas dinner with them, and then when he'd said that he did, she'd got in touch with the farmer whose land the POWs worked, to tell him what she wanted to do, and he'd got in touch with the Camp and now it was all official and settled that Wilhelm would come back with her and Tommy after church on Christmas morning to have his dinner with them, and that he'd be picked up by the camp transport on Boxing Day to be taken back.

Of course, Emily had made sure her neighbours knew about her plans, and she'd invited them round for a bit of something on Christmas Day evening. It wouldn't do to set tongues wagging – not that there was any cause for them to do so.

After that thrilling declaration Wilhelm had made to her back in the summer, neither of them had referred to their feelings for one another again, and nor had they displayed them. It was enough that they both knew how they felt. Wilhelm was a true gentleman, very proper and correct. There'd be no crossing over any lines with him, and Emily liked that about him. It showed proper respect for her.

When the time came for things to be different – after the war was over – then they *would* be different, but right now it was enough for them both to sit opposite one another either side of the warm Aga in the kitchen, on those days when Wilhelm came round to work on the vegetable plot, drinking their tea in a shared companionable silence, occasionally smiling at one another, whilst they listened to the radio, Wilhelm warming his feet by the Aga, her doing a bit of mending, the two of them content in one another's company.

Wilhelm, bless him, like the kind person he was, had offered her his rations to help with the Christmas dinner, but Emily had been scandalised at the thought of taking his food, although she knew of plenty who were doing exactly that to some POWs under the guise of 'welcoming them into their homes'. Mind, she didn't want to be uncharitable. It was easy enough for her to refuse, after all, when she had a larder full of bottled fruit and chutneys and the like, thanks to Wilhelm's good husbandry, a lovely fat goose to roast, thanks to the farmer, and even some home-made sloe gin, thanks to her neighbour's recipe. Yes, it was going to be a lovely Christmas, at least for her – although of course there was still a war on. And for all that the bells had rung out in November to mark the British victory at El Alamein there'd be a lot of families mourning loved ones lost in that desert battle.

Con glowered as he stared up at the house in front of him. Ruddy Whitchurch. What the hell had Emily wanted, coming out here? He hated the country, and right now he wasn't feeling very warm towards Emily either, with all the trouble she'd caused him taking herself off and leaving him high and dry in Liverpool. As always when it suited him to do so, Con conveniently ignored the many advantages he'd been enjoying as a married man whose wife was 'elsewhere' in favour of feeling sorry for himself because he no longer had easy access to Emily's money. And right now money was of prime importance to Con, which was why he'd had to come all the way out here on a ruddy unheated slow-moving train, just so that he could sweet-talk the wife who should have been close at hand in Liverpool when he needed her – or rather when he needed her money – into giving him what should have been his anyway. He'd had a hell of a time dodging his creditors, and dodging Eva as well, who thought he'd gone to visit a sick elderly relative. None of the mess he was in now would have happened if Emily had behaved as a wife should behave and had stayed in Liverpool. He intended to make sure that she understood just how badly she'd let him down, and what he expected her to do to recompense him. She'd always been a soft touch, and Con reckoned he could easily get five hundred pounds out of her.

Con opened the gate and went up to the front door.

Christmas Eve. How different everything was this year, Jean reflected soberly, as she stood at her kitchen sink peeling the potatoes for the family's Christmas dinner.

For one thing, there'd be no Lou, because she hadn't got leave, and there was certainly no chance of Luke coming home to surprise them as he had the first Christmas of the war.

Jean's busy hands stilled.

Her heart still lurched into her ribs every time she thought about the morning the telegram had coming telling them that Luke had been wounded in action.

She'd stood here in the kitchen, on her own,

with Sam and Sasha both at work and Grace and Lou miles away, her heart thudding with sick fear, hardly able to see the words for her tears. It hurt her to think now that at the very moment she and Sam had been marvelling at the bright uniforms of the military band and enjoying being at Buckingham Palace, Luke had been fighting the enemy. Of course, no one had known then that Monty had given the order for the assault against Rommel to begin except those who needed to know, but nevertheless it hurt Jean to think that she hadn't somehow sensed that Luke was in danger.

That morning when the telegram had come, though, all she'd been able to think was that wounded in action could mean so many things. It could mean that Luke was injured and recovering, or it could mean that he was injured and dying, and she, his mother, had no means of knowing which it did mean.

In the end she'd done something she wasn't at all proud of. She'd put on her hat and coat and she'd walked as fast as she could to the telephone exchange, where Sasha worked, where she'd asked if she could have a word with her daughter 'on a matter of urgent family business'.

When Sasha had been released from her work to talk to her, her daughter hadn't looked at all pleased and her first words to her had been, 'Mum, if you've come to tell me that Lou's getting another medal, then you needn't have bothered.'

But her manner had changed completely when Jean had shown her the telegram, and she'd willingly put through a telephone call to the hospital in Whitchurch where Grace worked, so that Jean could tell her eldest daughter what had happened and ask her if there was any way that Seb could find out anything more.

Seb had done his best, but what a relief it had been when Luke's letter had arrived, explaining to them what had happened and how he had been on board a hospital ship off Alexandria, having had an operation to 'sort him out', as he had put it, but was now on his way to South Africa, where he would remain until he was considered fit to return to duty. He wrote,

I've been very lucky. The doc told me that the bullet only just missed an artery and although they weren't able to get all the shrapnel out of me in one go, when the original wound became infected they realised there must be some left and they opened me up again and found it, and just in time, otherwise they might have had to amputate. Now they say that I'm going to make a full recovery and that I'll be back in uniform by the spring.

Back in uniform, but not back here in Liverpool, where Jean could see him and hold him, and assure herself that he was as whole and well as he said.

Christmas Eve, and Rainbow Corner was frantically busy. So busy, in fact, that Katie had been asked if she could possibly work over Christmas and New Year. She'd agreed with an enthusiasm she

338

would never have expected herself to feel on that first dank November evening when she'd walked uncertainly into the building, accompanied by her supervisor, to be interviewed by a somewhat intimidating American Red Cross official who had made her feel as though she would never quite be good enough to mix with their GI customers.

Once she had started her voluntary work, though, Katie had discovered that Carla Wannafeld's bark was much worse than her bite and, rather shamefully, that the American had good reason to suspect the motives of some of the British girls who were so ready to welcome the American military.

'Homely' pursuits were not exactly what members of the so-called Piccadilly Commandos, those women who hung around Piccadilly eager to entice GIs to part with their money in return for 'sexual favours', had in mind when they approached American men on leave, and Katie could quite understand why the American Red Cross ladies, on behalf of the mothers, wives and girlfriends 'back home' would want to vet any young woman coming into contact with their men.

For some girls the embargo on those who worked at Rainbow Corner 'dating' its customers might prove onerous, but for Katie it was a bonus.

One of Katie's main jobs was to be on hand to answer the GIs' many questions, which ranged from advice as to what shows to see, to enquiries about the denominations of English money, and covered everything in between. Katie had got used now to the arrows in the lobby – one pointing to

Leicester Square, one to Berlin, and a third to New York, just as she had got used to American accents, the smell of donuts and hot coffee, hamburgers, hash browns, waffles and sodas, and the juke box pumping out favourite American songs.

The Rainbow was designed to be a real home from home for Americans, where they could get a haircut, a shoe shine, a bed to sleep off a heavy night, and where they could play pool, watch a boxing match or teach willing British partners how to jitterbug at the Rainbow's five-nights-a-week dances. As Katie loved to dance, partnering young Americans in the kind of energetic dancing they favoured was fun, but far and away her favourite job was sitting downstairs close to the coffee bar, helping Irene Whittaker in her self-imposed task of providing an instant sewing and darning service.

As Irene had warned Katie the first time she had sat down to help her, as much as anything else, the young men who came to their table to have tears mended, socks darned or stripes and insignia stitched on, wanted someone they could talk to just as they might have talked to their mothers and their sisters at home whilst they were engaged in the same homely task. That was the part of her voluntary work that Katie most enjoyed: listening to the young men who sat beside her whilst she worked on the sewing task they had handed her, telling her about their home lives and those they had left behind, unburdening themselves to her in the safe privacy of the calm environment Katie created around herself, whilst she put in the occasional encouraging word where required.

It was amazing the number of young men who came back to her to tell her how much they had appreciated her 'advice', when all she had actually done was listen to them. Without her planning for it to happen, Rainbow Corner was, Katie recognised, becoming the antidote to her own pain. She had lost count of the number of requests she had had to 'save a dance for me won't you, honey' for the New Year's Eve dance, or how many gifts of sweets, cigarettes and stockings she had been offered and firmly turned away.

The New Year would soon be with them, and Katie was going to step into it with a determination to make a fresh start.

'Got a minute, Campion?'

The sound of Verity Maitland's voice had Lou straightening up from the engine on which she had been working and climbing out of the cockpit of the Lancaster. She stepped out of the hangar and into the afternoon daylight, shielding her eyes from the sun as she did so.

She'd seen Verity Maitland on several occasions since her first visit, although normally the ATA pilot only had time for a passing nod of recognition on her way to either deliver or pick up new aircraft.

Verity tugged the strap of her helmet free and sighed with relief as she let it drop to the floor along with her leather gauntlets.

'Beastly things, and so damned ugly.'

She was wearing the same RAF-issue leather flying jacket that the RAF pilots wore, and looked enviably dashing, Lou thought, glancing down at her own oil-stained, slightly oversized overalls.

'Thought I should let you know that if you're still interested in flying, ATA is recruiting for pilots,' Verity told Lou once she had offered Lou a cigarette, which she refused, and then took herself one. As always, Verity's nails were painted a glamorous shade of red. Lou felt like hiding her own hands, which were stained with engine oil.

'With Bomber Command and all the fighter units at full stretch, we're having to transport more and more planes, and further afield,' Verity continued, before drawing on her cigarette and then exhaling.

Lou's heart, which had soared with excitement, dropped back against her ribs with sickening disappointment as she remembered a few realities.

'ATA only take girls with flying experience and I haven't got any.'

'That was the case,' Verity agreed, 'but now there's been a rethink from on high. We're training girls up from scratch, and the WAAF is one of the places where we looking for them. But of course the girls most likely to get onto the training courses are those who are recommended because they show promise or already have some of the skills that are needed.' Verity stubbed out her half-smoked cigarette and announced, 'If you were to be interested then I'm prepared to recommend you.'

If she was interested? Lou felt as though she'd just been handed the very best Christmas present in the whole world.

'It would be a dream come true for me,'

she admitted, not sure if she was shivering slightly because she was excited or because of the cold sharp wind whistling round the corner of the hangar.

'Well, though I'd stop off here on my way home for Christmas and see if you wanted the chance to apply. After all, if it wasn't for you, my bro certainly wouldn't be sitting down to Christmas dinner with the family tomorrow. I can't promise anything, mind, but it never hurts to put a few words in the right ears, and as a family we certainly owe you that.'

Verity was already pulling her leather helmet back on over her curls and picking up her gauntlets, obviously getting ready to leave.

Lou was torn between feeling proud and listening to her conscience, and in the end her conscience won.

'I wouldn't want to be put forward for something I'm not up to,' she felt obliged to say.

'There's no question of that,' Verity assured her. 'We always need good flight engineers, so if for some reason we can't get you on board as a trainee pilot then we could think about getting you drafted over to us as an engineer. If we could get you based at White Waltham, for instance, then we could start you off with a few unofficial flying lessons and then get you transferred onto a proper training course. You'd be better off based there, or at Barton-le-Clay near Luton, for that matter, because that's where they do the training courses. I dare you'll have picked up a few tips from working here?'

Lou could only agree. It was true, after all. She had learned a lot from watching the flying instructors in training being put through their paces, ready to train up the RAF's new pilots.

'So what do you say?' Verity asked. 'Do you want me to put your name forward?'

'Oh, yes please.'

'Good-oh. I'll drop a word in the right ears and get things started. Should warn you, though, that you'll probably come up against a good deal of flak from some of the RAF flight crews. Most of them are decent sorts, but you do get some that don't think women should fly planes.'

Long after Verity's plane had disappeared, and she was back in the hangar working on the Lancaster, Lou was still lost in bemused disbelief. She was going to get the chance to become a pilot. If Sasha had been here then the very best way Lou could have shown how she was feeling would have been for the two or them to burst into one of their favourite energetic jitterbug dance routines to celebrate. But Sasha wasn't here, and even if she had been Sasha wouldn't have understood how Lou felt, and nor probably would her family, Lou reminded herself, especially her mother, who would worry and imagine all sorts of terrible fates overcoming her.

It was sometimes difficult to deal with what war did to relationships, Lou acknowledged. She longed to share her exciting news with those closest to her – her family – but she knew already that she wouldn't in order to protect them.

*   *   *

The last thing on Emily's mind as she opened her back door was Con, her estranged husband, and the marriage that had brought her so much heartache and humiliation. But Con was the first person she saw as she stepped into her kitchen. There he was, as large as life, taking all the heat from the Aga as he stood in front of it whilst Wilhelm and Tommy stood together to one side of him, Wilhelm's hand resting protectively on Tommy's shoulder.

The blood came and went in Emily's face, registering her shock at Con's unexpected and most definitely unwanted presence.

Con was equally surprised by Emily, although for a different reason. The wife he had despised and mocked so much had been transformed in the time they had been apart into a slender not half bad-looking woman, he realised. Con, who had been passing the time whilst he waited for Emily to return imagining how easy it was going to be to sweet-talk her into doing what he wanted, was taken aback to see the way that she looked at the German POW. Con knew exactly what that kind of soft-eyed tender look from a woman to a man meant. He'd been on the receiving end of enough of them from a wide variety of women over the years, after all.

He was taken aback and not at all pleased. So that was the way the wind was blowing, was it? Well, if some ruddy POW thought he was going to step in and get what was rightfully Con's he was going to learn his mistake and so was Emily. Con judged all men by his own standards, and he knew there was only one thing that he'd have been going round to a woman's house for: cosying up to her. It was obvious to him that the ruddy German POW had been sniffing around Emily, and Emily, of course, was daft enough to be taken in by him. Well, she could have her POW if she wanted, and her kid, but she was going to have to pay for having them, Con decided grimly. And the five hundred pounds he intended to get off her now would only be the start of it; enough to get Ed Mulligan and the rest off his back, and give him a bit of breathing space. Con reckoned that the best thing he could do would be to have a fresh start – in London, perhaps – but fresh starts took planning, and money.

'Well, here's a fine thing. I come all this way to visit my wife and I find she's got a ruddy German POW making himself at home,' Con accused Emily grimly, ignoring the fact that she was still holding her shopping, so that it was Tommy who came to help her, relieving her of the heavy bags.

Emily felt too mortified to look at Wilhelm, far more concerned about his reaction to Con than she was about Con's to him.

Normally Wilhelm would have taken the shopping from her, but with Con being here he'd naturally hold back, expecting her husband to help her. Some hope of that, Emily thought bitterly.

She couldn't imagine what Wilhelm must be thinking. Well, she could, but she didn't want to. It was her own fault. She should have told him about Con properly and let him know just what the situation was. Not that she'd meant to deceive anyone, of course; the thought horrified her. The truth was, she realised, feeling both miserable and guilty, that she'd been so happy, both to be away from Con and in her own life, that it had been easier for her to simply 'forget' that Con even existed. She'd never spoken about him, not because she had wanted people to think she was free, but because she had never really thought about him. Now, though, she could see that she should have said something.

It wasn't just Con's presence that was worrying her. It was why he had come. She knew Con well. Only one thing could have brought him here and Emily knew exactly what it was. He wanted something, and in Emily's experience that something could only be money.

'I'd like to know what the authorities have to say about a ruddy German POW acting like's got a right to be here.'

Con's voice was as ugly as the words he had spoken. Con might be good-looking but inside he was ugly, Emily knew. Ugly and mean and selfish.

Tommy, bless him, had moved closer to her whilst Con had been speaking, obviously wanting to protect her. He'd grown taller and stronger since they'd left Liverpool but he was still only a boy and no match for Con. Emily instinctively stepped forward to half-screen him from Con's vengeful gaze.

'Wilhelm has been looking after the vegetable garden for us,' she spoke up determinedly. Con could have as high an opinion of himself as he liked, but she certainly didn't share it, and she certainly wasn't going to allow Con to insult Wilhelm, who had done nothing wrong.

'Oh, he has, has he?' Con sneered, obviously not in the least bit calmed by her words. 'Well, I reckon that the vegetable garden isn't all he's bin taking care of.'

Before Emily could even react to his accusation, he continued, 'You and me need to have a talk, 'cos I've got a few things I want to say to you, in private. So you can hop it, mate,' he told Wilhelm.

'I do not go anywhere until Emily tells me to go,' Wilhelm responded staunchly.

Emily's heart swelled with pride at Wilhelm's response. She looked at him with gratitude. He had every right to turn his back on her and walk away from her in disgust, and the fact that he wanted to stay – for her sake – despite the way that Con had insulted him only confirmed what Emily already knew: that Wilhelm was a true gentleman and knight in shining armour.

Even so, 'You'd better go, Wilhelm,' she told him, more for his sake than for hers.

'Well, this is a fine turn-up for the books,' Con announced when Wilhelm had left and Tommy had gone upstairs to his room. 'I must say, I never thought you'd be the sort to get yourself a fancy man. Didn't think you'd got it in you, to be honest.'

'Wilhelm is a . . . a friend, that is all,' Emily defended her relationship with fierce dignity.

She wasn't going to lie and pretend that Wilhelm was just someone who did some work for her, but neither was she going to allow Con to besmirch

Wilhelm's good reputation with all his nasty talk and insinuations.

'Come off it. It's plain to see what he's after, and I'll bet there's plenty round here that think the same. Looks like I turned up just in time to save you bringing disgrace on yourself and breaking your marriage vows. I reckon I've done you a real favour coming here.'

Emily didn't say anything. She didn't trust herself to. There was no point in antagonising Con, she knew. The only person he ever did any favours for, in her opinion, was himself.

'What is it you've come here for, Con?' she asked him. 'What do you want?' How much do you want would be closer to the mark, Emily suspected.

Immediately he gave her a falsely injured look. Managing the Royal Court Theatre might mean that he mingled with actors but he certainly hadn't learned any true acting skill from them himself, Emily thought critically.

'I've come here to see my wife, of course. What other reason could there be? Mind you, I'm not going to say that it wasn't a shock to come in here and find that German, acting like it was his house and the brat his kid.'

'Wilhelm and Tommy get on well together.'

'I'll bet your neighbours think it's a funny setup, you here with no husband and a kid that's calling you his mum, and that German making himself at home. I'm surprised no one's said anything to you about it.'

'Why should they?'

'Well, for one thing that kid ain't yours, and if you was to ask me I'd say that he ain't even that cousin's of yours you reckoned was his mother. And for another, you're a married woman and we all know what decent folk think of married women wot consort with other men, when their husbands are fighting for their country.'

'But you aren't fighting, Con.' And you aren't even really my husband, not properly, Emily was tempted to say, but she didn't want Con going into one of those moods of his when he started imagining he could coax her into bed, just as he had done in the old days, before she had come to her senses and realised what he was.

'Not fighting, mebbe, but I'm still doing war work, keeping people entertained. Do you know what I reckon, Emily? I reckon that if your neighbours round here knew what I know about you, that you've got a poor husband you've deserted, wot's having to live by himself in ruddy Liverpool, and what's bin going on, they'd have some questions to ask about that kid and where he really came from, and about you and that German.'

'That's nonsense, Con. You were the one who was unfaithful to me – and not just the once – and as for Tommy, you might have this daft idea that my cousin wasn't his mother—'

'Daft idea, is it? Well, I reckon if the authorities was to be asked to check up, they'd pretty soon find out the truth one way or another, and then there's the matter of you taking the kid on without my agreement.'

Emily's heart had started to beat uncomfortably fast.

'Records don't mean that much when there's a war on,' she retaliated despite her anxiety.

'Well, as to that, I reckon things could be left as they are, with the kid, if you and me can come to an agreement about one or two things, like, for instance, you recognising that a man needs a decent amount of money to live on when he hasn't got a wife to look after him.'

So she had been right: Con had come to Whitchurch in the hope of getting some money out of her.

'You've got your wages,' she pointed out to him.

'Huh, a pittance. There's girls working in munitions that earn more than I do. I've got a position to maintain, Emily; I've got to entertain the right people, and be seen around with them, and that takes money, you know that. Look, give me five hundred quid and we'll say no more about . . . anything.'

Anything being Tommy and Wilhelm, Emily guessed, but she knew Con too well to put that into words.

Five hundred pounds, though! It was a small fortune! Emily wanted to refuse. Was Con in some kind of trouble? If he was, did she really want to know?

She might wish she could tell Con that there was no way she was going to let him blackmail her, and that there was no way either that she owed him anything either financially or as his wife, but she knew that she couldn't, not after his threats to her. It wasn't just the disgrace she would suffer, there was Wilhelm himself to think of, and there was Tommy. If the authorities were to start asking questions there was no saying where things might end.

'I haven't got that kind of money in cash, Con,' she told him truthfully. 'It will have to be a cheque.'

Con felt relief filling him and smiled triumphantly. He'd won, just as he'd known that he would. Con loved winning.

'A cheque and twenty quid to cover what it's cost me to come out here.'

Emily hesitated. She knew that she shouldn't give in to him and give him the extra twenty pounds he was demanding, but what else could she do?

'And if I give you that, do you promise me that you won't come here again?'

Con nodded.

Ten minutes later the cheque was written and in Con's pocket and the twenty pounds in five-pound notes was lying on the table.

As he picked it up, Con leaned towards her, the smell of his hair oil and the cologne he wore making Emily's stomach muscles clench with distaste. How could she ever have thought she loved him? He was nowhere near the man that Wilhelm was. Wilhelm was worth ten of him, and more.

Stuffing the money into his wallet, Con was oblivious to what Emily was thinking. He'd got what he'd come here for, and he was satisfied with that – for now.

TWENTY-FIVE

'Con isn't going to tell anyone about me, is he?'

Emily hugged Tommy to her. Not even the excitement of the new bicycle had been able to drive the look of worry from Tommy's eyes completely, and now as they walked to church he had finally come out with what was bothering him.

Never once in the time they had been together had Tommy ever referred to the fact that she had no business calling him her cousin's child, and nor had he ever offered any information about his own life prior to her finding him in the alleyway behind the Royal, Court Theatre.

'Of course he isn't,' Emily assured him stoutly. 'What is there for him to say, after all, exceptin' that you're my cousin's boy?'

'Nothing,' Tommy answered her vehemently.

Emily squeezed his hand in the smart navy gloves she had knitted for him out of her father's old pullover, and he squeezed hers back.

'And it's all right for me to call you Mum still?'

Emily's heart melted. 'I don't see any reason

why you shouldn't, although if we ever had to explain it for official reasons, like, we might have to say that you call me that on account of you not having a mum.'

She waited, holding her breath, wondering if perhaps now Tommy would say something about his past, and when he didn't she wasn't sure whether she was disappointed or relieved. The truth was that if Tommy ever did tell her where he'd come from and where he belonged, she'd then be honour bound to restore him to his rightful family and she didn't think she could bear that. He was so much a part of her life now that sometimes she actually forgot that he wasn't hers, or at least her late cousin's.

Would Wilhelm still want to come and have his Christmas dinner with them after yesterday? It had given her ever such a lovely feeling the way he'd told Con that he'd only leave if she asked him to, but then Wilhelm was a gentleman and that didn't mean that he wasn't shocked and put off by what Con had had to say.

Emily was guiltily aware that she'd never really spoken to Wilhelm about Con, but then she'd never spoken to anyone in Whitchurch about him. Not deliberately on purpose; it was just that somehow the subject hadn't come up, and the truth was that she'd preferred to forget all about Con and the misery of her marriage to him. He might be her husband, but he'd never been much of one, never a proper husband to her, not the kind of husband that a man like Wilhelm would be.

*   *   *

'Isn't Wilhelm going to have Christmas dinner with us now?'

Emily could hear the disappointment in Tommy's voice.

They were back home, their coats hung up in the hall, and the kitchen filled with the mouth-watering smell of the roasting goose. Emily tried to feel enthusiastic about the day for Tommy's sake, whilst really aching inside for the reassurance of Wilhelm's presence. The trappings of Christmas were only that – trappings – without having the man she loved to share them with, Emily knew, as she tried to make an effort to bustle round the kitchen, opening the door to the lower oven of the Aga, to lift out the heavy roasting tin and put it into the top oven so that the fat from the goose would heat up for the roast potatoes. Emily had seen Wilhelm in church along with the other POWs, but there hadn't been any chance to speak to him, and when her neighbours had suggested walking back with them, she'd had no option other than to agree.

'I don't know, Tommy,' she was obliged to admit, both of them immediately looking at the door when someone knocked on it. Emily's heart leaped so hard that she had to put her hand on her chest, whilst Tommy rushed to the door and opened it.

His, 'Wilhelm, you *are* coming. Good,' told Emily all she wanted to know.

Even so, she felt awkward and self-conscious, hesitating, not wanting to look directly at him, and yet at the same time longing to do so as she went towards him and then stopped. And then when he came towards her she stepped forward too, so that they had almost bumped into one another in a way that would have seemed comical if she hadn't been so nervous.

'I wasn't sure whether or not to wait for you at the church,' she said him as she took his coat and scarf from him, every bit as delighted as Tommy, although of course she couldn't show it. It was easier instead to bustle about, hanging up his things, keeping her back to him.

'There was transport for us to take us all to those who had kindly invited us. I must go with that so that all is in order.'

'Well, you're here now, and that's all that matters.'

She put down the old tea towel she'd been using to lift the roasting tin from one oven to the other, and then picked it up again, her movements betraying her tension.

'I'll just get the roast potatoes on and then we can go and sit in the front room. We've got a nice fire going in there, haven't we, Tommy?' Emily knew that her voice was stilted but she couldn't help it. She was so desperately afraid that Wilhelm wouldn't want anything more to do with her because of Con.

'Yes, I set it just like you showed me, Wilhelm, and we can put the tree lights on as well. I've got some binoculars, and some books, one of them about birds, with really good pictures in them, and a game.'

She couldn't put it off, Emily knew. She was going to have to say something, explain . . . apologise.

'Tommy, why don't you go upstairs and take off your good clothes?' she suggested.

She couldn't talk to Wilhelm as she knew she had to with Tommy there. They needed a few minutes on their own. She couldn't let what had happened with Con go without trying to do the right thing, no matter how embarrassed she felt about doing so.

Even so, once the door had closed behind Tommy it was several seconds, during which she wiped her already dry hands on the tea towel she had picked up, before she could begin.

'Wilhelm, I'm ever so sorry about yesterday.' Emily paused and then admitted, 'What you must think of me, I don't know, me having a husband and yet letting you . . .'

Oh, this was so hard to do. Poor Wilhelm must think she was a dreadful person, having a husband and not letting on to him.

'I should have told you about Con, and that's a fact.'

Wilhelm hadn't said anything so Emily risked a quick look at him. He was so nice to look at, was Wilhelm. Looking at him made her feel so happy normally, but today she was far too on edge for happiness.

'I should have told you,' she repeated, twisting the tea towel in her hands, and then putting it down when she realised what she was doing, only to snatch it up again as though somehow keeping a tight hold on it helped her. She certainly needed to squeeze it tightly when she told Wilhelm, 'But the truth is that I didn't want to think about him once I'd left Liverpool. I dare say you think that's no way for a wife to speak about her husband. But me and Con – well, he's never been what you might call a good husband to me. And when I first came here I reckoned that he'd be pleased to be rid of me.'

She had to turn away from Wilhelm; there were some things that it was very difficult for her to talk about because they made her feel so ashamed of herself.

'The thing is that Con never wanted to marry me, not really, and there'd always been girls that he'd be seeing, lying to me and to them. In the beginning it was them I used to blame, thinking they were trying to steal him away from me, but then I began to realise that he was making just as much of a fool of them as he was of me.

'He only married me for my father's money, but I was that much of a fool I believed him when he said it was me he wanted. I should have told you, though . . .'

'Emily.' The sound of Wilhelm saying her name in a voice that held such obvious kindness had Emily standing still and looking at him directly for the first time. Would he understand or would he turn his back on her? She was so afraid she might lose him.

'You have already told me all I want to know when you smile at me, and I can see that you feel about me as I do about you, Emily. This man, this Con, he is no true husband to you, I could see. He comes here, trying to make trouble. Upsetting you, upsetting Tommy. I did not like that, but he does not upset me, other than for you. He does not change the way I feel about you. He cannot. No one can.'

Emily was overwhelmed with relief, and flooded with love and joy, so much so that she had to reach into the pocket of her pinny – her Christmas one that she had had since she had first been married, the white linen embroidered with red berries and green leaves – to find her handkerchief, so that she could give her nose a good blow to stop herself from crying.

'Oh, Wilhelm you are so good,' she thanked him, her voice muffled by her feelings.

'It is you who are good, Emily. You bring out the goodness in me. You are a very special person.'

'Con certainly doesn't think so, but then he never did. All he came here for was money. Once I'd given him that he was more than happy to leave. Wilhelm,' Emily hesitated, and then plunged on, 'there's something more. Something I have to tell you about Tommy.' She had to make a clean breast of everything. It was the right thing to do. She didn't want there to be any more secrets between them.

'He . . . he isn't mine even though he calls me Mum. And Con's right, he isn't my late cousin's son either. The truth is that I don't know where he came from or who his family were. I found him outside the stage door to the theatre where Con works, you see. Starving and in rags, he was, and wouldn't speak. Not a word. I thought that maybe he couldn't at first, but I knew right from the start that he was a bright little lad; there was no mistaking that.'

She could see that Wilhelm was frowning. 'What is it? Do you think I've done wrong keeping him? I did ask him if he had a family, if he wanted to be with someone else . . .'

'No, you haven't done wrong. Anyone can see how devoted you are to him, and he to you. No, it is just that he looks so like your husband that I am surprised that he is not your own.'

'So like Con? Tommy?' Emily shook her head. 'Well I've never noticed any likeness between them, I must say, and poor Tommy would be mortified if you were to suggest that to him. Against him right from the start, Con was. Threatening to walk out if I didn't send Tommy away. Poor little lad, as if I'd ever have done that. Oh, there's Tommy coming back downstairs. Just so long as you don't think badly of me, Wilhelm.'

'I think you are an angel of goodness,' Wilhelm told her.

Her cheeks flushed with pleasure, Emily bent to open the Aga door again, announcing practically, 'I'd better get those roasties in.'

'Well, I don't see why me and Bobby shouldn't get married. You were only eighteen when you married Dad.'

'I was nineteen, Sasha, and anyway, it was different with me and your dad.'

'How could it be different? I love Bobby and he loves me.'

'And me and your dad have said that if both

of you are of the same mind come your next birthday, then we can talk about the two of you getting engaged.'

'Engaged won't do. Can't you understand? Bobby says he doesn't think it's fair to ask for a transfer out of Bomb Disposal unless he's married.'

'So that's what all this is about? You're worried about Bobby, and that's only natural, love, but you know you really are too young to be thinking of marriage. Marriage is a big commitment, especially now when we're at war.'

'You didn't say any of that when Grace wanted to get married.'

'When Grace and Seb got engaged, it was on the understanding that they would not get married until Grace had finished her nurse's training, because if they had married before she had done so, then the hospital wouldn't have kept her on.'

'Well, I'm not training to be a nurse, and me and Bobby know what we want to do.'

Sasha's voice was rising with her emotions, and it was very hard for Jean to keep her own feelings under control. Of course she sympathised with her daughter, and of course she understood how she felt. She had been young and in love herself, after all, but Sam had put his foot down and said that Sasha was too young to rush into marriage just because there was a war on.

'I know why you won't let me get married to Bobby. It's because of Luke, isn't it? Because he broke off his engagement to Katie. Well, that's not fair. Just because Luke changed his mind that doesn't mean that I'm going to do the same. If anything happens

361

to Bobby now because you won't let us get married, then it will be Dad's fault.' Sasha accused her mother bitterly, before rushing out of the kitchen in tears.

Jean closed her eyes briefly. She hadn't been expecting it to be a good Christmas, what with Luke injured and on his way to South Africa, Lou not having leave, and no Katie now that she and Luke were no longer engaged, but she had not anticipated the dreadful row that had erupted when Sasha had announced to her father that she wished to marry Bobby as soon as possible, when they were on their way home after the midnight carol service, which had always been such a special beginning to Christmas for Jean.

For once Jean's first thought when they had all got back home hadn't been the struggle she could face getting her turkey into the oven. Instead she had been more concerned with calming the angry atmosphere that had developed between Sasha and Sam.

Now, as she heard Sasha's angry and upset footsteps running up the stairs, Jean acknow-ledged that if someone had told her this time last year what she would be facing this Christmas she would never have believed them. Then she would have said that Sasha had never really given them a minute's trouble, and it was Lou who was the one more likely to do that; that Sasha simply got dragged into things by her more demanding twin. And now look what had happened. Lou had taken to the discipline of the WAAF like a duck to water, and Sam, who had been so against young women joining the Forces and going into uniform, was as proud as punch of her. Now it was Sasha who had got on the wrong side of her dad and got his back up.

Sam was a good father, a loving father, who had always been softer with his daughters than he had with Luke, and softer with Sasha than with either Grace or Lou, but Sam didn't like having his decisions questioned. What man did? He certainly hadn't liked the way Sasha had ripped up at him when he told her that she was far too young to rush into marriage.

Mind, Sasha herself was partly to blame for that, Jean admitted fair-mindedly. Jean had seen the tight pale look that had set Sam's face when Sasha had announced that she and Bobby 'had to get married'. Of course Sam had thought the worst, and that she and Bobby had been doing what they shouldn't, and that Sasha had gone and got herself into the kind of trouble no decent girl should bring on her family, despite the way she and Sam had brought them up. Jean had thought the same thing herself. It showed too just how young Sasha actually was that she hadn't realised how they were likely to interpret her words, Jean reflected tiredly.

Of course, by the time she had told them that the reason she was in such a rush to marry Bobby was because she was afraid for him, being in Bomb Disposal, and that she wanted to marry him so that he could transfer out, the damage had been done. Sam, not given to speaking his feelings, had let the shock and anger he had felt at the thought of her doing wrong and bringing disgrace on the family spill out by way of a furious warning to Sasha that she was not to even think about marriage as she was far too young.

The arguments and the angry unhappy atmosphere they had caused had rumbled on all Christmas Day, despite Grace and Seb's attempts to cheer everyone up. Sasha had even rowed with Grace, saying that it was all right for her to say, 'Let's not spoil Christmas' because she'd got what she wanted and she was married to her Seb.

Jean was just thankful that Bobby had gone home to Newcastle to see his own family over Christmas because she didn't know what Sam might have said to him if he'd been with them. And that was such a shame, because Sam had really taken to Bobby, and if Sasha had just been sensible and bided her time, Jean suspected that Sam would have agreed to them getting engaged on Sasha's birthday and then Sasha could have coaxed her dad into letting them get married sooner rather than later afterwards.

No, she had never known a Christmas like it, Jean admitted, blinking away the threat of her own tears. It wouldn't do for her to let Sam see she was upset; he'd only go blaming Sasha for upsetting her and that was the last thing she wanted. Jean felt for her daughter, she really did, but at the same time she believed that Sam was right and that Sasha wasn't mature enough yet for marriage, no matter how much she might think that she was.

TWENTY-SIX

Francine had everything clear-cut in her mind, her decision made and her determination not to be persuaded to change it immovable, or so she had thought until she had Jean's letter telling her about Luke. Jean was lucky. Luke had survived. Francine knew how grateful Jean would be feeling that Luke had been spared, and that he hadn't lost his life in the desert fighting for his country – as Marcus might easily have done, if he hadn't still been on leave when the battle of El Alamein had taken place.

She moved tensely through the apartment, picking things up and then putting them down again. The apartment was furnished and decorated by the hotel, with very little in it that was personal except for the few things on what had been Brandon's desk, which Francine had kept exactly as he had liked it, in his memory. There was a silver-framed photograph of them on their wedding day, put at the angle on which he had always insisted, so that he could see it whilst he wrote his letters and made his telephone calls, and the dark green leather-covered desk set she had bought him from a small second-hand shop in the Strand.

Francine picked up the blotter and then put it down again, rearranging the silver cigarette box she had also managed to find in an antique shop, and on which she'd had his initials engraved. Brandon had loved it. Francine stroked the cold surface.

Brandon. She knew what he would want her to do. He had wanted her to be with Marcus.

The apartment felt so empty with just her in it, like her life would be without Marcus.

She shivered, despite the warmth of the gas fire. In the mirror above the fireplace she could see her own reflection. She was wearing an oyster-coloured cashmere twinset just a shade or so darker than the pearl earrings and necklace that Brandon had insisted on giving her, the colour of her twinset picked out by the soft cream and brown tweed skirt she was wearing – part of a suit, a copy of a Chanel design she had had made in Cairo. Francine closed her eyes and then opened them again.

Marcus might have been spared the fighting at El Alamein but his leave finished the day after New Year's Eve, and then he would be returning to his unit. She had thought that she would be relieved to see him go. He had meant it when he had said that he intended to do everything in his power to show her how much he loved her and how much he wanted to make up for what had happened in Egypt. It had been hard for her to hold him at arm's length. She still loved him, after all – that had never been in any doubt – but she was determined not to put herself in a position when she could be hurt again. She had a duty to carry out Brandon's wishes as a trustee of the foundation; doing so would be an act of faith and an act of love. She couldn't allow herself to take the risk of getting emotionally involved with Marcus again. Or at least that was what she had told herself until she had read Jean's letter and realised what she would feel if she sent Marcus away and he were to lose his life in battle. No fear of him stopping loving her was powerful enough to hurt more than losing him without them having shared the love he was offering her. She knew that now. If she were ever to learn that Marcus had lost his life on a faraway battlefield she didn't want to regret and weep for what they had not had as well as for Marcus himself. What was holding her back wasn't common sense, as she had told herself, it was cowardice, and fear.

She looked at the telephone. All she had to do was pick up the receiver and asked to be put through to Marcus's room. He was staying in the hotel, and had suggested to her that they spend Christmas together.

She, though, had refused. And she had deliberately offered to stand in for the lead singer in a popular West End show so that she could spend Christmas with her family. That way, Francine wouldn't be tempted to change her mind, but now the singer was back and there was nothing to stop Francine from being with Marcus except her own fear.

She reached for the receiver, then released it back into its cradle when the bell to the apartment buzzed.

She wasn't expecting anyone. She had agreed to attend a reception at the American Embassy tomorrow but tonight she was spending the evening alone.

Frowning slightly, she got up and went to the door, her heart hammering against her ribs when she opened to find Marcus standing outside.

'I had to come,' he told her simply. 'I know we agreed that I wouldn't. I hadn't planned to, and in fact I'd decided to join a party of fellow officers on leave for dinner, but I had the most extraordinary feeling all of a sudden that I had to come here. You can send me away if you wish.'

Francine looked at him. It was impossible, of course, for her heart to have called out to him. Logically, that sort of thing belonged in a novel – a romantic fantasy, not real life. But then perhaps sometimes things happened in real life that overturned the rules of logic; sometimes perhaps two hearts could know best. Sometimes, through the loving generous actions of a special person, another person got a second chance to have what they most longed for.

This, after all, was what Brandon had wanted for her.

'I've got to know if there's any chance that you can find it your heart to forgive me, Francine,' Marcus continued.

'And if I say that I can't?'

'Then I'll say that I can't stop loving you, but

that I can and will respect your wishes, and that you can send me away if you wish.'

Send him away? The feeling of anguish that swept through her only confirmed what she already knew. These last weeks of seeing him, being with him, had shown her how much he meant to her and how bleak and empty her future would be without his love. It was time to put pride and past to one side.

'I'm glad you're here,' she told him, abandoning the defensive pretence she had been clinging to, as she held the door wide so that he could come in. 'I was just about to telephone you.' She took a deep breath. 'The hotel is holding a dinner dance on New Year's Eve and I was wondering if we might go, together.'

She could feel the fierce burn of the intensity with which his gaze searched her face.

'There is no one I would rather greet this and every New Year with than you, Francine,' he answered her. 'You know that, just as you know how much you mean to me and how much I love you.'

Her throat had gone very dry but she wasn't going to stop now.

'Show me,' she asked him softly, holding out her arms to him. 'Show me how much you love me, Marcus. Hold me, love me and promise me that you'll never ever let me go.'

His response was to reach for her, wrapping his arms tightly round her, kicking the door closed behind him as he did so, before bending his head to kiss her with all the love and passion she had missed and longed for so much.

'We won't make plans,' she whispered to him. 'We'll just live every day as it comes, love one another every day we have. I don't want to be cheated of any more happiness, Marcus.'

Being on duty over Christmas had been much more fun than Lou had expected. They'd worked hard, of course – planes still needed servicing and repairing – and the sergeant had still bawled them out when they were too slow, but there'd been hot mince pies at their morning tea break, and Christmas cake in the afternoon as a special treat, and then on Christmas Day itself the officers on duty had served them, in the proper Forces tradition. The canteen staff had put up decorations and there'd been a real party atmosphere, just as though they were all part of one big family, which in a way, of course, they were.

And she'd got her wonderful exciting hope for the future to hug to herself. It was there in the morning, when she woke up and opened her eyes, filling her with a joy she knew she could never properly explain to others.

There'd been presents to open from her family, and she'd thought of them, and pictured them at home opening theirs, missing her as she was missing them, but she'd missed them in a happy sort of way, knowing that she'd got something so special to look forward to.

On Boxing Day they'd entertained the children from the nearby village, with the sergeant dressing up as Father Christmas. They'd played games with the kids – blind man's bluff and hunt the slipper

– and if a handful of the men had tried to turn the situation to their advantage by changing the game into a grown-up version of sardines, well, it was only the girls who made it plain that they wanted to join in and permit a few stolen kisses that got targeted, and since Lou wasn't one of them she'd had a very jolly time playing with the children.

She'd missed her family, especially Sasha, and it had felt lonely waking up on Christmas morning without her twin to snuggle up in bed with, whilst they explored the contents or their stockings, even if she had been in a hut full of other girls.

When would she hear about the ATA? She was so excited and yet still half afraid to believe that it was true and that she could get the chance to train as a pilot. Please let me be chosen, she begged silently in her prayers. I'll do anything, if only I get that posting, she promised inwardly, anything and everything I can to be picked.

TWENTY-SEVEN

There was a change in the air, everyone was saying so, with the turning of the year from 1942 to 1943, and the victory of El Alamein. The bleak despair and hardship that had hung over the whole country during 1942 was giving way to a new spirit, not just of hope but the actual belief that the possibility was there that the war could be and would be won, and that Hitler would be defeated.

No one was saying that it was going to be easy, or that many more lives would not be lost, but the country's mood had changed. Heads and shoulders that, in 1942, had been bowed were now lifted and straightened; the austerity of daily life, which had dragged people down, had now become a proud badge of endurance. The country felt deep within itself that the tide was ready to turn.

For Bella, still waiting to receive her first letter from Jan since she had heard of his captivity, the significance of what was happening meant that she could dare to hope that the war would end with the Allies the victors and that Jan would be safely restored to her.

To Jean the good news meant less; Luke had rejoined his unit and the Allies were still fighting in North Africa.

To Lou, waiting nervously for the all-important letter that would signal that she was being transferred to ATA for pilot training, the days were filled with anxiety and hope. Verity had stopped off at the base in the middle of transporting a Spitfire, on a freezing cold February day to tell Lou that she had put her name forward and set things in motion.

To Sasha the winter's slow crawl towards spring was as irritating as it was long drawn out. As she hurried to meet Bobby at Lyons after work, the March wind coming off the Mersey buffeted her with its boisterous embrace.

'Have you spoken to Captain Harrison yet about you getting a transfer into another unit?' was the first thing she said to Bobby when she found him waiting outside the café for her.

'Let's get out of this wind,' he suggested, going to take her arm, but Sasha pulled back.

'You haven't, have you?' she demanded angrily. 'Bobby, you know what we agreed. You promised me that you would tell him.'

Tears of anguish and disappointment stung her eyes. Why could no one understand how she felt: how miserable and afraid Bobby being with Bomb Disposal made her feel, and how envious she was of the other girls she worked with, whose men were safe in reserved occupations and not risking their lives like Bobby had to?

Sasha didn't know when she had started to feel like this, when being proud of Bobby's bravery had become instead a terrible fear for his safety, which had grown from that into a feeling of fear and anger that boiled up inside her, blocking her throat, making her heart thud frantically, filling her with a sickening feeling of panic that she just couldn't explain to anyone, but which made her afraid almost to move. Thinking of what Bobby had to go through every time a bomb had to be defused made that feeling worse. Sometimes at night she couldn't sleep for remembering how she had felt when she had been trapped in that bomb shaft, thinking she was going to die. She had had Lou to hold on to her, and then Bobby to take her place so that she could be safe, but who was there to do that for Bobby, and what would she do if anything happened to him and she lost him?

'It isn't as easy as that, Sash. We lost two good lads last month and it isn't easy getting replacements. I'd feel that I was letting the unit down if I asked for a transfer out now. It affects everyone's morale when we lose someone.'

'You don't want to let them down but you don't seem to mind letting me down' Sasha stormed, without allowing him to finish. 'You promised me, Bobby, you know you did.'

Bobby frowned. He was an easy-going young man, who genuinely wanted to do whatever would make Sasha happy, but there were some things a chap just could not do, not without letting down team mates who relied on him. He'd tried to explain this to Sasha but she'd got herself so

374

wrought up about the danger of his work that she just wouldn't listen.

'I know that I said I'd have a word with the captain, Sash . . .'

'You *promised* me you'd tell him that you wanted to transfer out of Bomb Disposal.'

'That was before we lost Wrighty and Thompson. Wrighty had been with our unit from the outset. Captain always used to say he was our good-luck mascot. If I'd told the captain I wanted to leave after we lost them, it would have looked like I was being a coward, walking away from the other lads and letting them down.'

As Bobby struggled for the words to explain to Sasha how he felt he could tell that she didn't understand, and he hated seeing her so upset.

Bobby loved Sasha. He knew beyond any doubt that she was the girl for him, and he had known it since he'd found her stuck down the bomb shaft and looking like she was going to die there. There was nothing he wouldn't do for her, except walk out on his mates when they all needed to stick together. He couldn't do that and still call himself a man.

Sasha felt like bursting into tears, but of course she couldn't because they were inside Lyons now, and the last thing she wanted to do was draw attention to herself.

'Look, there's a table there,' Bobby told her, nudging her. 'You go and sit down and I'll go and queue up and get us our tea.'

'If you really loved me like you keep saying you do then you'd tell the captain, instead of keep saying you will and then not doing,' Sasha hissed. 'You know what I think, Bobby. I think that you don't really love me at all.'

Before he could say anything Sasha marched over to the table he had indicted and sat down at it, keeping her back to him.

Why was it that no one understood how she felt: not her mother and certainly not her father, who had refused to let her and Bobby get married; not her twin; and not Bobby either, it seemed. Sasha swallowed against the lump of self-pity blocking her throat. Why could none of them understand how afraid she was for Bobby? All she wanted was for him to be safe, instead of doing some of the most dangerous of all war work – defusing enemy bombs.

She was tired of people treating her like a child, telling her one thing, promising her one thing, but then doing another, just like she didn't really matter at all. Why, anyone would think that Bobby didn't love her at all from the way he was behaving, not asking for a transfer when he knew all she wanted was for him to be safe. Left alone to dwell on her increasing unhappy thoughts, Sasha had worked herself up into a very bad mood indeed by the time Bobby arrived at the table carefully carrying a tray with two plates of beans on toast on it, along with tea for both of them.

'I know what it is,' she announced as soon as Bobby was sitting down. 'You want to stay in Bomb Disposal really because those girls at the Grafton the other Saturday made such a fuss, saying how brave they thought you were. You'd rather have them fussing over you than please me.'

Bobby laughed. 'Don't be daft. Of course I wouldn't.'

There! It was just as she'd been thinking. Everyone treated her like a child, even Bobby. Well, she wasn't! And she wasn't going to be fobbed off either.

'And I'm supposed to believe that, am I, just like I believed that you'd do what you promised and tell the captain that you wanted to transfer out?'

'Aw, come on, Sash. It isn't the same thing at all,' Bobby told her, tucking in to his beans.

Sasha was in no mood to be mollified. She pushed away her plate. 'Well, I'm telling you now, Bobby, that unless you keep your promise to me and tell that captain that you want a transfer then it's all over between you and me.'

Bobby's good-natured smile disappeared and he too pushed away his food. 'Come on, Sasha,' he pleaded. 'You don't mean that. I know you're upset. But—'

'I do mean it,' Sasha told him. 'And if you loved me as much as you say you do then you'd do it.'

'Sasha, it isn't that easy. Like I've tried to explain to you, I can't just let the other lads down. Look, finish your tea otherwise we'll be late for the pictures.'

Sasha stood up. 'I'm not going to the pictures with you, Bobby. In fact, I'm not going to see you again until you come and tell me that you've left Bomb Disposal.' She pulled on her coat as she spoke.

'Sasha, wait . . .' Bobby begged her.

'I mean it, Bobby,' she told him, before she turned to slip through the crowded restaurant without looking back.

Bobby caught up with her within a few yards, reaching for her hand and then offering her his handkerchief when he saw that she was crying.

'Don't say things like that, Sash, please. You mean the whole world to me, you do.'

'Oh, Bobby . . .' Sasha wept as he took her in his arms. 'I just want us to be married and for you to be safe, that's all.'

TWENTY-EIGHT

'Welcome back, Corp. We've missed you.'

The vigorous manner in which Andy pumped his hand as he welcome Luke back to the unit confirmed how pleased he was to have him back, even if he couldn't resist joking, 'Pity you missed the fun, though, and we had to rout Jerry without you. Mind you, at least you'll get to see King George, even if you didn't see Rommel's backside.'

Even before he had been declared fit to return to duty, Luke had been itching to get back to his men, and he was delighted to have rejoined them in Tunisia, where it was already being rumoured that they would shortly be on the move, joining the assault on Italy.

'I owe you one hell of a lot,' Luke told Andy later on when he'd managed to snatch a few minutes alone with his friend. 'You saved my life.'

'Repaying the debt I owed you for saving mine, wasn't I, mate? We're even stevens now,' Andy grinned.

Knowing that the other man used his jokes to cover his deeper feelings, Luke didn't press the subject. There was, after all, no need. They both understood that in war you did your best to protect your comrades, and that your loyalty to them and theirs to you, the things you shared mattered more than the things that set you apart from them; that the trust you gave them and they gave you had to be all encompassing, and an act of faith rather than a reality that had to be constantly examined for flaws and weaknesses.

Luke frowned. Wasn't that the kind of trust that should exist between a chap and his girl when they loved one another? Wasn't it the kind of trust that Katie had tried to tell him they should share, but which he had withheld from her? Why was he thinking about Katie so much? She seemed to have found a way to keep pushing into his thoughts when he didn't want her to be there. It was over between them, after all, and surely it didn't matter now that he hadn't given her the trust he had just identified. But somehow it did matter.

It had happened at last. The CO had sent for Lou and told her that with immediate effect she had been posted to Barton-le-Clay, in the Bedfordshire countryside and, so she had been told, not far from Luton and Bedford itself, to begin her initial training to become an ATA pilot. Lou was beside herself with excitement and delight.

Admin had given her her travel warrant and she been told to pack her kit ready to leave the base at Lyneham first thing in the morning, in RAF transport, to be driven to the nearest railway station, and then north via London to her new posting.

Hilary had been a bit miffed. They'd got forty-eight-hour passes coming up, and Hilary had been trying to persuade Lou to go to London with her, instead of Lou going home as she'd originally planned, but now of course that was out of the question, as Lou's new posting meant that her leave would probably be cancelled.

'I thought I'd have had a letter back by now,' Bella told Bettina anxiously as they stood together under a shared umbrella whilst the heavy April rain fell from Wallasey's grey skies.

They'd met up in Wallasey by chance, on this wet Saturday afternoon, their unplanned meeting giving Bella the chance to talk to someone who would understand about her anxiety over the absence of any letters for her from Jan.

'It's the same for us,' Bettina assured her. 'Sometimes Mama and I think that we must have dreamed hearing from the Red Cross that Jan is still alive and a POW.'

'Oh, don't say that, please,' Bella begged her, shuddering. 'I couldn't bear it if we were told now that they'd made a mistake.'

'I'm sure they haven't,' Bettina comforted her, changing the subject to ask, 'How is your mother?'

'She can't stop talking about Charlie, my brother. He and his wife are expecting their first child.' Bella frowned. This new baby would not be Charlie's first child. He already had a daughter, after all, with Lena, and Bella resented on Lena and her baby's behalf her mother's constant enthusing about this other coming child.

381

'Mummy was hoping that they would come up to visit her over Easter, and I suspect that Charlie has only told her about the baby to head off her complaints because they didn't.' And possibly to ask her mother to help him out financially, Bella suspected, although she didn't want to say so to Bettina.

'I've always wanted to get married in June, but I never imagined there'd be so little time to organise everything. But, well, with the war and everything, and all this talk about invading Italy, we've decided to just jump in and get married as quickly as we can. After all, even though everyone is saying that we've turned the corner and that we're going to win, there's still a long way to go, and Leonard is bound to be posted soon and see action, so we don't want to waste a minute.'

Katie smiled, happy for her friend as Gina confided her good news about her engagement to Leonard and their plans to marry.

They were in Hyde Park, sitting on the grass, enjoying the May sunshine, the park busy with Londoners and visitors alike, doing the same.

'Of course, I want you to be my bridesmaid, Katie. After all, if it wasn't for you we'd never have met in the first place. Leonard is asking Eddie to be his best man, and Eddie says that he's looking forward to seeing you again. You know, I rather think that Eddie has a very soft spot for you.'

'And for all the other girls he knows as well,' Katie laughed, determined to dispute her friend's suggestion that Eddie had any partiality for her, and to make sure that Gina didn't get any match-making ideas into her head, as girls very much in love and soon to be married seemed to do.

'Mummy's thrilled to bits, needless to say. She adores Leonard, and of course with both our families having friends in common and knowing one another, it makes everything so much easier. I never thought that this would happen to me. I thought there'd never be anyone else I'd want to marry but, well, Leonard and I get on so well together.'

'You deserve to be happy, Gina,' Katie reassured her, sensing that that was what she wanted. 'You both do.'

Katie smiled again. It didn't do, of course, to reflect that it was two years ago this month that she and Luke had got engaged. That was all behind her now and she was a very different Katie from the one she had been then.

'I must go,' she told Gina, glancing at her watch. 'I'm on duty at Rainbow Corner in half an hour and I've promised to show a group of American flyboys "Sherlock Holmes's London".'

Rainbow Corner provided a variety of London tours for Americans on leave in the city, and even had bicycles that they could hire by the hour if they so wished. Not that Katie was sure they'd be so keen to hire them if they had read in the press, as she had done, that more people had been killed in road accidents since the beginning of the war than had died in combat.

Half an hour later, Katie was just about to cross Piccadilly Circus, her thoughts busy with her duties for the afternoon, when she felt a light touch on her shoulder and heard a warm female voice saying to her as she turned round, 'Katie, I thought it was you.'

Francine! Jean's sister, Luke's aunt, and the fairy godmother who had so generously made it possible for Katie to wear the most lovely clothes she had ever seen. Even now Katie still felt guilty about the fact that Jean had given her the beautiful grey silk frock she had been wearing the Christmas Eve she had first met Luke, and which in reality belonged to Francine.

'How are you?' Francine asked her. 'Do you have time for a cup of tea?'

They were virtually outside Lyons and Katie didn't want to appear rude, so she nodded her head, but explained, 'I'm due on duty at Rainbow Corner at half-past. I work there as a volunteer,'

'And you don't want to be late. Quite right, you mustn't be, but that still leaves us time for a quick cuppa and a catch-up.'

'I still have your dress,' Katie reminded Francine as the latter took her arm and guided her toward Lyons.

'My dress?'

'The grey silk. Jean sent it to me.'

'Oh, yes, of course. Well, you must consider it yours, Katie. It would be far too young for me now, and besides, I should like you to have it. You look well, and happy. Does that mean that some young American you've met at Rainbow Corner has put that sparkle in your eyes?'

Katie laughed. 'No. They are lovely boys, but so far away from home and sometimes so new to this war that it wouldn't really be fair to get involved with them.'

'Those are very wise words, my dear. When one has been hurt by love, one is so much more aware of the hurt it can cause others. You'll have heard the news about Luke, I expect?'

Katie was glad that they were now sitting down, as her heart lurched into her ribs. What news was it that Francine expected her to have heard? That he had found someone else? Well, she'd warned herself that that was bound to happen, hadn't she? The news couldn't be that something bad had happened to Luke; after all, Francine was smiling.

'Jean and I don't keep in touch,' she answered Francine cautiously. 'We both agreed that we shouldn't, although I did see her when they came to London for Lou's medal.'

'Oh, I see.' Francine looked conscious-stricken. 'Then perhaps I shouldn't say any more?'

'No, please,' Katie pressed her, unable to conceal her anxiety. 'You have to tell me now.'

Francine looked at her for a minute and then nodded her head. 'Yes, I think I do,' she agreed. 'The fact of the matter is that Luke was injured in action – El Alamein—'

Now Katie's heart was rolling into her chest wall again but this time in slow motion, and with a sickeningly anxious thud.

'He's—' she began, poised anxiously on the edge of her chair.

'Safe and well now, thank goodness,' Francine reassured her immediately. 'Although it's taken him a long time to recover. Oh, Katie, I'm sorry, you look quite pale. I didn't mean to upset you.' Francine patted Katie's hand.

'I was thinking of Jean,' Katie rallied determinedly. 'She must have been so worried.'

'Well, yes, she was, especially when the telegram arrived. Of course, she's worrying just as much now that he's been pronounced fit to return to duty.' Francine gave a small sigh. 'Life isn't very easy for her at the moment. She misses Grace, of course, and Sasha desperately wants to marry her young man, but both Jean and Sam think that she's too young. I know how sorry she was about you and Luke, Katie, and how much she wanted you as a daughter-in-law.'

'I wanted that too,' Katie admitted, before finishing her tea, and taking her leave of Francine, with an apology for having to dash away.

'No, you must go. I understand perfectly,' Francine assured her, giving Katie a quick and unexpected hug that reminded her immediately of Jean and made her eyes sting a little with emotion, as she left the café and hurried into Rainbow Corner, darting between the mass of uniformed men as she went to her post.

American accents, American uniforms, American music and food and customs – that was what Rainbow Corner was all about, and it worked. Even Katie, who was familiar with it, often felt when she entered the building that she was stepping into another world. Rather guiltily, though, today instead of thinking about the young men she would be showing round her city, she found it was Luke who was filling her thoughts.

It had been such a shock to learn that he had been injured, and it hurt that she hadn't known. What was even worse was the realisation that he could have died, might still die, and she wouldn't know. Feelings of despair and need gripped her, filling her with a foolish longing to see him and touch him just to reassure herself that he was still alive. Why should she feel like this? She didn't want to. Perhaps once you had loved someone, some of that love stayed imprinted on your heart.

'There you are, Katie. I was beginning to worry that you were going to be late, and that my chap would be left wondering where I was.'

The voice of the volunteer she was replacing was slightly sharp. Katie forced a smile. It wasn't her fault, after all, that she was thinking about her 'chap', not knowing that Katie was also thinking about a man who had meant an awful lot to her.

TWENTY-NINE

The train was pulling into Lime Street. It had been so long since Emily had been to Liverpool that she had somehow expected the city to have changed, but it hadn't. It still stood proud amongst the rubble of its own destruction, its citizens going about their business.

It was the smell that caught Emily's attention first when she stepped out of the station into Lime Street proper, the smell of sea air, salt and sharp, brought off the Atlantic by the wind to mingle with the dust of bombed buildings and city life, and that added, uniquely Liverpool, pinch of the cargoes brought into its docks. When Emily had been a child that pinch had been exotic and exciting, a mix of spices and luxury goods, of the food from the foreign restaurants that catered for the seamen, but now it was the smell of engine oil and metal and war.

She felt very nervous. She was tempted to open her bag and read the letter again, even though she knew every word of it by heart.

It had arrived nearly two weeks ago now, on a

388

bright sunny morning, although she had had to admit to herself that she couldn't really say that it had come 'out of the blue'. The fact was that she had been expecting it from the minute Con had stood in her kitchen on Christmas Eve, asking her for money. She had known then that that wouldn't be the end of it and that once he knew he could get money out of her by threatening to go to the authorities about Tommy he would be back for more.

Not that he'd asked outright in the letter for more money. No, he'd simply said that he thought it would be a good idea if she came to Liverpool so that the two of them could have a 'bit of a talk', 'and don't bring the brat with you'. Not that Emily would have dreamed of dragging poor Tommy all the way to Liverpool and back, when she knew how much being in Con's presence worried and upset the boy.

Instead she'd asked her neighbour and Wilhelm if they would keep an eye on Tommy for her because she'd got to go to Liverpool to attend to some family business.

'It's just some council business I've got to sort out because of letting the council use my house to billet people in,' she'd fibbed to Wilhelm and Tommy.

It made Emily feel bad knowing that she had lied, but she knew how Tommy would have worried if he'd known the truth, and Wilhelm too, and there was nothing that either of them could do.

She arranged to meet Con at the theatre; she

hadn't wanted to go to the house. After what had happened to her there when she'd been attacked, she didn't want to go back, daft though that was, because nothing was likely to happen to her there now.

And anyway, the theatre was also closer to the station than Wavertree.

Because she had known that Con wouldn't be satisfied with what he'd already had, it came in one way almost as a relief when she had finally received his letter, she'd been worrying about him getting in touch that much, and not sleeping for fear of what he might do.

It didn't take her long to reach the theatre, cutting through St John's Market, and noting sadly the empty space where Lewis's had stood before it had been bombed and burned down. Everywhere she looked there was still evidence of the terrible pounding the city had taken during the May blitz of 1940, three years ago now. So many years of war and hardship, there were little ones growing up now who had never known anything else, Emily thought compassionately.

Con was reading *Picture Post*, with his feet up on his desk in his favourite pose, when Emily opened the door to the cubbyhole he called his office.

'Emily! What the devil are you doing here?' he demanded as he swung his feet to the floor and stood up.

'What do you think I'm doing? You were the one who wrote and said you wanted to see me.'

'Well, yes, but I wasn't expecting you to just

turn up without a by your leave. What if I hadn't been here?'

'But you are,' Emily pointed out.

'Look, I'm busy at the moment. I'm expecting a phone call about this act I've got booked. Why don't you go and get yourself a nice cup of tea at Joe Lyons and I'll meet you there later?'

Emily knew Con in this mood. It meant he was up to something, trying to hide something, or rather someone. During the early years of their marriage Con had forbidden her to visit him 'at work', claiming that it would give him a benefit that others didn't have if he had his wife calling round every five minutes. However, the truth had been that he hadn't wanted her there because of his girls, the young women – chorus girls, singers, actresses and the like – he flirted with and sometimes far more.

Same old Con, Emily thought grimly. Silly fool, did he really think she cared any more what he did or with whom?

Well, never mind that. Turning up here when he hadn't been expecting her and when he was quite obviously anxious to get rid of her could give her an advantage over him.

Hellfire and damnation, Con thought angrily. It was ruddy typical of Emily to turn up when she wasn't wanted, causing him even more trouble than he already had. Women, the whole lot of them, were sometimes more trouble than they were worth. He did want to see Emily, of course. He wanted more money from her. He had quickly realised that by keeping up the pressure on her, he could force her to continue to give him money. Not as much money as his card game racket had been giving him, but enough to keep Ed Mulligan and the other bloodsuckers at bay. Not that he'd need to do that for long. Con had plans, big plans. Plans he wasn't intending to share with anyone, least of all Eva, whose jealousy seemed to grow stronger by the day.

What he intended to do was slip away quietly from Liverpool and set himself up in London, and for that he needed Emily's money, but typically she'd chosen her time badly. Any minute now Eva would be here for rehearsal, and if she found Emily with him, there'd be hell to pay. Con was beginning to seriously regret ever having got involved with the fiery singer, with her circus background.

She was tired of touring, she kept telling him pointedly. She wanted something more permanent, somewhere more permanent and someone more permanent, and that someone, she had made very plain, was Con. That was the very last thing that Con wanted.

Con's 'office' was extremely small. The large desk upon which he liked to rest his feet took up most of the limited space, and now when someone suddenly thrust open the door, Emily was almost knocked off her chair with the force of it slamming into the back of it.

The woman who burst into the room, was heavily made up, with a mass of dark curls.

'Ah, my dearest love,' she began theatrically, clasping her hands to the expanse of bosom swelling over the top of her low-necked blouse, only to stop speaking when she saw Emily, an expression of mingled fury and grief worthy of a pantomime dame replacing her previous look of adoration.

'Who is this?' she demanded.

'Oh, I'm nobody, my dear,' Emily tried to calm the emerging Virago, only to recognise that the other woman had no intention of being calmed. Con would involve himself with these highly strung and oh-so-dramatic women. Personally Emily thought it must be dreadfully wearing.

'Look, Eva, why don't you go and rehearse? Emily means nothing to me. She's just my wife, that's all,' Con said hastily.

'Your wife! But you cannot be married. I intended to marry you and be your wife.'

Too late Con realised where his desperation to ward off Eva's fanatical jealousy had taken him. He had treated his marriage in such a cavalier fashion and cared so little about it that it had simply not occurred to him that it would matter to anyone else. For all Eva's talk of wanting someone permanent, he had never imagined that she was seriously thinking in terms of marriage.

Poor woman, Emily thought sympathetically.

If only Con was the honourable sort who would now agree to 'arrange' to be caught as the guilty partner in their marriage, then they could divorce and this Eva would be welcome to him, but knowing Con as she did, somehow Emily thought that marriage to his current mistress wasn't likely to be part of Con's plans. The trouble with Con was that he lived in his own imaginary world where the things that mattered to other people didn't intrude into his fantasy of how he wanted his life to be.

'You have broken my heart, dishonoured me with your false promises, and now there is nothing left for me but this.'

Emily's eyes rounded as she saw the knife the other woman was now brandishing wildly, holding it as though she was about to stab it into her own heart.

Poor dear. She wouldn't do it, of course. It was all play acting – anyone could see that – but she did have her pride to think of so Emily was willing to play along out of sisterly solidarity and beg her not to hurt herself.

The minute Con saw the knife he panicked. She was going to do it, she was going to kill him just like her father had killed her mother, just as she was always warning him she would do if she caught him with someone else. She had him up against the desk with no way to escape because she was standing between him and the door. He was stronger than her, though. He could overpower her, take the knife from her.

'My dear—' Emily began, but then stopped as Con suddenly launched himself at the woman, reaching up for the knife. For a few seconds they both struggled for possession of it and then the woman burst into tears and released it, leaving Con holding it before throwing herself against him, begging him not to break her heart.

To Emily the observer, helpless to intervene, knowing what must happen when the full weight of such a well-built woman fell against the knife now clasped in Con's hand and pointing towards his body, time seemed to have slowed down, each second of intolerable length as she saw the woman's expression change from theatrical drama to bewilderment and then genuine shock. Her hands went to Con's chest and were removed, her eyes widening, as she looked down at them and saw the blood on them. She began to scream, an awful high-pitched, terrified sound, like an animal caught in a trap, Emily thought as she went first to the telephone, quickly telling the operator who answered that a doctor and an ambulance were needed, giving her the theatre's address, and then going to the woman, gently but firmly urging her away from Con, who, supported by the desk behind him, was slumped over, his hands still clutching the knife, which was buried deep in his chest.

The woman had stopped screaming now and was simply sobbing loudly, but Emily could still hear the steady drip of Con's blood onto the floor.

His eyes were wide open – shocked with disbelief. He was still alive, though, because as she went to him Emily heard him saying her name, like a child lost and afraid and not understanding what had happened.

Poor Con. He never meant any harm, not really. He was just foolish, that was all.

None of the cast had appeared yet to see what the screaming was all about but then they were probably used to angry females screaming at Con, and had learned not to get involved.

He was trying to say something, Emily saw, his hands on the knife as he looked imploringly at her.

Blood had started to trickle from the corner of his mouth. Emily opened her handbag and removed her handkerchief, gently dabbing it away.

She could hear the sound of an ambulance siren growing louder as it got closer, and then ceasing; its silence was followed the sound of the outside door being opened, and then male voices.

'Up here, she called out, relieved to hear feet pounding up the stairs.

One look at the face of the doctor who had come with the ambulance confirmed how serious things were. But Con was still conscious, still watching and looking so terribly afraid, silently begging for comfort and reassurance, that she couldn't say anything.

Whilst they were taking Con downstairs to the waiting ambulance Emily put a telephone call through to Whitchurch post office, and asked if a message could be sent to ask her neighbour to take Tommy in for the night because she had been delayed in Liverpool and couldn't get back.

Strangely, she had no anxiety about Tommy's welfare. Somehow she just knew that he would be safe and looked after, and that she need have no fears on his account.

'I do wish you would marry me, Francine.'

'Marcus, we've already been through that, and you know how I feel. I'm afraid that if I marry you then I'll lose you and that the best way for me to keep you and our love safe is for us to stay as we are. After all, there's nothing I haven't given you that I would give you if we were married; there's nothing I've held back from you.'

They were in the apartment and alone, so Marcus was free to take her hand and carry it to his lips to press a fierce kiss into her palm before saying thickly, 'No. You have given all of yourself to me with more generosity and love than I had any right to expect, but I still wish you would marry me, Francine, for your own sake as much as mine. The world is not always kind to a woman who lives outside society's rules.'

'You mean that society will shun me because I am your lover and not your wife?' Francine gave a dismissive shrug. 'Let it. I don't care. We are both adults, Marcus, and old enough to choose for ourselves how we live our lives.'

'There is your family to think of. You may not care, but they will. One day the war will be over and what is permitted and permissible now will not be then.'

'Marcus, it's no good. Please try to understand. I love you too much to marry you. It's silly of me, I know, but I have this superstitious feeling that if I marry you . . .'

'I might die? Because you married Brandon and he died?'

'No . . . I . . . I don't know. I don't know why I feel the way I do, I just do.'

'It's illogical and crazy and, God, Francine, have you thought of what could happen? If there were to be a child . . . my child?'

He said it with such passion and longing that

Francine knew immediately how much he hoped for that. But then wasn't it natural for any man, knowing that he must face war and possibly death, to want to feel that he had left something of himself behind him in the living form of his child? She couldn't blame him for that and she didn't.

'We haven't always been as practical as we might,' Marcus reminded her.

'Be careful,' Francine warned him, 'otherwise you'll have me suspecting that you've deliberately been "less than practical".'

'The last thing I think about when I hold you in my arms is tactics – of any kind,' Marcus told her truthfully. 'The reality is that whilst the battalion is currently posted to home duties, the way the war is now progressing means that the threat of invasion is more or less over. However, we are going to need more troops in Europe if we are fully to rout Hitler and win this war.'

'You mean that you are likely to be posted overseas?'

'I didn't say that and I can't answer that question. You know it's against regulations,' Marcus told her.

Francine didn't want to think of him being posted abroad and her not being able to see him with the freedom they were currently enjoying. Perhaps she was being selfish but she couldn't help it.

'Let's just stay as we are, Marcus. Please?' she begged him.

'Very well,' he agreed, but Francine could sense that he was disappointed.

* * *

'Well, at least your mum has said that I can talk to your dad about us getting engaged,' Bobby tried to comfort Sasha as they sat together at a table in the Grafton, watching the dancers jitterbugging.

'If he agrees,' Sasha replied. She felt so miserable and low, so frightened deep down inside herself that she was going to lose Bobby to a bomb.

Sasha was beginning to think that the only thing that would make her feel better was the war ending, but even when it did there would still be bombs that needed defusing. There were so many of them lying out of sight, hidden and dangerous, deadly, killing people. Sasha could feel the panic starting to grow inside her again.

'Let's dance,' she said, pushing back her chair and reaching for Bobby's hand. Perhaps if they were dancing and Bobby was holding her close she might be able to stop thinking about bombs and Bobby being killed.

THIRTY

One of the mechanics on the ground removed the blocks keeping the training plane's wheels and thus the plane itself static, whilst the other spun the propeller for her, both of them standing back as Lou gunned the engines, her heart thudding almost as fast as the propellers were spinning, or so it seemed to her, as she eased down the throttle until the small two-seater training plane, with her instructor in the back, and Lou herself at the controls, bumped across the grass and then began to taxi down the runway.

This was what it was all about – all those hours of lessons and diagrams in the base's classrooms, listening intently to lecturers explaining the actual workings of flight to them – this rush of adrenalin and delight, mixed with awe and fear of failure. Determinedly Lou increased her pressure on the throttle, whilst the engines whined in response, and she listened intently for that note in them that would tell her that she had the right combination of speed and power to enable the plane to lift into the sky. It was a 'sense' that good pilots developed, they had been told in the class-room, an awareness, a feeling that went beyond anything that any fancy equipment inside the cockpit of the plane could replace; a skill that could mean the difference between life and death for a pilot with nothing to guide them other than their own well-honed instincts. Would she develop that 'sense'? There it was, the infinitesimal drop from a high-pitched whine to something slightly deeper, the sound throbbing through her as Lou held her breath and gripped the wheel as she gave the engine more power.

There, the bumping had stopped and the nose of the plane had started to lift as though by magic. She was so excited and thrilled that for a second Lou almost felt as though it *had* happened by magic and forgot that control of the plane lay with her, but once again her attentive ear caught the warning increase in pitch of the engines and she quickly gave them the power they were demanding.

She'd done it. They were airborne! What a thrill! She hardly dare let herself believe that she *had* actually done it, but she had.

Relief hollowed out her stomach that, after all these weeks of lectures, schoolroom lessons and tests, followed by bumps and lifts over the training school's grass airfield, she had finally done it and had got a plane successfully into the air. This was no time to relax, though. Instead she must concentrate on what she was doing, on feeling the controls of the plane respond to her touch, on listening to the sound of the engine.

'Right, now level off.'

Lou nodded in response to the shouted instruction from her instructor. Her palms felt wet and slippery as she eased back the speed just enough to stop the plane from climbing any further; she couldn't afford to give in to any nerves now. Instead she must listen to the plane and let it guide her and teach her. Beneath her the countryside would be spread out like a patchwork quilt just as it had been when Verity had taken her up for that thrilling never-to-be-forgotten first spin, but she wasn't passenger now, she was the pilot. Determinedly she scanned the empty sky, shaken by the thought of how it must feel not just to have to fly a plane, but to have to fight in one as well.

Half an hour later, having brought the plane safely, if somewhat bumpily, down, Lou climbed out of the cockpit, dragging her parachute and its harness with her, feeling both apprehensive and euphoric. Euphoric because she had actually flown, and apprehensive because she was expecting her instructor to tear her performance to pieces.

Pushing back her goggles, Lou stood anxiously in her overalls and helmet, waiting for his appraisal, not sure whether to feel relieved or disappointed when he merely nodded his head and dismissed her.

'Well, that's that then, I suppose. I always told him that he'd come to a bad end, the way he carried on.'

Emily listened quietly to Con's sister, Alice, with the morning sun pouring into the quiet hospital waiting room, understanding that her apparent lack of concern for Con's death came not from not caring but from her shock at the unexpected-ness of it.

Poor Alice. She had lost her husband before the war and now she had lost her brother as well.

Emily thought she'd have been shocked too if she'd been summoned from her bed to be told that Con was in hospital and not expected to survive the night.

It was strange in a way that the two of them should be here like this, supporting one another, just as they had both supported Con through his last hours, sitting either side of his bed, waiting for what they knew to be inevitable, since they had never really got on as sisters-in-law.

Alice Mallory, Con's sister, had never wanted him to marry her. She'd said so right from the start, and of course Emily had been hurt by that.

'He never should have married you. I always said that,' Alice announced now, as though she had somehow followed the direction of Emily's own thoughts. She was a raw-boned woman, dark-haired like Con, but without his good looks, the mother of five children, with her eldest son in the RAF. A strong woman; if Con had got the good looks then Alice had got the strength.

'I knew straight off what he was after, and that it would all end in tears. Not that I haven't admired you for the way you've put up with him. He might be my brother but that doesn't mean that I don't know his faults. Always was too fond of women, was Con, and too full of himself. Still, I never thought it would end like this. Him being stabbed through the heart by one of them.'

403

'It was an accident,' Emily told her, repeating what she had already said to the police the previous evening when they had come to the hospital to interview her. 'She was just play-acting really, wanting to get Con's attention and make a bit of a fuss. She never meant it to happen.'

'Well, it has, and it was just as well that you were there to do what had to be done, else he'd have probably died in that ruddy theatre.'

'I've been thinking,' she told Emily abruptly. 'Well, wondering really how you'd feel about him being buried with our mam and dad. There's a space there, you see, unless you wanted him with your parents so that you—'

'No. I think that's a good idea,' Emily assured her hastily.

'What about the church and that? Do you want me to sort it all out, seeing as you're living in Whitchurch now?'

'Why don't we do it together?' Emily suggested. 'I'd like to give him the kind of send-off he'd have wanted, you know, a . . .'

'A proper wake, you mean? Well, it will be that all right, if all them girls of his turn up,' Alice told her with dark humour.

They looked at one another in mutual understanding.

'You've been a proper brick and no mistake,' Alice sniffed, reaching for her handkerchief. 'I reckon Con was a fool not to have realised how lucky he was to have you, but then that was Con all over, wasn't it?'

*　　*　　*

Poor Con, Emily reflected later when she was finally on board the train what would take her back to Whitchurch. Everything had happened so fast that it was still hard to believe that he was actually gone.

Oh, she'd known from the look on the faces of the nurses that he was going to die, but somehow, what with sitting with him, holding his hand, and then later when Alice had arrived trying to help her over the shock, the reality of what was happening had mercifully been pushed to the back of her mind.

The woman whose knife had killed him, Eva, had been in a dreadful state and had needed a doctor herself.

As Emily had said to the police, from what she had seen, Eva hadn't intended to hurt Con. It had all just been a terrible accident.

Last night, sitting with him whilst he slipped away, Emily had remembered how it had been when she had first met him, how handsome and wonderful she had thought him, and how disappointed she had been when she had realised that all there was to him was just his good looks and his vanity. Poor Con indeed.

'What's wrong?' Francine asked Marcus.

They were having lunch at the Savoy and she'd known the moment he'd stood up from his seat at a table in the bar that something had happened.

'White lady, please.' Marcus ordered her favourite cocktail for her from the hovering waiter, before telling her, 'We'll talk in a minute, but first please let me tell you how beautiful you look and how lucky I am.'

'I'm sure that there can't be many women here who aren't looking at me and thinking how lucky I am in having such a good-looking and dashing major as my lunch companion,' Francine responded with a smile.

Marcus was good-looking, with a pronounced air of masculinity and authority about him, and the right height and bearing to wear a military uniform as it should be worn, but more important than those things, at least to Francine, was the goodness that was inside him, as a person.

She loved him so very much, her love for him growing with every day they spent together. She could see in her own mirror the glow that loving him and being loved back by him was giving her, and yet at the same time Francine knew that, as happy as she was, she was hurting him because she had refused to marry him. Marcus, man of honour that he was, had not returned to the subject of them marrying once she had declared it closed, but Francine knew how he felt.

'Only this morning in the hairdresser's she had overheard two other women talking, one of them telling the other, 'I had told him that there were to be no babies until this war is over, but now, with him about to be posted overseas, I can't help thinking that I'm being selfish.'

'Selfish, in not wanting to take the risk of being left alone to bring up a child should the worst happen? My dear, how can you say that?' her companion had asked.

In response the first woman had answered her quietly, 'It is selfish, because if Archie doesn't come back then he and his family have lost the chance to create the next generation for ever, whereas if I lost him, my heart might be broken but I would still, if I wished, be able to remarry and have children. I will survive this war, but Archie may not. I feel I owe it to him to do whatever I can to show him my love and to make him as strong as he can be.'

The women had moved out of earshot then but their conversation had lingered in Francine's thoughts and her conscience.

Marcus watched Francine. To him she was the most beautiful woman in the whole world. Everything about her was beautiful, from the way she smiled to the way she walked. He had seen the heads turn when she had walked into the bar in her sky-blue silk dress with its little white jacket, her matching sky-blue hat with a white trim perched just so on her dark blonde hair, her slender legs encased in silk stockings, which, like most of her current wardrobe, had been bought when she had been in Cairo.

'I feel guilty having such pretty things when so many women haven't,' she had told Marcus.

But he had shaken his head and told her truthfully, 'You have earned the right to wear them through your work with ENSA. Not many women would agree to travel so far and in such dangerous conditions to sing to troops in the desert.'

He loved her so much and he was so grateful to her for taking him back, and to Brandon for making it possible for him to ask her to forgive him. There was nothing he wanted more than her happiness, nothing he wanted more than to give her that happiness and to protect it and her so that she would have it for all time, but he knew that that wasn't going to be possible. His heart was filled with love for her, and heavy with what he knew he had to tell her.

'Marcus.' Francine reached out across the table towards him, pulling off her glove as she laid her hand on the table. Such a small delicate hand, so easily lost when he held it in his own, and yet such a strong hand, holding as it did the will to reach out to others, to help them as she had helped Brandon and as she would help so many more through the foundation Brandon had set up.

After this war had ended there would be much for her to do, and much for him to do also, but first he had another duty to perform.

He took a deep breath and told her, 'I heard this morning that we're likely to be posted soon.'

'Italy?' Francine guessed. Her gaze was fixed to his.

'It looks like it.'

Italy, which had to be retaken from the Germans, in the same way that Canadian soldiers had attempted to take Dieppe less than a year ago, only to be repelled; massacred.

'Can it be done?'

'It has to be, if we are to win the war.'

'When . . . when do you think you will go?' Her mouth had gone dry, her heart thudding painfully inside her chest, her pain at the thought of losing him even worse than it had been when she had stood on board the ship sailing from Alexandria, watching him stride away from her.

'Not for another month, so we shall have some time to—'

'A month is four weeks. That's three weeks in which to have our banns read and a week in which we can be married before you leave.' Francine was speaking quickly, the words falling over one another as she said them hurriedly, not wanting to allow herself to think about them, following instead the agonised cry of her heart, listening only to it, thinking only of Marcus and their love, putting aside superstition and fear, wanting to give him all that she could so that when he left her there would be no regrets, and he would have no doubts about her commitment to him.

For a few seconds Marcus neither moved nor spoke, but then when he asked her, 'Do you mean it?' his voice choked with his feelings and his hand gripping hers tightly, Francine immediately felt heart-wrenchingly aware of just how much her words meant to him and achingly guilty for having previously withheld from him what he wanted so much.

When she answered, 'Yes. It's what I want more than anything else in the world, Marcus, to be truly yours in every single way,' she was speaking with the passionate conviction of her own heart and not just out of her love for him, because suddenly and illuminatingly she knew that his happiness was hers; his trust in her, her own in him; his need, her need.

Their hands were still clasped, their fingers interlocking as perfectly and seamlessly as though they were made to be together.

The waiter had reached the table with their drinks. Without taking his gaze from her Marcus told him, 'We've changed our minds. We'll have champagne, please, instead.'

Bobby was so nervous as he paced the floor of the Campions' front room. It was a hot day and he was all trussed up in his uniform, his boots so shiny that he could have seen his own reflection in them had he been able to bend that far forward against the collar and tie he was wearing under his battledress jacket. The heat of the late May sunshine wasn't the cause of his discomfort, though. That was due to the fact that any minute now Sasha's dad was going to walk in through the door and Bobby was going to have to persuade him to allow him and Sash to get engaged.

He'd been rehearsing what he wanted to say all week, good-naturedly listened to and then coached by his mates in the unit, of which he was the youngest.

The door opened and Bobby's stomach churned. Sam Campion, Sasha's father, was the kind of man that other men naturally looked up to and respected, but he was also a bit of a stickler, the kind of man who had strict values and high standards.

Bobby already knew from what Sasha had told him that even though she had won her mother round, Jean Campion had warned her not to get

410

her hopes up that her father would agree, and, even worse, Bobby's request to 'speak' to him whilst he had leave had meant that Sam had had to give up his Saturday afternoon working on his allotment.

'Well then, lad,' Sam greeted Bobby. 'Mrs Campion says that you've got something you want to ask me.'

'Yes, sir. You see, the thing is that me and Sasha would like, that is, we were wondering if you would . . .'

'Come on, lad, spit it out; I've got me toms to get watered.'

'Me and Sasha would like your permission to get engaged.'

Sam Campion was frowning now and Bobby's heart sank.

'How old are you, lad?' Sasha's father asked him.

'Twenty-two, sir, almost twenty-three. Plenty old enough to know that Sasha's the one for me,' Bobby spoke up determinedly.

'Mebbe, but is our Sasha old enough to be sure that you're the one for her? That's what I have to consider. She's a few years younger than you.'

'Sasha told me that Mrs Campion was only seventeen when you and she got engaged,' Bobby pointed out, remembering what Sasha had told him to say.

'Told you to say that, did she, Sasha?'

Sam Campion's astuteness had Bobby flushing up and longing to be able to unfasten the top button of his blouson jacket. He felt as though the tie he was wearing beneath it was strangling him.

Sam felt a flicker of male sympathy for Bobby. The poor lad was doing his best, obviously coached by Sasha. Not that Sam had anything against him. Sam liked Bobby and got on well with him, and in different circumstances, if Sasha had been a bit older and there hadn't been a war on, Sam would have given his permission for them to get engaged without any qualms. As it was, it was only thanks to Jean that the lad was here sweating uncomfortably in his uniform and preventing Sam from getting to his allotment at all. She was the one who'd told him that she thought they should relent and agree to Sasha and Bobby getting engaged.

'She's not herself at all, Sam,' she had told him, 'and I reckon not letting them get engaged will do more harm than good. Bobby's a decent lad, after all.'

He might be able to stand firm against his daughter but he couldn't do so against the combined will of both Jean and Sasha, Sam recognised.

'Very well, lad,' he gave in. 'But there's to be no talk of any marriage until after this war's over,' he warned Bobby. 'And no doing owt that wouldn't be right either. I don't want to see my daughter hurt or disgraced in any way,' he added meaningfully.

Bobby went bright red and stuttered wholeheartedly, 'No, never, Mr Campion. You can depend on me for that.'

'Good,' Sam told him, extending his hand to

take Bobby's somewhat sweaty palm in his own. 'Well done, lad. And welcome to the family.'

One look at Bobby's beatific expression when he and her father emerged from the front room and came into the kitchen told Sasha all she wanted to know.

She flung herself into Jean's arms, tears rolling down her face as she hiccuped, 'Oh, Mum, I'm so happy.'

'Well, now, I'd better put the kettle on,' Jean announced once Sasha's tears had been dried and Sam had disappeared off to his allotment, leaving Bobby to stand proudly in the kitchen, his face still pink with relief.

'We've got the ring, Mum. Show her, Bobby,' Sasha commanded.

'Have you now? Well, that was a bit of a risk, wasn't it?' Jean commented drily.

Watching them she couldn't help contrasting this engagement with Grace's to Seb. Bobby was a lovely lad but there was no denying that Sasha ruled the roost with him and bossed him around in a way that Grace would never have done with Seb. Mind you, it took all sorts, Jean acknowledged fairly, and if Sasha and Bobby were happy together then that was what mattered. It was certainly a welcome change to see her daughter smiling and relaxed instead of anxious and on edge, the way she had been these last months.

Obediently Bobby produced the small jeweller's box from his battledress tunic pocket.

When his hand trembled when he tried to open it, Sasha said, 'Oh, let me do it, Bobby,' taking the box from him and opening it to show Jean the three small diamonds on the ring inside it.

It was a lovely ring, Jean acknowledged, and Bobby must have saved ever so hard to afford it. He was a good lad and he thought the world of Sasha, there was no doubt about that.

'Put it on for me, Bobby,' Sasha commanded, handing the box back to him.

Beaming with pride and pleasure, Bobby did as she had instructed. The ring was a perfect fit, the jeweller had seen to that when they'd first gone in and looked at it. It wasn't new, of course – new jewellery was hard to come by now – but Sasha had fallen in love with it the minute she'd seen it and that had been good enough for Bobby.

'Happy now?' Bobby asked Sasha tenderly an hour later when Sasha's mother had tactfully slipped out to go to the allotment with some sandwiches for Sam, leaving them alone in the kitchen.

Perched on Bobby's knee, her head on Bobby's shoulder, his arm round her waist holding her tight, whilst she admired the sunlight striking sparkles of light off her ring, Sasha nodded.

'Yes,' she assured him.

She was happy, wonderfully happy, but underneath her happiness, like a bit of grit in a shoe, there was still that feeling she hated so much. That fear was still there deep down inside where it lay waiting to leap out at her and drag her down with it.

THIRTY-ONE

She had done it. She had finished and passed her Primary Training. Lou felt so buoyant that she could almost fly without her 'wings' with the heady mix of excitement and relief.

Not that the last few weeks hadn't been without their disappointments and difficulties. She'd sailed through her twenty flying hours' test, and the over-confidence and the impatience to be trained that had given her had led to her thinking she was a lot better than she was, she admitted now. At the time it had been a crushing blow when she had been told that her forty flying hours' test had been so borderline that they had been tempted to drop her from the course. Not all the girls who were taking it were going to be good enough to be pilots they had all been told right from the beginning.

Of course, the shock of nearly losing her place had done her good in the end. She had worked like a Trojan to make up for that poor forty-hour result, but she hadn't taken anything for granted until yesterday, when she had been told that she had passed.

If she was up in a plane right now, she'd be doing loops and rolls and every other exuberant aerobatic manoeuvre she could think of, Lou admitted, so it was probably a good job that she wasn't because that would get her so many black marks that she'd be banished from ATA for good, and that was the last thing she wanted.

Little had she known that December day in Liverpool, when she had been filled with such despair and misery, that a chance meeting and a throwaway comment from another girl who had just enlisted with the WAAF would lead to her discovering what now felt almost like a missing part of herself. A part to replace Sasha, her twin? Lou clamped down on that unwanted question. Whilst the rebellious streak within her had made her feel back then in Liverpool that it would be exciting and different to learn to fly, she had had no real idea of what would be involved, or that something about learning to fly would speak to her on so many different levels. She had been so lucky; she could have remained in Liverpool, at the telephone exchange, feeling resentful and unhappy. She could have joined the WAAF and ended up in an office filing paper, feeling equally bored, but somehow fate had taken a hand and guided her into the perfect place for her, so that her life now fitted her as snugly as the cockpit of a Spitfire fitted round the body of its pilot.

Spitfires. Lou was longing to try one, but of course she wouldn't be able to do that until she had completed the next phase of her training – her Class 2 Conversion Course at Thame in Oxfordshire, where she would move on from the

416

basics she had now learned, to learn to fly a wider variety and twin-engined aircraft.

For now, though, excited as she was, it was almost enough to simply enjoy the thrill of actually being able to fly.

Lou reached into the pocket of her dark blue regulation ATA trousers to remove her cigarettes, lighting herself one and then pushing her hand through her hair to let the breeze cool her down. Her hair needed cutting; her curls were well below the collar of her light blue RAF shirt, thick and wayward, the soft brown bleached gold at the ends by the sun. Lou inspected her nails. It was a point of honour amongst ATA pilots that they kept their nails polished, the camaraderie of the service ensuring that girls willingly shared precious bottles of varnish. Dark red was the favoured ATA pilot nail varnish colour – it went sooo well with their dark blue uniforms, as Lou had heard one of the American ATA pilots drawl in her lazy Deep South accent.

Appearance was very important if you were to be welcomed and well thought of by the other pilots, and appearance covered not only the way one looked, but the way one acted. It was the 'done' thing to assume a certain degree of faked female helpless insouciance around male pilots that was totally at odds with the gritty ability and determination the girls really possessed.

'It stops the boys from feeling too jealous of us,' Verity Maitland had told Lou when she had paid her one of her brief visits, to check up on how she was doing and to gift her with a large number of verbal dos and don'ts.

Although Verity hadn't said so, Lou felt that she had in a sense taken her under her wing, and because of that Lou was determined to do her best to be worthy of Verity's support.

She finished her cigarette and stubbed it out. She still hadn't told her family just what she was doing. They'd got enough to worry about with Luke, she'd reasoned. That was all right where her parents were concerned, but what about Sasha? What was her excuse for holding back from her twin something that was such an important part of her life? After all, Sasha hadn't hesitated to write to her telling her that she and Bobby hoped to get their father's permission to become engaged.

That was different, Lou told herself. The importance of getting engaged was something that anyone could understand, even her, although she had no desire whatsoever to do the same thing. Her dream of becoming a pilot, though, was something that only those who felt the same could understand. It wasn't something she could share with Sasha; they weren't close enough any more for that. And that was her fault, Lou acknowledged. In Sasha's opinion as well as her own.

'Hey, Campion, stop daydreaming about flying Spitfires and come and listen to what Sandra's got planned for our next forty-eight-hour pass. She's suggesting that we all go to London.'

'Coming,' Lou called back. This was her life now, not Liverpool. She wished Sash well, but Lou knew she would choke on her own boredom if she had to return to the life she had left behind.

*   *   *

418

Weddings. Why was it that there was something about them that brought tears as well as smiles, Katie wondered, blinking back her own as Gina and Leonard emerged from the small grey Norman church into the June sunshine of the Dorset village where her parents lived.

Gina had worn her mother's wedding dress, hastily altered, and Leonard, of course, was in uniform. Katie, at Gina's request, had worn her, or rather Francine's, grey silk, and the two mothers had done the bridal couple proud with silk frocks and elegant hats bought before the war, but none the less appropriate for all that.

The wedding breakfast was to be held in the pretty Queen Anne house owned by Gina's parents, and Katie had been touched by the genuine kindness and warmth both families had shown her, especially Eddie's parents.

'They're sizing you up for the family jewels,' Eddie had warned her the previous evening after his mother had finished showing her a family photograph album. 'They're desperate to find a decent girl to take me on and produce grandchildren for them.'

The twinkle in his eye had confirmed, as Katie had guessed, that he was teasing her. She doubted that there would ever be any lack of 'suitable' girls willing to marry a man as attractive and from such an obviously well-to-do family as Eddie.

'What do you say?' he murmured to her now as they watched the bridal couple walk under the raised swords of their RAF guard of honour 'Shall we make it a double, and tell the vicar that he can start to call the banns. The parents would be jolly pleased, I can tell you.'

Katie laughed. She liked Eddie and felt all the more at ease with him for knowing that she would never be in any danger of falling for him.

'You are a wicked tease,' she told him, 'and it would serve you right if I took you seriously.'

'No, it wouldn't serve me right, dearest Katie, it would serve me very well, and better than I deserve to have such a sweet girl as you as my wife. You should think about it, you know. After all, the war isn't over yet and you could end up a very comfortably placed young widow.'

'Eddie, don't. You mustn't say things like that,' Katie told him fiercely. 'Nothing's going to happen to you, and when the war is over you'll find a girl who is far more suited to you than I could ever be.'

'How do you know we aren't suited? You haven't even let me kiss you yet.'

Katie gave him a stern look. He really was irrepressible.

'No, and I'm not going to either,' she told him severely.

Happiness was such a fragile thing, a chameleon in many ways, sometimes so intense you could hardly bear it, and other times, as light as a drift of cloud.

Perhaps it was cowardly of her, but really she preferred the light fluffy white-cloud kind of happiness that couldn't hurt you to the heart-stopping-intensity kind that could, Katie decided.

THIRTY-TWO

It was a hot day, and she had been working hard in the garden. Surely she deserved a few minutes of blissful uninterrupted peace and laziness, Bella thought crossly as she heard the squeak of the front gate, and resolutely kept her eyes tightly closed as she lay in a deck chair, wearing an old sun top and a pair of shorts, hoping that whoever it was would go away when no one answered the door, instead of coming to look in the back garden. After all, it wasn't often these days she got time to herself, and she wouldn't have it now if her mother hadn't been coaxed into manning a stall at the WVS bring-and-buy sale.

The sun was so warm and more than anything else she simply wanted to drift off and daydream about Jan.

Something was tickling her chin, a greenfly, probably, from the roses. Without opening her eyes she lifted her hand to brush it away, her body going rigid with shock and her eyes opening wide when hand took hold of her own.

The bright sunlight was dazzling but that wasn't

why she blinked and stared and tensed again, this time with disbelief, whilst all the while the hand holding hers stroked her fingers, and her lips formed the name it was surely impossible for the man standing over her to be.

'Jan. It can't be you. It can't be.'

But it was, and she was on her feet, laughing and crying, holding him tightly whilst he held her tightly back, and the joy of it, of him being here with her, filled her until she was overflowing with it.

Miraculously Jan was here, holding her and kissing her, and she was kissing him back, and she didn't care who saw them. She didn't care about anything other than this, holding the man she loved in her arms, the feel of him, the scent of him, the reality of him, all and everything she could ever want or need.

It took a while and a lot of shared intense kisses before she could come back down to earth enough to ask, 'Jan, how can you be here? We heard that you'd been taken prisoner, that you were a prisoner of war. I wrote to you . . . I . . .'

'I know. I got your letter.'

'You didn't write back.'

'I did but obviously my letter never reached you. Bella, before I answer any more questions, I've got one I have to ask you.'

Bella looked at him.

'Will you marry me?'

She didn't need to hesitate or think. Her fiercely determined, 'Yes, yes I will,' came straight from her heart. Against all the odds she had been given a second chance, and she wasn't going to risk losing it.

'I've thought of this moment more than you can

know, thought of it, dreamed of it and longed for it. You and loving you are what has brought me here, Bella, my heart. It was for you, to be with you, that I was so determined to escape from our prison camp so that I could tell you how much I love you and how wrong I was to say what I did the last time . . .

'No,' Bella stopped him, shaking her head. 'I am glad you spoke as you did. Those words, your love, the letter you gave Bettina to give me have sustained me, helped me, been my food and drink and the air that I have breathed these last months. They, you, gave me the will to go on. Because of you I was able to be strong. Have you seen Bettina and your mother yet?'

'Not yet. I wanted to see you first.'

'Tell me what happened, Jan.'

'Oh, well, I told Hitler that I was missing you and he said, well, why don't you go and see her?' Jan teased her, relenting when she shook her head, then telling her quietly, 'I got the opportunity to join an escape group. The group had been planning the escape for months. Then one of the chaps who should have been going to escape fell ill and the rest of us drew straws to take his place. I was the lucky one. We used a tunnel that went right under the perimeter fence. We went at night, as soon as it got dark, a couple of the guards were in a card school run by some of our chaps; they let them win – cigarettes – so we waited for a night when they were on duty. That gave us a head start, but we knew they'd come after us once they realised we'd gone. We split up to give ourselves a better chance. The plan was to head for Switzerland, but when I was waiting on the station for my train I saw some SS officers arrive, so I switched platforms and ended up in France instead.

Luckily as it happened I fell into the hands of the Resistance. They thought I was a German at first, of course, but eventually I managed to convince them that I wasn't. From there it was relatively easy. There's an established organised system in place to return aircrew to England and they simply got me on to that. Of course, there were several hairy moments, but I was lucky. I tell you, Bella, swimming out to get on board the boat waiting to bring us back – there were three of us by this stage, the other two the only survivors of a Lancaster that had seen shot down on its way back home – I prayed as I have never prayed before. To be so near to you and yet still so far away . . . Of course, once we did get back officialdom took over and it was all debriefings and medicals and the like, but finally, yesterday, they told me I was officially on leave.'

'On leave?'

'They've given me a month.'

'Could we be married by special licence, do you think?'

Jan reached into his pocket and produced an official-looking document, smiling at her as he did so.

'I already have it, just in case I could persuade you to say yes.'

She should perhaps take him to task for taking her acceptance for granted, Bella acknowledged, but then in order to do that she would have to tell him to stop kissing her, and really that was the last thing she wanted to do.

EPILOGUE

'Well, I know that June's the month for weddings, but I never expected both Bella and Francine to say that they were going to get married at such short notice,' Jean told Grace, as they sat together companionably on the back step, the door to Jean's kitchen behind them open to the fresh air whilst they hulled the first of the strawberries from Sam's allotment.

'It's the war, Mum,' Grace responded. 'People don't want to waste a minute when they might not have much time together.'

Both pairs of busy hands stilled as they looked at one another, both of them thinking of all those men who might not come home and all the women who loved them.

It was the end of the beginning, Churchill had said.

Everyone knew that the tide had turned, that the risk of invasion was over, but there was still a long way to go to victory and many lives to be lost, and everyone in the country knew it.

What's next?

Tell us the name of an author you love

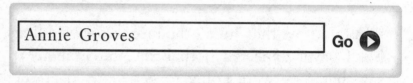

Annie Groves ⁣ Go ▶

and we'll find your next great book.

www.bookarmy.com